Charlie —

Enjoy!

Federal Agent: A Thriller

Sean Sweeney

Federal Agent: A Thriller
Copyright © 2012 by Sean Sweeney

All rights reserved. No part of this book may be reproduced or transmitted in any form or by any means, electronic or mechanical, including photocopying, recording, or any information storage and retrieval system, without prior written permission of the Author. Your support of author's rights is appreciated.

This book, an original publication, was registered with the United States Library of Congress Copyright Office in October 2012.

Cover designed by David Wood

ACKNOWLEDGMENTS

Special thanks go out to the following people:

"Big" Al Kunz and Kim Tomsett for their eyes, Trisha Reeves for the cover. Excellent job, gang. Steven Savile, Kent Holloway, Rich Steeves, Bruce Sarte: thanks for letting me bend your ears. Nickie Storey: I bent your ear, too—thanks for telling me that I got things right.

My boys and gal in the Indie Author Mafia: David Dalglish, David McAfee, Daniel Arenson, Robert DuPerre, Daniel Pyle, Mike Crane and Amanda Hocking.

Steve Green, as usual, was helpful with plotting. Phillip Norris was a great help with his firearms knowledge.

My girlfriend, Jen Slade: Thanks for letting me do what I do. I love you. Mom, Vicky and Mark, thanks for being in my corner.

And of course, I thank you the reader, for without you I'd just be talking to myself.

DEDICATION

For Pat Flaherty, my Junior Year English teacher at FHS:

When I told her I only wanted to be a sportswriter, she told me "Don't limit yourself."
I think I've heeded her advice.

Federal Agent: A Thriller

Sean Sweeney

Let us all hope that the dark clouds of racial prejudice will soon pass away, and that in some not too distant tomorrow the radiant stars of love and brotherhood will shine over our great nation with all their scintillating beauty. — Martin Luther King, Jr.

Racism isn't born, folks, it's taught. I have a two-year-old son. You know what he hates? Naps! End of list. — Denis Leary

Chapter 1
Georgia Diagnostic and Classification Prison
Jackson, Georgia
Friday, October 26, 2012
11:50 p.m. ET

Golden artificial light funneled down toward two sets of people, the lamp high on the black pole above not flickering. The people had encamped themselves in front of the Georgia Diagnostic and Classification Prison for the past five days in an Occupy-esque fashion, counting down the days, the hours and minutes, until the big event they all awaited—or dreaded—closed toward its inevitable denouement.

They awaited the execution of Bobby Ray Rayburn.

The two sets of people couldn't have been more different in their reasons for attending this show of legal homicide. On the right-hand side of the narrow entranceway was a group of pro-death penalty advocates, those who traveled from state prison to state prison as an execution neared to protest in favor of plunging the needle. They carried placards as if at a political rally, standing as one group. It was as if they represented the righteous rock of society, waiting for justice to be served for the condemned's heinous atrocities. They could not live on adrenaline alone: A food truck that only served those on that side of the asphalt, regardless if those on the other side waved one hundred dollar bills their way, had come and gone long before midnight approached. There would be no need for a late-night snack. Not today.

Another group, poised on the left-hand side of the entranceway, couldn't be more split in their reasoning. Closer to the entranceway stood those against the death penalty. They too carried placards, hand-painted and stapled to two-by-fours, and had chanted "Don't Kill Bobby Ray!" and "Pro-Life" in staggering fashion, the latter if only to enrage those on the other side. Several of them found it ironic that those on the right-hand side of the prison's entry believed in the death penalty, yet frowned on abortion.

To the far left, there was still another group. They were a group that those against the death penalty tried to keep away from, even if it meant intruding on the personal space of the protester to the immediate right.

The Ku Klux Klan had arrived two days prior to the execution date, and it wasn't long before stunned silence descended upon the shoulder of Highway 36. They had arrived in full regalia, their white hoods pulled down beyond their throats, their flowing, matching robes tickled green at the hem as they strode over the grass. They were there to protest against Rayburn's execution, for he was one of them. Georgia State Troopers assigned them a small corner on the left-hand side, near the triple-beamed fence set some thirty feet back from the road. They were peaceful and didn't cause any disturbances, other than trampling the grass with their heavy, booted feet.

Georgia State Police had assured the public that there would be law and order outside the prison as the execution date loomed. As the crowds grew, troopers on horseback patrolled the area, the authorities showing a great deal of force. No one wanted a disturbing the peace charge; all parties involved had assured police that their people would behave. Across the highway, scores of media vans and trucks, the trucks' dishes pointed to the heavens, recorded the scene for playback later in the day; in the case of CNN and Fox News, for live broadcast.

With midnight fast approaching and the late October temperature dropping steadily, a constricting silence took hold of both groups, so much so that even the crickets felt that making too much noise would be against their better interests. Tiny flames erupted from the center of people's hands, the placards forgotten, as the seconds ticked away. Soon, a chorus of Amazing Grace started slow and sonorous until it filled the entirety of the area as the clock reached 11:30 p.m. Even members of the KKK joined in, their voices a mix of bass and tenor, aiding the hymn in reaching the cold, aphotic sky above.

There was a nervous energy surrounding the prison and enveloping the crowd as the eleventh hour drew toward its close. With the closeness of unwashed bodies, the air began to stink, but no one could smell the other thanks to dulled senses. There were chattered whispers back and forth, wondering if anyone had tuned a radio to WSB to see whether Wallace Wellington Woodruff IV, the esteemed governor of the state of Georgia, had issued a stay in the execution. One wasn't expected. Even the anti-death penalty protesters knew the acts Rayburn had committed were beyond reprehensible and that no politician worth his or her salt would let him live. Maybe that would happen in the liberal, coddling northeast, but they admitted that would not happen here in conservative, Bible Belt Georgia. It was too late in the game. By now, prison guards had brought Rayburn over to the death house, and the young man sat in a lonely cell, a preacher nearby if he had wanted one. The death chamber was only twenty-one steps down the hall. Everyone outside had heard the stories of past executions, and knew that those twenty-one steps would take less than half a minute to occur. Five minutes later, the condemned would breathe his final gasps.

If Woodruff issued a stay, it would have to be within the next few minutes.

And if it did come, the reactions would be mixed: cheers of euphoria from the left-hand side, while those on the right would call for Woodruff's blood.

Time slowly ticked away.

***

This is it, the condemned man thought as he caressed the tiny wooden beads between his fingers. *The final hour is here.* He took a deep breath, then bowed his head and began to pray.

"Forgive me Lord, for I have sinned against you."

Bobby Ray Rayburn had sat on the thin cot for what seemed like years, the minutes dragging in slow motion toward his court-ordered death. Along with a borrowed set of Rosary beads wrapped around his fingers, the prison guards had allowed him to bring two other items from death row over to the death house, two earthly reminders for the rest of his life. He brought a Dale Murphy baseball card, 1987 Topps edition, as well as a picture of parents in a cheap plastic frame his cousins had bought him at a Wal-Mart two years back. He lifted his head and opened his eyes, the picture coming into clear focus.

At least they'll be with me in spirit, he thought, his eyes narrowing as he stared at the wall, the photo standing on a small shelf. His fingers moved across the bead, feeling the smooth wood between the pads of his thumb and forefinger. Holding Jesus between his fingers was supposed to sedate him. It wasn't working. He only grew more infuriated with each touch. He inhaled hard and gripped the beads tighter.

How many chances did they have to come see me, the bastards, and didn't? Did they stand by my side during the trial? No, they didn't. Good riddance. I'm better off, and I'll finally be rid of those—

Rayburn yanked his hands apart, snapping the string in two places. Beads collided with cold cement in a tinkling wooden rain, bouncing and rolling underneath the temporary bed.

He exhaled and dropped the strings, which softly clattered against the floor for only two heartbeats before it grew still. He ran his fingers across three days' worth of stubble on top of his head. Even though it was nearly November, he could feel sweat pouring off his scalp. He looked back to the photo, his eyes growing damp. He couldn't bring himself to curse his parents any further, even though they had chosen to abandon him to his fate.

Yesterday, the warden had come to tell him that his parents had rejected the prison's offer to be with him during the last day of his existence. He hadn't even acknowledged the man's presence. He had stared at the floor, hands clasped together, the veins on the topside of his palms throbbing.

Thirty hours later, all he wanted to do was wrap his hands around his father's neck and squeeze.

Rayburn could feel his heart punishing his chest's interior with repetitive, rapid beats. He begged it to slow down, aware that he needed to calm himself. He took a deep breath and stood up, the cot squealing as Rayburn freed himself from its grasp.

As he took three steps toward the shelf, a guard outside of the cell turned his bald head toward the prisoner.

"You okay, Bobby Ray?"

Rayburn nodded as he grabbed the picture frame and smiled.

"Yeah, Carl. I am. Thanks."

The large guard turned aside. Rayburn, even though he concentrated on the photo, heard the guard's shoes crunching as he shifted his weight, his keys jangling against the blue uniform pants.

He stared at his mama, the only woman who truly loved him. He had her eyes, nose and thin mouth, while the rest of him resembled the man who stood next to her. Rayburn didn't even look at him. He saw the man's face every time he looked in a mirror. His knuckles carried cuts and scratches from the times he shattered the glass. He flexed his right hand twice, as if he felt ghost pain rack his fingers.

Rayburn could feel his lip trembling as he pried the frame away from the photograph. He tore the photo in half, bringing the half that contained his mother's image to his chest. He left the other half on the shelf. He returned to the cot and lay down, staring at the ceiling with his hands grasping the torn picture. The springs held his weight, his body snug against the thin padding.

He didn't think about his crimes as he waited for the cell to open. At 23 years old and in prison for five years, he had known this day would come, ever since he heard the guilty verdict handed down. His attorney had fast-tracked the appeals process, hoping that someone in Georgia's judicial system would overturn the sentence to life, at the very least, or 25 years at the most. He was still a young man, and the lawyer believed that rehabilitation could serve Rayburn in that time.

Rayburn grinned. His lawyer was a patsy, but he was also a public defender. Rayburn wondered why the guy worked so hard for him, and on the people's dime, too. He wondered if the P.D. wanted to use this case as a springboard for public office. He probably did. Rayburn was young, but he had knowledge of what the real world was like. Everyone had an ulterior motive. There was something in it for him.

Eh, I couldn't care less, Rayburn thought. He checked the wall clock. *I'll be dead in less than half an hour anyway. What does it matter to me? I couldn't disappoint Wally, the jury, or the judges of good ol' Cobb County.*

He shrugged it off. He laid there silently, as if in a trance, unmoving.

At ten minutes of midnight, Rayburn heard the cell creak open and stop with a clank. He didn't even wince or budge. He heard everything, though: the guard's boots, the keys going back onto the belt. He felt his heart rate accelerating.

"Bobby Ray," Carl the Guard said. "It's time."

Rayburn smiled. He got up and slipped the photo of his mama into his pocket. The jail had procured him a suit for this event so he wouldn't have to die in the orange jumpsuit that Georgia's UDS's—inmates Under Death Sentence—wore on a daily basis. He flatted the pants a tad before he held his wrists out.

The cold steel snapped over his skin. He looked at Carl, his face passive as he stared into the big man's eyes.

Carl returned the look, his eyes warm.

"Good luck, Carl. And thank you."

Carl smiled.

"Good luck to you."

Carl led him out of the cell and turned left.

Rayburn did not appear nervous as he walked into the sparkling white death chamber. He held his head high, his visage full of arrogance right to the end. A curtain stood to his left, drawn together, keeping him from the view of those who won the right to watch him, a notorious killer, die by lethal injection. A gurney, brakes on, stood motionlessly in front of the curtain, several feet away. Two men in white lab coats stood off to the side. Rayburn saw several restraints on the gurney.

He gulped as Carl removed the handcuffs.

Oh, this isn't a drill, he thought.

They performed the drill two weeks ago. Guards brought in another prisoner, one they had locked in solitary. They performed this same procedure—the walk, the strapping down, the needle with the empty syringe sliding into a vein—in record time.

Rayburn blew out a long breath as he shifted his weight and sat on the gurney. Carl stood guard at the door, unmoving, albeit ready to pounce if Rayburn decided to revolt in the waning minutes of his life. He had his right hand on the butt end of his weapon, ready to draw it.

"Lay back, Bobby Ray," the tech said.

Rayburn did as he was told. His head hit the pillow, and the gurney's padding was cushioned to the point that his back sighed as he laid back.

Ahh, comfort in the final moments, he thought. He wet his lips with his tongue as the techs began securing him to the gurney.

The warden entered the death chamber three minutes later, at 11:54 p.m. The man looked smug, Rayburn saw, looking past his feet as he noticed the warden looking down on him. Rayburn's eyes narrowed and hardened his gaze as the warden stepped closer.

"Comfy yet?"

Rayburn's lip curled.

"Let's see. 11:55. I think you know who is sitting by the phone right now, waiting for me to call him." He grinned maliciously.

Rayburn wanted to spit at him, but his mouth had gone dry again, his salivary glands shut down. He knew that the warden was a flake, but the giddiness he showed over putting a man to death was sickening even to Rayburn, even after the crimes he had committed. And while he watched the warden move toward the door, he caught Carl reach into his pocket with his left hand from out the corner of his eye. Rayburn inhaled through his nose as his eyes flickered from the warden to Carl and back again. The warden picked up the phone and pressed a combination of digits.

Carl smirked Rayburn's way.

Rayburn turned his head to look at the warden, then let his eyes drop to the baseboards. He saw yellow tubing stretched across the joint that linked the floor with the molding. A gray substance resembling homemade Play-Dough lined both sides, securing it in place.

Rayburn's eyes danced. He tried to wet his lips again. They had turned to sandpaper.

He heard the warden speak to someone on the phone, but he didn't want to acknowledge the man at all. He knew he had to listen when he hung it up, because the sequence of the words to come were ones he had thought of for months. They haunted his dreams and every waking moment, so much so that there were times he wanted to yell for the words to stop.

Rayburn heard the click of the phone hitting the cradle. He watched as the warden nodded to another guard to Rayburn's right, before Rayburn heard the curtain open. He turned his head.

He saw several faces, including some of the faces of the people he killed, replicas all, staring back at him through the glass. There were several black faces, hatred, anger and revulsion, all mixed, hard and directed his way. He could feel their emotions.

Their emotions fed his life, his existence. He felt strong, potent.

He hated every single one of them.

Rayburn looked down the line and saw two white faces staring at him, too. They were his people, the proper people, by his line of thinking. He would have drank with them, shot darts, maybe shot a deer or two. They could have been buddies—if they, too, didn't look through the glass as if they wanted midnight to get here. One was a reporter from the Atlanta Journal Constitution.

The other was his lawyer.

Rayburn didn't even smirk. There was no reaction. Not even a word against the man. He turned his head and saw the warden staring over him, a sheet of paper in his right hand. He wasn't smiling, Rayburn could see.

He's smiling internally, though, he thought. *The bastard is enjoying this.* He clenched his teeth.

"Bobby Ray Rayburn, I have to read the death warrant to you. On the twenty-first day of October in the year of our Lord 2007, you willingly and maliciously kidnapped, dragged and hung a young African-American boy from a tree in rural Cobb County. After a three-day manhunt, you shot and killed two African-American sheriff's deputies in the township of Mableton. A jury of your peers found you guilty by a unanimous vote of 12-0, and ordered you put to death by lethal injection on this day, the twenty-sixth of October in the year of our Lord 2012. May God have mercy on your soul." He paused as he lifted his eyes from the document and looked at Rayburn. "There are no stays."

Rayburn did not look disappointed that the governor had not come through. He did not expect him to come through, either. Much like his attorney, the governor did not want to commit political suicide with the electorate. Rayburn understood that. He didn't grin, nor did he frown. He only filled his lungs with precious air, and thought of his mama before he looked over the warden's shoulder to the clock on the wall.

It was 11:58 p.m. He returned his gaze to the warden.

"Do you have any last words, Bobby Ray?"

Rayburn felt his lip curl on the left-hand side as he stared hard at him, wishing death upon him. Then, with every bit of malice he could conjure, he said it.

"Not to you, nigger lover."

Rayburn gleefully reveled in the look of pure shock on the warden's face. The man staggered backward just before the techs moved in with blue rubber gloves on their hands. One carried the first syringe, wielding it as if a mighty sword.

He watched with intense eyes as the needle closed in on him, as if in slow motion. It contained pentobarbital, used to bring about unconsciousness. A second needle contained Pavulon, in order to cause paralysis in the muscles as well as respiratory arrest. A third held potassium chloride to stop Rayburn's heart.

None of the needles reached his arm.

Shrapnel and plaster filled the room along with a concussion that rippled across the enclosure. A cloud of dust and black smoke began filling the death chamber along with the blood-curdling sounds of masculine screams. Flames crackled at the wall off to the right, the wall practically vaporized by the blast. Behind the glass partition, eyes widened, the shock registering on the faces there. The reporter's hands remained still. The needle clanked off the tiles, an almost forgotten element. The warden hit the floor.

So too did the tech to Rayburn's left, a piece of the wall embedded in the back of his head.

Carl moved. He drew his sidearm and quickly punched at a series of numbers on a wall panel, securing the door to the death chamber. With dust covered arms, he turned and shoved the barrel into the second tech's face.

The tech blanched, a gasp touching his lips.

"Take the restraints off him now."

The tech paused and looked down the barrel. The pungent scent of urine quickly rose toward the ceiling.

"Do it now!" Carl yelled.

The man scrambled forward and loosened the straps as fast as he could. Drops of sweat hit Rayburn's chest, slipping off the tech's nose. Rayburn lurched forward and punched the tech across the slick skin. The tech crumpled into the puddle of golden liquid below.

Carl drew another gun and passed it along to Rayburn just as several others, all dressed in black and toting Israeli-made machine guns, entered the death chamber from the hole in the wall. Their bodies sent the smoke swirling about.

"Let's go," Rayburn said, staring at the witnesses. Several had tears in their eyes. Rayburn could only surmise that they believed the killer of their sons was about to get away with every little thing. Carl and the others made their way toward the breach. "Wait."

They all paused and turned to Rayburn, who had lifted his gun toward the glass. He pulled the trigger without thinking. Glass shattered half a second later. From within, screams registered through to Rayburn's ears.

His grin was feral.

"Blast them," he ordered, a lack of emotion spilling from between his teeth.

Carl and the others brought their weapons up and unloaded a magazine into the witness box. Screams registered, then were silenced.

"Do you have it?" Rayburn turned and asked one of the newcomers. The newcomer nodded.

"Tag him," Rayburn said, pointing at the unconscious warden.

The newcomer pulled a white canister of Krylon from within his flak jacket. He shook it, the ball jingling inside several times. He pointed it at the warden's back and, in nWo-esque fashion, sprayed three letters across the man's shirt, from the bottom of his head to his bottom, in black spray paint.

KKK.

The tagger laughed as soon as he ripped the last stroke. The others chuckled along, too.

"Let's get out of here," Rayburn said.

Guns up, they exited through the hole in the wall. They made sure that no guards prevented their escape. They hurried across the grass to a hole in an outer fence.

"You guys sure did a bang up job," Rayburn noted.

"Keep your head down, Bobby Ray," Carl the Guard said.

Ten seconds later, they made it to the getaway car, a nearly-rusted out Ford Taurus. The driver turned the engine over just as they approached. They hopped in and sped north on Water Works Drive, making the left-hand turn and letting the Georgia back woods swallow them. Carl, in the back seat, grabbed a radio from the floorboards. He turned it on and pressed the transmit button.

"Free at last, free at last, thank God Almighty, Bobby Ray Rayburn is free at last! You good ol' boys, get ready. It's going to be a hot time in the old town tonight! Ha ha!"

He put the radio down as a chorus of "wooohooo!" chimed through.

"You doing okay, Bobby Ray?" one of the men in black said.

Rayburn, in the co-pilot seat, let his head smack the headrest before he passed the gun back to Carl. He let a smile drag its way across his face. Hot air spewed from the dashboard vents.

"Yeah," he said. "I'm great. I'm alive, thanks to you good ol' boys." He paused for a few seconds as they careened down the road. "Hey, what do I have to do to get a beer around here?"

They laughed as they continued on to their first stop.

***

Two hours had passed by the time prison officials came out to speak with the crowd of reporters across Highway 36. The assembled parties on either side of the entrance had seen the ambulances stream into the complex and openly wondered just what was going on. No one could confirm rumors. The warden wasn't answering his phone. Everyone had heard the explosions.

When the deputy warden came out with Georgia State Troopers on either side, the voices grew silent. The media tried to surround him, but the troopers kept them at bay. Pushing and shoving ensued, but when the deputy called for quiet—"There's been enough violence tonight," he had said—everyone calmed themselves. The reporters turned on their digital recorders. Videographers pointed their cameras his way. Within seconds, the red light came on.

"I have some tragic news to report to you all. Just before midnight, Bobby Ray Rayburn was set to be executed by lethal injection, but a situation occurred where the condemned escaped. We believe a prison guard aided him in his flight from the death chamber. This investigation will continue in the morning."

Shouts of "Where's the warden?", "Why so many ambulances?" and "Where is he?" went unanswered.

Instead, shouts of joy came from the far left-hand side. The anti-death penalty and pro-death penalty advocates, despite being on different sides, had looks of shock as the KKK danced. They knew what the deputy's announcement meant.

It meant that a killer was free.

They knew that Georgia wouldn't be the same again.

Chapter 2
The White House, Washington, D.C.
Saturday, October 27, 2012
7 a.m. ET

The timing of what happened in Georgia the night before was just too uncanny for Alex Dupuis' liking. When she had awoken at 5:30 a.m., she had found out about the incident on CNN. She learned what she could, then slurped a cup of coffee before showering and changing into business casual attire. After a phone call to Atlanta, she told her driver, as she did every morning, not to spare the pedal as they made their way to the Cottage. Traffic was relatively light on this raw, overcast morning. Washington D.C. was, for the most part, still asleep, and once the limousine pulled through the gates and up to the curb in front of the North Portico, the director of the CIA walked toward the Oval Office with a gait that stressed business, even on a Saturday.

Alex shucked off her tan leather trenchcoat and slung it over a chair mid-stride before she took a seat in front of an empty Resolute Desk. President Eric Forrister had not yet made his entrance. She checked her watch, pulling the sleeve to her cashmere sweater back to reveal her wrist. It was barely after 7 a.m., and she knew that on Saturdays, Forrister preferred to do several miles on the treadmill in the Residence before coming downstairs to work on the country's problems.

Healthy body, healthy mind, she thought. She crossed her legs, right over left, hooking her ankles together. She would show patience for the Commander in Chief, even though tapping a pen against the manila folder didn't quell her anxiety.

Ten minutes later, the President of the United States entered with a tall glass of orange juice in his right hand. Alex unhooked her ankles and stood immediately. Forrister wore a warm-up track suit in red, white and blue, the emblem of the United States men's national soccer team on his left breast. He bounced in as if on his heels, the exercising continuing into the Oval Office.

"Good morning, Alex."

"Good morning, Mr. President. Did you happen to catch what happened in Georgia last night?"

"Nope," Forrister said. "I was watching SportsCenter while Veronica and I played dueling treadmills. Can you believe it, though: the Yankees and the Dodgers, headed for a seventh game of the World Series tonight?"

Alex grumbled.

"No sir, I haven't paid much attention to the World Series after the Dodgers beat the Nationals in the NLCS."

Forrister smirked.

"Some fan of the game you are." The president sat down at his desk, putting the glass of orange juice on a glass coaster. "And no, I thought I'd wait for our morning briefing to hear about what happened in Georgia. I know they executed what's his name last night. Good riddance."

Alex gnawed at the inside of her cheek, taking away a bit of skin. A touch of copper slipped onto her tongue.

"Actually sir, they did not execute Rayburn."

"Wallace issued clemency?" Forrister said as he raised an eyebrow. "That's strange. I didn't think he was the type to have a soft spot for racist cop killers."

"That's not exactly what happened either."

The president leaned forward, resting his forearms on his blotter. He stared at the director with a look that said quite plainly that he didn't understand what she was talking about.

"What did happen?"

"He was broken out, sir."

Forrister's eyes widened.

"How can anyone just escape a death chamber?"

"It happens when someone on the inside helps the condemned out."

Forrister wore a sour look.

"Crap."

"My sentiments exactly."

Forrister leaned back, his orange juice forgotten. Alex then opened the manila folder and pulled out her handwritten notes, written with a hurried hand. She easily deciphered the chicken scratches on the white-lined paper.

"The execution appeared as if it would go off without a hitch, until an explosion—"

"If I had a nickel for every time you've said 'until an explosion,'" Forrister said.

"May I continue, Mr. President?"

Forrister smiled and nodded.

"The explosion took out the northern wall of the death chamber just before the clock struck midnight. From what I can gather from the Atlanta bureau, they had started the execution early. Witnesses to the execution who lived—"

"Oh, dear God, don't tell me."

"Witnesses who lived said that a guard pulled a gun on the execution staff just after the explosion and had him remove Rayburn's bonds. Other people entered through the hole in the wall, blasted the window away and proceeded to shoot those in attendance, including Rayburn's lawyer. One of the witnesses who survived was a reporter, and he managed to peer through the smoke to try to compile the story."

Forrister grimaced.

"Bastard could have been shot."

"Of course he could have, but as you know, Mr. President, reporters aren't exactly the smartest people in the lot."

"I can't argue with that," the president said with a wry grin, reaching for his orange juice. He took a long sip and put it back. "Has there been any word if he's been re-captured?"

Alex shook her head.

"No sir, he hasn't. It's like he evaporated."

"He'll be back."

Alex took her chance. She wet her lips.

"Sir, with the debate coming up next week and with this felon running about free, I'm concerned for not only your safety, but for Dick Bennett's safety."

Forrister grabbed an inch-thick folder and opened it.

"Has this Rayburn fellow made threats against me?"

"No sir."

"Has he made any threats against the city of Atlanta or the debate?"

"No sir."

"Has he made any threats against Dick?"

"No sir."

"Damn it."

Alex smiled softly, but it disappeared faster than it emerged. Back to serious.

"Mr. President, I want to beef up your security next week. Just in case."

Forrister turned his attention to the paperwork. To Alex's eyes, he looked like he was about to fall into a flood of bills as he picked up his pen.

So much like Sarah, she thought, *yet so different. In so many ways.*

"Fine with me, Alex. I'll let the Secret Service know you want to interfere in their jobs when I see the head later today."

Alex easily caught the sarcasm.

"Shall we continue with the briefing, Mr. President?"

Forrister spun his left index finger in a horizontal circle as he scribbled his name.

"Don't worry about Rayburn, Alex," he said. "The authorities in Georgia will handle it."

Alex continued, even though in the back of her mind she wanted to press her security clearance harder to get her way.

And it's not like I can't circumvent the system, she thought as she spoke about the situation in North Korea. *I can send someone in as backup without the president's authorization.*

She smiled.

Yeah, I think that's what I'll do. I just want more information before I send her into a dangerous situation.

***

Foggy Bottom Apartments, Washington, D.C.
Saturday, October 27, 2012
10:30 a.m. ET

Jaclyn Johnson waited impatiently for the phone to ring.

For the past three weeks the CIA special agent had been on leave, taking on new roles in her Foggy Bottom apartment: she was part time nurse, part time big sister, and part time cuddler. MI5 agent Tom Messingham, her boyfriend, was in the process of recuperating from injuries sustained at the foot of Robert Letts. Tasha, the young girl she had saved during her last mission in Las Vegas, was now her ward. At night, she held Tom in her arms while they slept. Things were, as they say, perfect.

For Jaclyn, the transition was somewhat rough going at first. Jaclyn thought that she would have no idea how she would balance her profession, where she had to be a bad ass killer, and her new-found home life, where she would have to keep the attitude in check, at least for Tasha's sake. It was her apartment though, and from the outset, Tasha, scared at her new surroundings and intimidated a tad by her new classmates at Woodrow Wilson High School in

Northwest Washington D.C., was grateful for Jaclyn taking her in. She didn't want to stomp all over Jaclyn's generosity.

Tasha automatically received a little bit of attention from the boys upon her arrival at Woodrow Wilson, which was something Jaclyn noticed right from the start. Tasha sat on the couch in her new forest green Woodrow Wilson sweatpants with the Tiger emblem resting on her right thigh, texting away with a slight grin dancing across her lips, her fingers moving at lightspeed. Jaclyn had bought her an iPhone and upgraded her own BlackBerry to an iPhone, too. They also had a little shopping spree at the mall in Arlington to make sure that Tasha had a new wardrobe. Jaclyn also converted her office into a bedroom for Tasha's use.

A teenage girl needs her privacy, Jaclyn had thought with a light grin, *and so do I. Especially with Tom here.*

Tom still couldn't speak, his jaw still wired from the damage Letts had caused after the terrorist figured out their ruse. Jaclyn had picked him up a small whiteboard so he could communicate with the girls. Tom had used harsh scribbles to tell Jaclyn that he could fly back to London and spend the remainder his convalescence at his mother's flat in Cockfosters, a small hamlet in Barnet, North London, but Jaclyn had shot that idea down. She wanted to spend as much time with him as she could before Alex called her back to work, and that meant a lot of cuddling in the chair during the interim down time. They spent quality time watching the football on Saturday and Sunday mornings—there was the occasional Thursday afternoon tie as Tom's beloved Liverpool had qualified for the Europa League after winning the League Cup the season before—as well as watching the World Series at night.

"How can you lot call it a World Series when it's just the United States playing? That's just rubbish! The world isn't just the United States!" Tom had scribbled. Jaclyn simply shrugged, not letting her boyfriend take the proverbial mickey out of her.

In addition, they watched a great deal of television together. Tom fancied Law & Order re-runs while Jaclyn was enamored with A Game of Thrones on HBO. And at 5 p.m. every day, Tom flipped to BBC America so he could watch Doctor Who. Jaclyn wouldn't tell Tom, but she started crushing on David Tennant, the Tenth incarnation of The Doctor.

"I don't get it," Jaclyn had said as they watched the episode Voyage of the Damned. "They made the Titanic a space ship?"

Tom nodded, then wrote, "You should have seen what happened in Time Crash, right before that episode. The Doctor needs to remember to put his shields up."

While she enjoyed all of these things, she had desperately wanted an assignment. She had been out of the game, as it was, for three weeks, ever since she stepped into the Sunrise Hospital in Las Vegas. Jaclyn made periodic trips to Langley, if only to catch up on things.

But with coffee in hand on this particular Saturday morning, they were watching the first half of Arsenal and Queens Park Rangers when Springsteen blared through the apartment, turning all three heads toward Jaclyn's iPhone.

"I think I better take this," she said. "I'll be in my room." She kissed Tom on the lips as he puckered for her, all while sliding her finger across the screen.

"Good morning, Chief."

"Are you secure, Snapshot?"

Jaclyn rolled her eyes as she entered her bedroom.

"Give me a second; I need to get the cube. Tom and Tasha are watching football."

"It's not noon yet," Alex countered.

"Soccer to you, Alex. Tom calls it football and only football."

"He's confused."

"Hey, that's my man you're talking about."

Jaclyn slid her hand into her MZ Wallace Paige handbag and grabbed the gray sound-dampening cube. She pressed the button, the noise-canceling waves pouring forth.

"Alright Chief. All set."

"Jaclyn, have you paid attention to the news today?"

"Nope. I woke up at 9:30. Tom was up at 7:30 watching Aston Villa and Norwich, and Tasha's been up since the crack of dawn, either texting with some horny teenager or running around the block. What's going on?"

"There's a small situation in Atlanta that I need you to keep an eye on over the next few days."

Jaclyn bit her lip.

"You need me to monitor it from here?" she said with hope in her voice.

"That's a negative, and you know that, Snapshot. You leave from Reagan at 1 o'clock. You've lounged around for too long. You're next on the docket, kiddo."

Jaclyn frowned.

"What's happening in Atlanta, Alex?"

"There was a jailbreak from the death chamber early this morning."

Jaclyn couldn't help but sit down on her bed.

"You're shitting me."

"I shit you not."

A small smile came to Jaclyn's face.

"What do we know so far?"

"There isn't much. We know that the prisoner, Bobby Ray Rayburn, escaped with the help of a prison guard by the name of Carl Dane. Police are keeping an eye out in Smyrna, his hometown, but I doubt that he'll return there. He'll be in hiding until he's ready to come out."

Jaclyn nodded.

"What's my assignment, Chief?"

"For the first day or so, you're going to pose as a White House Advance for the debate at Georgia Tech this coming week. You're to act as a liaison between Washington and Atlanta while keeping tabs on Rayburn. In essence, you're added security. The president doesn't think Rayburn will disturb the debate and wants the authorities in Georgia to handle it, but I wouldn't have the job I have now without erring on the side of caution every so often.

"Besides, having you there will make me feel a little more at ease. Your true assignment is to make sure no harm comes to either the president or Bennett during their stay in Atlanta. Both have campaign stops they will make in the interim. And Jaclyn, think about this: Should there be a potential strike against the hall, and you stop it, then perhaps Bennett will relax a bit on his whole down with the CIA kick."

"Yeah, and maybe the Mariners will do something in the off-season to replace Ichiro," Jaclyn replied sarcastically.

Alex chuckled.

"I don't take sucker bets, Snapshot."

"I know you don't."

"I'm having Salt draw up some false White House credentials for you to use. They will be on the Gulfstream before you take off."

Jaclyn lifted an eyebrow.

"Salt's working on a Saturday morning? What happened, he and the new girlfriend have a little tiff or something?"

"I don't think so. They didn't see each other last night, so he came in early today."

"Are you having him followed? I seem to recall you telling me something about knowing what I did with Tom after I saved London."

"Constitution and national security, Jaclyn. Get packing."

"Will I be working with someone in Atlanta?"

There was a moment's pause—Jaclyn thought she heard a light gasp—on the other end of the line.

"Do my ears deceive me," Alex said, "or does Little Miss Stubborn Secret Agent actually want to work with someone on this case?"

Jaclyn rolled her eyes and sighed heavily. She heard Alex's slight chuckle.

"Yes Chief, I want a partner. Tom's unable to work with me, and I'm sure I'll need someone to handle the grunt work while I'm piecing together what happened."

"About time you realized that, Snapshot."

Jaclyn sniffed.

"Tom has convinced me that I don't have to be SuperChickie every time I leave the henhouse."

"He's talking again? That's quick, especially after that kind of surgery."

"No, he said that to me when we were in the bowels of Herod's, right before he pulled me out of there." She paused. "I'll never forgive him for doing that. Or you, for that matter." She smirked. She knew she couldn't keep a straight face when it came to her emotions about Tom Messingham.

"He's a good guy, Jaclyn. And he speaks the truth." She paused. "Your parents would have liked him."

Jaclyn didn't know that she stood a little bit straighter all of a sudden.

"I know, Chief."

"Send Tasha to me, and I'll get Tom on a flight to London. I don't know how long you're going to be there. Enjoy Atlanta." Alex hung up in her customary way. Jaclyn pressed end soon after. She lifted her HUD Foster Grants and wiped her eyes before she headed back into the living room.

"Looks like I have a new case," she said, then turned to Tasha, who looked up from her phone. "You're headed to

Alex's for the time being. And you, sexy," turning to Tom, "are headed home. I'm sure your mum will want to see that I've taken care of her baby boy."

Tom tried to smile.

"What time am I going over?" Tasha asked.

"In a couple of hours. She'll have her driver get you to school every day, so don't worry about that. Just be on your best behavior for her, and no walking around the boys in your underwear."

"Of course I will, Jaclyn. I'm not going to fuck this up."

Jaclyn smiled, wondering if she meant that she would walk around the boys in her underwear or be on her best behavior. Her past was against her, but Jaclyn trusted Tasha.

"I know you won't. I'll have my phone on me if anything comes up."

Tasha grinned.

Jaclyn spun on her heel and headed back into her room to pack. Tom entered with the whiteboard half a minute later. He began to scribble and held it up for her to see.

A sly smile dragged across Jaclyn's lips half a second later.

"Well," she said softly as she walked over toward him, "since you asked so nicely, I'll just put the pillow in my mouth so Tasha doesn't hear me."

Tom grinned through the wires as Jaclyn pulled her t-shirt off.

Chapter 3
Republican National Committee Headquarters
310 First Street SE, Washington, D.C.
Saturday, October 27, 2012
11:30 a.m. ET

Unlike Alex Dupuis, Dick Bennett had his trenchcoat open as he scaled the granite steps with a healthy gait, the raw, late October winds that scoured the nation's capital this morning not affecting him. With his Secret Service escort next to him, Bennett entered the headquarters of the Republican National Committee to prepare his final assault on Eric Forrister's sham of a presidency.

During the past month, Bennett had waited for this moment, and he had yearned for it with glee. He waited for this moment with everything he had within himself: Every fiber of his being, all of his anger and hatred, had pointed itself Forrister's way over the last few weeks, mainly in regard to the way the interim president had treated him during the incident in London three months ago. Bennett had seethed when Forrister had turned on him, not hearing his counsel, not caring for the feelings Bennett had about the CIA and its staff, which had flouted the laws of the country, shooting first and asking questions later, especially the way Jaclyn Johnson operated the Boston mission and her search for a supposedly corrupt businessman. Bennett believed that he was only trying to save Sarah Kendall's legacy. In his mind, Forrister spat on that legacy without a care, and that was wrong.

The thought of Sarah's legacy toyed like that did not sit well with the new Republican challenger.

Of course, in order to get the Republican nomination, he needed to work his way into the GOP hierarchy. He had brought many pages of information, information that would down the Democrats and relegate the liberals to second tier status in Washington's political system, and once he won approval, he had to go and murder someone standing in his way to the nomination—the convention's choice, Senator Randy Jepson of Texas. These were papers that he believed wouldn't scar Sarah: he would use it and turn it against Forrister. The MBTA scandal in Boston and Jeff Harper's assassination—it didn't matter that he was in the room when these decisions were made, especially when Forrister gave the assassination order on Harper; the way he remembered it, he didn't want Harper to die, he only wanted Sarah's tormentor brought to justice.

The key to it all was not the planned assassination of Jepson, though.

The key was Jennifer Farrell.

Farrell's release from federal prison was important to Bennett's plans, as she had become his vice presidential nominee after securing her release earlier this month. Farrell had been the object of Johnson's "vigilante justice," as he called it, when the woman had tracked a Christian terrorist to Kingman, Arizona. Farrell just happened to be there as an innocent bystander—at least that's what she had told him when Bennett visited her at FCI-Dublin on a much rainier day than today. Even though Bennett knew the truth, he had overlooked it and had promised her that he would get her out. He had said he would get the charges dropped.

His promise worked: The RNC found a sympathetic judge to the conservative cause, a holdover from the Bush administration, a relic who ruled his courtroom with an iron fist and punished the poor with fines they could not afford to pay. With prompting from the GOP's attorneys, the judge released her on her personal recognizance and, at Bennett's insistence, set a pre-trial conference for the morning of January 21, 2013.

It was a sly move by the Republicans: January 21 happened to be the day after Inauguration Day, and the line of thinking was that if Bennett won the election, he would simply issue her a pardon as one of his first acts as president on January 20, making the case simply evaporate from the public's conscience.

It was simple, and it was exactly as the GOP hoped the judge would do. No one was keen to Bennett's plan.

Prior to her arrest in Kingman, Farrell was, for all intents and purposes, a two-term wallflower member of the Senate. She did enough to get herself re-elected a second time, and without a challenger from either party, the "enough" came in the form of taking out nomination papers in the fourth year of each term. She hadn't done much this term other than making sure that bills which had something to do with Nevada received the attention they deserved. Other than that, she enjoyed her time in Washington, living in a luxurious Georgetown home that rivaled the opulence of the hotels in her state's signature city. She was a rather thin woman of medium height, unmarried and in her late 30's, and Bennett knew her in passing as she and Sarah Kendall had served together, albeit in different houses of Congress, when Kendall had served the Tenth District of her native Massachusetts.

For Farrell, it took her a few days to get used to being on the outside again, but with her mind and her knowledge of how Forrister had secured the funding deal to rehabilitate not only Los Angeles but also the high-speed rail line between L.A. and Las Vegas, she was a great asset to Bennett and the RNC. Her information, Bennett knew, would help bring the Democrats down and return the Republicans to power. The bailouts to Las Vegas casinos were Farrell's doing, of course, on the prompting of hotel and casino owners, people who lined her campaign pockets with healthy contributions. Forrister, the Republicans believed, didn't have to agree to those conditions just to get Farrell's support and to get a bill passed.

And that's where Forrister trips up, Bennett thought with a slight grin. *Right at the finish line.*

He turned at the top of the stairs and gazed to the northwest. The Capitol Building stood off to the right while the Washington Monument, the white stone hardly seen through the thick fog that hung over the city, stood off to the left, the National Mall separating them with green arms spread wide. Various office buildings of the House of Representatives and the Senate dotted the landscape in between. From this vantage point, he could not see 1600 Pennsylvania Avenue, but he knew that the president was there, preparing to wage war in the home stretch of the 2012 election cycle. He entered the building, shucking off the trenchcoat as soon as the door closed, shutting out the cold. Bennett scratched at his red-tipped nose.

Even on a Saturday, the committee headquarters was full of life. Telephones looked as if surgeons had expertly sewn the receivers to ears, and as fingers danced across keypads, there was a look of seriousness on each face as they spoke to the voters. Pausing at the entrance to the headquarters proper, Bennett could see their determination and drive to get their candidate—a candidate that defected from the other side and needed subterfuge to get himself nominated, but that was beside the point—elected to the nation's highest office, and he appreciated every bit of their efforts. There would be jobs for them in his White House, even if it they had to fetch coffee for a living.

"Good morning, everyone," he said, hanging his coat on a tree stand next to the door.

"Good morning, Mr. President-elect," they chorused.

Bennett grinned. They had said that every day for the past two weeks. It tickled him that they showed so much confidence in his candidacy.

"How are we all doing today?" he said as he walked past several tables full of bright-eyed Young Republicans.

Some barely spoke to him. Bennett was the big shot candidate that had stolen their hearts and minds. He had been in Washington a long time, and knew his presence intimidated them.

Ignoring the "hold on, wait a minute" finger of Daniel Rubenstein, his campaign manager, he swept into Farrell's small office and closed the door behind him. Farrell was working that morning, too. Like everyone else, she was working the numbers, placing phone calls to her Nevada constituents, and mapping out her wardrobe for this coming week. She had planned to accompany Bennett to Atlanta for the debate and planned to stump for him as if she were running for president.

With her on my side, I cannot lose, he thought.

While Bennett was somewhat dressed down this morning—he wore a blue polo shirt with the logo of the Groton Country Club on the left breast, which he had picked up after playing golf there following an unusually easy campaign stop in uber-liberal Massachusetts—Farrell was in all black, right down to her stockings. Bennett liked that, and it gave him a charge every morning to glance down at his running mate's smooth legs. Thoughts of seduction had never entered his mind until he saw her the morning after the arraignment, when she wore this same outfit.

Besides, his wife was out of town on the campaign trail for him. He needed something to do to kill time between stops.

"Senator," he said.

Farrell looked up, her hair tossing about as she moved. She smiled.

"Good morning, Dick. What is on our agenda today?"

"We have to finish fine-tuning our plan of attack for the debate. Remind me again: Which casinos received bailouts from our esteemed Commander in Chief?"

"You name it, they got one. My whole argument for supporting the president's bill was based on the fact that Las Vegas's economy took a nose dive when the earthquake hit Los Angeles. He said he would ensure that funding went to the businesses on the Strip hit hardest. And that was pretty much all of them. Even Herod's received a cut of the pie to help get the project off the ground," she said, referring to the hotel that Robert Letts' organization had sent tumbling into the hot Las Vegas sands.

"What I'm surprised about," Bennett said as he perched his rump on the edge of her desk, "was that no one on the right-hand side of the aisle, in both the House and Senate, said anything about it."

Farrell flashed a wry grin his way.

"Oh, that. You do know that most senators and representatives don't actually read the bills they vote on, right? I've never read a single bill that's come across my desk, Dick. We have our aides take care of that; it's what they get paid for, along with everything else we have them perform for us. The aides tell us what is actually in the bill. I did hear from a few politicians on my side, and I convinced them not to talk about it to the press. Surprisingly, they agreed. It shocked me that they kept their mouths shut. The Democrats did nothing. Then I had to do a dance: What I had said on that dais in Las Vegas was true from a certain point of view. It was a great day for Las Vegas."

Bennett pursed his lips and tapped at them with a finger before he blew out a long breath.

"What else was in that bill that I need to remember to bring up Thursday night?"

"There's the fact that there's no need to have high-speed rail service to a city that doesn't exist."

"Very true, I remember thinking that when he signed the bill. Did you keep the pen from the signing?"

Farrell's face twisted in revulsion.

"I threw the thing in the fucking trash can before I left the convention center. I may have paid lip service to Forrister in my support speech about it last month, but it just makes no sense. Just like his plan to rebuild the monorail now, the high-speed rail project is just liberal pork barrel spending, plain and simple."

"And that is something that we will stop as soon as we're elected. The liberals have had their hands in the cookie jar of the American people for far too long. It is time to rein in the budget, the pointless entitlements. We will get the budget back under control far faster than our predecessors ever dreamed."

Farrell stood—the chair creaked slightly—and smiled.

"Yes, they have. And they've persecuted big businesses, our biggest campaign contributors, just as long. That will come to an end, too."

Bennett's grin widened.

"We think so much alike, Senator."

"We do," she replied. "You were just on the wrong side of the aisle for so long."

He leaned in and kissed her. She didn't seem to accept the kiss at first, but she was soon giving it back to him, deeper and wetter than Bennett could give.

"I'm on the right side now."

The pair couldn't help but laugh at the way fate had taken over the campaign. From their point of view, Forrister was finished—and it would be they who took him down once and for all.

Chapter 4
Reagan National Airport, Washington, D.C
Saturday, October 27, 2012
12:30 p.m. ET

Somehow, Tom and Jaclyn made their lovemaking work in the short time they had left together, and with Tom's current medical condition, there were certain aspects to sex they couldn't accomplish. With Tom taking an Emirates Airlines flight back to Heathrow and Jaclyn headed south on the agency's Gulfstream, it would be the last time they would experience each other's touch and kisses for some time. They made it work though, and they had emerged from the bedroom at about 11 to see Tasha standing in front of them, her arms crossed underneath her breasts, shaking her head at them. The couple, found out and caught, blushed furiously.

Alex's driver had come to pick up Tasha to take her to Arlington while Jaclyn's driver took her and Tom to Reagan. The trip did not take long. The two lovers stood on the tarmac—their diplomatic credentials pre-checked via Salt's supercomputer back at Langley—looking into each other's eyes, forehead to forehead, nose to nose. The Gulfstream rested only twenty feet away, gassed up and ready to blister the early afternoon sky.

"I'm going to miss you, Scouser," Jaclyn said.

Tom slipped his fingers through her silky blonde hair, his eyes growing wet. He pursed his lips and tried to speak through his clenched teeth.

"I'll miss you too," he grunted. They wrapped their arms around each other and held on, burning their partners' respective scents into their minds. Tom had the scent of Pert Plus pouring off his scalp. Jaclyn felt Tom's hands roam up and down the back of her navy blue sport coat. She also felt his breath, hot and steamy, against her neck.

She shivered and let her fingers pull at the back of his white button-down Oxford. The Gulfstream's engines, quiet at first, began to whine as they warmed up.

"I'm going to miss that most."

Tom winked.

"Text me when you get to London. I'll come see you soon. Christmas, more than likely. Tell mum to set a place for Tasha and I. I can't wait to meet your sisters."

They kissed once more, running their hands down the other's arms to hold hands. Tom brought Jaclyn's to his lips before they broke apart. She felt her heart skip a beat as lips found skin. Jaclyn smiled as she walked backward to the plane, its door open, ready to receive its highly classified passenger. She waved good bye to Tom before she ducked into the plane. Claire, her usual stewardess with an equally-high security clearance, closed the door behind her, sealing out the brisk air.

After she picked up the manila packet of false credentials from her seat, Jaclyn belted herself in before she took her iPad out and began reviewing the files Alex had sent her in the past two hours. Within a few minutes, they were ready to make their ascent into the rapidly clearing sky above the capital and northern Virginia.

"Agent Johnson, this is your captain speaking. Welcome aboard."

Jaclyn pressed a button on her armrest.

"Hi Kevin. Glad to have you working for me today. It's been what, two weeks? Feels like it's been a month."

"It has, hasn't it? It's always our pleasure to fly you around. We'll get you to Atlanta. Just relax."

Jaclyn smiled.

"That's why I always fly this airline."

She unclicked the button and leaned back, letting the flight crew run the Gulfstream through its pre-flight paces.

***

Hartsfield-Jackson Atlanta International Airport
Atlanta, Georgia
Saturday, October 27, 2012
3:15 p.m. ET

Captain Kevin gave Jaclyn a smooth flight and an equally smooth landing as the Gulfstream descended toward Hartsfield-Jackson Atlanta International Airport. The sun looked as if it were in the process of baking the runway from its mid-autumn tilt.

Jaclyn dressed in preparation of baking, too. Her last three high-profile assignments—Boston, London and Las Vegas—all occurred in seasonal climates with temps near roasting, and she expected Atlanta to be the same. But when she discovered that the temperatures at night would be something closer to her native Seattle, she nearly jumped out of her seat for joy.

"And I didn't even bring any warmer clothes," she said as Claire brought her a bottle of Nantucket Harbor, the company that Jaclyn had saved from financial ruin during the Boston incident sixteen-plus months ago. "I'm going to have to use my expense account to buy some new ones."

She grinned. That will have to wait, though, she thought. First things first. Rayburn and the debate.

The Gulfstream touched down at about quarter past 3 and spent a few minutes taxiing to a private terminal. Jaclyn deplaned and, after securing her luggage including her special essentials, she made her way to a Hertz counter. There she acquired a 2007 Hyundai Accent, which she believed would suit her until Parkerhurst—good ol' Parkerhurst—ventured south to deliver her usual souped up car in the next couple of days. Once she had her bags stowed, she hopped in the Hyundai and pulled out of the rental lot.

The seven miles from the airport into Atlanta proper effortlessly slid by in Jaclyn's estimation. Interstates 85 and 75 merged just south of the Langford Parkway, becoming the Downtown Connector. A few minutes later with traffic surging on either side of her, Jaclyn passed Turner Field on her right-hand side. With the skyline of Downtown Atlanta ahead of her, it was only a matter of time before she reached her first destination of this mission. It was nearly quarter of 4 before Jaclyn hit her directional and eased off the highway at Exit 250, with the campus of Georgia Tech on the left-hand side. The turquoise dome of the Hank McCamish Pavillion, the home of Georgia Tech's basketball teams, stood ready to receive her in its own unique way.

Jaclyn didn't question the reasoning behind holding the final presidential debate of the 2012 election season in this rustic old barn. She understood the logistics behind it: the Pavillion stood in the northeast corner of the campus, across 10th Street Northwest from CNN's broadcast headquarters. That would make it easy for that network to show the event without a lot of satellite hookups from the site. But she also knew that Georgia Tech had procured the debate in the refurbished building, once known as the Alexander Memorial Coliseum, in the hopes that it would be a draw to prospective students not only in the state, but around the country as a whole. It was a gamble, and a little voice in the back of her head told her that she needed to make sure that the gamble paid off.

She made the left-hand turn from 10th onto Fowler Street. A security guard held up his hand, forcing Jaclyn to stop just inside the sidewalk. She rolled down her window.

"Can I help you, ma'am? This area is off limits for the time being," the guard said, a southern drawl sliding from between his teeth.

"I'm from the White House," Jaclyn replied, pulling out the credential with her photo and her false name, Allison

Jennings. It showed her wearing regular eyeglasses, which Jaclyn now wore to keep up appearances. These eyeglasses, coupled with specially made contact lenses, worked just like her HUD sunglasses. She still had those packed away just in case she needed them for a nighttime surveillance, which she was sure would come up at some point. "I'm supposed to meet some folks from the Secret Service in a few minutes." She sounded bubbly and perky, which made her stomach roll.

"Let me radio you in," the guard said, pulling the mic clip from his shoulder and pressing the call button. Jaclyn remained calm through it all, tapping her fingers on the steering wheel to a tune only she could hear.

A minute later, the guard waved her through the gate area. She parked a little way down the street, her rental pointing toward downtown Atlanta. The Bank of America Tower appeared to burn rust in the fading sunlight. She could see the press box of Chandler Field, Georgia Tech's baseball stadium, off to the right a bit. And through the light towers of the softball field, she saw the north end zone seats of Bobby Dowd Stadium. Fraternity Row laid somewhere in the middle of it all, slumbering through the day, ready to party hearty tonight.

Jaclyn grimaced and sighed.

Another thing I missed with the hand God dealt me, she thought.

She entered the arena, trying to keep a smile on her face.

Jaclyn could only describe the interior of the arena as organized chaos and sensory overload as workers tried to convert a standard Division 1 on-campus basketball arena into a pit of political upheaval. They hurried around the circular floor area, setting up white folding chairs in long equal rows, a five-foot walkway running down the center toward a steel dais with seven yellow vertical Georgia Tech banners as a backdrop. Large messageboards stood on either side of the dais, where larger-than-life-size images of President Forrister and former White House Chief of Staff Bennett would appear during the debate. Workers were also moving a long horizontal graphics board, which would display an American flag with a digitized wind making it flutter across the screen, as the debate proceeded. Workers barked at each other as they milled about, stepping over heavy duty cables. Banks of lights sat in cases, ready for hanging.

This debate was to be the one that turned undecided voters' minds toward their chosen candidate, Jaclyn knew from watching the news. There were plenty of those people remaining, wondering whether to continue with Forrister's presidency and the ideals of Sarah Kendall or try something new with Dick Bennett. There was a third party candidate involved, but Jaclyn, a keen follower of current events, also knew that a majority of the voting public wouldn't give that candidate the time of day.

Jaclyn turned her head and looked to the upper level of the arena, where the three major networks as well as CNN and Fox News were in the process of setting up their broadcast positions for the next five days, the dais in the background of their camera angles. She had read the intelligence report on the plane: the networks wanted to give this debate around the clock coverage over the course of the week. Jaclyn hoped that none of the networks would come to her seeking information about the candidates, and wondered just exactly when Alex would free her from this disguise as an advance. She hoped that she wouldn't bury a bullet in anyone's brain for misidentifying her as a lowly paper-pusher.

That would be hard to explain away, she thought as a man wearing a suit approached her position. She turned to face him. He paused mid-stride as if to gauge her, she figured, before he continued moving her way. He had his hand out-stretched as he came within a few feet or her.

"Miss Jennings, I presume? I'm Gary Tuck with Campus Police. I understand you're from the White House? It's an honor."

Jaclyn shook his hand.

"Yes, I am."

"What can I do for you?"

"I'm here to make sure things are in order and that the Secret Service is doing its job."

"Did you expect them not to do their jobs, Miss Jennings?"

"I never take that chance, Mr. Tuck. After what happened in Colombia, it's standard to check up on them. They can get away with murder sometimes."

Tuck said nothing, and only nodded grimly.

They walked toward the dais, Jaclyn taking the lead.

"How many workers do we have here, Mr. Tuck?"

"There are about fifty, ma'am. Why do you ask?"

"Have they all been cleared by the Secret Service?"

"As far as I know. Why do you ask?"

Jaclyn spun on Tuck and immediately dropped the bubbliness.

"I need not remind you what happened in London in July, or in Las Vegas earlier this month, do I? We don't need more Americans dying, or the president's life put in danger because of lackadaisical security, do we, Mr. Tuck?" Jaclyn fixed the man with an incredible stare through the false contacts. Her eyebrows furrowed toward each other. She had never before done this, having had her eyes constantly covered.

Tuck gulped and blanched.

"No," he said, shaking his head. "We don't want that to happen at all."

"Good," Jaclyn said, feeling the sweat roll down her back, her heart beating wildly as she continued to walk toward the dais. "Let's make sure that none of these people will sneak any explosives or anything that may be construed as a weapon of mass destruction. We're going to have a few thousand people inside this arena in five days. I hope we can keep them all alive until they choose a new president or re-elect the current one." She paused to breathe for a moment, then turned to the security officer. "Can we continue the tour, Mr. Tuck?"

He nodded and followed her.

Tuck wasn't a large man, but he wasn't a small one, either. He was of medium build, yet slightly taller than Jaclyn. He had a full head of black hair that, Jaclyn noted, had sprinkles of gray just above his ears. He had his hair trimmed somewhat short, but not in crew cut fashion. Jaclyn gauged him to be around two hundred pounds, and she noticed that the man sweated a little bit as he walked.

Maybe I made him a little nervous just now, she thought. *Good. I like keeping men on their toes, especially when it comes to the security of the president. I'm glad he's taking this as serious as I'm taking it.*

They walked around the steel awning and stepped onto the dais a few seconds later. The two lecterns were not in place just yet. Jaclyn saw them under black curtains in the rear of the stage. From here, Jaclyn saw the breadth of the arena, where the candidates would try to cut the other down with facts and/or innuendo when the debate began. She hadn't decided from where she would watch it all take place, but she knew she would stay on site Thursday.

She could feel Tuck's eyes on her as she looked out on the sea of white.

Jaclyn turned toward him.

"Everything is looking good out here. How about you show me where the president and Mr. Bennett will be during the beginning of the program?"

"And don't forget the governor, too."

Jaclyn blinked.

"The governor?"

"Yes ma'am, Governor Woodruff let us know that he had planned on attending. He said his staff let the White House know about it."

"Funny," Jaclyn said, trying to keep her expression smooth. "I was not made aware. Perhaps his staff didn't follow through. I have to talk to the governor anyway."

"Oh?"

"Yes. I'll need to speak with his security detail."

As they walked toward the backstage area, Jaclyn bumped into a wall of a man standing just beyond the curtain.

She looked into the face of a tall, husky-sized man that towered over her. He looked as if he could break Jaclyn in two, but she knew that he had a weak spot and she could take him down any second that she wished. His eyes bore holes into her forehead, though, and Jaclyn immediately felt a shiver wriggle up her spine.

"Agent Johnson," he said.

Jaclyn looked perplexed. Tuck, on the other hand, looked confused.

"Yes, I know who you are. Mr. Tuck, if you'd excuse us please," the large man said. Tuck looked back and forth before he left the man and Jaclyn alone.

"Who are you?" Jaclyn demanded as soon as Tuck's footsteps trailed away.

"I'll ask the questions around here, Agent Johnson. I'd like to know why the CIA is snooping around. The other one couldn't give me a straight answer."

"Was that a question? I didn't hear the inflections of inquisitiveness in your voice." Jaclyn smirked. She didn't even hear him say anything about the other one.

The man fumed. Jaclyn could see his nose hairs trembling under the strain.

"You're being evasive."

Jaclyn nearly laughed in his face.

"Well gee, I work for the CIA and I have no idea who you are or how high your security clearance goes, so take a guess why I'm being evasive. That's my job. How about you answer a few of my questions, and then maybe—maybe—I'll answer a few of yours? How about that?"

The man's nostrils flared, but he took a deep breath.

"Alright."

"Who are you with?"

"The Secret Service."

Jaclyn snorted.

Yeah, she thought, *his clearance is pretty high.*

"Obviously."

"Who is the other person here from the CIA?"

"At the moment, I'm the only one here, as far as I know."

"And why are you here?"

"I'm providing extra security for the president and for the challenger, with everything that happened last night."

The Secret Service agent blinked.

"You mean the Rayburn matter?"

Jaclyn touched her nose.

"Are you investigating it?" he asked.

"I will be. I need to go to the prison in a little while and check in there. Where is this other person from the CIA?"

"She's over here. Let's go."

The agent turned and walked away. Jaclyn followed him.

"And what's your name, Agent—?"

"Agent Peters."

Jaclyn saluted him as they walked.

"Glad to know we're on a last name basis, Agent Peters."

It wasn't half a minute later that a young woman emerged from a side room with a manila file folder in her hand. Jaclyn nearly paused mid-stride upon seeing her. She was an attractive African-American woman who was slightly taller than Jaclyn, with skin the color of creamy mocha. She had black hair falling off her scalp in cottony waves, and her facial structure, Jaclyn noted, was near to that of the actress who had played Martha Jones, the Tenth Doctor's assistant, before her departure from the TARDIS in Last of the Time Lords.

Jaclyn's heart inexplicably ached for Tom's touch. That episode was one of the last they had watched during Tom's convalescence. She bit her lip.

"Ah, here she is. Agent Johnson, meet Agent Jasmine Anderson. She's been waiting for you." The Secret Service agent looked at both women before turning away and retreating toward the arena proper, leaving them alone.

Anderson held her hand out. Jaclyn grasped it. Anderson had a strong, tight grip.

"It's a pleasure to meet you, Agent Johnson."

"Likewise."

"I've heard a lot about you."

A light smile danced across Jaclyn's face.

"I bet. I haven't met anyone in the past three months who has managed to avoid hearing my name."

Anderson's lips parted, and Jaclyn believed that the look on her face was a tell: Anderson was worried about offending her new partner.

"I didn't mean—"

"Jasmine, don't worry about it. I have a thick skin. I've learned how to ignore things like that. I don't get angry about it any longer."

"You only get even?"

"Only if I don't like you."

Anderson couldn't help but bite her lip for half a second.

"I'll try not to get on your bad side, then." She inhaled quickly. "Has the director given you an update of what's going on yet?"

"Not really. I haven't been in contact with her since before I left Washington."

"Rayburn's gone to ground. There's no sign of him anywhere."

"As she expected. She believes that Rayburn's going to make a scene here at some point, and I don't disagree with her. Alex usually has good intel about the situations she sends me in to, and if she believes that Rayburn will make an appearance Thursday, then we need to keep our eyes open."

Anderson nodded.

"Right."

"Everything looks like it's all set here. Did what's his name tell you where the Secret Service will be positioned during the debate?"

"He did."

"Show me."

Jaclyn and Anderson went back into the arena proper, their heels clicking on the floor before yelling workers drowned the sounds out. Anderson pointed out the locations. Jaclyn wished she had her HUD to record the information on the device's microchip.

"Let's take a drive," Jaclyn said. "We'll take my car."

"Where are we going?"

"First, the hotel. I want to check in and get my gear stowed away. Then I want to take a drive down to the prison. I want to see how Rayburn avoided his death sentence."

"You're the boss."

The two women left the arena and made their way to Jaclyn's Hyundai.

Chapter 5
Westin Peachtree Hotel, 50th Floor
Atlanta, Georgia
Saturday, October 27, 2012
4:35 p.m. ET

Thanks to his associates' planning prior to busting him out of prison, Bobby Ray Rayburn found his way to Atlanta proper within a day. After spending the night in an abandoned farmhouse just off the back roads, they waited for daylight to make the full escape work. They had changed cars twice, ditching their prior methods of travel along the side of the road and torching the cars. They wouldn't need them again, and they sped off to the next destination.

Using unique disguises, Rayburn and Carl the Guard managed to avoid capture by patrols; Rayburn had dressed like a clown, while Carl, who drove, portrayed his bumbling, colorful assistant en route to a child's birthday party. Thankfully, they weren't stopped, and the pair changed disguises at the second destination, a sleeper cell of the KKK.

By the time they had reached Downtown Atlanta, Rayburn was exhausted. He had slept little in the farmhouse, for his nerves, even though the beer had settled them a little, had returned to flare up. The sounds of chopper blades above kept him awake, but the helicopters passed the farmhouse by just as fast as they had approached. Rayburn's co-conspirators had taken the initiative and hid the first getaway car inside the farmhouse with them, and there were no recent tracks to alert authorities in the sky where they were located. In the morning, Rayburn had a hot cup of coffee for the first time in memory—jailhouse coffee was not exactly the best for prisoners—and he tried to scarf down a couple of doughnuts that another sleeper cell had managed to sneak to them. Rayburn felt glad someone else drove, because he couldn't keep his eyes open to keep control of a vehicle.

They let the anonymity of Atlanta's streets swallow them. Rayburn's eyes drifted toward the dome of the State Capitol building as they passed. His eyes narrowed.

"Oh, Wally," he whispered. "Wally, none of this had to happen."

"Did you say something, Bobby Ray?" Carl asked.

Rayburn quieted himself, but he tried to peek at the dome again as Carl slipped further away.

Shortly after 4:30 in the afternoon, they pulled up to the front of the Westin Peachtree Hotel, a 73-story, 723-foot-tall building that seemed to dent the clouds above, its cylindrical shape making it appear like a steel-and-reflective glass tube standing in the heart of Atlanta's downtown. They had changed into matching suits, making them appear to be important businessmen visiting Atlanta. Rayburn, wearing a false hairpiece, checked into the hotel using the name Woody Bristle, a southern-sounding pseudonym that wouldn't attract attention to anyone in this state.

Rayburn took the card key for his room while Carl did the same before they turned and walked toward a bank of elevators. A small crowd of people stood waiting for one that would take them to their rooms, or possibly upstairs to the Sundial Restaurant, the rotating eatery at the very pinnacle of the building with scenic displays of Atlanta and the surrounding area. He studied every face, making sure there were no cops nearby, ready to haul him and Carl in for what had happened last night.

Two pairs of elevator doors opened at the same time. Rayburn and Carl entered the elevator on the right. A blonde-haired woman as well as another woman, this one of African-American persuasion, stepped off the other at the same time.

Rayburn paid them no mind as the elevator doors slid shut in front of him.

The elevator surged upward, carrying the escaped convict and his former guard—now a former employee of the state of Georgia—higher into the building, like bile surging up an esophagus. It stopped several times to let passengers disembark, but Rayburn and Carl didn't get off until it reached the fiftieth floor. There, a penthouse awaited their use, paid for by a Georgia politician with pro-KKK leanings, albeit silently. The view, the concierge promised Rayburn, faced southeast as he had requested.

Rayburn walked into the penthouse and, after setting his bag down and removing the piece from his scalp, walked over to the large window. He stared not at tall Atlanta City Hall, or even beyond to Turner Field, his home away from home during his youth.

He only had eyes for the golden dome of the Georgia State Capitol building.

He didn't hear Carl moving about, setting his own bag down or opening the door to the wet bar. Rayburn stared ahead, his brow furrowing toward the bridge of his nose. His cheek twitched involuntarily, and soon he felt his body grow warm. The sun had nearly reached the horizon, and its rays were nearly in his eyes, warming his bald head. He reached up and ran his hand across his scalp. It was saturated, and as he lowered it, he could feel the beads slip down his fingers and pool on the tips. He didn't hear the droplets plink off the floor.

He nearly had his lips primed to speak.

"Bobby Ray," Carl interrupted. Rayburn turned and found him carrying two longneck bottles of Bud Light. He handed one to Rayburn. "I just checked the radio, using code. It turns out that a lot of our followers are under strict surveillance. They won't be able to meet up with you yet."

Rayburn's lips twisted.

"Damn it. That's not exactly unsurprising. As we rode through the back roads, I wondered how quickly the cops would try to keep our friends under their eye. They'll want to prevent them from finding me, and I would hope, in turn, that our friends would be smart enough not to lead the police right to me. I'm sure they have Smyrna all blocked off to me right now, too. But there are other ways of communicating with them." He took a long sip of beer, letting the amber liquid slide into his mouth. He sat down on a long white couch.

"They'd have the phones tapped."

"Even their cellulars?"

Carl nodded.

"It'll have to be through email or snail mail, then."

"That's what I was thinking. Snail mail is too slow, and it's Saturday afternoon. If we want to get word to them, it has to be through the computer. They have this thing called Facebook now, but that's monitored heavily by the authorities. Email may be the only way to do it."

"Then let's do it that way. I haven't used a computer in five years." He paused and smirked. "I wonder if I remember how to turn the thing on."

"It's like a bicycle, Bobby Ray."

Rayburn chuckled.

"Tell me what's been going on other than breaking me out."

"The debate is coming up this Thursday. Forrister and some Bennett guy."

"Isn't Forrister the vice president?"

Carl laughed.

"You haven't been under a rock, man. You've only been in prison. Forrister took over when the broad was killed up there in Yankee country."

"And who's Bennett? He the Republican?"

"Yeah, he's one of ours. He was a Dem until he left over the summer. Some bull shit political thing. But they're not important." Carl stared into Rayburn's eyes. "Wally's going to be there."

A slow grin made its way across Rayburn's face. His mind whirled with the possibilities.

"How do you know?"

"It was in yesterday's paper."

"Do you still have a copy of it?"

Carl shook his head.

"It's at the prison."

Rayburn frowned.

"Shit."

"Sorry, man."

"No problem, don't worry about it. But he's going to be there? Perfect."

"We can wait until then to get revenge."

"We can," Rayburn said before taking a long sip. He leaned back. "Or we can do more than just lounge around until then." He smiled.

Carl's face was a mirror.

"What do you have in mind, Bobby Ray?"

Rayburn felt the left side of his mouth curl upward, so much so that his lip nearly touched his nose. Unbrushed teeth appeared.

"We're going to leave a little calling card for those nigger lovers."

Carl couldn't help but laugh, while Rayburn turned his head and looked at the State Capitol again.

I will have my revenge, Wally, he thought. *I will have my revenge. Everything that happens from here on out will be your fault.*

***

Rayburn didn't start out life as a racist. He was a good-natured boy during his formative years, his mother had said at his trial, but the jurors, all of them God-fearing Cobb

Countiers, didn't consider her testimony when they convicted him. The looks of disgust they threw his way as the foreman read the verdict and the subsequent sentence told him and everyone in the courtroom just exactly what they hoped God would do to him when he met his maker.

His story, though, was a tragic one, one that began with a movie during a friend's slumber party.

Young Bobby Ray was only twelve in 2002 when he attended his friend Timmy's thirteenth birthday party. He was only a couple of weeks away from turning thirteen himself at this time, and Timmy's special request was that he got to choose a PG-13 movie for him and his friends to watch without parental supervision.

Instead of the PG-13 flick, he and his friends took a chance and watched something else: his older brother's friend Chris worked at a video store, and instead of The Bourne Identity, with a nod and a wink, Chris handed over the DVD of Rambo.

From there, Rayburn's love of guns—his father had taken him hunting and let his son use his shotgun a couple of times to take down a deer, but that was between them; his mother didn't even know—developed from youthful curiosity into a carnal obsession. He needed to know about the latest guns; he craved that knowledge, much in the way gearheads know the in and outs of a car's engine, and the way that sports talk radio hosts devour the morning paper, stats and all. He could tell the uninitiated how to put together a Baretta and pull it apart in only a few seconds, and he knew the different types of ammunition that a hunter could use in a certain shotgun. He told everyone that all one needed was three pounds of pressure in order to fire a weapon. He lived, breathed and slept guns, so much so that he intentionally sniffed the harsh chemicals his father used to clean his own guns. To him, it was a high better than anything drugs or a double shot of Nyquil could give. To him, guns were drugs.

Target practice came easy to him. By the age of fourteen, Rayburn hit close to the bulls eye at the range, and a year later, he could hit it dead center with regularity. He especially loved semi-automatics and their ability to fire off multiple rounds.

It was around this time of his life that he fell in with the wrong crowd. A group of teenagers at his school had fathers who were fully-fledged members of a renewed Ku Klux Klan, and wanting to fit in, Rayburn and his friends spied on the men while they held a meeting in an abandoned farmhouse. They listened to the message—death to the blacks, every single one of them, for they have ruined the South since Doctor King walked the streets, the men had said—and sat outside the farmhouse in relative awe.

The speeches unsettled Rayburn at first. His parents were God-fearing Christians who taught him that Christ hated no one and loved everyone equally, regardless of skin color, creed, sexual orientation or religious denomination. He wondered what they would have said if they found out about this event. The fact these people spoke of hating another human interested him, and at the same time, had him hating himself for listening. He cried himself to sleep that night.

Yet drawn to the flame of bigotry, he went back for more. His curiosity was piqued. And much like his obsession with guns, Young Rayburn, only fifteen, grew into the life of the KKK. With time, he looked at people with different skin colors as if they had the plague. He would call those with black skin "coon," "monkey," and "nigger." He and his friends tossed bananas at their black classmates, a prank that, in suburban Atlanta, received a telling off but no substantial punishment and no mention of the incident on their permanent records. The principal, the students knew, was friendly with the KKK fathers. He had seen them at the meeting and smirked.

Then, at sixteen, he took part in a lynching. With shaking hands, he tied the rope around the young black girl's neck, making sure it was tight around her larynx. She was thirteen and barely conscious. He and his friends had cornered her on a back road near his house, but no one heard her pleas for help. They pushed her back and forth between them, calling her names. Flicking fingers at her ears. Then the spitting began, followed by the punching. She fell to the ground. The boys then put their feet into action. Her bones snapped. Skin swelled near the girl's lips and eyes. Someone pulled a rope out of a knapsack and handed it to Rayburn. He breathed in sharply, knowing what they wanted him to do. He grinned despite his rapid heartbeat.

He strung her limp body up, tossing the other end of the rope around what looked like a sturdy tree branch. They sent it up again before Rayburn wrapped the loose end around his fists, the rough material rubbing his skin red. He tugged once, hard, and the girl barely budged. She could have been dead weight, but the tall youth couldn't move her. Someone stuck a cloth into her mouth.

Two more friends joined him, and together, their efforts pulled the girl up from a prone position to one that had her hanging ten feet off the ground. Her feet didn't kick out, nor did she reach for the rope. She was limp, barely aware. Blood trickled down the left side of her head, sliding into the corner of her mouth. They all looked on and mocked her, throwing loose stones at her head. The force of the blows made her body sway.

It was when she finally awoke that her panic registered. Rayburn saw her eyes light up in alarm.

"She's awake," he said.

"Let's burn her!" another said.

"Yeah!"

Rayburn didn't freeze. He helped them gather wood and stacked it high. The pile came just under her feet.

Rayburn ran home and, after wiping any potential prints from the handle, fetched a red gasoline tank. There was half a gallon remaining; his father had used the first half gallon for the tractor. He poured it atop the pile and even doused the girl's shoes. The girl began crying for her mama around the makeshift gag. Rayburn's heart, hardened by hatred, felt nothing for her cries.

His friend lit the match and tossed it in close to the accelerant. The conflagration began, orange flames roaring around the pile in mere seconds, the fuel adding to the heat that poured from the pile of dead wood. The heat bathed their faces in a healthy orange glow.

The flames tickled her feet, but they couldn't hear her screams. Smoke rose, the fire melting the soles of her sneakers. Then the fire caught the gasoline Rayburn had poured on her.

She kicked at the flames, and the movement caused the branch to begin cracking. The snapping wood above went off like a gunshot, and the girl's body fell into the burning pile. Her weight sent wood scattering, causing the boys to jerk their bodies backward to avoid the kindling. They watched, wide-eyed, as the fire consumed the girl's body. She couldn't move. The stink of flesh charring filled the air.

They moved away, but not before Rayburn pulled out a gun with an empty soda bottle attached to the barrel. He had read about the ghetto silencer and was dying to try one out. Here was his opportunity. He reached over the flames, pointing the gun at her head. He didn't even flinch as the heat lapped at his forearm.

He didn't hesitate either. He pulled the trigger, his eyes dark, his mouth a thin line.

She didn't move again, the back of her head blowing away like a mushroom cloud.

The boys scattered. None of them were questioned, and it seemed as though the girl's death, despite anger from the black community, would be swept under the proverbial rug. The chief paid lip service to them and said his men would do everything possible to find the killer. They never did, and Rayburn never confessed to that killing.

Two years passed.

Nearly eighteen years old, Rayburn had turned from the sweet Christian boy into a young man who oozed hatred out of every pore. He had shaved his head in neo-Nazi fashion, right down to the skin so not a follicle showed, and his angst was not saved just for the African-American people, even though that was his true focus in life. He now hated gays, Hispanics, and Jews, too. Anyone who was not like him—mainly anyone who was not a white Southern bigot—faced his wrath. He had no use for Christianity. He had no use for liberals, either. Women's rights didn't upset him, but it wasn't something he supported. He was all about promoting the white race and exterminating the black race. Even before he was arrested, he had planned an attack against the NAACP's Atlanta office.

The day he turned eighteen, his transformation was complete.

His grandparents, oblivious to the changes in him, purchased him a hunting gun for his birthday, a Remington 870 Express Super Mag Waterfowl 12-gauge shotgun. It was a weapon that, in the brush and lake areas of the state, would be to his advantage: his prey would not be able to spot him coming for them due to the camouflaged chassis. The weapon was one that would stick out in an environment other than its intended purpose. They even bought him plenty of ammunition and a hunter's license. He enthusiastically thanked them with a smile on his face, even though the wheels in his mind whirled.

He had no plans to hunt birds or deer.

That night, he swiped his daddy's jug of moonshine, made within the last few months. It was a glass container, holding nearly a gallon of the home brewed liquor that the old man had left on the back porch. It was an easy swipe. He took his truck, a blue 1990 Chevrolet C1500 pickup, his gun and the 'shine and drove off into the distance. He sipped the 'shine as he turned the wheel around the bends until he came to a clearing. There were no houses nearby that he knew of, so he knew he wouldn't be disturbed as he fired away. The clearing had plenty of things he could shoot: trees, squirrels, litter. All he had to do was pull a cartridge from the rack, pump once, aim and pull the trigger. Rayburn felt the adrenaline rush through him as the weapon kicked into his shoulder, much akin to the way a horse bucks when agitated. The moonshine surged through him, too. He felt potent with both the alcohol numbing him and the gun's butt end resting on his thigh as he drank deeply.

The young black boy was out much too late, but he had heard the gunshots and, like every little boy, was curious as to the racket at this hour. He had sneaked out of the house, using soft steps as he crept along in his calf-high socks. He made sure not to step on the creaky floorboard, one that would make the house shudder. He made sure not to let the screen door slam; he didn't even let it snick against the metal lock. He then walked down the path, jumping slightly as the unseen gunman pulled the trigger, the sound of the gunshots jarring him. He wet his lips and continued walking, side-stepping stones on the fern-lined path.

Ten minutes later, he peered through the leafy underbrush, spying on the burly youth holding the shotgun. He held his breath as the young man some eight years his senior drank from the brown porcelain jug. He wanted to giggle as what looked like water dribbled down his cheek and neck. He heard the slurping before his ears heard an unmistakable belch pour forth from the young man's mouth.

Then the man tossed the jug some twenty feet, clinking against the dirt and stones. The boy couldn't see the jug through the darkness any longer, but he wondered if the jug had kicked up a small plume of dust like the way his football did when he missed a toss from his older brother.

He then heard the pump of the shotgun before he saw the burst of light pour out as the man fired it.

The noise, so far away when he first heard it, made him jump back. He couldn't stop his body from reacting. Nor could he stop himself from letting a scream of surprise dribble away from his lips.

"Who's there?" the man had said, a slur to his voice. He had stood up, pushing himself off the tailgate. "Come out and show yourself! If you don't, I'll fire in there. I have no quarrel with you, unless you want me to have one."

The boy hesitated, but he didn't want this drunken, gun-toting man to open fire on him. He stepped cautiously through the trees and held his hands up.

Rayburn saw the boy and grinned, his lips evil.

"What the hell are you doing out here, nigger?"

The boy's mouth widened, as if he no longer had control over his jawbone.

"You speak English, boy? I asked you a question," Rayburn said, walking as fast as he could. He grabbed him at the shoulder and tossed him to the ground. The boy winced.

Rayburn shoved the barrel into his little face. He pumped the shotgun.

The boy's eyes went wide. Rayburn saw the whites of his eyes enlarge.

"Answer me you stupid nigger, or I'm going to blow your fucking head clean off!"

Rayburn watched as the boy's mouth moved, but he didn't hear anything, not even a gurgle, uttered from his victim. Incensed by the silence, he snarled and grabbed him by the throat. He pulled him toward him, letting his putrid, drunken breath swarm the boy's face. He gritted his teeth together as he tightened his grip.

The boy gasped around the constricting fingers.

"Just what I thought: a muted fucking coon. That means no one's going to hear your screams tonight." He laughed. "This is my lucky day, I tell you something."

Rayburn dug deep and pulled the boy to his feet, but he didn't let the boy stand. He forced his stockinged feet to move as he dragged him toward the bed of his truck, the shotgun in his left hand. He tossed the gun into the bed and grabbed a rope, not letting go of the boy's neck.

"You're going to get what you deserve, spying on me without as much as an invitation to join my little party, you little fucking prick," he murmured. He slammed the boy's head against the side of the beat-up truck. He let go as the boy fell to the ground. The boy began to whimper.

"Oh, shut the fuck up, you black piece of trash. You're getting what you deserve. Not knowing your place, that's what you deserve."

Rayburn grabbed him by the feet and hurriedly wrapped the rope around his ankles. The boy tried to struggle, but Rayburn stepped over and on him, putting his weight on the boy's stomach as he finished wrapping and tying the knot. His nostrils flared as he worked, not feeling the sweat slide down his forehead to sting his eyes. He didn't think the boy would get loose. He had tied it fairly tight, so much so that the blood would stop flowing to the feet in no time. The Boy Scouts had taught him well.

He gave the boy a swift kick to the nose. He felt the boy's body shudder as he connected. Rayburn staggered the three feet to the bed and noticed he had plenty of slack on the rope. He tied it on the trailer hitch, securing the knot. The boy didn't weigh much. It wouldn't unravel on him.

He took the opportunity to step on the boy again, placing all of his weight on the boy's sternum. The boy groaned hard as the wind left him. Rayburn stepped off and walked to the truck.

"Get ready for the ride of your life, boy!" he called.

The boy couldn't reply through his tears.

Rayburn got in and shut the door. He turned the engine over.

The boy somehow pushed himself up, as if he tried to do a push-up. It was as far as he got though, as Rayburn put the truck in gear and hit the gas. Dust and dirt and stones kicked up with the spinning tires. The truck pulled away. The boy's head hit the ground, taking him away as the rope extended to its limit. Teeth snapped. Warm, coppery blood filled his mouth and slid down his skin.

The ride had begun.

In the cab, Rayburn cackled as he turned the wheel in his drunken haze, sending the truck into a swerve across the road. The rope followed.

So did the boy.

Rayburn dragged the boy for several miles across the back roads of North Smyrna, weaving across the narrow lanes. He looked in his rear view mirror and watched the shadow of the boy tumble helplessly, as if he were riding a tube behind a motorboat on a lake. At times, the boy was on his back, his shirt tearing to tatters on the dirt roads. He couldn't tell if the boy was bleeding, but it had to be a certainty.

The torturous ride continued. A line of white stretched across his knuckles as Rayburn's hands gripped the wheel. His eyes were wide. The alcohol had grabbed him, but he was sure to keep his eyes as wide as possible to see every bit of road, every tree, every car…

The headlights came toward him as he had maneuvered his way into the oncoming lane. The road had widened a tad here. Rayburn wanted to play a bit of Chicken. He eased the accelerator closer to the floor. He thumped the horn, blasting it to a rat tat tat in his mind. There was an answer that he barely heard over the blood pounding in his ears.

He turned the wheel before the other car could, as there wasn't much room for the oncoming car to move. Rayburn had turned right, bringing the truck to the right.

The boy's tumbling form didn't go to the right with him. It stayed left—

Rayburn heard the unmistakable sound of tires leaving the road for half a second, then steel crashing down to the ground.

He didn't slow down when the car rolled to a stop. He kept going, even though he felt his heart fall to a point near his groin.

A mile later, he finally slowed down, pulling off to the side of the road. He cut the engine and hopped out of the cab. Rayburn slowly walked to the rear of the truck and simply stared at the boy, still tied to the end of the rope.

"Wow," he gasped. "Wow."

He staggered forward and looked down at the boy's shattered body. Blood, fresh from the tap, covered his face, arms, torso and legs. Deep wounds covered his body, from his scalp all the way down to his ankles. His lips were fattened, as if he sported breakfast sausages on his face. Half of his nose looked like the road had rubbed it away. His shorts were wet; the scent of urine and feces rose to meet Rayburn's nose. He was absolutely broken, absolutely still.

Rayburn gasped again. He brought his hands to his head and rubbed them over his scalp. He didn't even recognize the day's worth of stubble that had sprouted.

Panic had set in. He checked the bed and saw that he didn't have his gas tank, so he couldn't burn the boy's body.

"Fuck, I can't believe this."

Whether he meant what had happened to the boy or that the tank was missing, he didn't elaborate. He reached in and grabbed his shotgun. He remembered he had a cartridge in the chamber. He patted it, calming him a bit.

He walked back toward the boy's body, but he paused as soon as he stood over the boy.

He felt his gag reflex take over. Seconds later, he retched, the alcohol and the remnants of his birthday dinner coming back up. His vomit covered the boy.

Rayburn's world started spinning as soon as the heaves ended. He could have fallen to the road, but he needed to keep moving. He pointed the barrel at the boy's chest, trying to keep it steady. He pulled the trigger. A hole several inches in diameter appeared half a moment later. Flesh exploded and covered Rayburn's pants.

It was at this moment that he detected flashing red and blue lights coming from around the bend. He gasped again, and as the headlights came into view some three hundred yards away, Rayburn stepped backward, the gun in his hand. He grabbed his backpack, which he kept his birthday ammunition inside, and rushed off toward a wooded area to the left-hand side. He disappeared into the darkened brush.

The police had caught a glimpse of Rayburn fleeing as they pulled up, but they didn't recognize him immediately. It was only after seeing the boy's dead body and running Rayburn's plates did they figure out his identity. Cruisers flooded the scene, from the Cobb County Sheriff to the state police, and Smyrna Police staked out the Rayburn family home. They called in the K9 unit and they managed to catch Rayburn's scent, but an hour had passed by that time, and Rayburn had already covered several miles and had splashed through a lake in order to throw off the pursuing pooches. He was lonely, cold and scared, but Rayburn was a survivor. He still had plenty of ammunition remaining, and over the first day-plus, he had lived off his adrenaline alone. It was his survival instincts kicking in: the manhunt had begun. It wouldn't end for several days.

Sometime during the night of his second day on the lam, he had taken to sleeping in a cemetery off Church Street in the town of Mableton, several miles to the southeast of Smyrna. It was his first bit of real rest in nearly two days. The fact that he had remained at-large was something of a small miracle: He managed to avoid main roads, and if he came to them, he made sure there was no one around as he crossed. The shotgun remained in his hand at all times.

Until that next morning. The shotgun slipped from his grip and clunked against the grass of an old grave. Rayburn, sound asleep with his head using the backpack as a pillow, didn't realize it had happened. He slept and slept. Not even the sound of a lawn mower firing up and dragging itself over the grass on the other side of the cemetery could wake him. He did wake up eventually, when the lawn mower drew closer.

The maintenance man for the cemetery had noticed him. A moment's hesitation had nearly cost Rayburn his freedom.

That same moment's hesitation cost the maintenance man his life.

He had recognized Rayburn's face, as all of the Atlanta networks had broadcast his picture to the masses. The recognition had caught the man by surprise and his jaw seemed to have locked when it dropped.

"What are you—?"

Rayburn gathered the shotgun up rather swiftly, pumped it once and fired.

The maintenance man dropped, taking the round in the upper left quadrant of the chest, missing his heart by inches. His shoulder, the press would discover later, could not be saved, and neither could his left arm.

Rayburn, adding an old man to his tally, panicked again. Someone had found him. It was time to run again.

This time, someone else had spotted him running from the cemetery, running southwest across the finely manicured lawns. He crossed the railroad tracks without looking for a passing freight train to jump aboard, but unfortunately, nothing passed. And with crossing the Veterans Memorial Highway an inevitability, he gritted his teeth and moved his feet forward.

It was at the Hawthorne Plaza Shopping Center, a small strip mall on the southern side of the highway, that the manhunt reached its conclusion. The Mableton Police had found him running and crossing the street with the shotgun raised and pointed at cars to get them to stop. Rayburn had continued to run and evaded capture, but his legs had grown tired. He had ducked behind a parked car just as two cruisers pulled into the lot and screamed to a stop. Two police officers—two black police officers—jumped out of the cruisers and used the doors as a shield.

"Put down your weapon, Rayburn!" the first yelled.

"You're not getting any further than here, boy," the other added.

"Fuck off, you nigger pigs!" Rayburn, crouched down near the front right quarterpanel, called over the hood, all while he dug into his backpack for a pair of cartridges. He slid them into the chamber. "I'll fucking die before you get me, you Godless bastards!"

He pumped the chamber and jumped up, shielding himself from the first cop. He pointed and fired within half a heartbeat.

The second cop's head vanished in an explosion of blood and bone even before he could squeeze the trigger of his own service revolver.

Rayburn, sweat rolling down his face, pumped the shotgun again just as another cruiser, this one a Cobb County Sheriff's Crown Victoria, bored its way into the parking lot followed by two Georgia State Police cruisers. Rayburn adjusted his body and pulled the trigger again.

The first cop's face imploded, showering the pavement with fluids.

Rayburn didn't have time to react, as the Sheriff's vehicle slammed into the other side of the car. The collision flung Rayburn backward, and his birthday present, devoid of ammunition, left his grip and soared through the air to crash through a window. Glass tinkled in a cascade to the sidewalk. Rayburn hit the ground hard, his head smacking the pavement. Police officers from both the Sheriff's Office and State Police swarmed his prone form and, after slapping him awake, hauled him onto his stomach. They cuffed him and escorted his 18-year-old ass to the third Cobb County cruiser.

Ten minutes later, a parade of police vehicles pulled into the Cobb County Courthouse in Marietta. A cadre of media, hearing of the incident on the police band radio, descended on the scene, cameras and notepads at the ready. Seven heavily armed deputies and state police had their guns pointed at the rear door as they dragged Rayburn out of the cruiser. They grabbed his arms and led him toward the door.

Rayburn seethed but didn't say a word. He looked at the assembled press and stared at them from underneath his heavy eyelids.

"Boy, you are popular today. Smile for the camera, asshole," a bald, heavy-set deputy said.

They moved him inside and sat him down in a wooden chair.

"The Sheriff's buying dinner tonight!" a woman in the office yelled. The others cheered, their voices raising to the ceiling.

"Don't you move, Bobby Ray. Don't you move. Don't even quiver," the Sheriff had said.

"Yes, sir," Rayburn said meekly.

And as he sat there, not moving, not quivering, Rayburn drew within himself and silently raged.

Chapter 6
Georgia Diagnostic and Classification Prison
Jackson, Georgia,
Saturday, October 27, 2012
5:20 p.m. ET

Jaclyn had called ahead to make sure that a short list of people she wanted to talk with didn't leave the scene of last night's breakout before she had arrived. She used her new alias over the phone and, even though the deputy warden questioned why the White House was interested in the incident, she deflected the answer and managed to convince the man to be ready to receive her by 5:30 p.m.

Their drive to Jackson on Interstate 75 was somewhat uneventful, but Jaclyn managed to glean some information about Anderson in their travels. Anderson was a rookie agent—*Just fabulous*, Jaclyn had thought as she learned this, gnawing the inside of her cheek as she drove, *a wet-behind-the-ears rookie*—that had only four months' experience coming into this assignment. She had recently graduated from Brown Mackie College in Atlanta and, from what Anderson had said, despised the white supremacists that had run rampant through the South, especially during her youth.

"I've been paying attention to the Rayburn case since high school," Anderson said as they drew closer to Exit 201. "It was that case that made me want to go into law enforcement. When I tested high, they were impressed. When I showed them my scrapbook about the Rayburn case, they thought I was obsessed."

"Are you?" Jaclyn asked as she changed lanes.

Anderson grinned.

"A little. What Rayburn did to that boy and those police officers is just shameful. I remember the trial like it was yesterday. The KKK tried to be disruptive."

"Were they?"

Anderson huffed.

"Of course they were," she replied. "They're the KKK. They're a bunch of hate-filled bigots who needed the spotlight on them and their agenda of eliminating the black race." She shivered. "It should have been about the cops and the boy." She sighed. "Luckily, the state was able to get a conviction."

"You sound as if that was in doubt."

Anderson's face twisted as if she didn't hear Jaclyn properly.

"This is the South, Agent Johnson. I don't know if you missed the memo, but there are a bunch of people here who still want blacks exterminated and the Civil War to resume. Those rednecks believe the South will rise again, and all that nonsense."

Silence descended as Jaclyn tried to wrap her mind around that statement. She was sure that still happened, but she was of the belief that some parts of the South had grown up and had assimilated with their neighbors to the north of the Mason-Dixon Line. Apparently, according to Anderson, there were people who needed to jostle their memories and remember that bigotry was out and embracing cultures was in these days.

Jaclyn took a deep breath.

"Hopefully this Rayburn guy won't get too far and he won't disturb the debate or either the president or Mr. Bennett's itineraries leading up to the debate."

Anderson made a sound that resembled a tire deflating.

"Bennett, what an asshole he is. His plan to eliminate our jobs won't work at all. What is he trying to play at? The day he signs that into law is the day I turn traitor and go after him for eliminating my job. Secret Service be damned."

Jaclyn grinned. She reached over and patted Anderson's hand.

"We're going to get along just fine."

She hit the accelerator and continued to zoom down Interstate 75.

The sun had nearly extinguished itself by the time the two women arrived at the facility. Emergency vehicles still filled Highway 36 nearly seventeen and a half hours after the incident. A Georgia State Trooper halted Jaclyn's Hyundai with a raised, gloved hand. Jaclyn showed her false White House credentials. Anderson flashed her CIA identification. The trooper stiffened slightly before waving them through. Anderson flashed a smile toward Jaclyn as they made the turn onto the property. Jaclyn frowned at the trampled grass near the gates, now devoid of protesters.

A few minutes later, Jaclyn pulled up inside the complex. Yellow police tape surrounded the small building set off to the left, along with a high fence with barbed wire running along its length. Smoke still hung around the building, Jaclyn could see with the telemetry inside her glasses. She could also see that it was about 58 degrees outside.

"Damn, I didn't bring a sweater," she said.

Anderson didn't say anything. The two women got out of the car and ducked themselves underneath the police tape, walking with an easy gait toward the death house.

"Hey!" a guard yelled. "You can't—"

But Jaclyn held up a finger.

"If you tell me I can't go over there, you're sadly mistaken."

The guard halted in his tracks as Jaclyn and Anderson passed.

"Where's the deputy warden?"

The guard hesitated before pointing to the thin man with the reddish-blond hair. Jaclyn thanked him and led Anderson to him.

Jaclyn didn't have much time to peruse the file the CIA had on the deputy warden, James Piermarini, before she arrived. He was a tall man, about 180 pounds, with Tom's build. Just thinking about her British boyfriend made her heart ache. She checked the chronometer inside the eyeglasses and saw that Tom was more than likely to land at Heathrow in about two hours. She reminded herself to send him a text when she got back to the hotel.

"Mr. Piermarini?" Jaclyn asked. The man turned toward her.

"You must be Miss Jennings from the White House."

"I am."

"Welcome to Georgia. I'm sorry it had to be under these circumstances."

But Jaclyn waved it aside with her model-like smile beaming away.

"I've always meant to come South. It would have happened sooner or later."

"You never said on the phone why the White House is so concerned about this particular incident, Miss Jennings. I'm sure it has to do with the debate this week."

"Of course it does. How well do you know our Mr. Rayburn?"

Piermarini frowned.

"Not very well, I must admit. Our late Mr. Green was more familiar with him than most, and that wasn't much. Apparently Rayburn hated the warden, and hated many others here, too. The only one he liked was, of course, the guard who helped him break out of here last night."

"What exactly happened last night, Mr. Piermarini?" Anderson said.

Jaclyn flashed her a look of warning that said, quite plainly, do not tread on my investigation.

Anderson didn't budge, as if she didn't catch the look.

"I'm sure you've seen the news reports. We were about to proceed with the execution, but the guard had other plans. We found traces of primacord and what looks like plastic explosives in the remnants of the death chamber."

Jaclyn felt a cold shiver wriggle its way up her spine as she stood there. Goose pimples sprouted on her arms. She wrapped her arms around her body.

Just like what happened in Las Vegas with the monorail, she thought.

"What did the guard do?" she asked.

Piermarini explained what the reporter had told him at some point during the early morning: that the guard had pulled a gun, sealed the death chamber from within to keep prison personnel out, then threatened the execution team to release Rayburn.

"What I don't understand," Jaclyn said, "is how the late arrivals were able to get inside the facility. This is supposed to be the most secure location in Georgia outside of the State Capitol Building."

Piermarini gulped. Even through the growing darkness, Jaclyn could see an embarrassed flush coming to the man's face.

"We haven't ascertained how that happened yet. How it happened, we may never know."

"How about you show us so we can make our own hypothesis," Anderson said.

Piermarini nodded and held an arm out. They walked toward the rear of the death chamber. Jaclyn could see a set of tire tracks in the distance as they approached.

It was when they reached the backside that Jaclyn heard an audible gasp come from Anderson. Jaclyn could understand her shock, her awe, and her utter fascination with what had happened here. She had done her level best to keep her emotions in check after watching Wembley Stadium tumble in on itself as she ran for her life with Tom's father and the man she practically dragged back in late July, and she had seen the results of what had happened to the Aquatics Center as well as the Las Vegas Monorail. Knowing something was there only minutes prior and then simply vanished in a cloud of tumbling steel and concrete was knowledge she could never erase from her mind. She thought back to September 11, 2001 and how the World Trade Center had stood for so long even after the planes had collided with them before they fell in on themselves.

And for her, the personal loss she felt as she found out that her parents had died in the attack on the Pentagon had rendered her numb, knowing that they'd never see her graduate high school, never see her walk down the aisle on her daddy's arm, and never enjoy potential grandchildren. She had cried for days on end, until Alex had flown to Seattle after the flight restrictions were lifted and gave her a new lease on life. The government would be her new family, and the government would train her in every manner of defense and attack known to man.

It meant that they would build something positive over the cicatrix that had formed on her healing heart, and while the pain may never go away, there was a way to make the pain easier to deal with as the days passed.

Jaclyn looked at Anderson, who stared at the hole in the building with wide eyes.

Rookies, she thought with a slight frown.

Jaclyn saw not only the hole, which left the walls smoking and crumbling, but also the lack of turf near it. She could see deep into the building, where concrete and plaster lay scattered. She also saw the destroyed observation window as well as the gurney Rayburn had lain on prior to the explosion.

"Mind if we go inside?" Jaclyn asked.

"Be my guest. They've already gone through it and they're making a report available."

"I'll want to see it, and I still want to talk to the psychiatrist."

"Of course."

Jaclyn and Anderson walked across the broken ground and stepped into the death chamber while Piermarini hung back. Jaclyn felt an eerie sense of foreboding as she stood in the room. She inhaled once, and the scent hung in her nostrils.

"Can you smell that, Jasmine?"

Anderson sniffed quickly.

"No, what is it?"

Jaclyn inhaled again. She held her breath for several seconds before slowly releasing it.

"It's death."

Out of the corner of her eyeglasses, Jaclyn saw Anderson blanch.

The two women grabbed a good look at the place. They stepped over plaster and a pool of blood from where the warden had fallen. Everywhere Jaclyn walked inside the room, the smell of death hung there, clinging to her clothes and permeating her skin. She peered around the curtain and saw blood splatters, nearly dried after seventeen-plus hours, on the walls, chairs and floor.

To her mind, the splatters were a Rorschach test gone awry.

She took a deep breath and closed the curtain again.

"This is sick," Anderson said from behind her. She turned to the deputy warden. "How many people died here?"

"About ten. A couple were taken to the hospital," Piermarini said. "They were treated and released, and they were definitely in shock."

"Of course they were; they were nearly blown away by a lunatic and his cronies," Jaclyn said sarcastically. "You'd be sucking your thumb and hoping not to pee your pants if that happened to you. Oh, wait—if you were actually here during the attack, you would have been laying next to the warden with a bullet hole in your forehead."

Piermarini jaw flopped open.

He huffed, "Miss Jennings—"

"Where's the psychiatrist?" Jaclyn said, cutting him off. "It's getting late and I'm sure he wants to go home."

"I'll have someone bring you to her."

Piermarini departed quickly.

"You were kind of hard on him, don't you think?" Anderson asked.

"Not at all," Jaclyn replied. "I don't think he needed to tell us that they were in shock. It was quite obvious to me that anyone who is shot at in a not-combat situation would be quite shocked that several lunatics brandished guns their way and tried to turn them into human planters.

"This is how aggressive questioning is done in the CIA, Agent Anderson. We don't give two shits about people's feelings, or whether or not we're going to offend people. That's not our job. Our job is national security, and if someone is in our way, or being a dipshit, then we treat them with the same courtesy with which they treat the emergency. I've browbeaten flippant police officers, MI5 video techs, state representatives, even the president." She cringed at the thought of what she had said earlier this month, but other than a slight talking-to by Alex, nothing came from it. "I don't give a shit who they are; if they want to fuck with me, I'll take them down."

"But the deputy warden is here to help us; he's not our enemy."

Jaclyn blinked.

"He's not our enemy, no. But he doesn't understand exactly what we're up against, especially with Rayburn free."

This time, Anderson blinked.

"I don't get it, what are we—"

"Don't worry about it for now." Jaclyn wanted to curse her mouth. "We have more important things with which to concern ourselves."

Jaclyn walked out of the death chamber toward the cell block. Anderson followed two heartbeats later, looking at Jaclyn as if she knew she wasn't being told the entire story.

Jaclyn paid her no mind.

The psychiatrist had waited for them inside the death house, albeit as far away from the chamber as she could get. Jaclyn saw that she was a raven-haired lady with a curvy figure, rectangular eyeglasses that matched her own, and a tweed jacket and skirt pairing. The top button on her white blouse was open, revealing a gold crucifix hanging from a thin chain, her alabaster skin a pretty backdrop. She met Jaclyn and Anderson with a smile and a firm handshake. Jaclyn was surprised that there was no complaint about a delay, especially on a Saturday evening.

"Thanks for sticking around to meet with us after your shift," Jaclyn said. Anderson introduced herself.

"It's no problem at all," the psychiatrist said in a sultry Russian accent. "My name is Olivia Seminoff. How can I help you, Miss Jennings?"

"I'd like to get your professional opinion about Bobby Ray Rayburn."

"There is only so much I can reveal to you. After all, doctor/patient relationships are confidential."

Jaclyn gave a weak smile.

"I understand that, however the government is of the belief that there is the possibility that Rayburn may be a disruption to the president and Mr. Bennett's visits to the Atlanta area over the course of the next week or so. We just want to get a bead on his mental condition, and since you are the person most qualified to deal with that—"

"I can tell you that in the past few days, Mr. Rayburn had remained in total control of his faculties, even with the execution looming." She paused, biting her lip.

Jaclyn, ever the observer of details, noticed this. She let her eyebrow arch a tiny bit.

"Something you want to share with the class, Doctor Seminoff?"

Seminoff's lips quivered.

"I really shouldn't."

"Whatever you say will not be used against you. It's very likely that if I catch up with Rayburn, he won't step foot in another courtroom. I can assure you that anything you tell me will remain confidential." Jaclyn didn't smile.

Neither did Anderson.

Seminoff looked to the ceiling, as if she had tears in her eyes and held a deep, dark secret. Jaclyn noticed that the doctor needed to take a deep breath before she continued.

"Rayburn did exhibit some moments of delusion and paranoia prior to the execution date, mainly at night."

"Go on."

"I observed him while he slept. Generally in the weeks before an execution takes place, we will isolate the UDS in a small, secure room with a one-way glass partition. He was perfectly fine during the daylight hours. He would read old science fiction paperbacks, mostly. A lot of Frank Herbert's Dune work. But at night, after he had gone to sleep, he began to mutter things to the darkness."

"Like what, for example?" Anderson asked. Jaclyn nodded.

"It may be better if I let you listen to it. If you'd follow me, please."

The three women left the death house and walked across the lawn to the main facility. Seminoff had Jaclyn and Anderson register—Jaclyn nearly signed her real name at first, but made sure she corrected it as soon as the pen hit the paper—before guest passes were issued. They continued walking through the brightly-lit hallways, the floors polished to a shine. A few twists and bends later, Seminoff had led them to her office. It was small, almost the size of an overlarge broom closet, but it had a desk with towering case files on what Jaclyn suspected was the entire roster of inmates, and maybe a few members of the staff, too, in the middle of it. A small lamp stood obelisk-like in the right-hand corner.

Seminoff walked to a filing cabinet, opened the top drawer and pulled out a video cassette. She brought it to a TV-VCR combo unit that looked like it was about fifteen years old.

Anderson shut the door behind her before she took a seat. Jaclyn sat on the right-hand side. Seminoff pressed play, turned the television on, then walked with the remote control to her chair.

Rayburn, laying on a cot, appeared on the screen. He was in the throes of a dream, it appeared, tossing and turning, his orange jumpsuit rumpling as he shook the cot. His body thrashed about, his head trembling. It went on like this for several moments, where the only sounds coming through the speakers were the sounds of the cot creaking away.

"It gets better in a second," Seminoff said, pointing the remote at the television. A green volume bar appeared, and the gauge rose as the seconds passed. "Keep your ears open for—"

"Wally," Rayburn croaked. "It all comes down to... it all comes down to Wally."

He thrashed twice more before he rose himself off the cot and screamed "WALLY!" in such a manner that Jaclyn felt the hair on her arms stand on end. The scream was lengthy and high-pitched. Anderson held her fingers over her ears for a second.

Seminoff ended the recording right there.

"Interesting, isn't it?" she asked as Jaclyn and Anderson turned to face her.

"To say the least," Jaclyn answered. "Who is Wally?"

"Your guess," the doctor replied, "is as good as mine. Whenever I tried to question him about it the next morning—and keep in mind, this went on for several days—he would clam up. He would ask me where I got that information, but when I offered an exchange, he would clam up again." She sighed. "He wasn't very cooperative, to be honest, and he was like that right until the day he escaped. The whole thing about Wally ended on Thursday night. I didn't talk to him yesterday."

"Doctor," Anderson said. "Did Rayburn exhibit any tendencies of being bigoted while inside?"

"Of course he did, Agent Anderson. He treated many of the African-American guards with disdain, and any of the Caucasian guards who sympathized with the African-American prisoners, which there were a fair few, were ones he would rather not deal with, either. There were times where he would get into fights with the African-American prisoners over the littlest things. I'm actually surprised he made it to his execution day, because I was wondering who would be the first to try to drive a shank into his skull."

"And what about the guard that helped free him this morning?" Jaclyn asked.

"What about him?"

"Did he display those tendencies?"

Seminoff grimaced.

"From what I can tell, Carl Dane was a model employee of the state of Georgia. He never once showed that he was a member of the Ku Klux Klan, and his background check, as I've recently read, was about as spotless as brand new paint. But as I'm sure you know, Miss Jennings, credentials can be faked."

Jaclyn gave Seminoff an appraising glare. She didn't know if the good doctor knew that she wasn't who she said she was, but she had the feeling that if she did, there was a good chance that her true identity wouldn't get out, not from her. At least while Jaclyn kept her own promise to the woman.

Jaclyn and Anderson thanked Seminoff for her time before they both departed. They didn't say anything as they re-traced their steps out of the complex. They walked in near-perfect tandem out to Jaclyn's rental.

"What do you think?" Jaclyn asked Anderson as they shut the door.

"I think Bennett was right about you."

Jaclyn stared.

"What do you mean?"

"You're not like any other agent I've met in the service before. You have spunk," Anderson replied. "I think I like it."

Jaclyn chuckled.

"Why, because I don't take shit from anyone?"

"Pretty much."

Jaclyn smirked.

Rookies, she thought.

"You really haven't seen anything yet, Jasmine. You haven't seen me really pissed off, and the deputy warden was stroking my BS-o-meter something hard. We didn't need him to tell us that people went to the hospital; that was in the report Alex had sent me this morning."

"You're on a first-name basis with the director?" Anderson's look was incredulous.

Jaclyn nodded.

"I am. If you want to be on a first-name basis with her, you should really listen to me when it comes to handling an investigation."

The two women were quiet as Jaclyn eased the Hyundai through the gate toward Highway 36. They made the right-hand turn, and seconds later, returned to Interstate 75.

"One thing bugs me, though," Jaclyn said.

"What's that?"

Jaclyn took a deep breath.

"Who is this Wally character, and why did Rayburn say everything comes down to him? That makes no sense to me."

Anderson remained silent for several minutes as they drove north. She didn't speak again until they passed the State Capitol Building.

"To tell you the truth, it makes no sense to me, either. I wonder what it means."

"If you find out before me, clue me in."

"You got it."

The women drove on.

Chapter 7
Westin Peachtree Hotel, 67th Floor
Atlanta, Georgia
Saturday, October 27, 2012
7:10 p.m. ET

Jaclyn had dropped Anderson off before she returned to Downtown Atlanta and her hotel room just as twilight was in its death throes. She parked the car, locked it, then headed inside, making the long elevator trip go a tad faster by closing her eyes and leaning her head against the wall.

What I wouldn't give, she thought, *for Tom's hands on my shoulder blades right about now.* A soft smile drizzled across her face as she mewed lightly, thinking about her handsome British agent.

She pulled out her new iPhone and began typing a message that she would send across the Atlantic: the agency had accorded her unlimited transatlantic texting, and she had a feeling that it would get plenty of use until she could see him again in December. She lightly tapped at the touchscreen keypad, occasionally grimacing as her fingers hit the wrong key.

"Have you landed yet handsome?" she typed. "I'm just now settling into the hotel room after a couple of long drives and a long flight. Need a hot shower, and your strong hands all over me." She added a wink to the end of her text message.

Jaclyn smirked as she sent her text toward London with a veroop. She wondered how quick it would take for it to reach Tom's phone just as the elevator dinged. Its doors slid open, and Jaclyn walked out of its air-conditioned maw. She used a healthy, hurried stride and made her way to her room.

It was just as cool inside the room as it was in the elevator, she noticed. She chose to put out a pair of pink sweatpants as well as white bikini briefs and a loose-fitting

Seattle Seahawks t-shirt (also pink) before she slid out of her work clothes and the special contact lenses, a light shadow passing across her vision. She padded to the bathroom wearing only a white bra and panties. She shut the door behind her and, after unsnapping and shucking the bra to the side, she hooked her thumbs into the waistband and dropped her underwear to the floor. She stepped into the shower, turned the water on, and immediately sank into her thoughts as the spray peppered her scalp and skin.

The fact that there was a racist killer on the loose didn't have Jaclyn's skin crawling, which shocked her. She didn't care for racists or anyone who lived with a 1950s mindset, that much was true. There was no evidence that she could determine that would make Rayburn hit the debate or any of the stops that President Forrister or Bennett were planning to make during this trip. But Alex's voice rang in her ears: she would need to stay vigilant, because Alex would tear her face off if something happened to the president on her watch.

She ran her fingers through her wet hair. Water plinked off the floor of the tub. She grabbed the bottle of floral scented shampoo.

Anderson is an interesting person, too, she thought as she lathered her hair. *A young agent who has compassion is something I rarely see these days. Usually that is drummed out of an agent right from the start of their training, but I guess that compassion could be used as an asset, too. I've been compassionate with Tom in the past*—her thoughts about her consoling him on a lonely London road the afternoon after terrorists killed his father at Olympic Park made her grin, if only for half a moment—*and I was somewhat compassionate with Kerri Davis, long before I found out she had played me for a fool in Kingman. That is why compassion can be a blinder. Not where Tom is concerned, but with those who stand in the way of a result in a case. Davis tried to blind me to the truth.*

She took a deep breath before grabbing a washcloth and her bottle of Warm Vanilla Sugar shower gel from Bath & Body Works.

I'll drum it out of her. Jaclyn worked a foamy veil into her skin. *She can't walk around feeling sorry for everyone. That's not our job. National security does not mean compassion. It means being hard on those who wish to bring harm to our shores and our interior. No tolerance is no tolerance, plain and simple.*

I will admit, though, that she does not care for this Rayburn fellow, Jaclyn's mind continued. *I must get her to continue thinking like this. There are people in this country who think like him and are great dangers to national security. The list of people who are like him runs for miles, their dossiers bulky.* Jaclyn rinsed her hands off. *Maybe if she only gets select cases, such as those terrorists and targets with racist tendencies, she would be an exemplary agent.*

I don't see her going far in the agency if she can't put the compassion behind her.

Jaclyn rinsed the rest of herself off before stepping out of the shower a few minutes later. She wrapped her body in a large, soft bath towel. The troubles of Atlanta vanished as she pulled it around herself, locked in a cottony cocoon.

She walked back into the main room, where she found her iPhone alight with a text message from Tom. She slid her HUD onto her face before she slid the bar to unlock the phone. She read his text:

"Just arrived at Heathrow. Flight was rubbish, lots of turbulence. I miss your lips on mine."

Jaclyn felt her heart skip a beat as her HUD passed over the words.

She typed:

"I miss your lips too, handsome. I'm only wearing a towel right now." She added a wink. "Just to give you something to think about as you head home. Who's picking you up?"

She pressed send.

Jaclyn sat down and crossed her legs, right over left, while she awaited Tom's reply. She took a moment to wet her lips as her foot tapped away to a song only she could hear. She checked her email and then typed a long message out to Alex.

She wrote:

"Chief,

"I have met with Agent Anderson. She seems competent, but I'm not sure she would be the right partner for me. She is a little too compassionate, and I'm afraid she may not take my methods of investigation too well. If there is another agent who is a little more like me, I would be open to a switch. I can work with her, but I just want to make sure you are aware of my first impressions, just in case the issue comes up during the course of our investigation.

"We traveled to Jackson and the prison. Chief, it doesn't look like Rayburn will attack the president, but I'll keep an eye on things here. The doctor I spoke with didn't exactly answer my question about that, but he's not crazy from what I can gather. He's not a Chillings or a Letts. Not that I was able to glean from the psychiatrist."

Jaclyn elaborated further on her conversation with Doctor Seminoff to Alex, mainly about what Rayburn had screamed in his sleep, and fired it off to D.C. before she checked her text messages. Tom had sent one as she had typed to Alex.

Seeing it immediately made her smile.

"Ugh, I may have to find the loo and relieve a little tension, love. Lien's coming to get me; she's bringing a new boyfriend for me to meet, which is actually the smart thing to do, since I can't tell her if I despise the bloke.

Jaclyn, I so wish I was with you in Georgia instead of back home. What is going on with your case?"

Jaclyn bit her lip. She knew she shouldn't tell Tom what was going on, as he was no longer officially on an American case, but she recalled that she didn't hesitate in asking him about his opinions regarding the Las Vegas matter. She had called him up without thinking about doing so. He had decided to fly over and assist.

Fat chance of that happening now, she thought.

She typed anyway.

"So far, a whole lot of nothing. Right now, we only know the guy is a racist bastard who killed a few people on two occasions and, despite screaming the name Wally a few times, seemed to be in complete command of his faculties leading up to yesterday's escape. My partner is a tad too compassionate. Not for the perp, far from it; she has a vendetta against him, somewhat. She's a little too compassionate toward witnesses. That may become a sticking point between her and I later, I think."

Jaclyn sent the message before standing up and heading into the brown-and-tan Presidential Suite Guest Bedroom, where she dropped the towel and, after putting the phone on the bed's white linen, started getting dressed into that evening's clothes. She had considered sending a naughty picture or two Tom's way, but she didn't want to take the chance of him opening it with his sister next to him.

Maybe later, she thought with a sly grin as the phone beeped. She pulled her shirt on and felt her cheeks grow flush and warm.

She picked it up and read Alex's message.

Jaclyn grimaced and felt her heart drop as she read it.

"Snapshot,

"I can very easily transfer you to the Human Resources Department if you feel like you have a proper bead on Agent Anderson. I'm sure the person that hired her would approve your request, but I won't. You will work with her.

I paired you with her in order for you to show her the way we really do things.

"Your objection is noted.

"As for Rayburn, keep a tight eye on the president and Bennett. Did you meet with the Secret Service agents at the debate site?

"Keep me updated.

"AD"

Jaclyn hurriedly typed "Yes" before pressing send. She took a deep breath before she switched apps to her text messaging. A message from Tom had just arrived.

She smiled as she touched it with her fingertip.

It read:

"Perhaps she is the one who will soften the edges on Agent Snapshot." A wink accented the tail end of his sentence. "Lien's here. Ta."

Jaclyn lowered her iPhone and stared at the far wall, rubbing her lips together. When she leaned back into the bed and, in turn, looked at the ceiling, she couldn't help but sigh.

What does he mean by that exactly? she thought, lifting her arms above her head. *Why would he say that? Am I too much of a hard ass? What does he see that I can't?*

Jaclyn grimaced.

My training has forced me to be a hard ass, has forced me to be a cutthroat cog in a government machine aimed at ending terrorism. I can't be Miss Goody Two Shoes. I kick ass because that's my job. My job is being a hard ass on anyone and everyone I come across. If they're a good person with a good heart, they have nothing to fear from me. If they're an asshole or someone trying to deal a blow to the American psyche, then I turn up the hard-ass-edness. If that turns people off, that's their problem, not mine.

She sighed.

But Anderson said she kind of likes my approach, even though she wondered why I treated the deputy warden the way I did. Jaclyn exhaled a sharp breath. *Maybe I'm jumping the gun on her a little. She'll learn. It'll take some time, but she'll learn.*

She'll learn, or she'll find herself working a desk job in Fargo.

She thought a little more about what Tom wrote. The left side of her mouth turned up a notch and she texted back.

"I thought you were supposed to soften my edges, Scouser. I can tell you that I've felt a tad soft when I'm with you." She added a kissing face emoticon before sending the message.

Another message from Alex appeared. Jaclyn opened it.

"Did anything open your eyes, so to speak, while you were there?"

Jaclyn smirked and typed.

"Other than the fact that the Secret Service guy knows who I am? I also think the psychiatrist at the prison knows I'm not who I say I am. I think Bennett has really blown up my spot. At least I'm not being followed by paparazzi, though. So I have that going for me. Which is nice."

She sent the message before she decided that it was time to eat. She called room service and ordered her dinner before Tom replied to her text.

"And some of your hard edges have rubbed off on me, too." Another wink.

Jaclyn's smile filled the bottom half of her face. Her fingers danced.

"Oh they have, Tommy. They have. How far from home are you, sexy? It's after midnight, right?"

She waited for his response, which came two minutes later.

"It is. It's nearly 12:30 in the morning. It'll be awhile before we get to mum's. We're on the M4. By the time we get to the house, it'll be nearly 2. Lien drives slow." Jaclyn saw that Tom had added several W's to the last word.

She typed back:

"As slow as we made love that first time in Vegas?"

She bit her lip as she sent it.

The ensuing reply made her arms tingle and her hair shiver.

"About as slow, but not as pleasurable."

Jaclyn's fingertips barely stopped.

"I never told you, but I still think about that night. If I close my eyes and think hard enough, I can still feel your lips and hands all over me."

She eagerly awaited his next text—only to find a new message from Alex.

She grimaced and opened it.

"That wouldn't shock me with the Secret Service man, Snapshot, but I am surprised at the doctor knowing your identity. Did the doctor give you anything about Rayburn's accomplice?"

Jaclyn typed back:

"Yes, she did, mainly how he was a model employee and that he never exhibited tendencies attributed to the KKK. How much longer shall I play the advance role? And for the record, all of these work inquiries are interrupting a hot sexting session with my sexy British man. Just saying."

She sent it, adding a second message with a wink.

Tom's message then plinked in. Jaclyn shook her head.

"Now I know what it's like to be a multi-tasker on a computer," she muttered as she opened Tom's message.

She bit her lip.

It read:

"I can still feel yours on me, love—although that was only a few hours ago, too. I can even still smell you; I have your bloody scent lodged in my nose. It will have to do until I can have you in me arms again."

Jaclyn felt her eyes moisten as she typed back.

"I know, handsome. I can't wait for that, either. You make me so happy; I can't stand that we're apart like this.

But I'll make sure I get to you in one piece. I love you. Text me back when you get to your mum's."

Jaclyn sent the message just as a knock on the door startled her.

She launched herself out of bed and grabbed her shoulder holster, pulling out her Walther P99. It was more than likely the kitchen staff bringing her order to her room, but she had to make sure that it wasn't anyone who wasn't welcome in her suite. That was standard operating procedure within the agency, and it was something she would have to teach Anderson if the time came. She checked the peep hole and saw a young woman dressed in the livery of the Westin Peachtree standing outside her room. Jaclyn breathed and stashed her gun into the back of her sweatpants, then opened the door.

"Room service," the young woman said as she rolled the cart inside as soon as the door opened wide enough. Jaclyn saw that a six-pack of Corona was on ice. A high stainless steel dome covered her meal in the center of the cart. "Is there anything else that you will require tonight, ma'am?"

Jaclyn shook her head. The young woman held out a piece of paper on a rectangular tray with an uncapped Bic pen rolling about. Jaclyn picked up the pen, signed her alias to the sheet and added a couple of bucks for the tip, before the young woman bowed and departed without another word.

The phone began ringing just as Jaclyn reached for the cover's handle, the dulcet tones of Bruce Springsteen echoing throughout her suite.

She ignored it.

"Alex won't begrudge me a meal, I don't think," she said. "I can call her back later."

Jaclyn sat down and tucked in, eager to sate her hunger.

Yet as she slid her fork into steaming chicken parmigiana, there was a nagging thought scratching at the backside of her brain. She recalled the conversation she had with Alex near Downing Street back in August, where she had said, rather flippantly, that anarchy, chaos, life insurance pay-offs, destruction, fire, death, and other crazy things happened when she's around.

If her previous missions were true to form, there was going to be some craziness in Atlanta over the next few days, and she wondered what site Rayburn would hit first—and if he'd do so with the same material he and his accomplice used to bust him out of prison.

Chapter 8
Atlanta, Georgia
Monday, October 29, 2012
10:15 a.m. ET

Jaclyn didn't do much on Sunday. While state and local authorities remained on the lookout for Rayburn, Jaclyn managed to stay busy. She did a little brainstorming of the crime's particulars first—she had taken a drive up to Smyrna and had met with the Cobb County Sheriff, someone who knew Rayburn and his family rather intimately— and did a little shopping afterward, something that always perked up her spirits.

She managed to keep the case in her mind as she peeked through a window display at a pair of reasonably priced Jimmy Choo's, a pair that would make Alex cringe when she saw the bill on Jaclyn's expense account. She wondered just exactly how a prison guard—*if that's what he truly is*, she thought—managed to get a hold of primacord and plastic explosives. She wrote that down, just in case she found herself face-to-face with the guard. She also wrote down a note that made her shiver slightly.

Why on Earth would anyone want to kill someone based on the color of their skin?

She had gone to sleep with that thought, and it woke her in the middle of the night. She reached out for Tom's comforting presence and frowned drowsily, remembering that he was now in England and not next to her. She wanted to text him to tell him her concerns, but she knew that he had his phone off, wanting to sleep off the effects of jet lag immediately, something she didn't do when she made her transatlantic flight during the Wembley incident. Even though it was just after 3 p.m. in London, she wanted to receive a text from him before she sent him one, regardless of the turmoil she was in over the question.

Jaclyn knew that racial problems were still rampant throughout the South, even in the 21st Century. It carried on with a wink and a nod, as if they didn't care for racial equality laws. But going as far as murdering someone because they were a different race? It didn't settle well with her, and Jaclyn fought the urge to vomit.

Yet as Sunday turned into Monday, she needed to prepare to defend several people from this racist nutjob, especially as the debate neared: Dick Bennett and his Republican entourage would arrive at Hartsfield-Jackson at about 10:30 a.m., and Jaclyn planned on being there to welcome him. The president and his entourage would follow a few hours later, and she planned on returning to the airport to greet the Commander in Chief.

As Jaclyn drove south on Interstate 75, she could not help feeling a bit of trepidation in her heart. She and Bennett had never met before, yet she knew that Bennett loathed her. She knew that Bennett had outed her and wanted to disband the CIA. Jaclyn fondly remembered telling Jennifer Farrell, now Bennett's vice presidential candidate, that she hoped Bennett wins the election so she could take her out for everything that happened in Las Vegas. The grin turned feral, and she felt her knuckles go white as she steered her rental toward the airport.

The man is a bastard, she thought, *and the woman is a bitch and a half. And I have to protect them? God help me.*

She drove on.

The Lear carrying Bennett and Farrell had not yet touched down, but she had called the tower and, after identifying herself, requested they not give clearance to land until she had entered the airport proper. Jaclyn had received a little bit of static on their end, but she made sure to threaten a phone call to the FAA if her orders were not followed. There was a pause, and within seconds, the flight control room had told her that they now acknowledged her orders.

Jaclyn couldn't help but smile.

Ten minutes later, Jaclyn pulled up to the airport and showed her credentials at the gate. She didn't bother with the Allison Jennings pseudonym this time. There were no appraising, judging glances, double takes or checks over the walkie-talkie. Jaclyn Johnson was here, and she was here to escort the Republican presidential candidate to his hotel as well as to any campaign stops he needed to make prior to the hotel.

"And I'll be back to welcome the president in several hours. I'll expect this gate to be open and ready for my arrival," she had said.

"If you call ahead," the Georgia State Trooper said with a slight twang in his voice, "we can have the gate readied for you."

Jaclyn nodded.

"I've always heard of southern hospitality," she said.

The State Trooper tipped his hat and waved her through.

Jaclyn dialed the tower and let them know that she was on federal property now. She gave clearance for Bennett's Lear to touch down.

Five minutes after Jaclyn pulled onto the tarmac behind a Republican National Committee limousine, the sleek luxury jet soared toward the runway like a javelin coming in for its own landing. It touched down with a squeal as rubber met asphalt. It coasted and rolled to a stop near the limousine. Photographers were perched near the nose of the plane, and near the terminal proper, a pool video camera captured everything.

Jaclyn stepped out of her rental as soon as the door to the Lear lowered. She smirked as Bennett made his way out of the jet, and the smirk grew into a smile as soon as she saw that he had noticed her. Farrell poked her head out and tried to walk down the few stairs, albeit trying to pass her running mate. Jaclyn saw that Bennett was in a full suit and blue tie while Farrell was dressed modestly in a blue two-piece skirt and blouse. Pearls dangled near the woman's breasts.

Party time, she thought as she began walking toward the man.

Bennett took two more steps before his feet hit the warm tar. Farrell followed, her shoes clicking against the steel. Within mere heartbeats, Jaclyn had come face-to-face with the man who wanted to dismiss her and the CIA of their jobs, as well as the woman who would have helped wipe her home district off the map had it not been for Jaclyn's intervention earlier in the month.

Neither spoke for several moments. In the background, shutters clicked away, unknowingly capturing this tense moment. The shutters, she noticed, camouflaged her heart beat from pounding in her ears.

"Mr. Bennett," Jaclyn said. She held out her hand. Bennett let it hang there for several moments before he finally grabbed it, remembering the cameras.

One for me, she thought. *He doesn't want to look any more the fool than he already is.*

"Miss Johnson," Bennett said. "I wonder what you're doing here?"

"I wonder why your running mate is not in prison right now, but that's neither here nor there. I guess conspiring to take out Las Vegas isn't exactly a crime in Republican circles these days," Jaclyn snapped back.

Farrell fumed. Her eyes darkened.

"You're going to pay—" she said through gnashing teeth.

"Jennifer," Bennett cautioned, touching the inside of her elbow. "There are cameras around. We don't want to cause a scene that will leave a bad impression with the electorate." Farrell seemed to shrink a tad, but her stare was potent and never left Jaclyn's face. Bennett returned his gaze to the agent. "I ask you again, Miss Johnson. What are you doing here?"

"I would have thought you're up to date on current affairs, Mr. Bennett. I'm sure you've heard about the escaped convict in this state." Jaclyn crossed her arms beneath her breasts, feeling her forearms rub against the fabric of her blouse. It felt a tad slick, and it wasn't from the pallid heat pouring off the late October sun.

Bennett didn't raise an eyebrow.

"Yes, I have. I didn't expect the CIA to handle something like that, though. Seems a little bit of," he said, pausing for effect, "overkill for you folks, is it not?"

Jaclyn smirked again.

"When Alex feels the need to send the very best—"

"Alexandra wouldn't know the best if it landed on her face naked and started to wiggle in front of her." Bennett stepped closer to her. "There has to be another reason." Bennett tried to search beyond Jaclyn's HUD, but the tint was too much for him to pry through. His eyes darted back and forth. "You're here to spy on me."

Jaclyn's smirk evaporated.

"No, Mr. Bennett. I'm not here to spy on you. I'm here to protect you from a potential attack from a dangerous man."

Bennett nearly spat his laughter.

"Are you joking? You, protecting me? You are joking, aren't you?"

"I'm sorry, Mr. Bennett, but no one in the CIA has a sense of humor. If you'd like to speak with Alex, I'm sure—"

"I have several well-trained Secret Service agents at my disposal, Miss Johnson. Do you seriously think you're better equipped than they are to defend me?"

"Apparently you're forgetting something, Dick," Jaclyn countered quickly, not letting the arrogant man get the best of her. "You're forgetting who saved London. You're forgetting who saved Boston. You're forgetting who saved Las Vegas—and no, it wasn't the bitch next to you, I can assure you." She didn't even look as Farrell's eyes narrowed. "I see your Secret Service escort, yes, but can any of them run down a dangerous terrorist in heels?"

Bennett opened his mouth to answer, but he couldn't get words to form. He seethed instead.

Jaclyn's smirk lingered.

"I didn't think so. I understand you have several campaign stops you want to make today before retiring for the day. Where to first?"

"I would prefer it if you weren't anywhere near my cam—"

"I don't give two shits where you prefer I be," Jaclyn said, raising her voice a bit and adding a hint of steel to her tongue. "I'm under orders from my boss, who just happens to be the one who'll hand over the nuclear football codes to you if you should happen to win the election in eight days' time, to keep an eye on you. Trust me Mr. Bennett, I would rather skinny dip in a shark tank than watch over you and this bitch after all the bull shit you've said about me and about the CIA and everything she's trying to avoid. By the way, great job in getting her case continued until January 21st, trying to get the voters to forget all about her crimes by Tuesday. But I don't think the people will forget my testimony as soon as you lose."

Bennett looked as if the breath had left him with Jaclyn's vicious parry. He managed to regain control.

"Don't get in my way, Johnson," he warned.

"I don't intend to be close to you, unless the escapee wants to take you out."

Jaclyn turned and headed to her rental, her sarcasm lingering over the two Republicans as she powered away. The fact she wanted to testify at Farrell's trial, a fact she had never admitted before, seemed to shock the two members of the GOP into silence. She ordered her HUD to give her a 180-degree view. A soft chuckle came to her throat as she saw the looks on their faces.

That'll teach you to fuck with me, she thought. Jaclyn opened the door, slipped into her rental, and waited for Bennett and Farrell to make their way to their limo. She watched as they walked, each of them casting a look of disgust her way.

The Boss erupted from her drink holder. Jaclyn jumped and grabbed her phone immediately.

"Jeez Chief, give a girl a heart attack, why don't you?"

"What did you say to Bennett?" Alex demanded.

Jaclyn's heart raced.

"Would you like the Cliff Notes version or verbatim?"

"The Cliff Notes version would be sufficient, Snapshot."

Jaclyn explained their conversation, hoping the director would understand the vitriol she had to spew toward the man that betrayed not only her and the CIA, but the United States as a whole with his words.

"And he has the nerve to run for president," Jaclyn added.

"Jaclyn," Alex said, "I don't have to remind you how to do your job, but be careful with him. He could win, especially with all the shit he has on Forrister. Hell, he has shit on you, too."

"And I have shit on Farrell," Jaclyn countered. "That bitch should still be in prison, but Bennett has somehow meddled with justice. After what he has done, Forrister should declare the man an enemy of the state."

"You can't hit him, Snapshot. You're not under an order to do so."

Under the HUD, Jaclyn blinked.

"Since when do you read minds, Chief?"

"Ever since your de-briefing after Vegas. I remember what you said about telling Farrell off in Kingman."

Jaclyn grinned as the words came back at her in a rush.

"And what happens if I'm out of a job, Alex? I won't be a free agent or am I confused by that?"

"Don't even think of that. I've talked to the House and Senate leaders. There's no way that bill goes through."

"I've heard that before, Chief." Jaclyn started the car as Bennett's motorcade began to pull away from the tarmac. "I have to go. Bennett's going to try to lose me on 75."

"Don't lose him, wish death on him, or anything like that."

Jaclyn grimaced, but smiled at the end.

"Damn it, on to Plan C."

"Report in later."

Alex hung up without another word. Jaclyn ended the conversation too, before she kept her eyes on Bennett's taillights. The Secret Service trailed her. The motorcade looked odd, with Jaclyn's Hyundai out of place between the limousine and the SUV.

She wondered how long it would take the Secret Service to be on her if she had one of Parkerhurst's souped-up cars available for her use today. She grinned as she thought about flipping a switch and letting her STA missile rack rise from the depths of the trunk, then hitting the button to blast the Republican challenger and his running mate to kingdom come.

Jaclyn snorted.

"No, I can't think about that, either. On to Plan D."

They headed toward Atlanta proper.

***

Monday, October 29, 2012
11:45 a.m. ET

The Republicans made two campaign stops. The first was at the State Capitol Building, where Bennett and Farrell paid a call to the governor of Georgia, Wallace

Wellington Woodruff IV. The second was to the Coca-Cola plant.

Jaclyn had done her homework on Woodruff during the flight from Reagan to Hartsfield-Jackson, pulling up the man's dossier on her iPad as soon as Captain Kevin leveled the Gulfstream off. She had a feeling that she would run into the governor at some point, especially with the debate in town, and having an edge on him, or at least a bit of knowledge about the man, was important to her. She never liked being behind the 8-ball, as it was, when it came to potential meetings.

Woodruff was in his early 50s, but looked older due to the stress of running the state. Some called him the albino governor, as the shock of white hair that sprang from his scalp shot off in all directions, untamed by comb or brush. His photo, Jaclyn mused, made him look like mixture of a crazed Colonel Sanders from Kentucky Fried Chicken and, thinking of Tom's viewing habits for a brief moment, of Peter Davison's fifth incarnation of the Doctor. He wore glasses that resembled the pair that John Lennon owned, and in all shots that the agency had on him, he wore a white suit that reminded her of Boss Hogg. He was a Republican, but a moderate that had hoped to change the state's—by his mind—antiquated gun laws. Of course, he was smart enough to know that the Second Amendmenters that resided in Georgia—in a word, nearly every single citizen—clung to their guns much akin to the way children held onto a stuffed animal as they drifted off to sleep, and wouldn't allow a change to the laws. He had argued, though, that if there were gun control laws in place, incidents like the one involving Rayburn would never have occurred.

"Good people," he had said, "will use a gun responsibly. It only takes one bad egg, like Mr. Rayburn, to spoil that for everyone. The fact that we don't have stricter gun laws in our great state is because there are some people who are too lazy to go through the extra red tape."

Jaclyn looked further back into Woodruff's life with a flick of her finger across the iPad's touchscreen.

Woodruff was born in the town of LaGrange, which was located in Troup County on the western border with Alabama. He attended Georgia Tech—Interesting, Jaclyn thought, that the debate is being held at Woodruff's alma mater—where he received a Bachelor of Science in Economics and International Affairs before he received his Master's at Georgia Tech, as well, studying in the College of Sciences and Liberal Studies, graduating in 1982. His file noted that he was interested in going for a Doctorate in Public Policy at Georgia Tech but instead began serving his home district, District 69, in the Georgia General Assembly. After a few years of serving in the legislature, Woodruff made the worst kept secret in state politics official when he announced he was running for governor.

He ascended to the governor's mansion in a landslide, and held it ever since.

Jaclyn didn't care that Bennett would make a campaign stop there. She figured that he would call on the top Republican in the state and ask for his support at some point during his near-week-long stay in Atlanta.

The fact that he made the stop now made Jaclyn's job just a little bit easier.

Jaclyn stood off to the side as the two men—and Farrell—exchanged pleasantries.

"I'm glad you came to see me, Dick. There were several things I wanted to discuss with you regarding the election next Tuesday," Woodruff said.

Bennett slid his hands into his pockets as he stared at the governor.

"What did you have in mind? It may not be proper to speak now, though." Bennett gestured over his shoulder.

Jaclyn wanted to snicker, but held it in.

"I can always make an appointment with you for later in the week if I have to, but yes, it's a rather important issue that needs discussing."

"We can do that," Bennett replied. "I always have time to listen to the ideas of fellow Republicans like yourself. If you'll excuse me, Miss Farrell and I have another stop to make before we head to the party fundraiser this evening. We will see you there, correct?"

Woodruff nodded. They all shook hands and departed—but Jaclyn stayed where she was for just a second. She waved Bennett and Farrell out before she closed the door behind them, leaving her and the governor alone.

"Can I help you, Miss—?" Woodruff said, startled by Jaclyn maintaining her presence in his office.

Jaclyn walked several steps, her heels clicking on the hardwood under foot.

"The name is Johnson. Jaclyn Johnson. Perhaps you've heard of me, sir."

Woodruff's face paled.

"I have. Say, aren't you the woman who Dick—"

"Outed a few months ago? Yes, that's me. And you're probably wondering what I'm doing hanging around him right now if I'm supposed to be this huge traitor to the United States."

Woodruff nodded, his mouth still somewhat open.

"I'm handling security for the debate and for the candidates," Jaclyn explained. "Ever since this Rayburn fellow—" Woodruff stiffened "—escaped from prison, my boss wants to make sure nothing happens to the candidates, even though one of the candidates wants to destroy the CIA as it is presently."

Woodruff grinned.

"You mean Dick."

"Of course," Jaclyn said, her smile mimicking the governor's.

"That's one thing Dick and I disagree on, but not what I wanted to speak about with him. I feel you CIA folks do a good job, keeping us safe. It's the other people in Washington that do their best to destroy us. But that's only one old man's opinion, of course. Now," he said, patting his middle, "what can I do for you, Miss Johnson?"

"I understand that you're planning on attending the debate on Thursday night."

"I am. Georgia Tech is my alma mater, several times over, and I called in many favors in order to get that debate for our great city."

Thanks for confirming that information for me, Governor, Jaclyn thought.

"Will you have your own security team with you?"

"I have several state troopers who plan on accompanying me, yes ma'am."

"I'll want to meet with them the day before, just to iron out security procedures on who enters and leaves first and whatnot. I'll be on site for the entire evening."

"Very well," Woodruff said, walking around his desk and sitting down. "I'll have them available for you on Wednesday." He looked up and saw that Jaclyn remained where she was and made no move for the door. "Is there something else you wanted to discuss, Miss Johnson?"

"Actually yes, there was. I wanted to know why you didn't grant a stay of execution to Rayburn. I do understand that it was an option."

Woodruff waved it off.

"It's always an option. I chose not to grant clemency because the people of the great state of Georgia and Cobb County, in hearing the evidence presented at trial, decided to convict and put Bobby Ray Rayburn to death. It wasn't in my best interests nor was it in the best interests of the great state of Georgia that I grant him clemency, or stay his execution, or put him behind bars for the rest of his natural life; they wanted him dead, and dead he was to be. Besides, what happened in that death chamber yesterday morning would have happened to another part of the building, and I'm thinking that more prisoners than just Rayburn would have escaped into the back woods. But that's just a small theory from an old man," he said with a smile.

Jaclyn grinned and nodded.

"That's a good theory, sir. What makes you think that?"

"The guard was a follower of his, right? It just makes simple sense to me, at least. The building's walls are old, unlike those at the death house. The blast of C4 or whatever he used—let's face it Miss Johnson, any explosive would have reduced the state prison to gravel in half a heartbeat, and like I said—"

"Yeah, I got it," Jaclyn interrupted. "Have you heard of any reasons why the state police have not caught up with him yet?"

"Not a word. I understand they were slow in responding, but we didn't expect anything to happen."

"And there were no guards on the rooftops?"

"Why the third degree, Miss Johnson?" Woodruff asked. "If you're handling security for the debate, I don't know why this Rayburn business would be any concern of yours."

Jaclyn smirked.

"Governor, I'll be frank with you."

"Good, it's about time."

"My boss has me here to protect the president and Mr. Bennett from potential attacks from not only terrorists, but potentially from Mr. Rayburn."

"The man's an escaped prisoner, Miss Johnson. I highly doubt we'll see him as President Forrister and Dick Bennett go at each other's throats. Why would he risk his freedom to attack the president? It just doesn't make sense to me, but then again, I'm just an old man with opinions."

Jaclyn smirked and thanked the governor before she stood and left his office. She walked through the halls of the State Capitol alone, making her way to the entrance. Her heels rapped against the linoleum, much like rapid-fire gunshots. Yet as she walked, she couldn't help but feel something nagging at her spine. She didn't know what it was, not yet.

It was when she opened the door and prepared to make her way down the stairs toward Capitol Avenue that she thought she figured out the reason for her distress.

Bennett's motorcade, save her rented Hyundai, were nowhere to be seen.

"Fuck me," she muttered, pulling out her iPhone in the process. She quickly unlocked the device, pressed the phone icon and scrolled to Alex's name. "Please don't be mad, please don't be mad, please don't be mad," she whispered as the phone rang.

"What's up Jaclyn?"

"Bennett's gone, Chief."

Silence echoed through the phone for several seconds.

"You didn't kill him already, did you?"

Jaclyn smiled.

"No Chief, I didn't. We were just at the State Capitol Building and I stuck behind to talk to the governor for a brief moment, and now Bennett's left without me."

"How long was a brief moment to you?"

Jaclyn tapped her lips with her fingertips.

"I don't know, four or five minutes?"

"And he probably grew impatient and decided to leave you to your own devices. Funny though, since he doesn't like it when you do that. I'll call the Secret Service and tell them to wait for Anderson. You can head down to the airport and wait for Forrister, after you call Anderson and tell her to meet Bennett's motorcade at their next stop, which is?"

"Coca-Cola. I'll call her right—oh, wait."

"You don't have her number?"

"That's a big 10-10, Chief."

Alex sighed.

"I'll call the Atlanta office and get her there. You just get to the airport. Air Force One is en route. It'll be there in half an hour."

Alex hung up without another word.

Jaclyn sighed as she walked down the stairs.

"Great, some Secret Service agent I'd make, can't even keep my eyes on a presidential candidate." Jaclyn paused mid-step and shivered. "I can't believe I put Bennett and presidential candidate in the same sentence. I need a vacation really bad."

She hopped into her rental before weaving her way to Edgewood Avenue and Interstate 75 South.

Chapter 9
Hartsfield-Jackson Atlanta International Airport
Atlanta, Georgia
Monday, October 29, 2012
12:33 p.m. ET

Half an hour came and went rapidly.

Jaclyn called ahead just as she merged onto 75 and let the authorities know she was en route. They told her that the tower had caught Air Force One's signal and was in the process of guiding the blue and gray-colored Boeing VC25 toward its destination.

Much like it had when she had first made the approach to retrieve Bennett, Jaclyn's heart raced with trepidation as her meeting with the president neared. This was her first time in Forrister's presence since she had wheeled on him and berated him for risking his life on the Las Vegas Monorail. And even though she knew that he had said he would forget it, there was a part of her that believed he wouldn't and would hold that incident against her for the rest of his term.

However long that lasts, she thought as she pulled into the airport proper.

Jaclyn had several minutes to think as she waited for the president's arrival. She could see, through her HUD, a group of airmen from Fort Benning preparing to welcome their Commander in Chief. They walked across the tarmac in formation, right leg then left, in perfect synchronization. She considered the airmen a distraction, since her thoughts rolled from Bennett's reluctance to accept her protection, all the way back to her last meeting with Forrister, something she hadn't thought of over the course of the past three weeks.

Why did I have to be such a bitch to him? Jaclyn thought as she tightened her grip on the steering wheel. *He had risked everything during the London incident to send me support after everyone else was against me. I should be kissing his feet for sending Parkerhurst over with the car. Lots of things wouldn't have gone the way they did if it wasn't for the president doing what he did.*

But he did take a chance with his life that should never have happened if his Secret Service detail had done its job, her thoughts continuing, still stewing over the reasons Forrister rushed back onto that monorail car, risking his life for a simple man who, Jaclyn later found out, wanted to die then and there. *What right did he have to do that?*

She continued to think about that meeting—a meeting she knew deep inside of her that she would regret for the rest of her life—as the Boeing made its descent. It landed in a squeal of peeling rubber against asphalt, a puff of smoke pouring away from the point of contact. The plane started decelerating after nearly half a minute and rolled toward the agent's location. Cadillac One, the president's armored limousine, stood parked and ready to take Forrister to the hotel. Another Cadillac stood behind it. An ambulance, filled with Forrister's blood, was also a part of the entourage, as well as several SUV's. Secret Service agents had perched themselves on running boards, assault weapons at the ready.

Jaclyn looked at the interior of her rental and cringed.

I'm definitely out of my element, she thought as she opened the driver's side door and hopped out. She flattened her skirt before she walked to the set of rolling stairs that was in the process of connecting to the plane. The soft scent of gasoline wafted on the air a bit, but that didn't make her wary. She let the HUD scan away as she walked, remembering to keep the president's security her top priority. If anything were to happen near her, the Secret Service would do its job—and she would do hers.

Too bad the necessities are back at the hotel, she thought.

Jaclyn ran her tongue over her lips as the door to Air Force One swung open. Forrister sprang out first, with his wife Veronica on his arm. As always, Veronica Forrister was an angel, her blonde hair, as blonde as Jaclyn's, tossing about in a light breeze. She wore a tan pantsuit over her hourglass figure while the president wore his traditional navy blue. Behind him, White House Chief of Staff Melanie Ruoff followed, briefcase in hand. Behind her, though, was a woman with whom Jaclyn wasn't really familiar. It took her a few seconds to recognize Lucia DiVito, the new vice president, walking down the stairs.

That makes sense, she thought, *since Bennett brought Farrell. Having DiVito here will help Forrister sway female voters. At least, in theory, that's what he's trying to do.*

There wasn't much in the way of interaction between Jaclyn and DiVito during the first year of Forrister's interim administration. DiVito wasn't nominated for the vacant vice presidential seat until six months after Sarah Kendall's assassination, and in a bit of irony, she had been Kendall's second choice to be the vice president. At the time, she had been a fellow member of Congress from Massachusetts, representing the First Congressional District in the western part of the Commonwealth, which also consisted of north central Massachusetts, near the New Hampshire border. She lived in Westminster, which wasn't far from the Little League field that Jaclyn had gone to investigate Grant Chillings' liquid attacks, and had arrived at the scene after Jaclyn had departed with a case of sports drinks. Jaclyn was in the process of bringing the potentially poisoned beverages back to Boston only hours before she had to chase Chillings into the bowels of the MBTA's Green Line subway.

DiVito was still rather beautiful for someone in her early 40's: Jaclyn's HUD telemetry indicated that the woman stood 5-foot-6 and was roughly 130 pounds, her slender physique not a detriment to her in either chamber of Congress, where she now served as the president of the Senate. The sun's rays caught her brown hair and made it stand out against her Mediterranean features, and she had a hand up to her eyes, shielding the blue tint from the blinding light.

I'll hand her my HUD when she gets down here, Jaclyn thought with a wry grin while the president, first lady and vice president stepped off the mobile staircase. The airmen saluted the president as his feet hit the tarmac.

Forrister held his hand out. Jaclyn, surprised a bit, shook it.

"Why hello, Agent Johnson," he said. "I didn't expect to see you here."

"Added security, Mr. President. Alex wanted to make sure—"

"She wanted to make sure that this escaped prisoner doesn't have a clear look at me," Forrister finished. "I told her that the authorities here could handle it."

Jaclyn noted that there wasn't a touch of impatience in the president's voice. He smiled, too, and that had her on edge a bit.

She shrugged and smiled.

"You know Alex, sir. She never takes anything to chance."

Forrister nodded.

"Yes, that's her alright. Either way, I'm glad to see you. Have you met my wife before?" He indicated Veronica, and the two women shook hands.

"A pleasure to meet you, Agent Johnson," the first lady said.

"Likewise, ma'am."

"Melanie, you already know. And this is Vice President DiVito of Massachusetts."

Jaclyn and the vice president shook hands.

"I understand that you were instrumental in the incident that happened in my home district," DiVito said. "I never got the chance to thank you in person."

"Thanks are unnecessary, ma'am. I was just doing my job."

"Nonsense," DiVito said, having none of it. "You helped save countless citizens. You should be celebrated."

Jaclyn felt herself turning red at the praise.

"That's not a part of the job description, ma'am, but thank you."

"I understand Dick has already arrived," Forrister said. "Did he say anything?"

Jaclyn smirked, shifting her red cheeks a fraction of an inch.

"Isn't my profession the job of secrets, sir?"

Forrister chuckled.

"It is."

"We made one stop together, to the State Capitol, if that's what you're wondering. Then he bolted and lost me. He's not too keen on having me around, Mr. President."

"With all that he's said about you and the CIA," DiVito added, "I'm surprised he even let you shake his hand."

Jaclyn's face immediately twisted in confusion.

The first lady picked up on it immediately, even through the tinted lenses of the HUD.

"We watched the coverage in the onboard Oval Office," she said. "Eric was shocked to see you with him."

The secret agent smiled softly.

"I'm sure I would have been surprised to see me with him, too, especially the way he drones on about liberals. I'm sure if he didn't leave, I would have gotten a headache from it all."

"I hope the American people feel the same way as you do next Tuesday," Forrister said.

They laughed. Cameras clicked away.

Jaclyn took a quick breath. "Where would you like to go first, Mr. President?"

"I'd actually like to check out the debate facility first," he said. They began walking toward the motorcade. Several steps behind, Jaclyn noticed the Secret Service kept their eyes on the surrounding area. "It's at Georgia Tech, right?"

"Yes sir," Jaclyn replied. "I checked it out yesterday. Everything is running smoothly, from what I can tell. The Secret Service, however, knows who I really am." She explained her alias.

Forrister laughed as the door opened.

"Jaclyn, everyone in the Service knows who you are. Even the agents keeping watch over Bush have your look memorized. They all know you wouldn't hurt someone with high ties to the White House, even if they're Republicans."

Jaclyn's smile faltered.

"Yeah," she said, "I wouldn't dream of it."

Forrister smiled and jumped in before the first lady and Ruoff did likewise. DiVito jumped into the second limo. Jaclyn shut the door to Cadillac One before she walked to her rental, trying to keep the flush out of her cheeks.

So much for hitting Farrell if I'm out of a job in January, she thought.

Nearly half an hour later, Jaclyn and the president's motorcade arrived at Georgia Tech. A group of students applauded the president as he stepped out of the limo. Some booed. He waved to every single one before they entered the facility, Jaclyn two steps behind the president, first lady and vice president. Their footsteps echoed off the hardwood.

And while DiVito and the first lady marveled at the debate dais, Forrister's gaze was focused on the other party inside the arena proper. It took Jaclyn a moment to realize what was going on, but her heart leaped into her throat as she saw who the president had taken the moment to acknowledge.

Dick Bennett and Jennifer Farrell approached with hurried steps. Bennett's face was inflamed, and Jaclyn could see his nostrils flaring as he hammered away. Farrell's eyes were narrowed. She also saw Anderson trying to keep up with the Republicans, her face a mask of emotions.

"So," he barked, "you abandon my safety so you can watch over the liberal savior, eh? I knew it; the CIA wants him to win!" He pointed at Forrister as he stared at Jaclyn. "You're an evil bitch!"

"Mr. Bennett," Jaclyn said calmly. "If you would calm down and look at the facts intelligently, you would come to the same conclusions the rest of the world has: One, I didn't abandon you. I had a matter with the governor that needed to be addressed before we continued. You decided to hot-foot it out of there without me."

"You could have waited until I was secure in my hotel room before you went back to the Capitol."

"Actually," Jaclyn replied, "I couldn't. I had our computer techs at Langley check the governor's schedule for today as soon as I learned we were going to the Capitol Building, and that was the only time I could meet with him."

Bennett fumed.

"That doesn't answer why you are with this liberal rabble."

"Dick—" Forrister said.

Bennett's eyes darkened as they turned the president's way.

"Shut up. Everything that's happened is your fault. Sarah's death, the death of her son, the bailouts for the hotels in Vegas. It's all your fault. And I will expose you for the piece of shit you are."

Forrister rolled his eyes as a click barely registered.

Half a moment later, a blistering gunshot nearby made everyone duck. The women—all except one—screamed. The Secret Service drew their guns, but when they saw who had their gun out, they didn't aim to fire.

"That's enough," Jaclyn said, holding her Walther P99 in both hands. They saw it pointed to the ceiling. Wisps of smoke lingered over her head. "From all of you. Another argumentative word before the debate begins, I'll pop the first one who speaks. I don't care whose side you're on. The CIA doesn't take sides." She stared daggers through her HUD at Bennett. "You of all people would be best to remember it."

Bennett's lips moved uncontrollably, but no sounds emerged. Jaclyn detected a little more nostril flaring, but she ignored it.

"Since I'm leading the security team for the debate, your Secret Service details will be following my orders," she said. She turned to Melanie Ruoff and to Bennett's aides. "I want your itineraries forwarded to me each day by 5 a.m. so I know exactly where you are at every minute of the day. Agent Jasmine Anderson will handle your side, Mr. Bennett. I will handle the president's side.

"We have a killer on the loose in Atlanta, and we don't know for sure, but he may or may not attack the debate. We don't want to take chances of him hitting you before you get to poison the country with your rhetoric," she continued, looking at Bennett as she spoke that last sentence. "Don't take unnecessary risks. Follow our orders and no one will get hurt. I'll expect to see you alive and well on Thursday.

"Mr. President, is there anything else you wanted to see before retiring for the afternoon?"

"I would like to see the back rooms, Agent Johnson." Forrister was slightly stiff, and Jaclyn noticed his face was a tad flush. She waved him through and, after a look to Anderson—she'd have to get her number from Alex—

followed the president's entourage deeper into the arena proper.

She did notice that the president looked to her as she approached, holding the black curtain open for her.

"I'm sorry for discharging my weapon so close to your wife, sir," she said.

"Did it shut Bennett up?" he asked.

A small smile touched Jaclyn's lips.

"Yes it did, and no sir, I won't do it at the debate."

Forrister frowned.

"Damn it."

The entourage continued walking, eager to put some space between it and Bennett's.

Chapter 10
Westin Peachtree Hotel, 50th Floor
Atlanta, Georgia
Monday, October 29, 2012
10:13 p.m. ET

Rayburn had kept a low profile for most of the day, electing to stay in his room instead of venturing out into the city on this the third full day of his freedom. He had followed the arrivals of the presidential candidates on television intently—"Boy, this Fox News is right on top of things the way I want to hear them," he had said to Carl—especially the Republican candidates. He slept without fear of anyone waking him up, and he managed to decide that it was time for his followers to sneak away from whatever surveillance the authorities had them under to meet up with him.

He wanted to plan his first strike of terror right at the heart of Atlanta itself, and he wanted to do it tonight.

Over the course of his 17th year, he had taken part in several KKK ritualistic exercises, mainly in the form of cross burnings throughout rural Georgia. Effigies were also a specialty of his, and he had no problem with stringing up a handmade doll resembling a certain person's likeness. He took great glee in it all, and it wasn't rare for him to watch everything taking place from afar, a pair of binoculars up to his eyes.

But tonight's activities were ones he could watch right from his hotel room, without leaving its air conditioned comfort.

The men he had counted on being there had arrived within the past two hours, waiting patiently for him to go over his plans. Rayburn had called room service ahead of their coming and made sure that they were fed and ready to go, as well as making sure that the bill was sent to the

KKK's generous benefactor. He could afford it, and Rayburn spared no expense.

The telephone ringing made Rayburn stir from his meditation a little after 9 p.m. Carl reached over and answered it, before handing it over.

"Hello?" Rayburn said.

"It's me," the male voice said. "I've just returned home from the debate site. The president and the challenger were there."

Rayburn rolled his eyes.

"That's good news, I take it."

"They had a woman with them."

"Their wives?" Rayburn asked.

"No, a woman named Jaclyn Johnson. She's pretty tough."

Rayburn sneered.

"I couldn't care less about her. Call me back when you have something more tangible for me." He hung up without another word.

He finally emerged from his sleeping quarters at quarter past 10 that evening, Carl trailing behind him carrying an easel under his armpit. The former prison guard set it up in front of the men and unrolled a map, blown up to show wide streets and blocks representing buildings. He secured it on the easel with thumbtacks, then stepped away as Rayburn slowly walked in front of his followers. They weren't dressed in white robes with pointed hats, but each wore hatred on his face as if it were a second skin.

Rayburn sneered at all of them.

"My brothers of the Klan," he began, "it is time for us to reclaim the South, starting with this very city. Too long have we been second-class citizens to those bastards from the North. Too long have we had to hold our tongues as the niggers and the other races gained ground in what had been a pure society, long before Lincoln emancipated our great-great-great-granddaddy's property. That ends tonight.

"Our simple strike targets the heart of Atlanta." He paced slowly, his hands at his inner hips, his thumbs hooking into empty belt buckle loops. He measured his words, not wanting to mix his message. "We will wait until the dead of night to undertake this mission. We do not want to arouse suspicion. Carl here has informed me through his contacts that certain buildings in this area have security forces that take coffee breaks at the exact same time in the early morning hours. If we coordinate together, we should have no problem in causing a great deal of havoc and instilling a great deal of fear with this one act.

"And I want us to be on the same page throughout this operation."

The men in front of him, nearly twenty of them in all, nodded in unison.

Rayburn grinned.

"We're only going to erect one cross tonight," he said. "It will be one of the larger ones, and we'll need four or five strong men to carry it. It should be placed here," he pointed to a small courtyard between the street and the building, "so that all branches see it in the morning. A group of three people will take the dummy and hang it nearby. As soon as the cross is lit and the dummy is hung, do not wait around for security to identify you as Klan members. Get the hell out of there as quickly as possible.

"Are there any questions?"

There were none. Silence reigned throughout the suite.

Rayburn's cheek twitched before he took a long steady breath.

"Be prepared to receive Carl's text. You will roll out as soon as you receive it, and you will meet the other team at Turner Field. Disembark from there and head to the target. We're trying to make sure that area is secure for your operation.

"Good luck."

The men rose and left the room, all heading to several banks of elevators, leaving Rayburn and Carl alone in the room. Rayburn waked to the window facing southeast. The lights of Atlanta streamed in.

"They are good men, Bobby Ray," Carl said. "They'll do the job."

"Of that I have no doubt. They were trained well, and they know what's at stake. Especially with what else I have planned for the next few days."

The two men stared out the window, waiting for a patch of earth to light the sky.

***

Westin Peachtree Hotel, 67th Floor
Atlanta, Georgia
Monday, October 29, 2012
10:30 p.m. ET

Jaclyn made sure that nothing went wrong for the rest of the day. She had called Alex and explained what had happened in the arena—she had received a little bit of a tongue-lashing over that—and had secured Anderson's number so she could stay in contact with the younger agent during the course of the next few days. Using the number, she was able to text updates in both directions, learning of where the Republican challenger was heading next.

By the time 10:30 p.m. had rolled around, Jaclyn was running on fumes, her energy sapped. She was secretly glad that Tom was not around, or else her energy would have flat-lined a long time before now. She collapsed in her bed and found several unanswered texts from her honey waiting for her. She smiled weakly.

"God, I wish I was in his arms right now. I could really use a back rub," she said. She continued smiling as she slid her arms back and forth over the comforter.

She replied to his text:

"Just got back to the room; my God baby, what a long day. Picked up both Bennett and Forrister, Bennett lost me. Then Forrister and I (and first lady and VP) met up with Bennett at the debate arena, and I had to discharge my weapon in order to get Bennett to shut up. Liberty ripped me a new asshole for that. Ugh. I need your arms."

She sent the text with a veroop.

Jaclyn then texted to Alex:

"Back to the room. Nothing out of the ordinary happened after I updated you last. Anderson kept a close watch on Douchebag. I had Eagle under my sights. And yes, we can now consider using Douchebag as Bennett's code name."

Veroop.

She laid her head down with the iPhone on her chest, still wearing her work clothes. She slipped her HUD off and, after cutting the lights, felt her eyes close. She didn't feel the slight vibration as her iPhone signaled multiple incoming texts from London and Washington.

It was nearly 1 a.m., she was hungry and feeling as if she had drunk a box of wine when she blinked the sleep from her eyes. She checked out the clock on her phone and groaned.

"That wasn't the nap I was looking for," she muttered before she checked out the missed text messages, sliding her HUD back on her face.

Alex's read:

"Good. Have a good night, and check in with me in the morning. AD"

"That was a quickie."

She then checked Tom's message.

"Oh bloody hell Jaclyn, you're lucky you still have a job. Again. Don't let that bellend wanker get to you any longer; and you know that I'd love to have you in me arms, love. Mum sends her best and can't wait to see you again."

Jaclyn smiled. She took a deep breath and closed her eyes, content in the knowledge that both Tom and Alex cared enough to try to keep her in line, and thankful that her crazy day was finished.

For now.

***

Georgia State Capitol Building
Atlanta, Georgia
Tuesday, October 30, 2012
2 a.m. ET

The two white vans swept toward their intended targets just as the digital read out on the dash turned to 2 o'clock. They both decelerated to 20 miles per hour, crossing two empty lanes of traffic and pulling up to the State Capitol Building on Washington Street, directly across from the Central Presbyterian Church. Doors opened and shut, and feet shuffled quickly on the concrete to the rear of the vehicles. The driver opened the rear compartment, revealing a near-empty bay.

With gloved hands, the men, all wearing black from head to toe, heaved at the object until they felt their backs spasm, pulling the large wooden structure from within its steel gullet. Not a sound came from wood scratching the bay floor, as they had laid a rubber mat beforehand. Within a minute, they had the cross out, and four men, one at each branch, hauled it across the sidewalk and up the eight steps on the western entrance side. Another man followed, carrying what appeared to be the wooden equivalent to a Christmas tree stand. He managed to skirt the men carrying the cross and reached the spot before them. Off to the side, two black blurs rushed past them on the left-hand side, a rope and a large burlap sack under their arms as they made their way to a tree.

They would work in tandem, erecting the cross at the same time that the others swung the extra long rope around a sturdy branch. As the rope went up the first time, the men held the wood as another poured gasoline over its length and width. The combustible liquid spilled down the wood and overflowed onto their clothes. They could only hear the squishy sounds of the gasoline flowing from the red plastic can as they worked. Within a few minutes, they had the cross upright and in the stand, while over on the lawn, the men had just untied the sack and had pulled the effigy out. The stuffed doll wore white, and soon, it wore the rope around its cottony neck.

The men holding the rope gave a thumbs up to the other group and immediately began pulling the effigy upward, turning the tree into a makeshift gallows. Seconds later, flames erupted from the cross, the others standing back as the heat poured off the burning wood.

The driver of the first van, standing in a puddle of petrol, burst into flame too. He fell to the ground writhing in agony, his screams penetrating the darkness. No one had seemed to notice the trickle of fire that shot along the concrete toward his position.

The men, foreheads slick with nervous sweat and faces wide-eyed from the shock, backed away further, making sure they weren't caught in a similar situation.

Remembering Rayburn's words from earlier in the evening, they didn't dawdle. They hurried away from the burning marker and into the vans. The dead driver had left the keys in the ignition, and within rapid heartbeats, they motored away from the scene before any security guards could pour out of their respective buildings, before they could hear the telltale sounds of fire engines racing toward the solitary inferno.

They were home free.

***

Several blocks away, Rayburn looked toward the southeast and saw the sky near the State Capitol Building turn an orange hue right on schedule. He smiled and took a deep breath.

We are back, he thought.

He turned and headed to bed with a spring in his step even before the flashing red lights swarmed the scene.

Chapter 11
Georgia State Capitol Building
Atlanta, Georgia
Tuesday, October 30, 2012
9 a.m. ET

Jaclyn awoke to a text message alert blaring in her ears. Her eyes remained closed as the sun streamed into her hotel room until she flopped to the opposite side. She could feel the warm tears flowing across her face, the pain coming to her as if God himself had stabbed her in the retinas with needles.

As soon as she regained control and slid her HUD over her eyes, she was able to read Alex's text message:

"Snapshot: Word has reached me that there has been a small, contained terror strike at the Georgia State Capitol Building. Take Anderson there and learn what you can. Remember to keep your eyes open—yes, I know, figure of speech—and report in ASAP. AD"

Jaclyn firmed her lips as she typed away.

"Will do, Chief. Can I presume then that I am off this pseudo-White House Advance duty?"

Veroop.

She checked to see if Tom had sent her a good morning text, but her heart sank when she saw that he hadn't. She typed out a quick good morning and a mwah, then sent it across the Atlantic.

Then she scrolled to Anderson's number and called her. It rang twice before her partner answered.

"Hello?" she said. It sounded as if Anderson had spent half the night partying, her mouth filled with cotton.

"Jasmine, it's Jaclyn. Are you awake? We have assignments this morning." Jaclyn didn't exactly sound chipper, either, but she sounded more awake than her younger counterpart.

"Yeah, I-I-I-I am," Anderson yawned mid-reply.

"How long will you need to meet me at the capitol building?"

"An hour, I think? I need to shower."

Jaclyn checked the chronometer in her HUD. It was nearly 8 a.m.

"I have to shower, too. Meet me at the capitol at 9. Bring coffee."

"Is Starbucks okay with you? It's all I ever drink."

Jaclyn smirked.

"That'll be fine. Get me a vanilla latte with whipped cream. See you in an hour."

Jaclyn hung up without saying good bye before she saw Alex had texted back the word "Yes." She sighed. She didn't reply, as she needed to get in touch with Melanie Ruoff.

She scrolled through her contact list and found her number. She called her.

"I know, I know," Ruoff said as soon as she answered, "I haven't sent Eric's itinerary yet, I'm sorry—"

"Melanie, don't worry about that. I won't be able to keep an eye on you guys for an hour or so. Something came up."

"Oh?"

"Yeah, something unavoidable, I'm afraid. Alex needs me to check something out."

"OK, don't worry about us too much," Ruoff said. Jaclyn noticed that there was no impatience in her voice, which she found refreshing, especially after the look Ruoff had shot her after Jaclyn had torn the president a new one in Las Vegas. "What time do you think you'll be able to get to us?"

"That I don't know. I'd keep your cell handy just in case you're out and about. What's your first appointment of the day?"

Ruoff rattled off the beginning of the itinerary, mainly about Forrister meeting with Senate Democrats from Georgia during a brunch at 10:30 a.m.

"I may be able to make that," Jaclyn said. "I'll keep you updated."

"Don't worry about it if you can't make it; the Secret Service guys are good."

"Is it the same guys from Vegas?"

Ruoff, Jaclyn noticed, paused.

"Yes," she said, drawing out the ess a bit.

"I'll make sure I get there for that reason alone. They better have scrambled eggs," Jaclyn said before hanging up and tossing her iPhone to her pillow. She hurried out of bed, finally discarded yesterday's clothes and walked to the shower. Within heartbeats, she felt the needle-like shards of water pelt her bare skin before she rinsed her hair, the strands turning a dark caramel. She closed her eyes and inhaled, opening her ears to the sounds of the water slapping against the shower floor, rapping against her bare feet. Jaclyn cupped her hands and ran them over her scalp before dropping them to her breasts. Soon, water droplets covered her body, along with soapy shower gel and shampoo.

By 8:30, her shower was complete and she had a clean towel wrapped around her body. She tied her hair back in a ponytail, not bothering to dry it, before she dressed in a new pantsuit with her blouse untucked as per her custom. She grabbed her HUD, a Walther and her CIA credentials before she headed to the scene in her rental.

Good Lord Alex, she thought as she drove south on Peachtree, *when is Parkerhurst coming to give me my new car? I can't be driving this piece of tin for the next three days.*

Within five minutes, Jaclyn had reached the State Capitol Building, and Anderson was nowhere in sight. The chronometer read 8:50 a.m., so she still had a few minutes to spare before Jaclyn grew anxious. She saw plenty of Ford Interceptors bearing the blue body and red lettering of the Atlanta Police Department as well as Fulton County Sheriff, Georgia Capitol Police and Georgia State Police cruisers all lining Washington Street.

"Everyone's going to want a piece of the action," she muttered.

Instead of waiting, Jaclyn, who parked at the church across the street, exited her rental and walked across the street. A uniformed Atlanta cop halted her, but a flash of her identification had her past the yellow police tape barricade without another word. She grinned as she walked.

The grin left as soon as she saw the steaming hulk of the cross through her advanced pair of Foster Grants. She paused as she came toward it and the dead body, which a firefighter had covered some time ago.

"Good Lord," she whispered. She took out her iPhone and snapped a photo of it before sending it to Alex and Tom. The time it took her to send the two messages to Washington and London was plenty of time for Anderson to slide underneath the barricade with two venti-sized cups of Starbucks.

The agent handed Jaclyn her cup in silence. They each took a sip.

"The KKK did this, didn't it?" she finally asked.

"Yep. At least that's what I'm thinking. I haven't spoken to an investigator yet, but that's just how the evidence is pointing, as you can see. Come on," Jaclyn said, sipping her latte, "let's see what we can find out."

They walked to the right of the cross and found an Atlanta Police detective named Jackson. He was a bald man of African-American descent, and Anderson, Jaclyn saw, looked the man up and down with a sultry smile as he spoke with other investigators and pointed over to the tree.

"Would you like a bib, Jasmine?" Jaclyn asked, leaning over to her partner.

Anderson blinked.

"What?"

"You're drooling over him."

Jaclyn noticed that Anderson began to grow a tad flush in the cheeks. She figured it wasn't from the coffee. She grinned, and she let Anderson know it.

"Detective," Jaclyn said after pulling her HUD away from Anderson, "I'm Jaclyn Johnson, and this is my partner, Jasmine Anderson. I wonder if you have a few free moments to discuss what happened last night, and before you decline, I must tell you that it's a matter of national security."

The detective grinned.

"I do have a free moment, ladies," he said, his voice slightly baritone in timbre. Jaclyn didn't need to look at Anderson to know that her partner had just turned into a puddle. "What would you like to know?"

"A little bit of everything, if you could," Anderson said.

Jackson nodded.

"At about oh-two oh-one this morning, Atlanta Fire received a call from a security guard from the State Supreme Court Building about a burning cross on the steps of the Capitol Building. Several engine companies responded and found not only the cross fully engulfed, but also the charred remains of a man we have determined was Albert LeMoyne, a man known to Atlanta Police."

"And how is he known, Detective?" Jaclyn asked at the prompt.

Jackson took a deep breath.

"He's KKK. At least he was before Rayburn was taken down in 2007."

Anderson, Jaclyn saw, looked like she was going to shiver at those words. But Jaclyn's training prevented her from doing any such things.

"Tell me, Detective. How this man was connected to Rayburn?" she asked.

"Come over here and we'll talk," he said. Jaclyn nodded and waved Anderson forward. Jaclyn followed.

They walked under the front façade of the building, a four-story portico that resembled, to Jaclyn's impaired vision, a stretched North Portico of the White House. They stood between the southernmost Corinthian columns, and Jackson made sure that no one from the media or any stray ears were eavesdropping.

"Rayburn and LeMoyne took part in several lynchings when they were teenagers. Remember that Rayburn is only 23 years old, but what he did is famous all across Georgia and many members of the Klan revere him. We had tried to keep all of his fellow Klansmen under surveillance since before the execution date, but—"

"I'm going to hate hearing this, aren't I?" Anderson said.

Jaclyn threw her a look that shut her up.

"But we lost a few of them over the last two days or so," Jackson continued. He didn't bow his head. "I'll be the first to admit that we're not perfect."

"No one is, Detective, we understand that. LeMoyne's connection with Rayburn is clear, but what evidence is there that suggests Rayburn was truly involved?"

"Yes ma'am, there is something. If you'll follow me," Jackson said before leading the women across the lawn to the tree that held—

"Oh my God," Anderson gasped. Jackson turned his head.

"Jasmine, quiet," Jaclyn warned. She turned her HUD toward Jackson. "What do we have here, Detective?"

"Quite frankly, ma'am, it's an effigy hanging. Sort of what the KKK did to numerous people over the years. Rayburn was believed to have hung several black children and took part in the hangings of several adults, too."

"But that doesn't truly mean this was Rayburn's handiwork." Jaclyn didn't want to poke holes in the detective's theory, much in the way she did in London while standing in front of Wembley in its final minutes before the stadium crumbled in on itself, but that was what she did. Right now she believed that there was only pure conjecture that Rayburn had a hand in any of this. "The fact that LeMoyne was an accomplice of Rayburn's is a coincidence."

"A coincidence that's hard to ignore, Agent Johnson," Jackson said.

Jaclyn ignored it. She then stared at the hanging bundle, which tossed about lightly in the morning breeze, swinging by the rope that the KKK had wrapped around the branch twice before they tied it around the trunk. She saw their plan as simplistic, but smart—even if the authorities were to cut the rope between the trunk and the branch, there was a good chance that the effigy would continue to hang. The rope was taut around the branch. Someone would have to climb a ladder and pull it off.

Yet something gnawed at Jaclyn's mind as she stared at the effigy for several minutes.

Her eyes, hidden by the HUD, widened.

"This representation is white, though," Jaclyn blurted. "Weren't all effigies in the Klan's heyday mainly of black victims?"

"Not necessarily," Anderson said. "There were Klan groups that engaged in hangings of carpetbaggers from the North in the 1800s, and anyone of white skin who was sympathetic to blacks found themselves assassinated."

This time, Jaclyn felt her skin crawl. She shook it off before she looked at the effigy one more time.

"I wonder who this is supposed to represent," she mused. "The Klan wouldn't switch to attacking white people, would they?"

"I hope not," Anderson said. "I just wish they'd go away entirely."

Jaclyn barely heard her. She kept staring at the swinging effigy, her mind a tumble of thought.

***

Atlanta, Georgia
Tuesday, October 30, 2012
11:25 a.m. ET

Forgetting about brunch and her stomach rumbling with hunger, Jaclyn managed to shake Anderson for a brief spell at lunch. After making a quick stop at Georgia Tech to get an update on the debate set-up, they drove west on 10th Street before hanging a right onto Northside Drive, choosing to pull into a Burger King that appeared to have been shoehorned into the lot. Jaclyn had ordered a Whopper Jr.—no cheese, no onions, light lettuce, extra pickles—and had Anderson bring it over while she ducked into the ladies room.

She had her cell phone and the gray cube out even before the door closed and, after manipulating the touchscreen of her iPhone and the center button on the cube, placed a call to Alex. It rang once.

"Snapshot, what's going on?" her boss said as she picked up.

"Quite a bit, Chief," Jaclyn said before she had bounced into her narrative. She mentioned that one person was dead—"Roasted is a better word here," she had said—and that they had found a dummy swinging from a rope.

"Hmmm," Alex said. "Who does the dummy represent? Any clues stick out at you?"

"No idea."

"Are you going to look into it?"

Jaclyn shrugged.

"I don't know, to tell you the truth. Right now, police believe that Rayburn is behind it."

"Stay vigilant, Snapshot. I don't think Rayburn wants to attack anyone in particular, but you never know. I'm getting a bad vibe from this. Keep your HUD on the president and Bennett, and protect them over and above the call of duty."

"Anderson's watching Bennett and she's reporting his movements to me. We have them pretty much covered and protected. They thankfully had nothing planned for this morning, but we have a full afternoon scheduled." She sighed. "Thank God I'm only human or else I would sleep through to Friday after today."

Alex chuckled.

"Can't be two places at once?"

"Not at all."

"I'm sure you can manage something if you put your mind to it, Snapshot. Check in if something happens." Alex hung up without another word.

Jaclyn pressed the end key-home circle-lock button in sequence before stuffing the iPhone into her jacket pocket, then canceled the eavesdrop-proofing waves in the gray cube. She stared through her Foster Grants at her reflection in the large mirror, biting her bottom lip. She felt her heart hammering away. She didn't know why, but she felt sweat sliding down her spine and beading on her forehead.

Get a grip, Jaclyn, she thought, firming her lips. *It's not like you haven't protected a president before.*

But thought caught up with her half a heartbeat later.

Of course, you had on your jumpsuit then. Good luck catching a bullet in just work clothes.

She grabbed a paper towel and wiped the sweat away before she returned to Anderson's side, ready to eat.

She hoped Anderson hadn't touched her French fries.

Chapter 12
Cobb County Courthouse
70 Haynes Street, Marietta, Georgia
Tuesday, October 30, 2012
12:05 p.m. ET

The Honorable Jeffrey A. Cameron couldn't help but roll his eyes as the defense counselor, looking away from the judge, rambled on about his client's perceived innocence. The attorney, Cameron saw, had barely put any effort into his wardrobe, and had put the same amount into his client's defense. He noticed that the defendant looked nervous, shuffling his feet underneath the desk even though he looked at his counselor as if he were God, and God was about to deliver him from the death chamber.

It's a pity then, Cameron thought, *that the defendant didn't choose a jury trial instead of letting me choose his fate.*

Cameron had sat on this bench for nearly four decades, and every day and every case brought him closer to his retirement. He could have retired a decade ago, but he felt his life was more useful on the bench, dispensing justice and pruning society's dead weight. It was either that or helping dispense prune juice for his fellow senior citizens at the retirement home, or helping his wife of nearly five decades prune her rose bushes.

As it was, this case would be his last. Those rose bushes beckoned, calling his name with a voice as sweet as their scent.

Cameron grimaced.

If only I could stretch the final arguments a few more days, he thought as he leaned back into his comfy chair, a cushioned seat just as black as the robe he wore over his white Oxford shirt and blue bow tie. *I could always call my grandson and have him come do it; he does a good job with* *the lawn, and I stopped mowing it ten years ago. I'll give him $20 to help his granny while I sleep the day away.*

Cameron blinked his distraction away, his heavy, thick lenses hiding his eyes from the gallery. He had already perused both counselor's summations—the defense counsel's brief ran ten pages—before falling asleep in his recliner last night. Jeopardy! was on the television, a cold beer resting on a coaster. His wife puttered around the kitchen, putting the dishes away after washing them. He didn't know why she still hand-washed them; after all, the kids had bought them a fancy new dishwasher as part of the renovations, and she barely used the blasted thing. Cameron had re-read the summation over his morning coffee and breakfast—two eggs scrambled with hash browns, ham and toast—and knew it word for word, along with every piece of evidence and every bit of testimony. He could bang the gavel and rule on the case now if he so desired, but he wanted to stretch this out. Just a little bit longer.

The counselors expected the old coot—he knew they called him this, even though they were polite near him—to take a few days to deliberate over the facts and do research over sentencing guidelines. He wanted to show these young pups, all more than half his age and practically out of law school, if he wanted to guess, that he was still as sharp as a whip.

He had presided over thousands of cases, and this one, he could tell, wouldn't go down as one of his more memorable.

One of them, without a doubt, was the trial of Bobby Ray Rayburn.

Cameron couldn't help feeling a cold chill rush across his skin every time he thought about that trial: the mix of the KKK and an angry mob of African-Americans—at his age, he still called them negroes, even though he meant them no ill will—standing out on Haynes Street, chanting and hurling epitaphs at the other group. He distinctly remembered their voices carrying upward to the seventh floor courtroom he now sat in, distracting the participants. He recalled how he ordered the sheriff's office to move the protesters two blocks to the west, to Marietta Square, regardless if they complained.

And he remembered how Rayburn struggled against his handcuffs and the Cobb County sheriffs as he yelled that he would get his revenge on everyone, even though he would spend the rest of his life behind bars, until that needle slid into a vein and pumped him full of pentobarbital, Pavulon, and potassium chloride.

"Get him out of my courtroom!" Cameron had bellowed. "Get that killer out of here!"

"I'll get you, nigger lover!" Rayburn had said, his teeth gnashing together. "I'll get you if it's the last thing I ever do!"

Cameron gasped as the bailiffs finally managed to haul Rayburn's skinny ass out of the courtroom. He turned and found everyone staring at him, each person in the gallery wearing a look of pure shock. He banged his gavel twice and dismissed everyone, and as he walked out, he didn't hear a single murmur emitted from the departing crowd. His ears still rang with Rayburn's threat.

And now, three days after the day that Rayburn was supposed to meet his end courtesy of a lethal injection, Cameron recalled that case, wondering if the escaped convict would do as he had promised.

If he does, Cameron thought, *he'll have to take his best shot. I'm an old man, but I won't go down easily.*

He reached for his left side and rubbed his robe, feeling the Smith & Wesson M&P340, a .38, secured in a shoulder holster underneath. There were five rounds available and one already in the chamber, which made him feel at ease. Thankfully, his wife made no mention of Rayburn's connection with her husband—actually, he recalled, she had said something to the effect that she hoped the police would capture him quickly, but didn't say anything to me about recognizing me as Rayburn's judge—when they watched the news Saturday morning. He made sure that the gun was on him at all times beginning Saturday afternoon, when he and his wife went shopping.

At least she's not worried about me, he thought, *and that eases my mind more than the gun does.*

The defense counselor continued to drone on in his rambling even as Cameron reminisced. He sighed audibly.

"Counselor," he said, "do you have a point to your summation coming any time soon? The court would like to eat before Halloween."

The gallery chuckled. The defense counselor's face grew flush, he saw. Cameron knew that kind of line could hurt him in an appeal, but he neared 82, and his patience was somewhat limited, even if it meant growing closer to putting in winter windows. He didn't care if this guy filed every appeal known to man.

"I'll wrap this up quickly, Your Honor," the defense counselor said, pulling at his collar.

"That would be greatly appreciated, thank you." Cameron couldn't keep the sarcasm out of his tone, as much as he tried.

The counselor continued, wrapping up his summation in a neat two minutes. Cameron looked at the clock. It read 12:04 p.m.

"Not bad, only a few minutes after noon. Prosecution will begin its summation at 2 p.m. sharp. We're in recess until then. Enjoy your lunches, y'all." Cameron picked up his gavel and rapped it once. He stood just as the bailiff instructed the gallery to rise as the judge departed. Cameron had his robe unzipped and off his body the moment he turned the corner. He entered his office and tossed the robe over the back of his chair. The robe slipped off the headrest and slithered to the right armrest. It stayed there.

Cameron shrugged as he grabbed his sport coat. He headed for the elevator, humming an old tune that he and his wife had danced to some time ago. It may have been their wedding, but he wasn't entirely sure. The elevator ride was swift. He stepped off the elevator and headed outside toward the parking lot, his 2000 Buick LeSabre waiting for him on the Lawrence Street side. He could have walked to the Celtic pub two blocks to the west, but he felt like pizza and a beer today. Marietta Pizza was a little further down the street, but he didn't mind the drive. Crossing traffic, though, was a different story.

He dreamed of tangy sauce as he walked through the open door and barely acknowledged the young secretary who held the door open for him.

It was such a distraction that he didn't see or hear the bald headed man walk up to him from the side of his car. It was the feeling of cold steel, felt even through the jacket, that made the judge freeze in place.

"You knew this was coming, didn't you old man?" the man hissed.

Cameron nodded slowly. He didn't even look at his assailant.

"You could have stopped everything and let Bobby Ray go free. People died the other day because you didn't stop that heinous trial." The man's breath, so close to the judge's right ear, made his skin ripple and shiver in disgust.

"I did what I had to do," the judge said sternly, regaining some of his bravado. He turned to the side and looked right into the face of—

Cameron staggered backward as the gun erupted. He felt a sharp, stabbing pain in his throat, and the bullet's momentum carried him toward his car. His body collided with the driver's side mirror, but the pain in his throat overrode the new pain in his lower back. His weight bent the mirror backward, and as his feet finally faltered, he fell to the pavement, landing hard on his right arm. He felt the wind leave him even as his arm grew numb. Nearby, a secretary screamed. Another yelled for a security guard.

The man Cameron soon recognized as Carl Dane—the man's Georgia driver's license photo had been displayed on television the past three days, so it wasn't hard to identify him—stood over him, the gun pointed right at the judge's heart.

"The Klan always gets its revenge, Judge," he said. "You should know that by now."

Cameron couldn't say anything as blood pooled into his esophagus. He felt his eyes growing wide with panic as respiratory arrest kicked in during the intervening heartbeats, now rapid and too close together. He wished he could reach for his sidearm, if only to go to his grave with the intent of protecting himself. He wished he could prune his wife's rosebush before he died, and he wished he could kiss his wife goodbye one last time. He knew that this was the end, and even though it was the last thing on his mind at that moment, he knew that some other poor schmuck would have to listen to that poor defense counselor's summation a second time.

Somehow, that comforted him as he looked up the barrel of Carl Dane's .44.

Carl didn't hesitate. He quickly pulled the trigger.

Cameron lurched upward as the bullet sheared through flesh, bone and lung. He gasped, his life concluded, dispensed and disposed of with two bullets.

Carl took off on foot toward Cole Street, hopping into the getaway van and quickly meandering its way to Interstate 75 South.

***

Westin Peachtree Hotel, 50th Floor

Atlanta, Georgia
Tuesday, October 30, 2012
12:14 p.m. ET

Rayburn had fallen asleep on the couch an hour ago with The Price Is Right on the television. He shook awake as his borrowed cell phone blistered his ears, ringing just as loud as the current commercial for an Atlanta car dealer. He quickly wiped the sleep from his eyes, digging his left thumb and forefinger into the corners as he brought the phone to his ear. An eyelash and eye gunk came away.

"Hello?" he rasped.

"Did I wake you?" Carl said.

"No," Rayburn lied. "I was just resting my eyes. What's going on, Carl?"

"Oh. Well, the hit is done. I executed the judge as you wanted."

Rayburn couldn't help but smile. He stood up from the couch, feeling his joints creak. He winced.

"Good. That's two down, including my good-for-nothing lawyer." He walked toward his kitchen. "Who's next?"

Dane told him.

"I want you to handle that one personally. Call the others out of seclusion via the radio. They have other tasks I need them to complete."

"Like what?"

Rayburn grinned, baring his teeth.

"Something worse than burning crosses and hanging pitiful effigies," he said.

"When did you come up with it?"

Rayburn shrugged his shoulders.

"Not too long ago. We're going to meet at that abandoned farmhouse we were at the other night. Have everyone meet me there."

"And just how will get there, Bobby Ray? You don't have a car, and it's not like you can just get up and walk through Downtown Atlanta."

Rayburn ran his hand over his scalp, where several days' worth of stubble had sprouted through the skin.

"I'll get there, trust me. Don't we have a cab driver loyal to the cause?"

He heard Carl spit.

"Golly, I don't know. You can always use code if you got to make sure he's legit."

Rayburn smiled.

"Right. I'll be in touch." Rayburn disconnected the call and tossed the phone on the couch. He walked to the bathroom and, after shutting the door, disrobed until he stood there naked.

"Time for a little switcheroo, and time to get the fuck out of here. I shouldn't have stayed here this long anyway," he muttered to himself as he filled the basin with hot water. Once full, he turned the faucet off and scooped water into his palms. He winced a bit, but he accepted the pain and bowed his head.

Hot water slipped over his scalp as he lifted his hands up and over his head. Air slipped through his teeth as it cascaded across the sensitive skin half a heartbeat later. Rayburn lathered his hands with shaving gel before rubbing it all over his scalp, covering every inch from the top of his forehead, back around his ears to the nape of his neck. He rinsed his hands and grabbed a Bic razor, the stainless steel blades gleaming underneath the artificial light. He began to scrape the stubble away, using broad strokes as the blades glided across his cranium. He cleaned the blades in the water and repeated his actions several times until his pate was completely bare.

Rayburn showered the excess away, and by 1 p.m. he was dressed in a Braves t-shirt and jean shorts, ready to check out of the hotel even though his benefactor had paid for an extra two nights. He didn't care; it wasn't his money. It was Klan dollars, which he knew were unlimited.

He made one more phone call, this time to a cab company. He asked for a cab to come and pick him up at the hotel by 1:15 if it was possible. The dispatcher told him yes. Rayburn hung up, before he collected the few clothes he had and headed downstairs.

At 1:10, a cab bearing the markings of the company he had called pulled up. The driver popped the trunk, and after Rayburn stashed his bag, he slid into the backseat.

"Where to, pal?" the cabbie asked as he looked in the rear view mirror.

"It's a simple farmhouse out in the country," Rayburn replied. He gave him the address. "You can't miss it."

The cabbie shrugged. He pulled out into traffic seconds later and turned onto Spring Street headed north. He flicked on a local news station on the radio. As they drove, the station spoke of the escaped convict, "who may be looking to hook back up with his KKK cronies."

"Boy, I'll tell you. I hope they never find the guy," the cabbie had said. "Not enough proper folk any longer."

By the time they crossed over Interstate 85, Rayburn had observed the driver for several minutes. He licked his lips.

"AYAK?" he said, a questioning inflection coming to his lips as he used code for *Are you a Klansman?*

The driver merged onto West Peachtree. He narrowed his eyes as he looked into the rear view mirror again. His eyes widened slightly, and Rayburn believed recognition clicked on in the driver's mind.

"AKIA."

A Klansman I am.

Rayburn grinned.

They drove on, heading out of Atlanta proper without drawing attention to themselves.

Chapter 13
Children's Healthcare of Atlanta at Hughes Spalding
35 Jesse Hill Junior Drive Southeast
Atlanta, Georgia
Tuesday, October 30, 2012
1:37 p.m. ET

After Jaclyn and Anderson split up to head to their respective security details, Jaclyn caught up with the president and his entourage having a quick lunch at a Subway restaurant on Edgewood Avenue Northeast. The president made several campaign stops, stops that Forrister's Chief of Staff, Melanie Ruoff, knew the Republicans would avoid on principle: a homeless shelter and a children's hospital, the hospital practically right around the corner from the State Capitol Building. Jaclyn hung back at a safe distance while the president mingled and shook hands with workers—at least at the shelter; there weren't many homeless folks who wanted to be caught on camera with the president, or caught on camera period—and with the young patients. There were no speeches for the press, Jaclyn noticed; no promises for funding that he couldn't deliver. She heard rounds of applause for Forrister, the cameras clicking away as he walked down the halls with his Secret Service detail just in front of her position. She couldn't help but smile as the little faces lit up as the most powerful man in the free world extended his hand and took a little one in his. A little boy high fived him. Another little girl's cheeks turned pink.

Jaclyn's HUD picked up the incoming call even before it rang. She saw that it was Alex calling.

She nudged Ruoff.

"I'll be right back, I have a call to take," she said as soon as the still-new Chief of Staff turned to her.

"No problem; I don't think the kids are going to do anything to him," Ruoff said.

Jaclyn grinned before she turned away, sliding her finger across her iPhone's touchscreen while digging the gray cube out of her MZ Wallace handbag.

"Hi, Chief. Give me a second to get secure."

"Half a second—"

Jaclyn quickly rolled her eyes as her spine straightened, every inch of her body squirreling with annoyance.

"I know, I know, half a second would be better, I know." Jaclyn pressed the button as she walked away from the president, her heels clicking off the linoleum. "I'm all set."

"Trouble's brewing up in Marietta, Snapshot. A judge is dead."

Jaclyn paused mid-stride.

"Ok."

"You're waiting for me to get to the punch line."

"I wouldn't think that there's something funny about someone dying unless I'm the one who killed the guy, but sure, I'll play along."

"Settle down, Jaclyn," Alex said, her voice stiff. "The judge just happened to be the one who presided over Rayburn's trial and conviction."

Jaclyn felt a chill.

"That sounds like something out of a Grisham novel, Chief. Do you have any idea what happened?"

"Nope. Cobb County informed us because of Rayburn. We had sent a request for information on him after the breakout, and they figured we'd want information. Can the president's entourage spare you for a few hours, Snapshot?"

Jaclyn shifted on her feet as she tried to remember what else the president needed to do today. She only knew about the $1,000-a-plate dinner at the nearby Hilton Nikolai's Roof restaurant, but that wasn't for another few hours. She looked down the hall and saw that he was now engaged in a fierce yet spirited game of Connect Four with a little boy.

She smiled and knew that he wasn't going anywhere any time soon.

"I think they can," she said, telling the director of the CIA what the president was up to at that minute.

Alex couldn't help but chuckle.

"I hope he lets the boy win. I'd hate to see how Fox News spins that."

Jaclyn smiled.

"Oh, I think I can picture it. They did a lousy job on what happened in Vegas." A cheer came from down the hall. Jaclyn turned her head and saw the boy celebrating. Nurses clapped their hands. Ruoff had a smile on her face as everything played out to its conclusion. Forrister's hands covered his face. "Looks like the boy won."

"The Facebook memes will criticize him for losing a war. I can see it now."

"Thankfully we don't have Facebook pages."

"Right," Alex said. "What time should I expect a report on what happened up in Marietta?"

Jaclyn checked her watch.

"It's nearly quarter to 2 right now, it'll take me a little while to get up there." She did some quick figuring in her head. "Probably by 3:30, 4 o'clock at the latest."

"That'll work. I want to know where Rayburn will strike next, Snapshot. I want this debate to go undisturbed. Do you understand me?"

Jaclyn didn't have to nod. Her lips were a thin line across the lower half of her face.

"I do."

"Call Anderson and have her come with you. Maybe she'll be able to provide some insight."

Jaclyn nodded.

"I'll call her right now. I'll be on my way in a few minutes."

"Good. Report in by dinner time. And just so you know, Parkerhurst is en route to Atlanta. He'll have a new car for your use. Meet him at Turner Field tonight at 8 o'clock."

She hung up. Jaclyn touched the screen and did so again to end it on her side. She felt her heart racing at the prospect of a new ride, one just a tad sleeker than her current mode of transportation. She had to admit that without the special modifications that Parkerhurst implemented in all of her cars, she felt a tad naked driving in the Hyundai. She wondered exactly what he would give her.

She shook away those thoughts and then called Anderson. It rang three times.

"Hello?"

"Jasmine, it's Jaclyn. Something's come up. I need you to ditch Bennett and come up to Marietta with me."

"What's going on in Marietta? And don't worry about me ditching Bennett; he's already done that."

Jaclyn froze.

"And you're just letting me know now?"

"I called our branch office, who in turn called the Secret Service. I don't think he cares, to be honest."

Jaclyn grimaced.

"No, I don't think he does, nor does he appreciate our protection given the circumstances." She bit her lip. "Damn it, it's like it's a running joke with him right now. What happened? What caused him to leave you?"

"I had to go to the bathroom, and he just vanished. One minute he was waiting for me, the next, he was gone. It's like he didn't exist."

Jaclyn tried to hold back a smile.

"I wish that were so, Jasmine. I really wish that were so. What's your location right now?"

Anderson told her that she was standing outside of a high school on the south side of Interstate 20.

"I'm not that far from you. I'll come get you and we'll head up to Marietta from there."

"You still haven't told me what's going on up there," Anderson said.

Jaclyn sighed and pulled the phone a little closer to her mouth.

"Apparently Rayburn had one of the judges killed today. We're going up to check it out."

"I'm willing to bet the locals won't like it, us infringing on their territory and all," Anderson replied after half a beat.

Jaclyn's lip twitched.

"It doesn't matter what they like or don't like," she said as a reprimand. "The locals will have to remember who they're dealing with here. Alex has already let them know that anything has to do with Rayburn falls under our jurisdiction. They're just doing the leg work for us. Be ready to go, I'll be there in less than twenty minutes."

"I'm not going anywhere."

"See you in a few then." Jaclyn hung up and walked back to where Ruoff stood. "I'm heading out. You guys should be fine."

"What's going on?" the chief of staff said, her eyebrow lifted in an arch.

"It's a classified situation outside of Atlanta. I'll check in with you in a few hours."

Ruoff shrugged it off and wished her luck before she turned back to the president.

Without anything keeping her there, Jaclyn headed to her Hyundai.

***

Cobb County Courthouse
Marietta, Georgia
Tuesday, October 30, 2012
2:27 p.m. ET

Jaclyn had hopped onto Interstate 75 before making the eastward swing from the Downtown Connector onto the Ralph David Abernathy Freeway, also known as Interstate 20. She was on this stretch of road for not even a mile before jumping off at Exit 59A. A right turn onto Boulevard Southeast followed by a left-hand turn onto Hansell Street brought the secret agent to the Maynard H. Jackson High School. The building stretched from north to south.

She found Anderson waiting at the front entrance. Anderson walked to the Hyundai and hopped in before Jaclyn pulled away and weaved her way back to Interstate 20.

Snapshot brought Anderson up to speed.

"Apparently, as I said, a judge was killed earlier today, and we suspect that Rayburn is behind it."

"Right. Do we know which judge?"

Jaclyn shook her head.

"All I know is we're going to Marietta."

"That's Cobb County," Anderson said. "There was an old judge who presided over the Rayburn case by the name of Cameron. Cameron was a fuddy duddy of sorts, very old school. He wasn't a racist by any means, but he had that damn you whippersnapper attitude: if you weren't over the age of 50, you were a snot-nosed punk to him. He wasn't keen on women lawyers, either. So anyway, he gets the Rayburn matter. Rayburn's attorney, a snot-nosed punk who doesn't like his client, if you followed his body language, tries to file for a change of venue. Cameron says no, says that the crime happened in Cobb County, it'll be tried in Cobb County." It was as if Anderson had morphed into a college professor, a lecture at the ready. "The scuttlebutt was that the attorney didn't want to move the trial to begin with; he just wanted to assault Cameron with an avalanche of paper."

Jaclyn smirked as she merged onto 75 North.

"Nice."

"It gets better. The attorney then tried to get Cameron removed."

Jaclyn was glad for her HUD. She turned her head sharply toward her partner.

"You're kidding."

"Nope. I don't kid."

"Why would he want to do that?"

"Because Cameron wasn't pro-white enough."

Jaclyn sighed.

"Oy vey."

"It was a smokescreen, of course. It was basically telling the potential jurors that even if they were to convict his client, he'd appeal on prejudicial grounds, saying that today's society is prejudiced against his client, who is prejudiced against anyone not like him."

"Which is one hundred percent true."

"Trial begins. The prosecution lays out the facts, the defense counters with saying that southern society—not just today's society, simply southern society—has made his client what he is: hateful.

"Which, if you think about it," Anderson continued after a heartbeat, spitting out her words as she crossed her arms underneath her breasts, "is also one hundred percent true."

Jaclyn didn't say anything for a few seconds, electing to keep her HUD on the road. She easily detected the vitriol Anderson used. It wasn't hard to detect Anderson's anger, and her body language said it all. Jaclyn could tell Anderson was upset with Rayburn's attorney, even if in her heart she knew he was right. Rayburn was a product of his environment: he lived an area where some people continued to breed anti-black racism among their youth, even though it wasn't openly acknowledged these days.

Jaclyn couldn't help but feel sickened by that.

"This area has gotten better at cutting out the racism, but there's always a few who spoil that image," Anderson said, a touch of emotion in her voice. "My parents taught me to like everyone, regardless if they were black or white. Growing up here, you could tell there were a select few people, both black and white, who hated the other race for everything that happened sixty or even one hundred and sixty years ago. Like I said the other day, some of them are the 'The South Will Rise Again' fools who are so anti-Yankee that they truly believe the Civil War isn't over."

Jaclyn smirked.

"The end of the Civil War was in all the papers, wasn't it?"

Anderson made a sound that resembled a tire deflating.

"That wouldn't help that crew much."

They passed the exit for Georgia Tech, continuing to drive north toward Marietta.

"So did anything else happen in the trial?" Jaclyn asked. "You seem so close to it."

"I studied that case so hard," Anderson replied. "I used to read the paper every morning with my corn flakes and coffee. I still have the scrapbook at home."

They drove on.

Twenty minutes later, they pulled off 75 at Exit 265 and followed Route 120 into Downtown Marietta. By 3:20 p.m., Jaclyn had brought her Hyundai to Haynes Street. A Cobb County Deputy Sheriff held up his hand and brought her to a stop. Jaclyn showed identification. The deputy had her pull over to the side before he radioed over to the sheriff.

"The sheriff will be waitin' for you over yonder," he said.

"Thanks for your help," Jaclyn said.

The two women walked around to Lawrence Street, their heels clicking along on the concrete sidewalk. The seven-story courthouse loomed above and to their right.

When they got to the other side, there were still quite a few officers on the scene, from both Cobb County Sheriff and Marietta Police. The body had long been moved, but a chalk outline and a few blood splatters on both the ground and the cars were on full display. To Jaclyn's HUD, it appeared as if it were the scene at the State Capitol Building all over again.

That was only six hours ago, Jaclyn thought. Had so much happened in so little time since then?

She never answered herself as the sheriff approached, making her blink back to the present. Jaclyn extended her hand. The beefy sheriff took it warmly.

"You must be the Johnson woman," he said, his accent giving him a twang in his voice. "I heard about you. And I know Miss Anderson well." He tipped his hat to Anderson. The agent nodded. "I take it y'all want to know what happened here, correct?"

Jaclyn nodded.

"Simple. Bald headed guy comes up and shot the judge twice."

"Which judge?" Anderson asked.

"It was Cameron."

Jaclyn caught Anderson's shiver out of the corner of her HUD. They shared a brief look.

"He was the judge in the Rayburn case," Jaclyn said.

The sheriff nodded.

"Yep, he was."

"Did the witnesses give you a better ID?"

"Not really, ma'am. Just said he was bald. They said it happened too quickly. Didn't really get a better look at the guy."

"Damn," Anderson said. She turned her head as if she was about to spit, her hands positioned right at her hips.

"Call me if you find out who did it, Sheriff," Jaclyn said, handing him a business card.

"I can do that, sure," he said. The sheriff grabbed his buckle. "But I wouldn't hold your breath, little lady. If it's Rayburn, he's going to try to stay hidden as long as he can. That's what happened the last time. I figure that's what he'll do again." He reached into his pocket and fetched a business card of his own. He passed it over to Jaclyn. "Let's stay in touch; if you come up with anything, give me a holler. I'll do the same for you if we figure out anything."

Jaclyn nodded. She and Anderson took one last look around the parking lot before they returned to Jaclyn's Hyundai.

"What do you think, Jasmine?" Jaclyn asked once she started the engine and headed north on Haynes.

The younger agent could only shake her head.

"I don't know. It sounds like Rayburn's carrying a hard grudge for the people who sent him away."

"That's what I was thinking. We're going to have to talk to that prosecutor. He's the only one left. Rayburn's done away with his own attorney and the judge."

Anderson had her phone out right away.

"I'm on it," she said.

"On what?" Jaclyn replied as she turned right onto Lemon Street.

"I'm getting him some agents to find and protect him. He lives over in Kennesaw. Take Route 3 North."

Jaclyn had to smile.

Smart thinking, Jasmine, she thought. *I just hope the agents are up to the task of protecting against an emotion and a movement rather than just protecting against an individual.*

They drove to the highway.

Chapter 14
Home of Allen Schatzenberger
Cobb County Assistant District Attorney
Kennesaw, Georgia
Tuesday, October 30, 2012
3:45 p.m. ET

Jaclyn didn't ease the accelerator much as they passed the Cobb County Airport. They had contacted the federal marshals' office and gave them the address, while Jaclyn called Alex and gave her a brief sit-rep.

"We're headed up to see Rayburn's prosecutor," she said. "He's the only one alive right now."

"Smart thinking."

"It was Jasmine's smart thinking this time, Chief."

"Good!" Alex said with an air of surprise. "I'll make a note of it in her file. Call me back when you learn more. And remember your meeting tonight." She hung up. Jaclyn slid her iPhone into the drink holder.

They approached Watts Drive in Kennesaw, passing small strip malls, hotels, automotive chains and the occasional church before Anderson told her to take a right-hand turn. They passed a community center with a set of ballfields behind it on the right.

"We're almost there. Any chance the marshals will get there first?"

"I doubt it. We'll wait for them to get there before we leave."

Anderson nodded and told her to take the third left onto Hillsborough Chase Northwest. A subdivision of about fifty small single-family homes, all sharing a lawn, unfolded before Jaclyn's HUD.

"Wow," Jaclyn said as she drove slowly around a bend. "They look cramped in here. It doesn't look like kids would have a big area to play in."

"True, but subdivisions like this form neighborly bonds," Anderson said. "I grew up in a small subdivision. You make a lot of friends and you have a lot of mommas. It's difficult to get in trouble in one of these, especially when all the adults have permission to whip your ass."

Jaclyn smiled and nodded.

"Where does he live?"

"He's down by the cul-de-sac at the end."

"Tell me when to stop." Meanwhile, Jaclyn's HUD scanned as they rolled through the subdivision. "Tactically speaking, this is probably the best defended residential areas I've seen. The houses are so close together that it's nearly impossible for someone to go undetected."

"That's true, and with the houses on the next street to the south so close, there's no chance of a sneak attack through the backdoor. We'll have to let the marshals know."

Jaclyn saved the mental note to her HUD as Anderson said, "That one."

She pulled the Hyundai in front of the prosecutor's house, not letting the tires crush a single blade of grass. The manicured lawn rolled away from the house, which was small, two stories high and painted yellow with black shutters. Jaclyn thought the house resembled a bumblebee ready to strike, stinger at the ready.

Both women walked to the front door, located right near the driveway. Jaclyn opened the screen door while Anderson knocked on the heavy black door.

Jaclyn's HUD then screamed in warning just before the door burst open halfway. A harried looking man holding a sawed off shotgun appeared, breathing heavily through his nose, just as Jaclyn drew her Walther P99. To Jaclyn's gaze a split second later, it appeared as if he were waiting for something—or someone, she thought—to come for him.

"Who are you?" the man screamed. "What do you want? I won't go down easily!"

Jaclyn eased her weapon into the air along with her left hand.

"Alright, just take it easy, sir. I'm going to put my gun away and show you some ID. I want you to put your gun down, too."

The man pumped the shotgun and stuck it right in Jaclyn's face, only inches away from her nose. The HUD whined, but she ignored it.

"I don't think so," he said through clenched teeth. Jaclyn could see saliva ready to spring from between his teeth. "Reach for it slowly. I'm about two seconds away from blowing your brains all over the ground."

"Calm down," Jaclyn warned as she reached for her badge, "or you'll find the butt end of that shotgun in your mouth."

The man's lip curled.

Jaclyn pulled out her badge and flipped it open for him to see. He peered at it.

"My name is Jaclyn Johnson, CIA. Are you the Cobb County prosecutor?"

Anderson nodded and reached for the man.

"It's okay, Mr. Schatzenberger, she's okay. She's on the good side."

Schatzenberger started to calm down, lowering the gun even though, Jaclyn noted, he still had his finger poised to pump the trigger. His breaths came slower yet sharper, and before long, the trigger finger slipped away.

"You heard about what happened at the courthouse then." It wasn't a question.

"That's why we're here," Jaclyn replied. "Can we come in?"

Schatzenberger was a little stiff in his movements, as his nod was rather quick. Jaclyn noticed that he positioned himself on the right as the door opened, as if to present a smaller target to any potential hitmen that may be lurking between the houses, even though Jaclyn already knew who was out there. Jaclyn and Anderson slipped in before Schatzenberger closed the door with a snap.

The two agents slipped into the man's kitchen. No light streamed through, as Schatzenberger had pulled the shade down and had drawn the curtains together. It seemed to Jaclyn as if the attorney had made his home a fortress.

Or a prison, she thought.

Jaclyn spun on the prosecutor.

"We're arranging to have you protected, Mr. Schatzenberger. Federal marshals are on their way. They'll secure the perimeter and will have bodies at the start of the subdivision to make sure that no one who doesn't live in this area comes anywhere near. We're going to keep you alive."

"That's a lot of inconvenience for just one man, Miss Johnson. I can assure you my neighbors won't be too happy with that; my neighbor three doors down has a birthday party scheduled for Saturday afternoon with guests coming from all over. Their addresses won't match."

"They'll get the guest list if they're still here," Anderson said. "We're going to have them try to stay as unobtrusive as possible to protect not only you, but the others around here. We really don't know what we're up against."

"You're up against Rayburn," Schatzenberger spat. "He's a fucking psychopath."

Jaclyn and Anderson shared a look.

"How do we beat him then?" Jaclyn asked. "You've spent time with him, we haven't. Tell us what you know."

Schatzenberger seemed to shrink, his body shaking. He leaned against the refrigerator, his right shoulder smashing against the freezer door.

"He threatened all of us," he whispered. "His trial was a circus from the start."

He moved away from the fridge and pulled out a chair, the legs squeaking against the linoleum tiles. Jaclyn and

Anderson did the same. Anderson sat at the opposite end while Jaclyn sat closer to the prosecutor. She leveled him with a stare that only the Foster Grants could manage to pull off. Usually, the HUD had people on edge, wondering what lay behind them. Schatzenberger didn't seem too interested in Jaclyn's face. Instead, he gnawed on the skin that lay near his fingernails. Jaclyn saw that he had already torn several nails away. The abrasions looked fresh, as if his nerves had triggered everything.

"How was it a circus?"

Schatzenberger looked up from his impromptu meal.

"The damned KKK was there, shouting racial epitaphs at prospective black jurors. The sheriff's department could barely control those devils. Some prospective jurors received threats prior to the trial. Some of them never showed up. Judge Cameron let them off, even though it set a dangerous precedent. People skipping jury duty just for the sake of skipping?"

Jaclyn wanted to say that those potential jurors didn't want to deal with being harassed or killed by the KKK, but she kept that to herself.

"Do you believe that Rayburn would stoop this low?" Anderson said.

"You've followed this case closer than anyone else, Miss Anderson. You know that he would. And he has."

Jaclyn blinked. She wondered just exactly how involved Anderson was with the case before she joined the agency. Did Anderson meet with Schatzenberger to discuss those clippings she had? Is that why she knew where he lived?

It wouldn't surprise me if she did, Jaclyn thought.

"We have no evidence—"

"Think, Miss Johnson, think. You have his statement at the trial. Judge Cameron is dead. He killed his own attorney. That's enough for an arrest warrant."

Jaclyn read between the lines: Schatzenberger wanted Rayburn picked up before he found the prosecutor. She could understand that.

The two women waited outside for the federal marshals, and while Anderson sat on the front stoop, Jaclyn took the time to think about what would happen next.

Her mind was blank.

Chapter 15
Sun Dial Restaurant, Westin Peachtree Hotel
Atlanta, Georgia
Tuesday, October 30, 2012
8 p.m. ET

Night had fallen upon Atlanta, and had done so with force.

By the time Jaclyn had dropped off Anderson, a northeasternly breeze settled on the city, making pedestrians shiver the early evening hours away. Jaclyn saw people walking about in heavy sweaters, while others pulled their jackets tighter around their bodies.

Inside her rented Hyundai, she was toasty warm as she made her way back to her hotel. After turning it in, she made her way to her room on the 67th floor, changing from her work clothes to something just a little more casual—she also checked her text messages and found one from Tom as well as two from Tasha, all of which she could answer at dinner—before she made her way all the way to the top of the hotel and the Sun Dial Restaurant. As usual, a Walther P99 rested on her hip.

The Sun Dial is a piece of the Westin that rotates in two levels: the top level of the restaurant completes its turn every thirty minutes, while its bottom level needs a full hour to complete a revolution. It is said that the views from the restaurant are some of the best in the southeast portion of the country, and that a customer's bill reflected the view.

Jaclyn shrugged that off as she surged the remaining six floors to the Sun Dial. The agency would pay for it.

She ordered a glass of water as well as a kumato tomato salad, along with grilled salmon for an entrée. When she was finished, she wiped her mouth, signed the check with the pseudonym Salt had given her and charged the room, then headed back down the length of the skyscraper to where she waited for a cab.

Fifteen minutes later, the cab dropped her off on the southernmost side of Turner Field, the home of the Atlanta Braves baseball club.

"Lady," the cabbie said. "You do know that there's no game here now, right? The Braves aren't in the World Series." He allowed himself a little snicker. "They really haven't been in it in some time."

"I know. I'm a Mariners fan."

"You admit that?" the cabbie said with widened eyes.

Jaclyn smiled and nodded.

"Are you sure you want me to drop you off here? I can take you back if you made a mistake."

She nodded again.

"I'll be fine. Thanks for the lift." She paid him and, with a curious glance back at his former party, the cabbie drove away. Jaclyn didn't move until she saw that his taillights had melded with the others heading into Atlanta proper.

Her HUD scanning away, she walked toward the parking lot on the north side of the building. As an insightful baseball fan, Jaclyn knew its history: Turner Field was originally built as the Olympic Stadium for the 1996 Summer Olympics, and then quickly transformed into a baseball stadium for the beginning of the 1997 baseball season. Atlanta-Fulton County Stadium, the Braves' home since they moved from Milwaukee in 1966, was then torn down to make way for the new ballpark's parking lots, with the only remaining edifices being an imprint of the diamond as well as a makeshift fence signifying the location of where Hank Aaron's record-breaking 715th home run landed in the old yard.

She smirked as she approached it.

And in many of the fans' eyes, he still is the Home Run King, she thought.

Jaclyn continued walking.

As she drew closer to the monument for Hammerin' Hank, Jaclyn could see the outline of a tractor trailer behind it, and she immediately felt her heart race. The last time that she knew of Parkerhurst using a tractor trailer to haul her car was in Boston. She figured that he had driven the Citroën C6 to St. James' Park in London himself, even though driving it from Heathrow would have been risky. And she knew that he didn't need a trailer to drive the Dodge Charger from McCarran to their meeting point one block to the west. Her pulse continued to quicken the faster she walked.

Two minutes later, Jaclyn saw the side door to the trailer swing open above a set of stairs, and from within the steel depths, Parkerhurst walked out and down to the pavement below. His smile was wide, and Jaclyn saw that he had dressed nearly as casual as she had. He wore a red polo shirt underneath a Red Sox pullover sweatshirt as well as blue jeans. The leg cuffs flared out a bit. He also wore a pair of well-worn Nike sneakers, and he wore a Red Sox hat on his head.

"Why, you don't stick out like a sore thumb here, Parkerhurst," Jaclyn said with a smile.

Parkerhurst only replied with a sarcastic smirk of his own.

"Enough of that, Snapshot. We have work to do."

"Why are you wearing all of that?"

Parkerhurst shot her a blank look.

"It's baseball season?"

Jaclyn sniffed.

"Yeah, in New York and Los Angeles."

Parkerhurst grimaced. Jaclyn thought he might have swallowed his tongue. He looked a little green around the edges.

"Don't remind me."

Jaclyn shifted her weight from her right to left, then crossed her arms underneath her breasts.

"What do you have for me, Red Sox fan?"

"Other than a knuckle sandwich," he said quickly, "which I would gladly deal out to you, I have nothing of interest for you but a new car."

Jaclyn jumped up and down on the front half of her feet, clapping her hands like a child receiving a new toy. "Oh, goodie gum drops," she said. "What is it, what is it, what is it?"

"Calm down and you'll see in a minute." Parkerhurst brought his fingers to his lips and blew a harsh whistle. "Alright, Charlie! Do your best."

Jaclyn heard a door open and slam shut before she saw Charlie, the same driver who had gently backed out her Porsche Spider 918 from the depths of the trailer in Boston, walk around the rear end. He fiddled with the latches and managed to free the twin doors with a squeal.

Jaclyn leaned toward her counterpart.

"Does he have any WD-40 in there?"

"Not that I know of."

"Put that on the list. Alex will expense it."

"Duly noted, Snapshot."

Charlie swung the doors open before pulling out a set of runway flaps that came to rest at Jaclyn's feet, the sounds of steel clanging against pavement meeting her ears. As Charlie worked to secure the runway, Jaclyn tried to peer into the dark morass in an attempt to see her new wheels. A latex tarpaulin covered the car.

She turned her head sharply toward Parkerhurst.

"What's up with the condom on the car? It's not a damned Camaro with the black bra on it, right?"

Parkerhurst smirked as Charlie walked up the ramp and disappeared into the darkness.

"It's just that potent a vehicle, Snapshot."

As he walked toward the opening, Jaclyn couldn't suppress a girlish giggle, even though the sounds of Charlie turning the engine over inside the trailer drowned her out.

The engine revved twice before the soft sound of the car going into gear—reverse—was only detected by the secret agent.

"He's going to be gentle with her, right?" she asked.

"He should," Parkerhurst replied. "It's not his first rodeo after all."

The car backed out slowly with Charlie handling her well. Soon, Jaclyn saw the white back-up lights grow closer as well as the red taillights that were set several inches across the frame. Then she noticed where the revving came from, as a pair of twin exhaust pipes came into her line of sight.

Every car Parkerhurst had given to her for missions had impressed her from first sight, and this one was no different: Jaclyn couldn't help but let her jaw drop as the car, now fully emerged from its mobile hangar, slipped down the runway ramps, its sleek lines immediately apparent from its emergence.

When it reached the level surface, Charlie revved the engine twice more before putting the car in park and turning the engine off. He grabbed the keys and got out of the car. He rolled the runway ramps back into the trailer before he tossed the keys to Parkerhurst.

Jaclyn snatched them just out of the man's reach.

Parkerhurst's eyes narrowed as she smiled and twirled the key ring around her right index finger.

"Your 2013 BMW M6 Coupe, Snapshot," he said, grinding his teeth as he spoke. "A beautiful display of German engineering, if I may say so myself." He walked around the front end. Jaclyn followed. "Using the feminine pronoun you've obviously already deemed to it, she'll go from 0-to-62 in less than four seconds with her 5.0 liter V10 engine, she has 560 ponies under the hood. Seven-speed automatic, rear-wheel drive transmission, 19-inch aluminum rims and wheels—she could have come with 20-

inch rims, but we weren't sure if you could handle the extra inch."

"All girls can handle an extra inch, Parkerhurst," Jaclyn snapped.

The CIA quartermaster blanched.

"So I've heard. Carrying on. It has a four-wheel ABS and she'll get seventeen miles to the gallon on the highway, eleven miles in the city, climate control. Power everything, of course."

"Good, I like more power. And need I ask the non-standard options?"

"The usual accoutrements are included, Snapshot: triple-plated armor in the windshield and chassis, side windows tinted and armored. Dual hood mounted machine guns, the usual full rack of STAs in the trunk. Registered in three states, Georgia, Florida and Alabama. Your personal security setting via your iPad, an autopilot setting with anti-collision sensors in the wheels and the perimeter to keep you out of harm's way on the road. A built-in Garmin GPS unit named Lucy that comes complete with detonators on each side of the device."

"Lucy?"

"Yes, Lucy."

"Why Lucy?"

Parkerhurst looked at her, dead in her HUD.

"Because for some reason, the company programmed her to speak like Lucy Van Pelt from Charlie Brown."

Jaclyn raised an eyebrow.

"At least the thing doesn't sound like the teacher. Wahwahwahwah, wahwahwahwah."

Parkerhurst sniffed.

"Turn left?"

Jaclyn shook her head.

"Keep right."

"Gotcha."

The pair stood in silence for several moments, staring at the car. The traffic on 85 whizzed by silently, not disturbing their vigil.

"No rocket booster again?"

"It's only been a month, Snapshot. The last I heard, the British are still tinkering with the Citroën to take the proverbial Velveeta out of it."

"Speaking of Velveeta, Parkerhurst," Jaclyn said. "My cars don't ooze Velveeta compared to the Italian job you flew back to D.C. in last month."

The young quartermaster smiled.

"You have to understand something, my old friend. Our positions in the CIA give us the ability to try out certain devices that other agencies don't have access to. For example, the Giulietta was an experimental flyer in the prototype stage. I was testing it out."

"And what were your initial conclusions?"

"That, Snapshot, is top secret at the highest levels. Not even you have a security clearance that high."

"Rats," she said with a grimace.

"But I will tell you that it's planned to be used as a manned drone by the military, one with better targeting abilities than the unmanned drones and better armament to protect the pilot. We're planning on implementing the design with American cars so that we get credit for attacks instead of Italy. Not a word to anyone, though. Not even your British boyfriend."

Jaclyn lifted a finger to her lips, trying to hide a bit of a smile.

"I promise I won't tell anyone."

"Good girl."

Parkerhurst turned and headed for the cab, but not before securing the trailer doors. Jaclyn headed into the BMW. She shut the door just as Parkerhurst disappeared. Jaclyn started the engine before reaching over and pressing the voice activation icon on the Garmin.

"Hello, Agent Snapshot. I am Lucy. What course shall I set for you this evening?"

What episode of Charlie Brown was Parkerhurst watching? Jaclyn thought. *She sounds nothing like Lucy Van Pelt.*

"Can you access Salt's database back at Langley to double check to see if a group of people are still living at where they had lived six years ago?"

Lucy's reply was automatic.

"I can. Salt's database has the ability to access the United States Postal Service computers, thereby allowing me to cross-reference addresses from up to twenty-five years ago."

Jaclyn grinned.

Salt thinks of everything.

"Good. Look up this up for me and plug in the directions." Jaclyn gave her the North Smyrna address. Within twenty seconds, Lucy replied.

"This address is currently occupied by the same people, Snapshot. Accessing directions from this spot." And then, "Drive to Fulton Street Southwest, then turn left."

Jaclyn put the BMW in drive before she pulled up next to the cab. She rolled down the window with one touch of her finger.

Parkerhurst, in the passenger side of the truck's cab, did the same.

"Have a safe drive back to D.C., Parkerhurst."

He smiled.

"You have yourself a safe mission, yourself. I'll see you back at Langley."

Jaclyn grinned as she hit the gas and headed toward Fulton Street Southwest, leaving Parkerhurst, the tractor trailer, and the imprint of the Launching Pad in her wake. She adhered to Lucy's voice, telling her to turn left before driving two-tenths of a mile before turning right onto the onramp, which swept underneath the myriad of on and offramps for Interstate 20, making like strands of concrete and asphalt spaghetti.

She followed the onramp to 85 North and merged easily with nighttime traffic.

Time to get some answers, she thought as she began her return to Cobb County. She flipped the autopilot on while she made a phone call.

Chapter 16
The Home of Mr. and Mrs. Chester Rayburn
Hickory Flat, Georgia
Tuesday, October 30, 2012
8:37 p.m. ET

Jaclyn didn't spare the pedal—well, the autopilot didn't—as the BMW brought the secret agent to the Rayburn Farm. She had called ahead and, even though she apologized for the lateness of the hour, asked the escaped convict's parents if she could come up to see them. She didn't tell them she was already en route.

They accepted, and the mother said she would put on a kettle for tea.

As the car drove for her, Jaclyn leaned back in the leather seat and pondered the questions she would ask Rayburn's parents. Certainly she would ask about his youth and how exactly he made his dramatic turn toward his life of hate, but there were other questions for which she wanted to receive answers.

She knew that, as an expert questioner, if she turned the right screws without letting the questionees know that she was doing it, she would get those answers without a problem.

She grinned at the thought, even though she wouldn't use her usual techniques on his parents. Him, though, she would. Oh yes, she would.

I would do that gladly, she thought.

Jaclyn pulled up shortly after 8:30 p.m. Streetlights dotted the landscape, and a small light above the Rayburn porch glowed. It looked friendly and inviting, even though it was the stereotypical redneck home: Jaclyn used her HUD to detect a slightly deteriorating structure surrounded by knee-high grass that began to resemble a growing wheat field. Dotted within the premises were a few rusted out cars lying like slumbering elephants. One of the cars, Jaclyn saw, was tire-less, its axles propped up on cinder blocks.

I wonder what the rest of the farm looks like, she thought, just as a large dog, a sheared black Newfoundland, barked and came out of his crouch on the porch. It came running up to Jaclyn with a hearty trot.

It leaped into her arms and began to lick her face.

"Aww, you're a good boy, aren't you?" she said, just before a loud, gruff voice called from the home.

"Heel, Diesel, heel!"

"Diesel's your name? You're as big as a diesel truck, yes you are," Jaclyn said, scratching behind the massive beast's ears just before the dog's front paws hit the ground. The dog padded away as the screen door's interior collided with the small, steel locking bar. The man with the gruff voice stepped forward. The porch creaked under his weight.

"You must be Miss Johnson," the man said. He had a healthy Southern accent that Jaclyn needed to concentrate on in order to understand. He carried a kitchen towel in his hands, and he was wiping what looked like motor oil off his skin. There was much more of the tar-like liquid still coating his hands rather than the cloth. He wore gray overalls over a white shirt. "I'm Chester Rayburn. My wife's inside. Come on in. Watch out for the dog shit over there. Sorry about the look of the lawn; damn lawn mower ran out of gas."

Jaclyn shrugged, wondering just how long ago that was. She made sure that her HUD picked up the pile's location so she could sidestep it as she walked toward the creaky porch. Several wooden beams were worn, and some were missing altogether. A small charcoal grill that had the look of a halved steel oil drum rested as far from the house as it could. The roof wasn't much higher.

Thankfully I won't have to duck, Jaclyn thought.

She entered the home, following Diesel inside.

The interior wasn't much better than the exterior, Jaclyn quickly surmised as she took a glance around the living room. Dust hung like gray curtains throughout the room. Plastic covered the furniture, while the outline of what Jaclyn believed had been a gun rack rested on 1970's-esque wallpaper over the mantelpiece. The soft, dulcet tones of Hank Williams choroused throughout the room, an unseen record player turning away, the scratchy old sound an easy tell. Dust, she noticed, still covered the mantel. A picture had been turned around, the photo not on display.

Jaclyn's heart raced. She didn't dare grab for it. She had a feeling who it displayed, though.

An older woman came into the room. She was a frumpy woman, as if her weight didn't settle in one spot; it seemed to have spread like rising dough. She wore a plaid dress that may, at one time, have been used as a tablecloth, with a white apron draped around her voluminous waist. She carried in a tea tray loaded with tea cups, a tea pot and what looked like a pie and small plates while not looking at who was in the room.

"Marjorie," Chester Rayburn said, "this here's the woman from the government." It sounded like he had said "gubmint."

Marjorie Rayburn nearly dropped the tray in surprise, but Jaclyn's HUD tipped her off half a heartbeat early. She swept in and had her hands on the stainless steel tray—a tray that looked like it was around at Appomattox—before the woman could let go. The woman gasped, but Jaclyn's disarming smile made her echo it. They eased the tray down to the table together.

"Hi, I'm Jaclyn Johnson," she said, holding her hand out to the mother of her prime target. The father stayed silent. "Thanks for meeting with me at such short notice and at such a late hour."

"It's not a worry at all," Marjorie Rayburn said. She had a soft voice that belied her girth. "We was about to turn in for the evening, but when someone famous comes a-callin' to my door, I can postpone my beauty rest a little while." She pushed her store-bought red curls up a little.

Jaclyn blinked.

"Famous? Is Hank Williams Junior joining us for tea?"

Marjorie laughed, and this time, the chortle came directly from her feet. Plates resting in a hutch rattled on the wall.

"No silly, I'm talking about you," she said, her face red with embarrassment. "You're a superstar, that's what you are."

Jaclyn hoped the large, old woman wouldn't break out into song.

"I take it you're talking about my magazine work," she surmised.

"I have a few of them in the bathroom. Chester," Marjorie bellowed, "be a dear and fetch those magazines with Miss Johnson on the cover. And bring a Sharpie, too!"

Jaclyn felt her heart make a beeline for her diaphragm.

"No, that's okay—" she said as she tried to prevent Chester Rayburn from carrying out his wife's will. Jaclyn usually didn't sign autographs; it was generally frowned upon by the CIA, and other than utilizing aggressive interrogation on suspects, she preferred not to break government policy.

And she didn't want to hear what Dick Bennett would say should he get wind of her signing autographs.

Chester Rayburn paid the secret agent no heed. He walked to the bathroom and fetched the magazines for his wife. Jaclyn could hear the man grunting as he lifted something out of the way.

A minute later, Chester returned with a stack of five magazines and the Sharpie. Jaclyn recognized the top issue. She had been garmented in a red jacket and a silk chemise. It was a fall 2011 issue of Vogue.

"I remember this shoot well," Jaclyn mused aloud, a soft smile dribbling across her lips. She grabbed the Sharpie and pulled the cap off. The harsh scent of toluene and other solvents mixed with black ink rose into the air immediately. "I was in Miami for this shoot, was late at night, the photographer had me waiting because he was plugging some chick on South Beach around dinnertime." She scrawled her name.

Marjorie Rayburn made the sign of the cross.

"That picture," Jaclyn continued, "was taken just before my phone rang. I remember the pose." She sniffed. "I had to fly to Boston early the next morning."

"Why? What happened in Boston? Those Yankees do something rotten? They always do."

Jaclyn blinked again as she realized what Marjorie had asked her.

"It's classified, actually, regardless of what Dick Bennett chose to divulge a few months ago. And if I were you, Mrs. Rayburn, I'd watch out when you erroneously refer to Bostonians as Yankees. They don't like that much."

"They're up north, they're Yankees."

And you're white trash living in Hicksville, Jaclyn thought. She kept it to herself as she signed the other four magazine covers. She put them on the coffee table. A plume of dust sprang out of its slumber. Jaclyn coughed.

There was one thing she noticed as she stared at the woman: Mrs. Rayburn was firm in her convictions. She filed that away.

"Tell me something about your son, Mrs. Rayburn. Did you ever get to talk to him after he was arrested, or after the trial?"

Marjorie Rayburn grew silent for several moments. She flattened out a crease in her dress and she grabbed a napkin and dabbed at her eyes.

"I did, a few times."

Jaclyn turned to Chester.

"And how about you, Mr. Rayburn?"

Chester Rayburn waved the question aside and continued his vigil, looking down on the two women with his arms crossed.

Jaclyn lifted her eyebrows underneath her Foster Grants and silently wondered what his problem was.

"He doesn't like talking about Bobby Ray," Marjorie said, leaning toward Jaclyn and lowering her voice to a tone just above a mere whisper. "He said during the trial that his boy shamed him by taking up with them damn—pardon my French—Kluckers. He says he don't have a son no more."

Jaclyn nodded. She now understood Chester's reaction.

"Tell me about his life before he joined the KKK," she asked.

Marjorie smiled wistfully. She dabbed at her leaking eyes again, all while her lower lip trembled.

"He wasn't like this as a boy," she said, putting her hands in her lap. "Not at all. He was a very sweet boy. He helped around the farm. He was very polite, said yes sir, no sir, yes ma'am, no ma'am, just like every good Southerner was raised: with respect for your elders and treated strangers with kindness. He even treated the colored children with respect and kindness.

"That all changed when he turned 13."

Jaclyn grimaced. She sent a mental command to her HUD to record the conversation; it would never see the light of day, so she did not ask for Mrs. Rayburn's permission.

"What happened at 13?"

"He joined the God damned Klan, is what he done," Chester Rayburn barked.

"Chester, watch your mouth in front of our guest," Marjorie chastised. "The good Lord'll bring locusts down on us if you use His name in vain again."

"It's okay, Mrs. Rayburn, I've said worse."

"You shouldn't use those kinds of words; you're a Christian lady."

Jaclyn felt her wrist sting with the invisible slap. She rolled her eyes.

"Be that as it may, ma'am, how did he join the Klan?"

"From what I recall from the trial, Bobby Ray had admitted to eavesdroppin' on Klan meetin's since 2001 or 2002, he didn't remember which. He was about 13 or 14 at the time. He and his friends would eavesdrop on the men there. They were the fathers of Bobby Ray's, well, I hate to use the term now, but they were the fathers of his friends. He had testified that he was sickened by what he heard, but apparently that didn't stop him from going back for more."

Jaclyn nodded.

Curiosity will always kill the cat, she thought. She wondered just what kind of cat Rayburn had become during his formative years.

Marjorie, with tears running down her face, told Jaclyn of the events that came right after another, up until he dragged the black boy and killed the black police officers in Mableton.

"We were worried sick about our boy until they caught him," she said. "We prayed ceaselessly, every night and day. We just wanted our boy home."

Jaclyn knew that he never returned to this home. His parents were unable to post his bond, and his father, she had read in the case file given to her by Schatzenberger while they waited for the federal marshals to arrive, didn't try to raise any money for his son's release. Jaclyn figured that if Chester's earlier attitude was anywhere close to a partial representation of his anger back in 2007, jail was the safest place for Bobby Ray Rayburn at that time.

She held in her smirk.

"Mrs. Rayburn," she said instead, "I'm investigating your son's break out from death row and several subsequent incidents that have happened since Saturday."

She paused before she returned her gaze toward the escapee's mother. She told her of the incidents at the State Capitol Building as well as the assassination—she couldn't think of a better word for what happened to Judge Cameron, yet since he was a public figure in Cobb County, assassination seemed proper. "Do you think that Bobby Ray had something to do with it?"

Marjorie held her lips together, as if deep in thought. She clucked her lips apart before she said, "The coincidences are too uncanny for my liking, Miss Johnson. If the evidence points in Bobby Ray's direction, though…"

She let her thought trail off.

Jaclyn smiled as she reached over and patted Marjorie's hand before she finally stood and made to leave.

"You have to go so soon? You haven't had any pie yet," Marjorie said, trying to lift her bulk out of her seat. She finally stood. "It's peach."

"Thank you for the offer, ma'am, but I must be going. I still have other things relating to the investigation to do before I go to sleep tonight."

Jaclyn made for the door. The Rayburns followed.

"Miss Johnson," Chester finally said as Jaclyn opened the door. She turned to him. "Will you end up killin' him?"

Jaclyn bit her lip.

"We had heard that you are rather handy with a gun, at least that's what Bennett said in the newspapers and on the TV," the father said. "Will you kill him if you get near him?"

Steeling her face to rid her flesh of emotion, Jaclyn could feel her heartbeat pulsing away. She couldn't hear a thing—it was too cold for crickets—and she couldn't smell anything, either. She could only send her gaze toward the two people who her brand of justice in this case mattered to most of all.

"He has many crimes to answer for if he is behind these recent events, as well as the death sentence he avoided on

Saturday. If I don't kill him if and when I catch up with him, the state of Georgia will end up doing the job anyway." She took a deep breath and, even though it wasn't a question she would expect to even consider asking a pair of civilians, she couldn't stop the words from spilling between her lips. "What would you wish me to do about that?"

Jaclyn steeled herself as she saw both Rayburns begin to choke up. Chester had his arm around his wife's shoulders. Jaclyn could tell that even the big, quiet man had trouble with thinking his son dead, regardless of the crimes he committed. Yet there he was, holding tears in while being a rock of support for the woman he loved.

Jaclyn could easily understand that.

Marjorie Rayburn nodded, shaking the tears out of their pre-arranged tracks and sending the secretions to the porch. With her sensitive hearing, Jaclyn heard each fat drop plop against the wood, making it groan under the stress.

"Take him down, Miss Johnson" she stuttered, all while the tears raged down her face. "Please, take him down. We'd rather he be killed humanely instead of being filled with chemicals. Do it for us, please."

Jaclyn forced herself to take a deep breath before she nodded.

"I'll make sure it's done cleanly," she said. Jaclyn turned and walked toward the BMW, sidestepping the dog poop again as she walked. Chester and Marjorie hugged each other, the woman's face buried in his chest.

Jaclyn slid into her rolling neutron bomb and closed the door. She smacked the back of her head against the headrest and looked at the roof. She suddenly felt five degrees warmer, even though it was rather chilly inside the BMW. The night had grown darker. Jaclyn checked the digital read-out on the dashboard.

It was 9 p.m.

"That's something I've never experienced before," she muttered while sliding the key into the ignition, "asking permission to kill someone's son. I hope I never have to do that again."

Jaclyn turned the engine over and after setting Lucy to lead her back to the hotel, she headed into Atlanta proper, wondering just when she would help Bobby Ray Rayburn meet his end.

She hoped it wouldn't take long.

Chapter 17
Westin Peachtree Hotel, 67th Floor
Atlanta, Georgia
Tuesday, October 30, 2012
10:15 p.m. ET

Jaclyn emerged from the shower within a cloud of lacy steam, a towel wrapped around her torso and another wrapped around her head. Not a trace of water fell onto the bathroom floor or to the living area's rugs as she walked. She plopped herself down on the bed and, after sliding her Foster Grants back on to ward off the glare, she grabbed her iPhone.

She had several text messages, including three from Alex, Tom and Tasha.

She checked Alex's first. Sent only five minutes ago, it contained three words.

"Sit-rep please."

Jaclyn bit her lip and checked the chronometer inside her HUD. It was a little late to call, but she knew that Alex would be awake and waiting for Jaclyn's reply.

She called anyway, Alex picked up after two rings.

"Did I catch you at a bad time, Snapshot?" she asked.

Jaclyn grinned.

"No, I was just finishing up a shower when you texted. What's going on?"

"I'd like to know what's going on with the investigation, primarily. You haven't checked in for a while."

Jaclyn turned over onto her stomach. The towel stayed where it was. She explained her side trips to Marietta, Kennesaw and Hickory Flat to her boss, especially highlighting her final conversation with Rayburn's parents.

"Wow," Alex said, as if breathless.

"Right? If I would bet that wouldn't happen again, I may be able to retire by the time I'm 30."

"Don't make bets you can't cash in on. What's your plan of attack then?"

Jaclyn sighed.

"That's a good question, Chief. I guess stay vigilant and stay close to the president."

"We have a dead judge in Cobb County, and federal marshals are protecting the prosecutor. That situation is secure. Don't worry about that end of things unless something happens."

"This isn't something they can fuck up, though. This prosecutor has a sawed-off shotgun, and I don't believe he's afraid to use it. He can probably defend the marshals, if it comes down to it."

"True. Continue doing what you're doing, and I'll monitor Atlanta Police from up here. I went to college with the chief and the commissioner, so they'll keep me updated on anything that looks like a Rayburn hit."

"How's Tasha doing, Alex?" Jaclyn asked, slightly changing the subject. "She sent me a text tonight, but I haven't read it yet."

"She's OK, as far as I can tell. She fell asleep on the couch a little while ago. She was quiet during dinner, though."

"Hmmm, I wonder if there's a boy issue going on. Is she behaving herself?"

Alex answered in the affirmative.

"Not walking around in her underwear?"

"Nope. The boys are, though. I've had to smack them a couple of times."

Jaclyn smiled.

"She hasn't come to you with a problem, has she?"

"Not at all. I don't think she completely trusts me; it could be the age difference, or she just doesn't really know me, period. I'll have her give you a call in the morning." Alex paused. "If it is boy trouble, do you think you'll be able to handle that aspect of her life, Snapshot? Remember that your development as a young woman was slightly stunted by 9-11."

Jaclyn's face was stony.

"I'll do my best to guide her the way my mother would have guided me," she said.

She could hear Alex's smile on the other end.

"I wouldn't expect anything less of you, Jaclyn Ann." Alex hung up without another word.

Jaclyn ended the call on her end before she put the iPhone on her chest. She looked at the ceiling.

Just how would my life be different if bin Laden and his cronies hadn't attacked the United States on that sunny September morning? she thought. *Would I have had boyfriends in high school? Would I have been able to go to the mall with my friends instead of with Alex? What would I have done with my life if the US government didn't choose to take me in and turn me into the force against terrorism that I am today? Would I have needed my mother's guidance during my adolescence?*

Tears filled her eyes as she thought of her mother, who she greatly resembled during her formative years. She closed her eyes tight, as if to control the flow. She took a deep breath and opened her eyes a few seconds later. She felt a tear slide toward her ear.

She answered her own question: of course she would have needed her mother's guidance.

Jaclyn felt an ache in her chest, just underneath the top of her towel. She didn't move to rub it.

"Mom," she whispered, "I don't know if you can hear me, but I need your strength right now. What would you say to Tasha if it is about boys?"

She didn't receive an answer, the answer cut off eleven years ago in a cascade of tumbling steel, concrete, and burning jet fuel.

Jaclyn lay motionless in bed for several more minutes before she checked her text message from Tasha.

It read:

"Hi Jaclyn, I just wanted to let you know I'm doing fine at Alex's. I do have a problem, though. There was a fight at school… two boys were fighting over little old me! "

Tasha had added a smiley face at the end of the first message. A second one followed: "I kinda don't know what to do here. This isn't what I'm used to; I'm used to taking a john's money and letting him do whatever he wants to me. This is outside of my area of knowledge. I mean, both boys are cute and all, although one may have a black eye tomorrow. Help?"

Jaclyn firmed her lips as she finished reading.

Yep, she thought, *it's about boys. But this is what I signed up for when I saved her from that disgusting pimp, right? Dealing with teenage girl relationship drama when I never went through it myself? Is this really something I need to deal with?*

She answered herself with a nod of her head. She took a deep breath and typed back:

"Are you awake, Tasha?"

Veroop.

Half a minute later, Tasha responded.

"Yep."

Jaclyn dialed the number and pressed call. It rang twice before Tasha answered.

"Hey."

"Hey yourself," Jaclyn said. "You give any thought to your problem?"

Tasha groaned.

"It's really all I can think about, Jaclyn," she said. She sounded half asleep, but she was able to form words that weren't slurred. "I mean, what do I do here?"

"Which one do you like more?" Jaclyn said, taking a stab in the dark.

"I don't know," Tasha replied, her voice unsure.

Jaclyn shifted her weight on the bed, turning onto her stomach. The towel came loose a bit in front. She ignored it.

"There's nothing wrong with seeing both boys, as long as you tell them that you're interested in both of them. Just don't string them along when you find out you're interested in one more than the other." She paused. "Does that make sense to you?"

"Yeah, a little."

"I'm sorry if it doesn't help, my development in this area was jilted a little. While girls my age were going through this kind of shit, I was learning about hand-to-hand combat and about how to disassemble a gun to clean it. I'm not exactly the world's best when it comes to relationships or developing them."

"Well, I know Tom's in love with you, so you had to have done something right."

Jaclyn blushed.

"Yes, that was an interesting way to develop a relationship: get involved with a sexy secret agent from another country, and one that happens to be across an ocean," she said.

"At least it's an allied country and not Iran or something like that," Tasha replied.

Jaclyn laughed this time.

"You're right about that. My advice: don't string the boys along, but get to know both of them if you want. Remember, you're the prize they're after, so you're holding all the cards."

"You're right, I am." Tasha made a sound with her mouth that sounded like she was slurping a bit of saliva. "How's your case going?"

"It's going fine," Jaclyn said a little too fast. "You know I can't tell you about everything, right?"

"Yeah, I know." Tasha sounded disappointed. "It's been on the news, though."

"Yeah, that doesn't shock me. What are they saying?"

"Not too much, although they think it's the guy who broke out of prison the other day who's behind it."

Jaclyn grimaced.

I wonder if those are leaks in the investigation or if it's the reporters adding one and one together, she thought.

"They aren't too far off, if that's what they think," she said. "We're looking into all possible angles. And I'm getting to hang out with the president a little."

"Wow, you get to do that?"

Jaclyn smiled this time. Tasha sounded as if she were eight years old instead of sixteen.

"Yeah, from time to time. I never met the queen when I was in London, although I told some blokes from the BBC that I was Her Majesty's Enforcer once."

Tasha giggled. It was as if they were having a girls' night over popcorn and cheesy movies.

"That's awesome."

"Alright kiddo, I need to scoot. Anything you need to tell me?"

Tasha said no.

"Get some sleep, and call me and let me know how it goes tomorrow. Leave me a voice mail if I don't pick up, OK?"

Tasha said she would. They hung up after saying good night.

Jaclyn took another deep breath and checked her text from Tom. She smiled right from the first word.

"Just checking on you, Snapshot. Haven't heard from you in a couple of days, so consider this me being an annoying boyfriend. Hope everything is alright with the mission. I know that if there was something the matter, Alex would let Sir David know, and he'd let me know."

Jaclyn felt her heart skip a beat. She knew exactly what he meant, especially after he went silent a month ago trying to get clearance to come into the country to surprise her.

All she wanted to do right now was hold her sexy British man.

"I'm feeling better. I'm seeing my physio in the morning, so I'll be able to give you a better read on how my jaw is holding up. Right now, it's sore, but I'm dealing with some of the painkillers.

"Missing your kisses, your scent, and your arms. Love you. TM"

Tears welled in Jaclyn's eyes. She slipped her hand underneath her HUD and wiped them away before wiping the secretions off on the towel.

She began typing.

"Everything's okay with me, Scouser. This is a crazy case over here. Judges dying, prosecutors carrying shotguns, burning crosses on the capital building's front lawn. You can't make this shit up. At some point though, this guy is going to get the Maqil treatment.

"I miss you too. I miss everything about you. Christmas can't get here soon enough. I'll text when I can. I love you, Scouser. JJ"

Veroop.

Jaclyn put her iPhone down and got out of bed. She separated the towel from her now-dry skin before she slid a pair of cotton briefs up her legs, bringing them to rest on her hips before she put her arms through the arm holes of a white tank top. The material hugged her sweeping curves.

She slid back into bed and grabbed her iPad, and even though she tried to finish reading Daniel Arenson's Wand And The Witch, there was a nagging sense in the back of her mind that told her something would happen tomorrow.

Something that would turn this mission on its ear.

Chapter 18
Outside of Atlanta, Georgia
Wednesday, October 31, 2012
8:10 a.m. ET

Bobby Ray Rayburn overslept again.

For the past five years, Rayburn had been used to constant 6 a.m. wake-up calls by the guards at Jackson, and for the past four days, he slept well past that designated hour. Carl stood watch over him to make sure no one interrupted his slumber, a shotgun at parade rest. Sunlight streamed into the small room that Rayburn had commandeered as his own, the dust dancing in the rays to a tune only it could hear. Leftover hay, unconsumed by the animals that had once called this barn home, lay scattered on the dirt floor. The smell of manure, long since mucked, hung in the air up to the rafters. Rusted out equipment was scattered about the farmhouse; a rototiller rested near where Rayburn slept, a sack of grain, leftover from the last owners, as a pillow.

Rayburn and Company had arrived at this abandoned farm outside of Atlanta proper just before 3 p.m. on Tuesday, and by 10 p.m., the word had spread to Klansmen all across northern Georgia: Rayburn was actively recruiting members to cause havoc in Atlanta, and they were invited to the farmhouse for a meeting.

There was a warning attached: Just keep everything quiet.

Rayburn stirred a few minutes after 8 a.m. He wore his heavy Braves sweatshirt and long pants instead of a blanket, as they couldn't find one among the detritus. He shivered slightly as the cold air rushed through cracks in the walls and through open windows. Over to the side, Carl moved a bit, feeling the blood rush to muscles that hadn't moved in hours. He brought the gun up and rested it against his shoulder.

"Morning, Bobby Ray," he said as soon as the escaped convict opened his eyes.

Rayburn dug his thumb and forefinger into his eyes. Glops of yellow eye goo stuck to the pads as he pulled them away.

"Morning," he replied.

"Let me get you some coffee."

Rayburn yawned as he nodded.

Carl busied himself around the makeshift kitchen, where other Klansmen, on Carl's orders, had brought a Mr. Coffee as well as granola bars and other things that would provide their leader with sustenance for the time being—until their leader could rest without worry for his safety. That time would come, they knew, when the world settled into a routine where blacks were once again subservient to the white folk. It was then that Rayburn could reveal himself fully, and hopefully, they thought, without fear of reprisals or assassination. Until that time came, though, they would not divulge the location of Rayburn's hidden base, and they would ferry supplies to the farmhouse—as long as they had to do so.

Rayburn got up and stretched, feeling the muscles and joints pop. Relief soon flooded him. As much as he didn't want to admit it, he yearned for the cot in Jackson, or his own bed in Hickory Flat.

He grinned.

Soon, he thought. *Soon.*

He stumbled into the makeshift kitchen and leaned against a wall. He shivered as the cool air meandered through the barn.

"How was it last night, Carl?" he asked.

The big man shrugged as he poured the coffee into the filter.

"I didn't hear a peep, and there wasn't any wind. Strange for Halloween morning, don't you think?"

Rayburn smirked.

"I don't seem to remember wind on Halloween morning. At least not the last five years or so."

Carl grimaced.

"Sorry, man."

Rayburn waved it off.

"It is of no concern to me. I see several futures in front of me that tell me that this could be the last Halloween I wake up to."

"Do you care to elaborate?"

Rayburn grabbed a Kellogg's Nutri-Grain cereal bar, one with apple cinnamon filling, and opened the wrapper. It crinkled as he worked it, then took a bite. He chewed for several moments. "The first future," he said with his mouth full of cake, "is the one I hope will happen; that the world will recognize the Ku Klux Klan as a legitimate empire and government, and that the southern states that support us will once again fight to secede from the Union." He swallowed. "Coffee ready yet?"

Carl shook his head in the negative.

"Two sugars, remember that. That future also will force all black police officers and politicians to stand down and return power to more qualified white people. Them black people are always trying to push their anti-white agendas on God-fearing people, and by God that'll end, damn it. I'll make them fear me. I'll tie every one of their black asses, I don't care how fucking big they are, to the back of a truck and drag them through the backwoods of the South. I don't care how. Those damn motherfucking niggers have no rights as far as I'm concerned."

"Damn right," Carl said.

"The second future sees me exonerated by a white-only jury, full o' rednecks and proper folk. I'll be damned if I have a nigger face on my jury again. What do they call that process, voila?"

"*Voir dire*, Bobby Ray."

"Right, *voir dire*. We'll select a jury that has no biases toward good, upstanding white folk like myself."

Carl grinned.

"Is there a third future?" he asked.

Rayburn's face grew dark, even in the growing sunlight. He stuffed his hands into the pocket of his Braves sweatshirt. Coffee began to percolate into the glass pot.

"We die fighting for what we believe in," he said. His voice was cold, as if backed by an Arctic wind.

Carl shivered.

"I see."

"Do you agree with that future, Carl?"

"What I agree with doesn't matter in the slightest, Bobby Ray," the ex-guard said without hesitating. "If we fight, we fight. There's a chance we get killed. I wouldn't bet against a gun-toting Southern boy, though. They'd send some gun-shy Yankee in with no sense of how us Southerners play when it comes to war."

Rayburn finally smiled. He took a step toward his friend and embraced him. They patted each other on the back.

"You're right, of course. They'll send us a silly Yankee, one who is too liberal for our liking, always wanting to put restrictions on our firearms. Well, let me tell you something Carl, we'll go after any fucking Yankee they send with two guns in each hand and a shotgun strapped to our backs."

The two drank coffee a few minutes later. Rayburn walked around the farmhouse, all while Carl, mug in hand, kept watch on the perimeter. Rayburn was in thought as he sipped. The coffee, he thought, was sweet enough.

He thought back to last night, where he laid out his plan to those in attendance, those who were curious to hear the words of the man who had escaped the death chamber. He didn't go into the gory details of what happened on Friday night, for he knew the newspapers and television stations had dissected his escape on an almost nightly basis. But he told of his plans to rid the South of the blacks, and how he was ready to recruit young, idealistic men who wanted to see the South rise once again, this time to defeat the cowardly North.

His skin rippled with excitement as he spoke of his plans, plans he had spent five long years thinking about, bouncing them all off Carl during the days when Rayburn was locked in solitary. He recalled Carl standing outside the steel door as he whispered to him, feeding the guard his propaganda, his racist agenda. He knew that Carl could have turned him in, but after using the code words, he knew Carl was on his side. He would help him when and if it came down to it, even though there were no plans to break him out as of yet. Those plans came afterward. He had spoken of a "clean, sterile" Atlanta, an Atlanta where there would be nothing but white faces as far as the eye could see. He could tell as he stood on a tractor-sans-pulpit that the men in front of him yearned for this. These were the same men, he learned later in the evening, who went to a "White Christians only" event over the Alabama border in Lamar County during the Fourth of July, where the message was the same; he wasn't going to burn a cross tonight, for he preferred to save those things for more public displays. They craved a world where the white man said enough is enough, and that they weren't going to take it any longer. Rayburn knew these were men who were sick and tired of the NAACP, and the fact that there were scholarships their children could not apply for due to their race; they felt it was reverse racism, and they despised being declared inferior. Rayburn knew these were men who wanted better lives, but they were only looking for someone to lead them to the promised land.

He smiled as he promised them deliverance. He barked out his plan, which would start that night.

"It will be a scary night for someone, I can assure you," he said, a chorus of laughter trailing his words.

He asked for volunteers to undertake this mission of terror—as well as another set of volunteers to undertake another mission, which he said would be concurrent with the other. He did so separately, leading the volunteers into separate rooms and explaining what he wanted done. He wanted no leaks, and no one else was to know of what the other group was doing in case they were captured by the authorities.

Rayburn smiled as he shook himself back to the present. He took another sip of coffee and looked at his borrowed watch. It was 8:30 a.m.

In another sixteen to eighteen hours, he thought, that next wave will just be finishing up, and the white vans will roll into the farmhouse, one with my quarry.

The real terror will begin Thursday morning.

He drank the rest of his coffee.

***

Atlanta, Georgia
Wednesday, October 31, 2012
9 a.m. ET

Jaclyn met the president's entourage at the Hilton Nikolai just before the clock struck 9 a.m. She had awoken at 7:30, showered and had breakfast before driving the souped-up BMW—Forrister needed a double-take when he saw it, but kept his mouth shut when he realized just what was under the fancy trappings—a few blocks to the east.

"Where are we headed today, Mr. President?" she said just as Veronica Forrister slid into Cadillac One.

"I only have a campaign breakfast and one campaign stop after that. And then I'm planning on playing golf at Augusta National today and tomorrow, if you can believe it," he said.

"Great," Jaclyn replied. "I do look good in a sweater and a golf skirt."

They spent nearly ninety minutes where the president and the first lady took part in a brunch, where Forrister's waistline expanded half an inch. The Secret Service had reported to Jaclyn that everything was satisfactory and that there was no trace of poison.

Jaclyn didn't even blink an eye when the lead agent belched. She only grabbed a plate for herself, sitting off to the side and letting her HUD scan away while the president addressed the crowd, asking them for their vote on Tuesday. She liked the scrambled eggs the best, noting a faint hint of cheddar. She also doubled up on sausage and home fried potatoes.

If I keep eating, she thought, *I may have to get into my fat pants. Luckily, the Lycra stretches.*

By 11 a.m., the motorcade was in motion again. It wound its way through Atlanta proper like a garter snake sluicing through short grass, until it stopped on a now-familiar street to Jaclyn's Foster Grants: Washington Street Southwest, and to her left, the façade of the State Capitol Building. She got out of the BMW and walked behind the president and first lady as they walked across the plaza toward the west portico.

Jaclyn noticed that both the effigy and the cross, not to mention the dead body, were all gone, and that the plaza had been scrubbed, the effects of the burning cross washed away with elbow grease and soap.

Several pairs of feet echoed along the corridor leading to the governor's office. Jaclyn eased next to Melanie Ruoff.

"Melanie, does the governor know we're coming?"

The White House Chief of Staff nodded.

"He said he would meet with us at 11:15."

Jaclyn checked the chronometer inside her HUD. It read 11:10 a.m.

"So we have a few minutes to kill."

Ruoff blinked.

"Figure of speech?"

"Yeah."

For the second time in about a month, the two women were acting like old friends. Jaclyn only wondered how long it would take before Ruoff didn't like her tone.

The president walked into the reception area, with the secretarial staff standing as he and Veronica Forrister entered, followed by the Secret Service, Ruoff, and Jaclyn. Jaclyn saw the aide that had escorted Bennett and Farrell into Woodruff's office stand a half second too late, but with enough time to move around his desk and make his way to the president. He extended his hand.

"John Monroe, Mr. President, an honor," the man said. Jaclyn smiled when she detected a certain effeminate lilt in his voice; she didn't remember the man speaking with it when Bennett came calling on Woodruff on Sunday. "Governor Woodruff will be with you shortly; there's a budget meeting for FY-14 going on, and he hopes to be out of it soon."

Forrister blinked, Jaclyn saw, before he recovered with a nod.

"Good, glad to see Wallace is hard at work. If you could let him know I'm here, though, I'd appreciate it." Forrister sat down as he held his arm out for the first lady to sit next to him.

"Of course, Mr. President." Monroe toddled off.

While the president sat patiently, Jaclyn fidgeted. She kept an eye on the chronometer inside her HUD as she let the device scan away.

Ten minutes passed.

Then fifteen more went by the wayside.

By 11:45 a.m., Jaclyn had taken to pacing the hallway in front of the governor's office, her heels clicking on the linoleum.

A short beep a few seconds later made her reach into her suitcoat and unhitch her Walther. She was able to relax when the governor, followed by Monroe, came up the stairs. She pulled her hand away from the gun.

Jaclyn slipped into the office.

"He's coming."

Forrister and his wife stood just as Woodruff came in.

"Governor Woodruff, good to see you again."

"Mr. President!" Woodruff said. "I didn't know you were here!"

Jaclyn saw Forrister raise an eyebrow.

"Really? I was under the impression we were meeting half an hour ago."

Ruoff opened her datebook and handed it to the president. Jaclyn's HUD caught the words "confirmed with governor's office" written in red ink underneath. Forrister handed it to Woodruff.

The governor looked at it and frowned. He looked to the president.

"I'm sorry, Mr. President, but I never saw this on my schedule."

Forrister looked to Monroe, who had a blank look on his face.

"Didn't you tell the governor I was here?"

Monroe slapped his cheek.

"Oh, I plum forgot. Sir," he said, turning to Woodruff, "the president is here to see you."

Jaclyn rolled her eyes underneath her HUD. She leaned toward Ruoff.

"Awkward."

Ruoff's eyes widened as she nodded.

Silence overtook the small office as Woodruff looked to Ruoff's datebook and back up to the president.

"I really must apologize for this oversight. Can we have lunch today? We can have a lunch meeting."

To Jaclyn's HUD, the governor looked truly sorry for what had happened.

Forrister smiled in return.

"We can do that; I only have to be at Augusta National by 1:30. I have a 2 o'clock tee time."

"Don't we all," Woodruff laughed. "Come on, let's head downstairs. And I see Miss Johnson is with you. My, my, she gets around with the candidates." He looked beyond the president to Jaclyn. "I spoke with my security chief, and he said that anything you want tomorrow night is fine with him."

Jaclyn felt a weight come off her shoulders for some reason. She just didn't know why.

"Thank you, governor. It's going to be fun tomorrow night, I think."

Woodruff smiled.

"I'm sure it will be a great time."

The governor led the president's entourage to the Capitol Commissary. Monroe, Jaclyn noticed, stayed behind them all.

"You know, Mr. President, you and I are very much alike," Woodruff said as they walked down the stairs.

Jaclyn rolled her eyes a second time.

"Really? I didn't know that Democrats and Republicans have that much in common."

Woodruff's laugh carried to the inside of the golden dome.

"Of course we do. I'm more of a moderate than my far right counterparts. There are some things that Mr. Bennett is against that I am for."

Jaclyn noticed the slight pause in the president's step.

"Such as?"

"Such as the fact that you made a huge statement last month in helping Las Vegas and Los Angeles with their transportation issues."

"Thank you; we worked hard on that bill. I'm glad your legislative delegation was in support of it, too."

They turned a corner. Jaclyn kept back at a safe distance.

"We're looking to improve our transportation system here in Atlanta, sir. With your help, Mr. President, I think we can get that done by 2030, right around the same time the southwest transportation system is finished."

"What needs to be done?" Forrister asked.

"Loads. We have one of the worst transportation systems in the country; well, we moved up one spot after Los Angeles was knocked out of commission by the earthquake. We have long commute times and some of the worst traffic in the Union. We're trying to improve our systems, but the voters don't seem to get it. All we're trying to do is make their lives easier and hopefully reduce the amount of carbon dioxide emissions into our airspace. The plan to create light rail services that will reduce air pollution, the voters want to clutch the purse strings a little too tightly. This is 2012, not 1912. Services like this aren't cheap."

"How much were you looking for back in July? Eight million, is that what I read?"

"No sir, eight point five billion, with a b."

Forrister whistled.

"That's a lot of peaches."

"It would have been a temporary sales tax that lasted ten years, tops. We're trying to resurrect one of the abandoned rail lines, the Clifton Corridor, which would put a light rail line at Lindbergh Center headed out to Avondale. We also want to dust off plans for an Outer Loop, make our subway stations more handicap accessible, complete the Downtown Loop streetcar plan, extend MARTA bus service into Cobb County, covert our buses to solar power and complete our Beltline project to help add more bicycling trails. All of that takes money, and it will ease the traffic on our existing freeways and make our city more viable for tourism. Remember, Mr. President: Atlanta hosts many important sporting events and we see fans from all over the Southeastern Conference coming into this city. We also have the NCAA Tournament every few years. These are things we need."

"And since the Atlanta voters turned it down in July, and with what I managed to win for Las Vegas and Los Angeles last month, you're looking at federal money for Plan B."

The governor paused.

"Precisely."

Jaclyn overheard the exchange and thought a little bit about it as they walked. She had arrived in Las Vegas only hours after Forrister had secured four hundred billion in funding for various projects in both Las Vegas and Los Angeles, not limited to building solar power stations between the two cities, a DesertXpress high-speed rail line, as well as money that would help rebuild L.A. During their girls' night out following the Las Vegas mission, Alex had told her about the little-known bailouts for the Strip's hotels that Jennifer Farrell managed to slide into the bill in exchange for her help to persuade the Republicans onto the president's side. Thankfully, that information hadn't been released to the public, but Jaclyn figured that Farrell, as Bennett's running mate, had told the GOP's nominee everything and expected that information to come out in the next four or five days, before the voters went to the polls this coming Tuesday.

The fact that Forrister already went to the well for four hundred million, plus another untold amount to rebuild the Las Vegas Monorail after Robert Letts had it destroyed in his plan to religiously cleanse the city, made Jaclyn believe the president would be hesitant to go to Congress for more money, this time for Atlanta.

There was also the fact that the rest of the country may not be too pleased with Forrister if he funded Atlanta, especially after Sarah Kendall had helped fund Boston's MBTA.

The dominoes have started to fall, she thought.

"Is it something that is desperately needed, Wallace?" Forrister asked.

Jaclyn turned her HUD toward Woodruff.

"Desperately needed is not the term I'd like to use, Mr. President. I'd prefer to think of it as a legacy. Every politician speaks of a legacy. Tip O'Neill's legacy was the Big Dig. Your predecessor, Sarah Kendall, her legacy was to stop a madman, wiping out all the bad things the right wing had said about her."

Jaclyn grinned.

"Your legacy is rebuilding Los Angeles and helping to bridge L.A. and Las Vegas. Mine, my friend, is to make Atlanta a leader in the transportation industry. We're an old rail town, and we're proud of that heritage. We want to embrace it further and wipe out the traffic problem that has mired our city. We're going to do this, by hook or by crook. Having you help us sell this proposal to the voters by throwing your support behind it with federal dollars will make the project a lock."

"I will have my people look into it," Forrister said, slapping Woodruff on the back. "We will give Atlanta the help we can. As long as the country can afford it, we will help."

Jaclyn heard hurried footsteps rushing up the stairs the way they had come. She turned her head and noticed that John Monroe, the governor's aide, had departed the group as if his pants were on fire. She saw that he had his cell phone out and was quickly dialing it.

Her lips twisted.

I wonder what he's up to, she thought.

She wondered if she should follow him or if she should keep to her mission parameters and continue to guard the president. She bounced on her heels as she weighed her options.

Alex wouldn't be too happy if I abandoned my post, she thought as the president moved further away. She breathed hard through her nose before she continued to walk down the stairs to where Forrister and Woodruff stood.

Jaclyn saw Ruoff looking at her, then mouthing, "What's wrong?"

Jaclyn shook her head in the negative. "Nothing, I hope."

They continued to the commissary.

Chapter 19
DoubleTree by Hilton Hotel—Atlanta
Sixth floor, 3342 Peachtree Road Northeast
Atlanta, Georgia
Wednesday, October 31, 2012
11:55 a.m. ET

Dick Bennett heard the phone ring, but he didn't pay it any attention. His attention was focused on Fox News, listening in as the anchors droned out about the liberals and how they were messing up the United States, ruining it for the upper class. He nodded along in agreement every few seconds, truly believing every word.

He heard Daniel Rubenstein's voice as the ringing ceased. He then heard the aide—Bennett had said the young man would be his new White House Chief of Staff when he was elected on Tuesday—approaching, his feet nearly silent on the rug of his Presidential Suite.

"Dick," he said, "there's a man by the name of John Monroe on the phone. He says it's urgent."

Bennett mouthed the name to himself, as if trying to recall where he had heard the name before. It registered seconds later. His eyebrows lifted a few millimeters.

"I wonder what he wants," Bennett said, taking the phone from Rubenstein's hand. "This is Dick Bennett."

"Mr. Bennett, this is John Monroe from Governor Woodruff's office calling."

Bennett nodded as he recalled the man's face.

"Yes John, what can I do for you?"

"You mean what I can do for you, sir. I have information."

Bennett looked to Rubenstein and lifted one eyebrow, then pointed to the other phone nearby. Rubenstein took the hint immediately and picked it up, covering the receiver with his hand.

"What do you have for me, John?" Bennett said as soon as Rubenstein had the phone to his ear.

"I just overheard the president offer to help the governor with transportation projects here in Atlanta. He offered a pledge of eight point five billion."

Bennett's grin was wide. Rubenstein's eyes were, too.

"Did the governor accept? Did he promise anything in exchange?"

"Yes to the former, no to the latter. The president said that he would give Atlanta the help they need."

Bennett nodded.

This is good, he thought. *The governor is a good Republican, being non-committal like that. And the aide was smart to call me and offer this information.*

"Excellent. Was there anything else in their conversation I need to know about?"

"Nothing imperative, sir. The governor explained things with our transportation system and what our needs are to the president, and the liberal fool that he is believed every word."

"Good. If anything else happens between them, let me know."

"I will do that."

"There may be an ambassadorship in it for you if I'm elected. Any information you have that can take Forrister down will bring us closer to victory."

"Of course, sir! I'm honored to help your campaign."

Monroe hung up. Bennett and Rubenstein did likewise. Then, Bennett turned to Rubenstein.

"What do you think of that, Daniel?"

Rubenstein began to pace slowly, his hands at the small of his back.

"We can use it, even though it's hearsay."

Bennett rolled his eyes and stood up.

"This isn't a court of law, Daniel, this is a presidential election. Hearsay wins elections. Randy would use it and you know it."

Bennett's remark did not hit the usual bull's eye: he recalled a month ago the two times he had invoked the name of Randy Jepson. Bennett had inspired Rubenstein simply by mentioning Jepson and what he would do in certain situations. Bennett recalled the way Rubenstein's back would straighten upon mentioning his name, the look of confidence the young man showed in him pouring from his face as he glowed.

Now, Rubenstein's face was pallid, not energized by hearing the manipulative words of his boss.

"Don't we have enough on Forrister already?" he asked, his hands spread apart. "We should be able to beat him with everything he and Kendall did while in the White House."

"No, we don't," Bennett countered. "What we have is not enough; a candidate can never have enough dirt on their opponents. This could definitely tip the scales our way, though. A transportation scandal in Boston isn't enough. Knowing that Forrister had ordered an assassination of a mere state representative may freak the people out a little. But the fact that he bailed out private businesses in Las Vegas and wasn't fully honest about it, and then privately pledged however much money Woodruff wants for a project that ninety-nine percent of the public will never use after doing what he did with Congress, that will be the straw that broke the camel's back, Daniel. And you can bank on that."

Rubenstein looked like he was in the process of mulling Bennett's words over in his mind. After a few minutes, he had firmed his lips before he nodded.

Bennett managed to smile.

Needed a little prodding this time, he thought. *Maybe he's not as much of a puppet as I originally thought.*

"Good. Now let's put all of our facts together, and let's make sure we have everything ready for the debate tomorrow night."

***

Westin Peachtree Hotel, 67th Floor
Atlanta, Georgia
Wednesday, October 31, 2012
7:30 p.m. ET

Jaclyn finally got back to her hotel room at 7:30 p.m.

The president had a full afternoon, including the aforementioned round of golf at Augusta National. Jaclyn stood off to the side, her HUD scanning away as Forrister worked his way from tee box to fairway to green. She figured that Rayburn wouldn't try to hit the president while he worked on his short game, but she wasn't taking any chances. She heard Alex's voice in her mind, telling her to be vigilant, even as Forrister chipped out of the bunker.

For most of the day, Jaclyn couldn't think about Rayburn and the current investigation. She hadn't received a phone call from Alex informing her of new hits, so she was of the belief that Rayburn was in the process of either a., laying low, or b., biding his time. Rayburn would strike again, quite possibly in the next 24 to 27 hours. The debate would end around 10 p.m. ET tomorrow night, which would give him ample opportunity to disrupt the debate, just as Alex had hypothesized.

Of course, the future hasn't been written yet, Jaclyn thought as she unbuttoned her blouse. She smirked. *This is what I get for watching Back To The Future with Tom and Tasha, quoting the movie.*

Jaclyn tossed her blouse onto the bed and reached behind to unsnap her bra. She shucked that off easily. She rubbed her shoulders where the straps had dug into her flesh.

He has struck in the dead of night before, she thought as she unbuttoned her slacks and shoved them down her legs, *and all we've done is react to his actions. I don't know if anyone's noticed so far, I prefer being proactive to reactive.*

She stepped out of her pants before hooking her thumbs into her bikini briefs. They went the same way as her pants, and within seconds, the secret agent was nude.

But not for long.

Jaclyn walked over to the walk-in closet, where she had hung her clothing bag. The maroon bag had a clear window to display its contents. As she spied what it held inside, a smirk developed across the lower half of her face.

She unzipped the bag and revealed her black Lycra jumpsuit, the item that made her the United States' greatest asset, and terrorism's greatest fear.

Jaclyn pulled it out and slowly wriggled her lithe form into it, zipping it up and securing the thin Velcro flap that ran the length of her torso. She then slid her six Walther P99s into place as well as wrapped the utility belt around her waist. She slapped the button near her navel.

The Kevlar lining inflated into place. She smiled, knowing that the interior bullet proofing was still operational. She pulled at the Velcro to de-pressurize the suit. Half a minute later, she re-attached the Velcro, sliding her hand down to secure it, before she slid into her long black trenchcoat. She tied her hair back into a pony tail, the hair pulled back tight.

Her stealth identity of Snapshot was ready for action once again.

Jaclyn grabbed the keys to her BMW as well as her iPad—she hooked the device to her utility belt, remembering that its case could attach itself to the jumpsuit with the Kevlar engaged—before heading out to patrol Atlanta's side streets.

As she headed to the elevator, she wondered just how long it would be before she could see some action.

Chapter 20
Near Spelman College
Atlanta, Georgia
Thursday, November 1, 2012
1:10 a.m. ET

The club was rocking, and Roseann Teague didn't want to leave the party. It was the start of Thirsty Thursday after all, and it was still Halloween night, even if the clock had already slid past midnight. The 21-year-old was decked out in a slutty nurse's costume, her breasts nearly spilling out of her half open top, a little bit of white lace from her bra peeking around the lapels. Her nurse's hat was a tad sideways and tilting toward her brow, and her white stocking tops came just below the hem of her skirt, which rested just above the middle of her creamy, caramel-colored thighs. She had drunk her fill of beer and then some, but she was still dancing away at this late hour, grinding her rear end into the crotch of a sparkly masked vampire that had come up behind her.

She giggled as the vamp nibbled on her neck with his false fangs, his hand tracing tiny circles along her waist line. Roseann made no effort to remove it. She seemed to like the attention—or the alcohol had numbed her to the fact that the vampire's fingertips were making their way south to her skirt. She grinned throughout the entire gyration, as if she knew what the guy behind her had packed in his pants. A Bud Light was comfortably settled in her left hand.

The speakers were pumping Fifty Cent throughout the bar, the costumed revelers shaking their asses on the small but serviceable dance floor. Partners changed as rapidly as the songs. Flashing lights made it difficult to determine who was who. The costumes caused that problem, too.

The vampire disappeared, leaving Roseann for a slutty cat a few feet away.

"Horny asshole," she said, her voice a slur as she brought the bottle to her lips once again. She downed the remaining beer and walked it over to the bar. She stumbled a little, but she managed to put the empty bottle on the edge of the bar before reluctantly moving toward the exit, alone once again while her girlfriends hung on the arms of muscle-bound studs, attaching themselves by their lips. Roseann had been 21 for only a few months, and despite her attractiveness, she could not get laid at a bar to save her life. She met tons of great guys at the bars around Spelman College, just north of Interstate 20, but for some reason they never wanted to separate her from her panties.

And that was a source of irritation for her, however chivalrous it was.

"What the fuck am I doing wrong? Am I not pretty enough?" she said as she walked west on Abernathy Boulevard, approaching Metropolitan Parkway. The cold late October air—early November, she reminded herself, checking her watch—didn't affect her, despite not wearing anything over her costume to ward off the stiff breeze coming from her back. "These boys don't know what they're missing at all."

She walked on, still glowering over not being picked up. Her heels clicked away on the pavement.

She crossed underneath the interstate and despite the sounds of several cars and the flashing blues of Georgia State Police cruisers passing overhead, she didn't let that distract her from keeping the tormenting thoughts out of her mind. She managed to shake them as she approached a set of train tracks, looking back and forth before she took off her heels and crossed to Peters Street. Her heels—white, to match her nurse's outfit—remained off as she turned left and made her way to Chapel Street.

The route she took would bring her practically to the front door of her dormitory. It involved a right-hand turn onto Chapel before she skirted the edge of the nearby tennis courts. Her dorm was located just to the north of the courts, where warm blankets and silky pajamas awaited her, as well as a soft pillow that would cushion her while her dreams of manly hands caressing her body played out.

In her stupor, Roseann didn't see the white van until it was too late.

The van turned its engine over and pulled out of Westview Drive at speed, then screeched to a halt as it approached the young black woman.

Roseann blinked, her eyebrows knitting together as she stared at the parked van, it's engine still running and revving under the driver's heavy right foot.

Her lips finally parted when the men—she could tell they were men just by their stature, their bulk—in white robes and hoods emerged slowly from the van, only converging on her with speed she couldn't believe existed before she imbibed with such quantities of alcohol. Hands grabbed her arms. She felt a cloth being shoved into her mouth before she could scream, the shock too much for her. She dropped her shoes, but she couldn't hear the clattering on the sidewalk.

They then picked her up and slung her over one of the man's shoulders, exposing her rear end to the chilly air. They carried her to the van, her feet kicking at air and hitting the same. The tossed her through the open sliding door, her left shoulder colliding hard with the steel floor.

A wave of pain and nausea passed through her, her shoulder separating under the impact. She could feel the tears welling in her eyes.

The men jumped into the van with her, one throwing a burlap hood over the woman's head, knocking the nurse's hat askew. She could feel the hood tightening near her neck, and then felt her arms being yanked behind her back. She then felt a rope being wrapped around her wrists, securing them as the door slammed shut. She heard the clicking of the transmission even through the hood, and then heard the sound of the tires peeling away.

Soon she felt the van turn once and then twice, and within moments she figured out that they were marring her sense of direction.

Even through her tears, she wondered where they were taking her, and what would happen to her.

She had a feeling it wouldn't be a happy ending.

***

Atlanta, Georgia
Thursday, November 1, 2012
1:19 a.m. ET

Jaclyn was just finishing up her sixth straight hour of driving around Atlanta, and she hadn't seen anything out of the ordinary so far. The cold weather had kept most people indoors, with only few partygoers in the places that she had passed in her BMW. She had checked in with Atlanta Police and let them know she would be patrolling the city, and she also inquired about the clubs that would be holding Halloween parties. She had remembered what had occurred in Las Vegas a month ago, of how the Disciples of Elam had hit a gay club as people were entering for the night. She only wanted to keep tabs on those places just in case a similar incident happened.

She had driven past the club near Spelman College at 9 p.m. and had seen the slutty nurse enter. She had shaken her head with a tight grin, knowing the young lady was about to have the sort of fun that Jaclyn never had the chance to enjoy when she was that age.

But now, with the evening dragging slowly to a close and with her nearing the Georgia Tech campus, Jaclyn was ready to call it a night herself. She yawned deeply and thought about utilizing the auto-pilot, but after blinking her eyes a few times at a red light, she managed to keep her wits about her and stay awake. She turned the air conditioning on and angled the vents toward her face.

It was then that she saw a white van make a hard left-hand turn onto 10th Street Northwest from Hemphill Avenue, tires squealing and headed in the general direction of the Hank McCamish Pavillion. The van sped up despite the posted speed limit signs.

Jaclyn eyed the van's taillights through her HUD and nibbled on her bottom lip.

"That just screams suspicious," she muttered. She exhaled sharply and firmed her lips, then nodded. "Yep, I need to see what they're up to."

Jaclyn checked both ways and found no one coming, despite the green light accorded to the Hemphill motorists. And despite the red light that halted her on 10th, she hit the gas and followed the van. She imagined the driver's handbook being thrown out the window as she crossed over.

Once she passed Center Street, she flipped a switch on the center console. Seconds later, she could hear the servos and gears turning as the under-the-hood machine guns flipped open, ready for action.

Just in case, she thought.

Jaclyn followed the taillights at a safe distance, slowing down and pulling over near the empty bus stop some one thousand feet away from the arena—which is where the van pulled up to, the back doors opening seconds after parking. She watched intently as several men in white robes and hoods spilled out of the sides.

"Oh boy," she said. "I wonder what they're going to—shit!"

She watched as several of the men pulled out a heavy wooden cross. The men, she could tell, were laboring under the strain of the structure. Four carried it, while another, the driver, stood off to the side with a sawed-off shotgun held at the ready.

Jaclyn smirked.

Time for a little fun, she thought.

She slammed the accelerator down as she turned the wheel, the tires burning rubber and bringing the BMW back into the non-existent traffic. She flipped another switch on the console, which preceded servos and gears churning away. The S-T-A rack locked into place, and Jaclyn hoped that it wouldn't topple against the force of her driving. She smirked as she put her finger over the trigger.

"What better way to announce my presence than with a missile launch," she said, pressing the button at the same time.

Steam vented away from the rack as the missile displaced air en route to its target.

Heartbeats later, the van exploded, sending fire and black smoke into the air, and hot, jagged shrapnel in all directions. The men dropped the cross, the wood hitting the sidewalk in front of the domed building with a clatter. Several of the men screamed as the van's remains cut into them.

The driver, seeing the missile fly, managed to get away without saying a word to his comrades. He began to fire at the oncoming BMW, the bullets smacking off the windshield without snapping it.

Inside, Jaclyn smiled.

"It's about time I got to test the armor on these things," she said as she slammed on the brakes. The tail end fishhooked a bit to the left as it came to a stop.

Jaclyn slapped the button on her utility belt as she made to unbuckle her safety belt. The Kevlar lining formed up. The driver of the destroyed van started to run toward the BMW, the shotgun up and pointed right at her. Several more bullets flattened as they collided with the windshield. They sank down to the reservoir with the windshield wipers and stayed there. Out of the corner of Jaclyn's eye, she could see the others, despite their injuries, get up and reach for sidearms through pockets in their now-dirtied robes.

She drew two Walthers and opened the driver's side door and rolled out just as the driver fired another round toward the car. She somersaulted forward and pulled the triggers just as she hit her knees.

The Klucker flailed backward, the shotgun sliding out of his grip and hitting the pavement before he did.

Jaclyn was up in a heartbeat, her Walthers aimed at the others. They, too, had their weapons out, and bullets hammered against both the car and against Jaclyn's Lycra jumpsuit. The shots didn't faze her one bit.

The Kluckers just stared as Jaclyn approached them.

She wondered if their mouths had started to hang on a hinge under their hoods, realizing that she could not be brought down by conventional means.

Jaclyn took advantage of their hesitation. She stalked in and fired two rounds from her Walthers. The first two hooded men dropped like stones, the bullets making flowers of red spread across their pristine white robes near their hearts and lungs.

The next two froze in place as they looked down on their fallen comrades. The fifth man took off on foot toward Fraternity Row.

Jaclyn fired toward the two that remained. They quickly pin wheeled to the ground as they caught her bullets in their respective necks and chests.

She ran toward the building, not worried that at least one of the Kluckers was not yet dead. She kept an eye toward the street that ran along the side of the Pavillion and saw the white robe fleeing. Jaclyn knew that the man would do his best to lose the robe and hood as soon as he made a turn away from the sports complex. And with the sounds of bullets flying and exploding vans waking students from their slumber, she was sure that even from a few blocks away, there would be people in various states of intoxication heading outside to see just what was happening near their school.

Jaclyn gritted her teeth as she saw the man finally make a turn. She thought about chasing him on foot, but she had waited too long.

"Damn it," she said, turning and high-tailing it back to the BMW, sidestepping the motionless Kluckers. An ambulance would show up soon, along with Atlanta Police, to clean up her mess.

She slid into the BMW, closed the door and dropped the S-T-A rack as well as the machine guns. She knew she was headed into a potentially crowded area, and she wouldn't risk civilians. Jaclyn pulled away from the Pavillion.

Unfortunately for her, Fowler Street was now blocked off by the burning van. She did a three-point turn and came back the way she came for about four seconds before she turned left onto Cherry Street, a road that, according to Lucy's display, wound around a pair of tennis courts, a building next to a soccer field, as well as Chandler Field's third base stands.

Cherry Street spat the BMW out at Ferst Drive, and like Jaclyn predicted, students were milling about en masse.

"Crap," she said. She parked the car and hopped out, and within seconds, several male students, inebriated from their Halloween debauchery, began wolf-whistling at her.

She ignored them. Instead, she scanned the area near the Greek houses for anyone who may resemble the size of the fifth Klucker.

No one stuck out, and there was no sign that she could see of a white robe, either on a person or on the ground. She figured the man fled through the yards of the fraternities. She returned to the BMW and turned onto Ferst, making her way to Fowler. She turned right. The north stand of Georgia Tech's football stadium, darkened in the early morning hours, loomed ahead.

Jaclyn soon realized that it would be difficult to find this man un-robed, forcing her to pull the souped-up BMW to a halt at 4th Street. She exhaled sharply through her nose before she slapped the steering wheel.

"Fuck," she said. "I can't believe the bastard got away."

As she made another three-point turn and returned north on Fowler to await the authorities' arrival, she couldn't believe she was giving up on the chase so easily.

Chapter 21
Rayburn's Abandoned Farmhouse
Outside of Atlanta, Georgia
Thursday, November 1, 2012
2:15 a.m. ET

Rayburn and his guard watched as the white van slid into the farmhouse carrying not only the prized capture that Rayburn had planned out the night before, but also the man that had escaped from what was supposed to be an easy get-in, get-out cross-burning at the debate site. From what Carl had told him after he ended the call, a woman showed up at the site, blew up the van, then killed the others before their agent made a run for it. Carl mentioned that the man smartly called the other team—which was headed in that direction anyway—and had them pick him up just south of the Tech Tower lawn and Georgia Tech's football stadium.

Rayburn's mind spun. Things had changed with that phone call. The fact that only one of the two things he wanted his men to accomplish tonight made him nervous; he rubbed his right palm over the skin between his left thumb and forefinger. To date, all of his attacks had succeeded. He had put the fear of the KKK in the city of Atlanta and the state of Georgia. Men—pure, white men—had flocked to his call. They listened to his message and wanted to make him proud.

And now, one woman threatened everything. One damned, lousy woman.

He didn't even know who she was, but Rayburn wanted her dead.

"Who is she, Carl? Why has she stopped my men?" he said after Carl had hung up and relayed what he had heard.

"I have a guess," the former prison guard said. "But I can't be too sure until I see more proof."

Rayburn stared.

"You have a guess," he said sarcastically. "How about telling me your guess." It wasn't a question.

Carl took several steps away from Rayburn's side and slid his hands into his pockets. Rayburn heard him sigh, before he had turned around.

"Remember our agent's call from the other day? The government has this woman secret agent that caused some mischief in London and Las Vegas. Apparently she's the genuine article when it comes to fighting terrorism. I'm thinking she's the same woman our boy called us about."

"We're not terrorists, Carl. We're God-fearing Southern Americans. We're the chosen people."

"The government has a pretty wild imagination when it comes to who is and who isn't a terrorist these days, Bobby Ray. You can thank President Bush and his Patriot Act for that."

"Tell me about this woman," Rayburn said, not hearing the remark about the former president.

Carl leaned against a rusted out tractor.

"Her name is Jaclyn Johnson. That Dick Bennett Yankee outed her back in August. She works for the CIA, but she kind of investigates like the FBI does. So she's like this superagent that the president calls on to handle stuff where an aircraft carrier and a battalion of good ol' boys isn't needed."

Rayburn's mouth made a sound that resembled a tire blowing out on the highway.

"Good ol' boys are always needed," he countered.

Carl conceded the point with a wave.

"She's a blonde bombshell that is supposedly a model, according to what Bennett told the papers. She managed to hide away for a month or so before she was involved in some shit over in Las Vegas."

Rayburn ran a hand across his shaven scalp. He paced slowly.

"And now she's in my city."

"If it's really her," Carl cautioned as he launched himself away from the tractor. "We don't know for sure yet."

Rayburn was quiet for several minutes as he paced. He smacked his dry, chapped lips together several times. He ran his tongue over them once, but that didn't seem to do anything. He took a deep breath, then turned back to face Carl.

"Didn't we get a report of a woman going to see my parents the other day? Yesterday, was it?"

Carl's eyes lit up.

"I think we did."

"Where is our informant?"

"I think he was one of the men this woman killed tonight."

Rayburn's face fell, blanching as it did.

"Rats."

"He did," Carl said, "leave his digital camera here, though."

Rayburn brightened a bit.

"That's good news then?"

Carl turned and walked into another part of the farmhouse, sidestepping moldy hay and a long wooden trough that smelled like rotten eggs and manure. After a couple of days there, the two men had grown used to the stench and chose to ignore it when they walked past. Rayburn had followed him.

"It might be, if I can figure out how to use it. We don't have a computer here to look at the pictures. We're lucky that we have power still."

Carl found the small Nikon camera and fiddled with the knobs and buttons until he managed to get old pictures to display. A few shots showed a naked woman using her mouth on an equally-naked photographer. Both men cringed. They continued flipping until they came to a wide shot of a yard Rayburn knew all too well.

"That fat bastard hasn't mowed the lawn in ages," he said. "Was he waiting for me to get out of jail to cut it? Damned fool."

"Look at the car," Carl said. "BMW."

Carl's lips turned downward, but it wasn't a frown.

"Nice wheels."

"Yep. Expensive." Carl pressed the button that flipped to the next photo. "There's the woman he was talking about. It may be Johnson; you can see the sunglasses, even in the darkness."

Rayburn's left eyebrow went up half an inch.

"Why would she be wearing sunglasses at night?" he asked.

Carl shrugged.

"Beats me."

Rayburn strummed his fingers on his lips.

"She went to see my parents," he said, mainly to himself. "Interesting."

Carl peered at his friend with narrowed eyes.

"What are you thinking about, Bobby Ray?"

Rayburn blinked and shook his head.

"Right now, nothing, other than wondering what this woman wanted at my parents' house. Save that photo and we'll show it to our agent when they finally get here." Rayburn yawned. "Hopefully that'll be soon."

Nearly forty-five minutes passed before the van arrived. Rayburn and Carl stood at the opening to the farmhouse, even though Rayburn knew it wasn't exactly prudent for him to do so: he didn't know if there were government snipers out there, ready to take him down with a well-placed bullet between the eyes. He felt his heart tapping out Morse code as the van backed up.

Squeaky brakes brought the van to a halt. The door slid open, the steel grating against steel.

Rayburn peered in and saw the slutty nurse, bound and hooded, lying prostrate on the floor, shivering. He smiled and licked his lips. He saw the girl's figure and found her desirable.

"Bring her downstairs and hook her up. I'll be down momentarily. James," he said to one of the men, "stay here."

The others hauled the young woman out of the van and brought her downstairs. Rayburn saw that the woman must have passed out, as the men carried her easily. To his eyes, Rayburn thought she looked like a fifty-pound sack of potatoes. They disappeared.

The man Rayburn wanted to wait here did so without question. Rayburn watched as the tired man stood there at parade rest, his hands at the small of his back. His robe was missing.

That's obvious, Rayburn thought. He didn't want to walk openly through the Georgia Tech campus after he ran away from the woman. It was prudent for him not to let anyone identify him—but leaving the robe will also give people another clue that the KKK is still active, even though they close their eyes to facts right in front of them.

"James, are you all right?" he asked.

The man nodded.

"I am. Everything happened so fast. Just a little tired, but ready for my next assignment."

Rayburn smiled.

"Your next assignment is to tell me if the woman on this camera is the same woman you spied at my parents' house the other night."

Rayburn handed him the camera. James knew how to work it, and within a few moments he had the camera on and flipped to the scenes where the BMW—and the mystery woman—appeared on the screen.

James held the camera near his face as he studied the image.

"It could be her," he said finally. "The car is the same color, make and model. And the woman tonight definitely had on those type of sunglasses. But why at night?"

"You're a journalist," Rayburn said. "Find out for me."

James nodded.

"I'll do that."

"Don't fail me."

The man gulped.

"I won't."

He turned and left the farmhouse, leaving Rayburn and Carl alone for several moments.

"He'll come through for us. He works for one of the biggest papers in Cobb County," Carl said.

Rayburn's answer didn't miss a beat.

"He better, or he'll be no more alive than the men he worked with tonight."

Carl smiled.

"Let's go see what our other unit brought us to play with," he added, slapping Rayburn between the shoulder blades and bringing him to the stairs.

When they hit the bottom step, they had seen that their followers had done as Rayburn had asked. The young woman was tied up against a wall, her arms outstretched and secured by ropes around her wrists. They gave the same treatment to her ankles, which hitched her skirt up and nearly exposed her crotch to the men. She still wore the hood, and it seemed as if she didn't struggle as they tied her up.

"Remove the hood," Rayburn said. "I want to see the bitch we've caught in our web."

A few of the men laughed.

"You're going to love this, Bobby Ray."

The speaker grabbed the hood and untied it before ripping it off. The nurse's hat was gone and her hair was disheveled, but Rayburn, stepping forward, got his first look at the young woman. She was asleep, either passed out from the alcohol that Rayburn could smell as soon as the hood came off, or she had fainted from embarrassment after pissing herself. He could see the trails of urine on her inner thighs.

He smiled at the scent once it reached his nostrils.

"You boys done good. You brought me a nigger bitch," he said. They laughed. "Get some water and wake this whore up."

They did as he asked, racing toward the spigot. The one who had driven the van got there first and had the bucket in hand. He walked back and flung the contents into her face just as soon as Rayburn backed away.

Roseann Teague's eyes snapped open several heartbeats later. She sputtered and coughed as water violated her mouth. Her black hair was drenched, and so was her white top and her chest, with droplets hitting the flesh after slinking off her chin. The top wasn't transparent. She looked back and forth and finally noticed her restraints.

The Kluckers laughed as she struggled against her bonds.

Rayburn stepped forward.

"Welcome, sweetheart. Welcome to the heart of the new Ku Klux Klan." Rayburn said it with an air of hospitality, as if the abandoned rambling farmhouse was a luxurious, whites only resort that specialized in torturing blacks.

Roseann's eyes widened.

"You!"

Rayburn smirked.

"Were you expecting Simmons? Or maybe Forrest instead of me? Or even David Duke?"

"My God, what are you doing to me? Oh God, my head," Roseann whined.

Rayburn reached up and stroked the young woman's cheek. He could tell that his prey's flesh quivered from disgust, not excitement. He sneered as he looked into her eyes.

"My dear, sweet nigger girl, your question shouldn't be what are you doing to me—it should be what are you going to do to me?" he said. "Can you say that?"

He saw tears begin to form in the woman's eyes. He smacked her. More tears followed, streaming down her cheeks.

"Say it, bitch!" he screamed.

"Wh-what ar-are you going to do t-to me?" she whispered, the tears careening into the valley that was her mouth.

"You're going to get what's coming to you good," he whispered, even though he knew she heard every little word.

Roseann's body began to shake with convulsions as the tears continued.

Rayburn snarled as he reached up and grabbed the lapels of her nurse's top with both hands and yanked them apart, revealing her breasts encased in her lacy white bra. Buttons tinkled off the cement floor, even though the young woman's screams drowned out the sounds. Rayburn ripped it completely off her before he made a move for the woman's skirt.

He pulled it off so easily that the fabric ripped like wet paper. He tossed the skirt aside. She screamed again, then tried to clench her thighs together in a futile attempt at modesty. The ropes prevented her from moving. All of the men stared at her urine-stained lacy panties with smirks on their faces.

Rayburn rubbed his crotch. A lascivious grin formed.

"You know something," he said as he grabbed her hair, "I ain't had a woman since I was 17."

The woman turned blubbery.

"I bet you got all dolled up tonight for your Halloween party looking like the little nigger slut you are so you could get some of that big cracker dick you so desperately desire," he said.

The young woman shook her head in defiance.

"Yeah, I bet you did. You're going to get a lot of it, too." He stood on tiptoes and licked her cheek. "You're going to get all you desire and more."

He lowered himself and turned around.

"Someone go get a fucking knife!" he snarled.

The men cheered and ran upstairs, looking for something with which to cut.

Rayburn looked at the woman and patted her cheek.

"I'm going to enjoy this, yes I am," he said.

The young woman continued crying.

Chapter 22
Westin Peachtree Hotel, 67th Floor
Atlanta, Georgia
Thursday, November 1, 2012
7:10 a.m. ET

Sleep didn't come to Jaclyn that night.

She returned to the Pavillion and met with Atlanta Police and Fire, receiving a tongue-lashing from the Officer In Charge for not informing them of what had transpired.

"Aren't we supposed to be on the same team here?" the OIC had said. "You know something, Bennett was right about you. You take matters into your hands too damn often. Y'all need to be reined in."

After Jaclyn gave him her side of what happened, she walked to the BMW knowing that Forrister had lost a vote. She did, however, learn that one of the Kluckers she had shot was still alive, which meant she could find out more about Rayburn's plans.

She hoped.

Knowing that it would be a while before she could talk to him, she returned to the hotel at 3 a.m., undressed—the jumpsuit's interior was slightly slick, prompting Jaclyn to take a hot shower—and tumbled into bed nude half an hour later. And after sending a quick text to Alex, she collapsed and managed to sleep until 7, when her iPhone blistered the silent sanctity of her suite.

Except it wasn't an alarm: the dulcet tones of Bruce Springsteen carried to her ears.

Jaclyn groaned and grabbed her phone, sliding the unlock mechanism with her finger and bringing it to her left ear almost at once.

"You're interrupting a really good dream, Chief."

"Was it sexy?" Alex Dupuis asked.

Jaclyn sighed.

"I don't remember."

Alex chuckled.

"Dream time is over, Snapshot. You have a lot of work to do today. I've just been on the phone with Atlanta P.D—"

"Does that OIC still want my head on a spike?"

"No," Alex said. "They're actually glad you left someone alive."

"Is he out of surgery yet?"

"They didn't do surgery. Instead, they took out the bullet and stitched him up before the police took him into custody. He immediately lawyered up once he was Mirandized."

Jaclyn grimaced.

"Shit."

"Were you hoping for a different conclusion, Jaclyn?"

"I was hoping to rough the bastard up and get him to talk. You know, the way I usually do things."

"I'm not going to say yes or no about that; besides, I don't think a no would stop you anyway."

Jaclyn flung the covers off and swung her legs over the side, managing to sit up.

"It may be hard to get away from the president today to begin with. It is the day of the debate, and I don't want Forrister without me close by today, especially if Rayburn is tracking him."

"That's what I thought you'd say, Snapshot. Keep me up to date with your movements."

Alex hung up without another word. Jaclyn tossed the phone on the bed, even as a text message from Tom filtered through.

"I can answer that later," she said to herself, stretching her arms above her head. She shivered. "I need some coffee and clothes first. Then I need to see what Forrister has planned for today."

She stood up and walked to the closet, looking for something to wear.

***

Rayburn's Abandoned Farmhouse
Outside of Atlanta, Georgia
Thursday, November 1, 2012
7:35 a.m. ET

Rayburn couldn't sleep, even after the evening he had.

He had raped the young woman not once, but twice, taking her by force after he had sliced her undergarments away with a long-handled machete that his followers had found in the loft. He had groped her hard, making her wince. He smacked her on the ass and on the face. It was a brutal rape, forcing himself on her with ease. Eventually he pulled out, unable to reach a climax after nearly half an hour. He punched her, snapping the woman's nose. Warm crimson fluid soon coated her lips and dribbled down to her chin. Carl then took his place while Rayburn pulled his pants up. He needed a drink, something to relax him.

Yet even as he sawed in and out of her for the second time, she made no sounds. She did not even emit a whimper as they violated her body. She had ceased crying, choking the tears back, and he had noticed that she had stopped saying anything while the third man had his way with her. No one had even gagged her. She was still alive, and her eyes were open—but she wasn't there, so to speak. It seemed to Rayburn, as he hovered over her, that she had chosen to accept her fate, that she would be repeatedly raped by these men and eventually killed after her usefulness to them had ended.

That turned him on. He had started to pound her, eventually pulling out with a groan. Semen covered her lower back. Rayburn grunted several more times as he stood over her.

Now, an hour later, with the sun fully up and the farmhouse nearly deserted, Rayburn was alone with his thoughts.

Did a black woman really arouse me? he wondered. *That's never happened before. All of my girlfriends as a teenager were white, and I had no problem getting it up for them. Black girls did nothing for me then.*

So why now? Why did I get a hard-on for this slut?

His lip began to curl.

Maybe it's because I finally had control, not after the last five years of not being in control.

He closed his eyes. Seconds later, his head bowed.

Damn them all, he thought. *They found me weak, and that's why they took me so hard. That's why this little black bitch got me hard. I had to prove I was strong. That's why I took her as hard as I did. To prove my superiority.*

Rayburn took a deep breath.

His mind became a tumult of thought once again. He recalled his earlier conversation with Carl, about the woman killing his agents. He didn't know if any of them had survived, only hearing from James on the phone that he had witnessed their falls after she had shot them.

Of course, there was a chance that James didn't see everything, Rayburn thought. *He had to have been in motion long before they fell in order to escape. One of them could have survived.*

"There's only one way to find out," he said, lifting his head and coming out of his crouch. He walked first back downstairs, where the young woman was covered by a blanket, asleep. Rayburn grabbed her purse and unzipped it, checking for the woman's identification. He found two plastic cards: her driver's license and her Spelman College ID. He then walked to the loft, where his followers had stashed a radio for his use.

He had grinned at their ingenuity. These types of radios were a more old fashioned form of communication.

Rayburn picked up the handheld, two-meter receiver and, after collecting his thoughts and his emotions, pressed the transmit device.

"This is Bobby Ray Rayburn contacting any and all local law enforcement agencies in and around Atlanta," he said, not utilizing an FCC code to transmit. "I'll continue my broadcast when someone responds." He unclicked the transmitter.

Nearly a minute later, he got one. It came through with quite a bit of static, as if the sender chose to transmit underwater.

"Go ahead, Bobby Ray. You have the Fulton County Sheriff's Department with its ears on, you copy?"

Rayburn smiled as he pressed the transmitter again.

"I just wanted to let you boys know that soon, y'all are going to hear about a missing person. My men kidnapped this bitch earlier this morning, and I be claiming responsibility for taking her." He paused and smirked. "She works it real nice, if y'all know what I mean. We took her at about 1 o'clock in the morning, so it hasn't been that long for a report to come in. But it will, boys. It will."

The response came right away.

"Rayburn, why don't you give yourself up? This won't end good for you if you don't."

"It won't end good if I do either, and you boys know that. So here's what I'm going to do for y'all. I'm going to help y'all notify this bitch's family that the Klan has their girl, and that they better pray to God I decide not to kill her—but y'all need to do something for me first."

"We're not going to bargain with you, Rayburn. Give yourself up."

Rayburn smirked.

"That's all y'all are saying here, and y'all know I'm not going to just give myself up after five long years in prison and almost takin' a needle in my arm. I don't know what y'all are smokin' over there in Fulton County, but I assure you I ain't going to give myself up. I will also assure you that I'll kill this whore if my demands aren't met, so shut the fuck up and get ready to write this shit down."

He paused and waited. A minute passed, then a second.

"Mr. Rayburn, what do you want to assure this girl's safety from this point forward?" a voice said.

"Who am I dealing with?"

"This is the Fulton County Sheriff."

"You a white boy or you a nigger?"

There was a pause.

"I am Caucasian, Mr. Rayburn. What are your demands?"

Rayburn smirked.

"First things first, I want to know what happened to all my men when I had the cross put up at Georgia Tech this morning."

"Alright, what's the girl's name?"

"I'm not done yet," Rayburn replied as he slowly paced across the loft. He held the transmitter down so the sheriff couldn't break in on him. "I want all of y'all's nigger officers to lay down your guns. They don't belong in a position of power like that. They be abusing the whites, that needs to stop. Third, I want the Brady Bill revoked. Then maybe I'll give you the girl's name."

"Give us the girl's name and I'll get you the first thing. I'll work on the others for you, but I doubt the second things will happen, Bobby Ray."

Rayburn's lip curled again.

"I don't know," he said.

"Show me some good faith, man. Give me the name, I'll get you the info you want."

Rayburn lowered his head, his lips tight. He gritted his teeth, then sighed a reluctant sigh.

He keyed the mike as he looked at the girl's ID's.

"Her name is Roseann Teague. She goes to Spelman." He also gave them her home address. He could imagine the

Fulton County Sheriff's Office working the phones, trying to figure out whose jurisdiction her hometown was in.

"Alright, we'll be in touch. Monitor this band, and I'll try to get you what you want." The channel went dead—until it began burning up with pro- and anti-KKK listeners-turned-transmitters. Rayburn listened to none of it. He simply walked out of the loft, tossing the woman's ID cards into the farm detritus. He walked over to the open gate, where a white van rested and waited for Rayburn's men to reclaim it. To the side of it, an older Volkswagen microbus rested.

He looked out toward the west, looking across the expanse of dying wheat. The sun's rays, coming from behind the farmhouse, caught the wheat and reflected the rays toward Rayburn's eyes.

He took a long, deep breath, exhaling slowly.

For some reason, a reason he couldn't be sure of, thoughts of the woman who had taken out his agents came into his mind.

Who are you? Are you really this perceived superwoman that Carl said can't be beaten? Are you truly up to the task of bringing me down? I bet she doesn't realize that if she cuts the head off of one branch of the KKK, another will sprout up in its place, for the Klan will never be truly beaten as long as there are good Southern men who will continue to nurture it in our youth.

Another breath rattled his chest.

I wonder what you said to my parents, he thought, *if it was really you who went to see them.*

He stared at the wheat for several more minutes, debating things over in his mind.

Should I stay put, even with the chance that one of my agents could still be alive and be forced to give up the location of my hideout, or should I leave on that fact alone? Where should I go?

A light smile came to his lips. He turned around and walked over to the Volkswagen microbus, stopping only to peer inside at the dashboard. A key dangled from the ignition.

His grin turned feral. He opened the door, slid in, then turned the key.

The microbus's engine turned over, revving away as he tapped at the accelerator. He had plenty of gas. He pumped his fist once before getting out of the Volkswagen.

Rayburn ran down to where Carl slept. He shook him awake.

"Carl, wake up. Carl!"

The former prison guard stirred and finally awoke with a snoring start.

"What's wrong, Bobby Ray? Is it the police?"

"No, it's better than that. Grab the girl. We're getting the fuck out of here."

Carl blinked twice, then leapt up from the floor. Rayburn had already turned and headed for the door. Carl followed.

"What? Where are we going?"

Rayburn turned and looked at his lieutenant with a smile on his face.

"We're going home, buddy. Get your shit and the girl."

Chapter 23
Atlanta, Georgia
Thursday, November 1, 2012
7:50 a.m. ET

At Langley, Salt had intercepted the all points bulletin that the Fulton County Sheriff's Office had put out shortly before 7:45 a.m., simply by using the keywords Bobby Ray Rayburn and Atlanta. He had disseminated the message and forwarded it to Alex Dupuis. Alex's eyes went wide as soon as she saw it, and she immediately called Jaclyn.

Jaclyn, fresh out of the shower with a towel wrapped around her hair and another around her body, answered on the second ring, silencing Springsteen.

"What's up, Chief?"

"I just found out that Rayburn kidnapped a college girl last night. Get over to Spelman College, and grab Anderson on your way. Consider this priority one for today."

Jaclyn shivered. She took the towel off from her head and tossed it on the bed.

"You got it. I have to call Melanie Ruoff first and tell her I can't be with the president for a while. I saw on his itinerary he's playing golf again before the debate tonight."

"Golf's off, Jaclyn. They all should stay in until you and Anderson are free to protect them. Rayburn's getting more and more brazen. I got your text about the near-cross burning at the debate site. Is there anything new to report there?"

Jaclyn shook her head.

"Not that I know of, Chief. I'll find out more and give you a call." She bit her lip. "I'm thinking you're going to call Bennett and give him the bad news?"

"No, I'm going to call the Secret Service and have them order him down. He won't countermand an order from them. I'll keep in touch." Alex hung up.

Jaclyn tossed her iPhone on the bed and whipped the towel off. She hurriedly dressed into business clothes, holstering one of her Walther P99's. She was ready to go in all of five minutes, not bothering with make-up. She was inside her BMW by 8 a.m., and twenty minutes later, she had picked Anderson up.

"Where are we going?" the younger agent asked as Jaclyn pulled away from the curb.

"Spelman College."

"My cousin goes there. Why are we headed there?"

"There's been a kidnapping."

Anderson blinked.

"And why are we wasting our time handling this? That's a job for local police, not the CIA. It's overkill."

"Overkill is what I do best, Jasmine," Jaclyn countered. "Besides, Rayburn is behind it."

"How do we know?"

"If Alex says Rayburn's behind it, then Rayburn's behind it. She didn't tell me how she knew; she just knows things. We can find out when we get there."

They slipped into traffic.

By 8:30 a.m., police had swarmed Spelman College, trying to contact the young woman's friends.

"I hope someone's trying to contact this girl's family, too," Anderson said as they pulled up. Yellow police tape cordoned off a part of the sidewalk, where Jaclyn saw—

"A pair of shoes. The girl left her shoes."

Anderson spied it, too.

"Yes, she did."

They got out of the car and walked toward the police tape. Anderson showed ID while Jaclyn swept underneath the tape.

"What do we have?" she asked an officer photographing the scene.

"Stiletto pumps. We're figuring she kicked them off during the struggle and Rayburn's men didn't notice the shoe was gone."

"How did Rayburn contact the sheriff?"

"He used the old radio," the cop said.

Jaclyn blinked.

"Huh?"

"Some people call it a ham radio," the cop said, rolling his eyes. "It's an older style of communication, but the police try to monitor it because there are some rednecks who prefer it to cell phones. Mainly the criminal elements prefer it."

Jaclyn nodded. Anderson's cell phone rang. She answered it, stepping away from Jaclyn.

"Can't say that's the smartest thing I've ever heard, but it makes sense. Makes it difficult to pinpoint where Rayburn is."

Anderson choked a scream. Jaclyn turned to her, only to find Anderson's face slacked, as if she had been frightened.

"What's wrong, Anderson?"

"That was my mother. It's my cousin," Anderson said, tears welling in her eyes. They quickly made their way down her face. "Roseann Teague is my cousin. She was the one taken from here last night."

Jaclyn's jaw dropped.

"Oh, fuck," she said.

Anderson began crying harder. Jaclyn vaulted forward as the woman slumped and fell apart emotionally. She lowered Anderson to her knees

It's a completely new ballgame, Jaclyn thought as she held her.

***

Hickory Flat, Georgia

Thursday, November 1, 2012
8:32 a.m. ET

Carl drove the Volkswagen microbus toward Hickory Flat, avoiding Atlanta proper and anything resembling law enforcement. Carl had wondered why Rayburn had wanted to use this old piece of crap instead of the white van, but the escaped convict had explained it succinctly.

"The police are going to look for a white van. From what you said last night, the Johnson woman blew up one of our vans. This van isn't white."

Carl had rolled his eyes, knowing the microbus wasn't as inconspicuous as the white van. White vans are a dime a dozen, while the VW microbus—at least this model—wasn't something seen in urban Atlanta, or in rural Georgia, to begin with. He didn't know the last time one of these were seen.

"We'll be fine. Do we have the weapons?" Rayburn asked.

Carl nodded.

"Under the seat."

Rayburn smiled and reached down underneath the passenger seat and pulled out a pair of Glock handguns. Each had a suppressor screwed into the barrels. They gleamed under the feeble sunlight that streamed through the windows.

"One for you and one for me?"

"I have my own under my seat, too. How's the girl?"

Rayburn looked over his shoulder and down to the microbus's floor. The captive was bound with her hands tied behind her back, her ankles tied together, too. The same hood covered her head, and Rayburn couldn't see it but he knew that another cord was tied around the lower half of her face, the rope in her mouth.

He smiled, knowing she wouldn't move or make a sound while he and Carl were in the middle of their current task.

"How far away are we now?" Rayburn asked, turning his attention back to the road.

"Not far," Carl replied. "We should be there by 8:30 or so."

"Good. He should be there then. He leaves for work at 8:45. At least that's the time he left before I was arrested."

"And everyone else should be gone by then, too. One of our agents reported in and said there were no foreign cars on your street, so there should be no witnesses."

"Good. Call him back and have him go to the farmhouse. I want that van retrieved. I don't want it to fall into the wrong hands."

Carl nodded.

"I'll make sure it's done after we take care of what we have to do."

They drove on.

Ten minutes later, Rayburn and Carl pulled into Rayburn's parents' driveway, pulling behind Chester Rayburn's F-150 pickup. They left the girl there. With weapons in hand, they got out of the microbus and walked around the dog poop.

Rayburn pounded on the door several times and waited for someone to answer.

He got his wish two seconds later as the door swung open. Chester Rayburn stood there, a hard hat on his head, a steel lunch box in his hand.

He gasped upon the sight of his son.

"You—"

He didn't get the rest of his sentence out. Rayburn lifted his gun and pulled the trigger, the suppressor reducing the sound from a firecracker to clapping hands.

Chester Rayburn took the bullet in the chest and dropped hard, falling backward, the collision resembling rolling thunder. His hard hat toppled off and collided with the fireplace. Half a minute later, Rayburn and Carl heard barking and padding feet.

Carl brought his gun up and fired as Diesel came into the living room.

The dog slumped as the blood poured out of the wound between his eyes.

"Did you have to shoot the dog?" Rayburn said, turning toward Carl. "I could have handled him."

Carl's look simply said sorry.

"Bobby Ray!"

Rayburn turned and saw his mother standing in the doorway between the living room and the kitchen. She didn't have the look of someone who was happy to see her son after so long.

Rayburn, on the other hand, looked at his mother with a wistful gaze, as if he wouldn't see her again.

"What in the hell are you doing here? What happened to your fath—oh my God," she said, noticing her husband on the floor, dying. Blood flowed from the wound to pool on the carpet. She turned her eyes toward her son.

Rayburn noticed that the woman—the woman he loved most in the world, the woman that gave birth to him, the woman he could count on most—had hatred in her eyes. Spittle flew from her mouth.

"You ungrateful little bastard," she screamed. "How dare you come into my house like this when you should be dead?!"

Rayburn took half a step backward, shock registering across his face. But within seconds, he was rational about everything.

Why am I shocked by this? Why am I not surprised? She didn't stand by me during it all, she didn't come to see me in prison. She didn't want to see me die. She wasn't truly one of my people to begin with, he thought.

He brought the gun up and pointed it right at his mother. He walked toward her with hurried steps.

Marjorie Rayburn couldn't move as her son approached with fiery wrath in his eyes.

"I'll be dead when I'm damn good and ready to die," he said, his teeth clenched. He jammed the barrel into the bridge of her nose. "But you're going to die now."

He pulled the trigger. Another clap.

Rayburn's mother crumpled at his feet. He and Carl had taken out his entire family. He didn't show any emotion or feel the weight of the world leave his shoulders. He had long since said good bye to his parents. Putting a bullet into them was the only other thing he hadn't done up until now. Now he was free of their influence forever. For good measure, Rayburn kicked at her as blood shot out of the wound like a geyser.

He turned to Carl.

"Go get the girl and make sure no one sees you," he ordered, pointing toward the door. "Then make sure we get that van out of the farmhouse."

Carl went out and did as Rayburn asked. Two minutes later, he returned to the house with the girl slung over his shoulder.

"Now we just have to bide our time. You said the debate was tonight, right?"

"Right," Carl said, dropping the girl on the couch. They both heard her moan as her body hit the plastic. "What are you thinking?"

Rayburn grinned.

Wally's going to be there, he thought, remembering what Carl had said the other day.

"I'm thinking that it's time we take our Klan movement to a national level tonight," he said, his grin growing, "and make sure that Wally sees every little thing we do. Then, he'll know we mean business."

Carl began to chuckle. Rayburn joined him soon after. Within heartbeats, a living room that had already filled with the smells of death was now filled with the sounds of laughter.

"I need to check the radio to see if there's any information. Call for the van, Carl. We're going to need it for tonight's activities. And get word to our man inside the debate hall—everything's going to happen tonight."

Carl nodded and pulled out his cell phone, all while Rayburn stroked the girl's feet at her sole, bringing it down to his crotch.

He grinned as he manipulated her foot, all while Carl relayed Rayburn's orders. He grabbed the radio, then pressed the transmit button.

Chapter 24
Atlanta, Georgia
Thursday, November 1, 2012
10 a.m. ET

Jaclyn found it difficult to console Anderson after she received the phone call no one wants to receive. She managed to find out a little about the victim when Anderson quieted herself enough to talk. Roseann was 21, studied nursing, and Anderson gave her partner a description before she tumbled back into a quivering puddle of grief.

Jaclyn bit her lip and excused herself, the sounds of Anderson's crying chasing her as she walked away for a little privacy. She slipped her hand into her MZ Wallace handbag and pressed the center button on her gray cube as soon as she slid into the BMW.

She waited a few seconds before Alex answered.

"What's up, Snapshot?"

"The fecal matter has hit the proverbial oscillation device, Chief."

Alex snorted. "That's a nice way of putting it. What happened?"

"Anderson's cousin is the victim."

"Oh dear," Alex said.

"She's not taking it well."

"I wouldn't think so. Is she okay to continue the mission?"

Jaclyn bit her lip again and peered out the window to where Anderson sat. She was on the tail end of an ambulance, and Jaclyn now saw that the EMT's had slipped an oxygen mask over her face. She grimaced.

Hyperventilating? Jaclyn thought.

"I don't think so."

"Is this your honest assessment or is this your Human Resources assessment from the other day, Snapshot?"

Jaclyn didn't smirk or grimace. She recalled her comments from the other day, comments that earned her a stiff tongue-lashing over text by Alex. Her thoughts weren't exactly confirmed by Anderson's emotional outburst today, but facts were facts—Anderson's impartiality was now compromised.

But if Mark Hansen could get away with it, she thought, *why can't Anderson?*

Her thoughts continued: But Ciara Hansen, an agent who had been one of the forty-seven killed during Grant Chillings' initial attack on Boston, was Hansen's wife, not a cousin. Hansen had been able to close down his feelings in order to help Jaclyn track Chillings down; in fact, she recalled how he had escorted her to an evening out in Worcester to get close to the businessman. Hansen was within striking distance of Chillings and hadn't done anything. She didn't know if Anderson would be able to contain herself the way Hansen had; after all, Hansen was a veteran agent, while Anderson is just a rookie. Vengeance could change people.

It had changed me, even though I wasn't the one who got to take out bin Laden, she thought.

"Honest assessment, Chief. She's handled herself well, even though we haven't had to go up against any of the things I've gone through in the past. She wasn't with me this morning, so it's not like she's had to shoot at anyone so far."

Alex chuckled.

"Fair enough. But Jaclyn, I want you to ask her if she wants to continue. I don't want her to feel that she has to go through with this. Her cousin was just kidnapped by a racist escaped convict. Her head may or may not be in the right place, and she may not recall that her duty to country comes first."

And my parents were killed by psychotic Islamic terrorists, Jaclyn thought. *Is there a difference between the two, Alex?*

"I'll go and check on her in a little bit." Jaclyn paused. "If she's not fit to continue, what is your pleasure about Bennett's security until he leaves? I can't be in two places at once, Chief."

Alex sighed.

"Yeah, I know. We can't lock him down."

"Even though we technically already are."

"Right. Let me talk to the Secret Service again. Bennett has to realize that the threats are real, especially with the arena targeted early this morning."

"I wouldn't bet the mortgage on that, Alex." Jaclyn bit her lip. "And what about the security for the vice president, Farrell and the first lady?"

"Crap. I forgot they were there. Damn it," Alex said before sighing. "We need to get them out of Atlanta. The security risk is too great, and I want to make sure the line of succession is secure before we send the president into that hall tonight. Just as a precaution."

"Just in case I fail?" Jaclyn asked.

"You won't fail," Alex said after a moment's hesitation. "I know you won't. You have nothing left to prove. But where the president is concerned, we take no chances. Especially after Las Vegas. Understood?"

Jaclyn nodded.

"Understood, Chief."

"Good. Check on Anderson, then call Melanie Ruoff and tell her what I told you. I want the vice president and the first lady on the next flight out of Atlanta. If we have to scramble F-16s or F-22s from somewhere close by or from Andrews, then we will do that. We're not going to let Rayburn get the drop on anyone. Not on our watch."

"Personally Chief, I think both the president and Bennett should be locked down, their engagements for today canceled."

"Forrister has another round of golf at Augusta National this afternoon," Alex replied.

"It's off. No one plays 18 holes without my say so."

Alex sighed again.

"I understand, Jaclyn. But it'll be your ass if Forrister's short game goes to shit," she said before hanging up.

Jaclyn unclicked the gray cube, cancelling the distortion waves before she slid it inside. She slipped her iPhone back into her pocket before getting out of her BMW.

She walked to the rear of the ambulance.

Anderson sat there, her face tear-streaked. She looked up at Jaclyn, her eyes full of defeat.

"How are you doing, Jasmine?"

Tears welled in her eyes again.

"Not good." Her voice was muffled by the oxygen mask.

"She suffered from hyperventilation," an EMT said, noticing Jaclyn's badge, putting one and one together. "Her heart rate is rather accelerated, too. We're going to bring her in for observation for a day or so."

Jaclyn slid her hands into her pockets, turning her attention to Anderson.

That'll take you off the mission, then, she thought. She licked her lips a tad, bringing moisture back into them. *And I didn't have to make the decision.*

"You take care of yourself then, and listen to the doctor."

"I'm sorry, Jaclyn," Anderson said.

Jaclyn saw that she truly meant it.

"Don't worry about it," Jaclyn said with a smile. "We're going to get your cousin back, and we're going to get this psycho for what he's done. I promise you that."

Anderson cried again. Jaclyn firmed her lips, patted her on the shoulder, then turned and walked away from the ambulance—and her former partner.

Jaclyn had her hand in the handbag, pressing the cube again. She quickly called Alex.

"She's out, Alex. The EMTs made that call, not me." She explained what had happened and that Anderson was in for observation as soon as they got her loaded in and on her way. She didn't know what hospital she would be taken to, but told her boss that she was in good hands. "I'm going to get in touch with Melanie now. What are you going to tell Bennett's people?"

"I haven't decided yet," Alex replied. "He's still hunkered down at his hotel, and he's probably chomping at the bit. I just checked his itinerary; he doesn't have any commitments until tonight as it is. I just want him to get Farrell out of there. That city is no place for a woman right now."

Jaclyn blinked underneath her HUD.

"And what am I?"

"A highly-trained terrorist killer that is going to kick Rayburn's ass if he comes within a hundred yards of Georgia Tech tonight," Alex replied.

Jaclyn smiled.

"Now that is a safe bet for your mortgage, Chief."

"Good. Report in when you get DiVito and the first lady on a plane."

Alex hung up.

Jaclyn put her phone against her chest. The realization came to her that she was now working solo again.

She could feel her heart beating against her breastbone as the thought came to her.

I've pretty much been alone on this case as it is, she thought. *But now that I'm really alone, I wish that Tom were here, wired up jaw and all, even though he'd be a distraction when I don't need one.*

She pulled her iPhone away from her chest and found Ruoff's number in her recent calls list. She one-touched the number, then waited for her to answer.

"It's Johnson," she said. "I need you to relay this information to the president and his people."

***

Hartsfield-Jackson Atlanta International Airport
Atlanta, Georgia
Thursday, November 1, 2012
11:35 a.m. ET

A portion of Forrister's entourage slid through the gate leading to the tarmac, where Air Force One rested, gassing up for its unscheduled flight back to Andrews. Jaclyn didn't want the full motorcade to make its way down 85. She wanted this escape, as it was, to happen with little fanfare. The White House press corps was not alerted, and Jaclyn instructed Ruoff not to tell the media until the VC-25 was in the air headed home.

At any rate, there was little static between Forrister and Jaclyn as she relayed Alex's order.

"Sir," Jaclyn had said over Ruoff's speakerphone, "I stopped a cross-burning outside of the debate site earlier this morning, and Alex believes it represents a threat to the debate. It is her wish that we evacuate the first lady and the vice president from the city to minimize collateral damage."

Jaclyn could picture the president's eyes widening as he heard her speak the last few words.

"If that's what Alex wants, then Veronica and Lucia will be out of here soon." He breathed. "I'm glad Alex disobeyed me, Jaclyn. I'm glad you're taking care of this."

Jaclyn felt goosebumps tickling her flesh as the president's praise sank in. Her heart swelled. She tried not to smile.

"Thank you, sir. I'll do my best to make sure that your wife and the vice president are safely aboard Air Force One before I return to the city." Jaclyn said she would head down to the airport now, while Ruoff said she would contact the pilots and let them know what was happening.

"Jaclyn," Ruoff asked as soon as the president left the room, "how serious is this threat against the president?"

"We take all threats seriously, Melanie. Especially after what happened in Las Vegas. Hell, we can go even further back than that. Remember Ford's Theater?"

Ruoff said nothing.

"We're protect the president, Bennett and the governor. Don't worry about that. We'll get everybody in and out without harm coming to anyone."

Jaclyn heard Ruoff's sigh.

"Thanks, I appreciate that. I'll talk to you tonight." She hung up.

Jaclyn sat in her BMW as she thought of that conversation, now with the abbreviated motorcade coming to a stop in front of her. She slid out of the car and walked over to Cadillac One.

Both the first lady and the vice president looked anxious as they stepped out of the armored car. Jaclyn noticed that Veronica Forrister had her arms wrapped around her upper body, while Lucia DiVito bit her lip as she smoothed her skirt.

"Madame First Lady, Madame Vice President, this way please," Jaclyn said, waving the women ahead toward Air Force One. The Secret Service followed, their sport coats unbuttoned, ready to draw a gun if they had to do so.

Jaclyn hoped they wouldn't.

They were, however, stopped by a man wearing coveralls.

"We'll let you board in a few minutes, ladies," he said. "We're just going over a few last-minute checks."

Jaclyn's B.S.-o-meter nearly pinged off the scale. She felt the little hairs on the back of her neck stand on end.

"Why? They always board first."

"We're taking the right precautions. Miss Ruoff called ahead and asked us to make extra checks."

Jaclyn bit a curse back.

That would be something Melanie would do, she thought. *Damn it all! I wanted this to go flawlessly.*

"I can't have them out in the open like this," she said to the engineer, motioning to the ladies.

"Then bring 'em back to their car," he replied. "Duh."

Jaclyn wanted to draw her weapon and plug the bastard for such dissent, but she had already discharged her weapon in front of the first lady before. She didn't want to do it again unless it was absolutely necessary.

She turned and asked the two women if they could return to the safety of Cadillac One. They nodded.

It was then that Jaclyn's HUD screamed in alarm.

Jaclyn hadn't heard her Foster Grants scream like that in a few days.

"Oh, shit," she muttered. "Get down!"

Jaclyn used her shoulders to knock Veronica Forrister and Lucia DiVito to the tarmac, then tried to cover both of them. The Secret Service stood there, not knowing with the agent was doing to their protectees.

Then the tail of Air Force One exploded. Jaclyn stiffened up and felt the heat wash over her. She felt as if she were on a large barbecue, roasting away.

She soon heard hurried footsteps even with the sound of crackling flames roaring away. She looked up and saw the man in the coveralls running away from the blaze.

Now her B.S.-o-meter pinged off the charts.

She immediately gnashed her teeth together as she saw that the man had a thirty-yard advantage on her. She sprang up from her position.

"Keep an eye on them," Jaclyn told the Secret Service agents, all of whom had their Sig Sauer handguns out and at the ready. She wiped sweat from just above her brow. "I'm going after that fruitcake."

The Secret Service agents saluted with two fingers before Jaclyn launched herself into action, leaping into the BMW, turning the engine over and speeding away from Cadillac One.

With a quick flip of a switch in the center console, Jaclyn chose her weapon.

"Let's see how you like bullet holes in the back of your legs," she muttered as the servos and gears churned away.

In mere heartbeats, Jaclyn caught up with the fleeing mechanic. Jaclyn angled her foot on the accelerator, pushing the upper half of the pedal closer to the floor. The seconds passed quickly. Sweat poured down her face, tickling her chin.

She pressed the trigger.

The machine guns sprayed bullets, the ratta-tat-tat tinkling off the asphalt—and piercing flesh at the same time.

The mechanic tumbled face first to the tarmac and rolled several times. Jaclyn knew she caught him in the knees and the hamstrings, but also knew the damage to the man's face would be just as bad.

She slammed the brakes and skidded to a halt, fishtailing to the right. She put it in park before she sprang from the driver's side, a Walther P99 in her hand. She whipped around the side and hot-footed it over to where the mechanic lay. Our of the corner of her eye, she noticed people running to assist her, while others rushed toward the burning carcass that had been Air Force One.

Jaclyn leveled her Walther at the man's back. He wasn't motionless; he writhed in agony, and Jaclyn wondered just how much pain this bastard was in.

I wonder if I have to inflict more, she thought with a slight grin.

"Turn over," she ordered. He didn't move right away. Jaclyn nudged him over with her foot and shoved the barrel into his face. "Alright asshole, who are you working for?"

The mechanic spat at her, but Jaclyn deftly dodged it. She lifted her right foot as she moved to the side, avoiding the spittle, then stepped right on his throat. She inched the barrel closer to the bridge of his nose.

"I'll ask again, and if you try to spit at me again, I'll break your teeth, got it?"

She felt the bottom of his chin hit her shoe.

"Who are you working for?"

She watched as the man's nostrils flared. She applied a little extra pressure to his throat. It was just enough to make his eyes widen.

"I'll tell you, I'll tell you," he screeched.

Jaclyn released her hold on his neck and kneeled.

"Who is it?"

He took a deep breath and said, "The KKK."

"Rayburn?"

He nodded.

"Was this supposed to be an assassination?"

He nodded again.

Jaclyn sneered.

Dumb move, asshole, she thought.

"How did you do it? How did you get a bomb onto the most secure aircraft in the world?"

This time, it was the mechanic's turn to smile.

"I'll never tell," he said. A Georgia State Police cruiser came to a stop near him and Jaclyn. The state trooper eased his way out of the car.

"Cuff the bastard," Jaclyn ordered. She kept her gun on him until the state trooper had him in the back seat of his Ford Interceptor.

Jaclyn drove her BMW back to Cadillac One, where the Secret Service waited for her and some answers.

She gave them quite an earful.

"There's no way that the KKK could have gotten past your security unless there's someone inside. Do you guys have any so-called good ol' boys in the Service?"

"No ma'am," they chorused.

Jaclyn firmed her lips and jaw as she stared at the men. She knew they were telling the truth.

"Have him checked out," she said, "from top to bottom. I want to know if he's really on staff here, or if he snuck his way in. I'm thinking the latter. Meanwhile, we need a private aircraft to take the ladies back to Washington. Check them out from top to bottom, too. I don't want them plunging into a mountainside. I want it all done quietly. Move."

Several of the Secret Service agents went off in several different directions, all while Jaclyn stayed with the vice president and the first lady. Another agent stayed at the door to Cadillac One.

He opened the door for Jaclyn. She slid in.

She noticed, as soon as she closed the door, that the two women were even more nervous than before. Veronica Forrister had a scrape on her chin. Lucia DiVito also had a red mark on her upper arm, and her knees were scraped up.

Jaclyn tried to smile.

"We got the mechanic. He was KKK," she said. "He won't be KKK much longer."

The two women tried to smile, too.

Chapter 25
Atlanta, Georgia
Thursday, November 1, 2012
2:11 p.m. ET

Jaclyn stayed at Hartsfield-Jackson until she saw the first lady and the vice president safely away. A small Lear with an Air Force veteran at the controls took off for D.C. a few minutes after 2 p.m. The Secret Service was extra careful as the airport's maintenance facilities fueled the jet up for the flight.

Jaclyn had already been on the phone with both the president and Alex in the time between her detaining the crooked mechanic and take-off, and she received an earful from both, mainly an earful of praise.

But Alex reminded Jaclyn to stay vigilant over the course of the next six hours—especially as both Forrister and Bennett traveled to the Pavillion for the debate.

"Bennett's chomping at the bit, Jaclyn," Alex said, speaking as if Forrister wasn't on the line with them. "He's not too happy with us cooping him up in the hotel, and he rejected Farrell being shipped out. It's like he knows we're behind this, somehow."

"Dick can settle down," Forrister said. "It's not like his wife was nearly roasted by a hate attack."

Even over the phone, Jaclyn could tell the president was furious at Rayburn and the KKK for trying to take out the first lady in an attack meant for him.

"One of these days, he's going to see that we're trying to protect American interests, and to a small segment of the population," Jaclyn said, "that includes him."

"Don't worry about what Dick Bennett has to say right now," Alex cautioned, "just worry about finding out all you can from these two idiots we've captured, and seeing if they can tell us where Rayburn is and where the girl is."

Jaclyn nearly forgot about Anderson's cousin. She nodded.

"Got it, Chief."

"Jaclyn," Forrister said, "thank you for protecting Veronica. I appreciate your efforts."

Jaclyn's chest swelled under the praise.

"You're welcome, Mr. President. And thank you for placing your trust in me again."

"You've always had it. I'll see you tonight."

The president hung up, leaving the two women on the line alone.

"You can't get higher praise than that, Snapshot," Alex said.

"No," Jaclyn answered, smiling, "you can't."

"Check in after you talk to these two morons."

"Will do."

They hung up. Jaclyn switched applications to her text messaging feature and typed out a quick message to Tom.

"The shit is getting deeper by the hour here. AFO grounded. My partner's done. Working solo. I'm telling you, you can't make this shit up. I'll tell you more later. Love you. JJ"

Veroop.

Jaclyn turned the BMW's engine over and made her way back to Atlanta proper. She had work to do before the debate began.

***

DoubleTree by Hilton Hotel—Atlanta, sixth floor
3342 Peachtree Road Northeast
Atlanta, Georgia
Thursday, November 1, 2012
2:15 p.m. ET

"If Alex Dupuis thinks she's going to pull a fast one on us," Dick Bennett told Daniel Ruebenstein and Senator Jennifer Farrell, "then she is absolutely dreaming. Let me tell you something: She is the one pulling these little strings in this campaign. She's the one telling the Secret Service what to do here. These threats aren't threats at all. She doesn't want us to win. She wants her liberal pals keeping us 'safe'."

All three laughed. Bennett sat down, a high ball glass full of Scotch tinkling against three ice cubes.

"Can you believe this garbage she's throwing about? A cross burning at the debate site? Total bull shit. Just another red herring, the so-called KKK. Why, I haven't heard anything about the KKK in the last few days. Just a couple of kids playing pranks after that Rayburn guy escaped. He's not going to show his face; he's a wanted man. Why would he risk his new-found freedom? That just doesn't make any sense."

"It's liberal posturing," Farrell said. "Making things up that don't exist to scare the people." She paused. A sly grin crossed her face. "It's about time they caught up to us in political maneuvering."

"Right?" Bennett said. He looked to Ruebenstein, who looked like he had taken the appearance of a wallflower. "Daniel, sit down, enjoy yourself. We're only hours away from winning. Once we attack Forrister's credibility and tell the people that he had a hand in much more than he actually did during Sarah's administration, plus what he's done with the bill in Las Vegas and Los Angeles, and what he plans to do here in Atlanta, there's no chance that he wins the election on Tuesday. He'll only have a few votes to his name, and we'll reclaim the White House in a landslide."

Bennett took a sip.

"The sheep on both sides of the aisle will want Forrister's head on a spike after everything tonight is all said and done," Farrell said. "And as soon as we're in office, we'll have him arrested for abusing his power, and we'll make sure that Jaclyn Johnson is taken away before she can threaten honest public servants ever again."

Bennett smiled and pointed to her.

"Very true. Alex Dupuis will be laid off, of course. She wouldn't even be able to get a job sorting mail after January."

Farrell couldn't help but laugh.

"Have you drafted the bill yet?" she asked.

Bennett pulled the glass away from his lips, swallowing and nodding at the same time.

"I have," he replied. "Daniel has a copy for safe keeping. It will easily pass once the liberals are all out of Washington. I have received certain, shall we say, guarantees."

"Good. And all the charges against me will be dropped?"

"That is the plan, Jennifer. Don't worry yourself over it. Everything will be pardoned in the minutes after I get the nuclear football. That, too, is in Daniel's keeping."

"Then we better hope no harm comes to young Daniel in the next two and a half months."

Bennett chuckled as he drank.

"No, he'll be safe. He'll be put in Fort Knox if we have to."

Ruebenstein said nothing. He simply looked at his shoes.

***

Hickory Flat, Georgia
Thursday, November 1, 2012
2:15 p.m. ET

After they both moved Rayburn's dead parents and the dog to the basement, Rayburn had Carl lock the girl in his old bedroom's closet. He had shoved a kitchen chair under the door knob to secure it. Carl had chosen to sit on Rayburn's old twin bed with the shotgun propped on his legs, just in case the girl found a way out of her temporary prison.

And now, five hours after storming into his old house to re-claim it as his own, Rayburn awoke from a long nap, his body recovered from his exertions from half a day beforehand. He yawned and stretched, then went in to check on Carl.

The former prison guard stared at the door and didn't acknowledge Rayburn's presence.

Rayburn ducked out of his old bedroom without another word.

There was plenty to do with regard to the plans that one of his followers had swiped from the debate site: the plans told him where the Secret Service's snipers would be located on the outside of the building, which is where Rayburn wanted to make his move.

If I could neutralize them beforehand, he thought, *then it would be easier for me—or Carl, or someone—to grab Wally.*

He smirked.

It'll be hard to do, but anything is possible when you put your mind to it.

His followers would be coming over at 6 p.m. That gave him a little under four hours to concoct a plan of attack for that evening's festivities. He still hadn't heard a peep from the Fulton County Sheriff about his agent in the hospital. He checked the radio. The power was still on.

Rayburn grimaced. Not having that information, he believed, would hurt not his efforts, but the girl's life expectancy.

He picked it up and pressed the transmit button.

"This is Bobby Ray Rayburn, contacting the Fulton County Sheriff. Do you have the info I requested earlier; I repeat, do you have the info I requested earlier?"

He let go of the button and waited. Silence endured for several moments, until the anti-KKK slurs started. He grimaced and turned it off, forsaking his agent's life—for now.

He studied the plans further, wondering just when he'd kill the girl—and wondering if there was time to put a slight twist in the plan.

He grinned at the possibilities while he grabbed his parents' old landline phone.

Chapter 26
Atlanta, Georgia
Thursday, November 1, 2012
2:51 p.m. ET

Jaclyn mulled her thoughts over while she battled traffic on Interstate 85 North—well, she mulled them over as the autopilot swerved into free spots between cars, the perimeter sensors working hard to guarantee the agent's safe return into Atlanta proper.

Her first stop was to the hospital to check on the Klucker she had shot earlier this morning. She hoped she would be able to get the guy to speak without his lawyer present. Not that she cared if the lawyer was present to begin with. She wanted information, and she would get information.

Besides, he was already in a hospital, she reasoned. If anything happened to him during her interrogation, he wouldn't have to go very far for treatment.

She smirked.

Yeah, she thought, *he may need something silver removed.*

She drove on.

She arrived at the hospital that EMS had brought him to earlier this morning. Jaclyn showed her credentials to the woman at the information desk, who didn't want to give out the information on the patient in question.

Jaclyn chose not to beat around the bush. She leaned forward, her forearms resting on the small counter made of cheap particle board.

"Ma'am, I'm a federal agent working on a matter of national security. This is far greater than what you can deal with. I'm going to need to speak with your boss—or the president of the hospital, for that matter. I don't really have a lot of time today, so you might as well call the president now. Or should I have my president call your president? I have my president on speed dial. Should we race to see who can get their president on the phone faster? I just saved my president's wife's life. Who do you think will carry more weight?"

The woman gulped hard.

"I'll call him right away," she said, pressing the button to his line.

"Tell him it's rather urgent and to get here as if his shoes were on fire."

The switchboard operator nodded.

Five minutes later, the man Jaclyn presumed was the hospital president walked to her with an extended hand and a courteous face.

"How can I help you?" he said.

"I'm Jaclyn Johnson with the CIA. Are you the hospital president? I need to see the prisoner I shot up this morning," Jaclyn said, not measuring her tone or her words. She knew that hospitals didn't give out information about their patients, especially those who had been shot; the hospitals and the authorities didn't want assailants to come and finish off their victims.

But I'm not just another assailant, she thought.

"I'm sorry, but we can't let you—"

"Oh, but you have to," Jaclyn interrupted, tiring of the man already. She chose to utilize a course of action that she used in Massachusetts a year ago. She stepped closer to him, getting right into his personal space. "If you don't, I'll have you placed under arrest for obstruction of justice." She nodded as the man's eyes widened slightly. "In addition, I'll have the President of the United States call the Georgia Department of Public Health and have them take a peek into your records for the past decade, shutting the hospital down in the process. Do you really want that to happen, sir?"

Jaclyn watched closely as the man pursed his lips, as if the wheels were now finally spinning within the deep recesses of his gray matter. She stared, hoping that the dark Foster Grants she wore would prompt a faster response out of the man.

Or at the very least, she thought, *a little bit of fear and a little loosening of his bowels.*

She tried to hide her smirk.

A few seconds later, the man had still not come to a decision.

"So, what's it going to be? Do I get access, or do you get shut down?" Jaclyn demanded.

The man sighed.

"He's in room 802. Eighth floor. I'll let them know you are coming up." He grabbed the phone and had the switchboard operator hit the button. He waited a few seconds before he spoke again: "This is Mr. Hicks calling. There's going to be a woman coming up in a few minutes. She's with the federal government. She wants to talk with the prisoner." A pause. "I understand that, but I'm of the belief that she won't take no for an answer."

Jaclyn nodded.

"Yeah, she won't take no for an answer, she just nodded." Another pause. "I'm also of the belief that she has ways of making a person talk."

Jaclyn smirked and nodded again.

"Alright, she's on her way, and your reservations have been noted." He hung up and looked at Jaclyn. "They're a bit nervous, and understandably so. We usually don't let an assailant near the patient they had just shot up. The nursing staff would be appeased if you left your gun at the nurse's station."

"That I can't do," Jaclyn said, "but I will allow a nursing supervisor to come in with me. That's as amenable as I can be, given the situation. National security is at stake, sir."

The hospital president shuddered.

"I understand. Happy questioning," he said before turning away and heading back to his own office.

I hope he wets himself on the way, she thought. She headed for the elevator.

The ride up was rather rapid, as if she had somehow stumbled upon an express lift. The electronic voice signaled her floor, and the doors opened with a ding, slowly sliding apart. Jaclyn half-expected to see a matronly woman waiting for her as the elevator opened to escort her to room 802, but there was no one standing there. She exited and walked across eggshell-white tiles toward the nurse's station. The smell of Lysol hung everywhere.

The nursing supervisor, a healthy buxom black woman, met Jaclyn at the station and then escorted her to the Klucker's room. They were silent as they walked, even though the woman's rubber shoes squeaked away. Jaclyn felt that the woman was annoyed by Jaclyn's presence on her floor. A pair of Atlanta Police officers tipped their hats as Jaclyn approached.

The supervisor knocked on the door and then poked her head inside the room.

"There's a woman from the federal government here to see you," she said. She sounded as if she smoked three packs a day for two decades.

"I don't want to see anyone," a voice said, his Southern drawl apparent to Jaclyn's ears. She also heard the tell-tale signs of a mid-afternoon soap opera on the television.

Jaclyn stormed in. The supervisor stepped back. Jaclyn crossed her arms under her breasts as she looked at her victim. He wore a generic hospital gown and had intravenous tubes running into his wrist. A sheet covered him.

"You!" the man said, his eyes narrowed. "Get the fuck out of here, you nigger lovin' bitch!"

"Mr. Hall! Get a hold of yourself!" the nursing supervisor said.

But before she could get the last word in, Jaclyn stepped toward the man and smacked him across the face, hard. It sounded as if she had shot him without even pulling out her Walther.

Jaclyn quickly turned to the woman and pointed a finger at her.

"Be quiet, right this instant, both of you. I am in charge now," she said. The supervisor's mouth swung up and down, as if the breeze caught her jaw and tossed it back and forth. She couldn't speak, her consternation great—and for that, Jaclyn was thankful. She turned her attention back to the Klucker. "I'm glad you recognize me. Maybe you can answer a few of my questions now."

"I'm not saying anything until my attorney returns with a court order to allow my release as soon as I am better," he seethed. "And my lawyer's gonna sue your sweet blonde ass for negligence."

Jaclyn reared back and laughed, her hands on her hips.

"Funny," she said. "Real funny. Suing me for negligence. God, if I had a nickel for every time I heard that one." Jaclyn walked around the front of the bed and slapped the TV's power switch. It blinked out before she sat down next to the man. She grabbed his chart and checked for the man's name. "Tell me something, Mr. Gerry Hall. Who put you all up to burning the cross at the debate site? Was it Rayburn? Honestly, I think it was Rayburn. I don't think the other KKK units have enough brains to copycat."

Hall's eyes narrowed even further. His lip curled on the left-hand side of his mouth.

"I'm not saying anything."

"You just said something," Jaclyn taunted, leaning in. "That whole right to remain silent thing is just getting thrown out the old window, isn't it?" She chuckled softly. "It was Rayburn, wasn't it? A nod will do. I already know it was him, Gerry. He practically left his calling card all over it: the white sheets, the burning crosses, the kidnapping." She let it hang in the room. She smirked.

His reaction was just as Jaclyn wanted. He turned his head sharply toward her, a look of confusion on his face.

"Kidnapping? What kidnapping?"

"Rayburn probably didn't let you in on his other group's activities. While you folks were at the Pavilion, rigging up your little wooden T and setting it alight, another group of you Kluckers were in the process of kidnapping a black girl walking alone." She paused. "That young woman just happened to be my partner's cousin." She smirked. "And now I want the kidnappers caught."

Hall's face turned dark.

"I don't know what you're talking about," he said.

Jaclyn snarled and launched herself at Hall. She grabbed a handful of hospital gown. The nursing supervisor didn't move to stop her.

"Bull shit! You know everything, Gerry. You know where Rayburn will strike next, and you know where he's hiding out. Tell me that, and I'll make a deal with the federal prosecutor for you."

Hall twisted his lips as he went into thought. He soon took the bottom one between his teeth and nibbled.

Jaclyn breathed sharply through her nose and reached into her coat, practically announcing that time to think about it had expired. She yanked out her Walther and directed it at Hall's nose.

This time, the nursing supervisor protested while Hall froze. She had called for the police officers that guarded the door, but they didn't make a move.

Jaclyn grabbed his throat while turning the gun on the older woman.

"Don't move any closer," she warned. "I told you who's in control here now."

"You know that statements made under duress can't be used against him in court," the supervisor said. "My husband is a judge; I know this stuff. If his lawyer is worth anything, he'll get any confession quashed right away."

"He won't live to see the courtroom anyway, and that offer of the federal prosecutor just went out the window," Jaclyn replied. "Get out."

"I'll have you arrested. They'll escort you out and you'll be the one in jail."

Jaclyn snorted.

"I'll be pardoned with one phone call, lady. Didn't you notice how those Atlanta cops treated me just a few minutes ago?" She watched as comprehension soon dawned on her escort. Jaclyn motioned for the door. "Get out of here. You can come back for what's left of him when I leave."

The woman left, her eyes widened with shock and fear, stumbling out the door. Jaclyn heard the woman yelling at the two cops for not doing anything, and then heard their reply:

"We have an off-limits order on her, ma'am. She has carte blanche to do whatever she wants," one of the officers said. "I like my badge too much to try to arrest her."

Jaclyn smirked.

She returned her attention to Hall. A wet spot soon emerged on the gown near the man's crotch, and the scent of fresh urine rose to Jaclyn's nose.

"Had a little accident, didn't we?" Jaclyn tsked. "We're going to have an even bigger, redder accident if you don't speak up."

"Please," Hall said, begging around Jaclyn's hand, which still held the man's throat, "spare me. I'll tell you anything you want! Just spare me, please!"

"Oh, spare me," Jaclyn spat, leveling the gun at his nose again. "You're worthless to Rayburn, and you're worthless to the human race. After I'm through with you, your family will think you're worthless. Rayburn hasn't even checked on your condition yet. Isn't that nice?"

Jaclyn knew that to be a lie; Atlanta Police already relayed that information to her.

"No! Please, I know where Rayburn is."

Jaclyn's lip curled.

"Tell me where he is."

Jaclyn eased up her grip on his throat. Hall inhaled deeply.

I hope his lungs are burning, she thought.

"There's an abandoned farmhouse outside of Atlanta," he said. "He's there. I don't know anything about a girl though, I swear."

"Give me the address."

He did as she asked. Jaclyn saved it to her HUD and let go of the man's neck. He began to sob.

"Oh shut up, you big fucking baby. You're a fucking disgrace," Jaclyn said before moving to the door. "If you're lying to me, I'll be back to deal with you."

She exited and slammed the door. She turned to the cops.

"The hospital may fuck with me after all of this," she said as soon as the large man leaned forward. "They may not inform the feds if he's moved. My guys could hack into their mainframe in seconds, but I doubt they'll update the information fast enough. Do me a favor: Radio back to headquarters when they move him—it's a guaranteed certainty with how I treated that bitch of a nursing supervisor—and have them notify Langley when they do, and there's a shitload of java in it for your department."

The cops brightened and nodded.

Jaclyn patted them on the shoulder and pulled out her iPhone as she walked back to the elevator.

"I just love Southern hospitality," she said as she scrolled to Alex's number. She pressed it and heard it start to ring.

Alex picked up half a second later.

"What's up, Snapshot?"

Jaclyn told her what she had to do in order to pry what she needed from her victim. She pressed the button that called for the elevator.

"Good job, Snapshot. I'll alert the Attorney General and prepare him for the inevitable complaint."

"I don't give a shit about that, Chief. We have an address."

"We do?"

Jaclyn smirked as she stepped into the elevator. She waved to the nursing supervisor as the doors closed, and caught the middle finger the supervisor shot her.

"Yep, we do. Ready the reserves, Alex. It's time to take Rayburn down. We're going to get the jump on that racist bastard, Branch Davidian style."

***

Jaclyn didn't have the time to go on the trip, as she was needed elsewhere. She still had to question the mechanic before hurrying to Georgia Tech for the debate.

Yet she would receive the news of what happened on her way back from that second interrogation, which gleaned little in the way of additional information regarding Rayburn's reasoning to attack Air Force One.

The farmhouse, the Reserves had discovered, was empty, save for rusting equipment.

Fuck, Jaclyn thought, *we missed the bastard. Hall just earned himself a one-way ticket to the morgue, though.*

There were two items that made Jaclyn's ears perk up, though: they found two cards—both belonging to Roseann Teague—in the discarded farm equipment. There was no sign of a radio, or of Rayburn himself. There were no white vans, either.

"She was there," Jaclyn breathed. "She may still yet be alive."

I hope to God that she is, she thought as she drove toward Georgia Tech via the Westin Peachtree—she had something form-fitting to pick up and put on before she entered the arena—*or else my promise to Anderson won't be worth shit.*

Chapter 27
Atlanta, Georgia
Thursday, November 1, 2012
6:38 p.m. ET

Jaclyn checked her HUD's chronometer as soon as she pulled onto Fowler Street. It read 6:38 p.m. She knew that the president, Bennett and Governor Woodruff would arrive before 7:30 p.m. She had plenty of time, but was glad that she was able to do a quick check before the dignitaries pulled up along 10th Street.

The Secret Service agent that Jaclyn had run into during her first stop here—she couldn't recall his name, after everything that had occurred in Atlanta since she arrived on Saturday afternoon—met Jaclyn inside.

"Do you recall the itinerary?" he asked.

She nodded as they walked toward the control room. He handed her an earpiece that contained a Bluetooth headset. She slipped it into her right ear.

"I do. Dick Bennett and his entourage will arrive at 7:10 p.m. We'll sweep him inside and get him to his waiting area in the visitor's locker room. At approximately 7:22 p.m., if everything goes right, the governor will arrive. We'll get him inside and into the arena. President Forrister is scheduled to arrive at 7:30 p.m., and we will have him inside rather rapidly. We've found out that he's that escapee's target tonight." Jaclyn explained what had occurred today, starting with the kidnapping and the attempted cross-burning.

Agent Peters nodded.

"We heard about that, too. Someone escaped?"

Jaclyn grimaced.

"I'm trying to forget that happened, Agent—I'm sorry, I forgot your name."

"It's Peters. I'm sure you'll remember it from now on."

"Peters, right. I'll remember. It all has to do with the president and making a statement. But as you know already, this president is a difficult one to take down."

"After what happened in Las Vegas?"

Jaclyn spun on him.

"No, because I'm here," she said. They continued walking. "We're going to get the president in quickly. I'm hoping that he doesn't choose to shake hands or do a lot of waving to the crowd. I don't want to give any of Rayburn's people an opportunity to get off a clean shot at him, or anywhere close to him. You got that, Peters?"

He nodded.

"I got it, Agent Johnson. Where will you be again?"

"Over the course of the next half an hour or so, I'll be making sure your people have done their jobs. Then I'll be at Fowler Street getting ready to escort them in. I want your people to join me, especially with Bennett and Forrister."

"What happened to Agent Anderson?" Peters asked. "Why isn't she here?"

Jaclyn paused and gulped.

"Agent Anderson is otherwise indisposed," she replied. "She won't be joining us."

Peters lifted an eyebrow, then shrugged.

Jaclyn went about her business for the next twenty minutes, checking on every little thing. The arena had begun filling, the dais all alight in cameras and floodlights, the marquis above the dais welcoming the attendees to the building as well as the final 2012 Presidential Debate.

By the time she had completed her rounds, it was nearly time for Dick Bennett to arrive.

This ought to be a great few minutes, she thought as she walked to the Fowler Street entrance. She found Peters and several other Secret Service agents ready to do their jobs.

"Let's head out," she said. "The limo should be here any second now."

They all headed outside. A brisk wind met them. Jaclyn nearly wished for a heavier jacket, as she began shivering under the wind's healthy overbite. But even in a sportcoat, she was well-protected from the elements—and anything else that came her way.

A minute later, Bennett's limo pulled up.

"Right on time," Jaclyn said, checking the chronometer. She pressed the button on her earpiece. "Bennett has arrived." She walked up to the limo and opened the door. She stuck her head in. She smiled as soon as she noticed that Bennett's face had turned from surprise to revulsion in half a heartbeat. Jennifer Farrell's did, too. "Right this way, Mr. Bennett. And you, too, Senator." She spat the word out as if someone had laced it with poison.

Jaclyn smirked as Bennett nearly shoved his way past her, but she managed to walk right next to him. Out of the corner of her HUD, she noticed that he was all smiles as he waved to the cheering crowd.

"Are we having fun yet?" she said. They grew closer to the doors.

"The only fun I'm going to have is smearing Eric Forrister's supposedly good name during this sham of a debate, and bringing you down with him." He waved to a supporter.

"You're not in his league," Jaclyn added. "Don't stop to shake hands. Just go inside and wait for further instructions."

"I will not be talked to that way, Miss Johnson. I don't care what Alex Dupuis has put you up to tonight, but you won't win. And neither will the liberals." Bennett didn't stop walking. Farrell did the same, Peters near her.

Jaclyn could breathe a little easier once they were inside. They walked to the locker room in silence. They could hear the sounds of the music inside the arena as they walked through the bowels of the building.

Everything took less than three minutes. Jaclyn, Peters and the rest of the Secret Service crew returned to the outside world, where they waited for Governor Woodruff to arrive. As they waited, a police officer came up to speak with Jaclyn.

"Agent Johnson, there've been a few more assassinations. More judges, ma'am. Two members of the state Supreme Court and a Superior Court judge. Happened about an hour ago at the State Supreme Court Building."

"Shit," Jaclyn replied. She shivered, and not because of the breeze. "Let me guess: they were the judges who denied Rayburn's appeal and upheld his conviction, right?"

The officer nodded.

"Fuck," Jaclyn said. "And the others?"

The cop told her the others were under guard now.

"How about Schatzenberger, the Cobb County District Attorney?"

"He's alive still."

Well, the federal marshals are doing their jobs this time. Fantastic work, boys, she thought.

Jaclyn thanked him. He departed.

This is getting way too serious now, she thought while the governor's limousine pulled up to the curbside. He arrived at 7:21 p.m., a minute ahead of schedule.

Jaclyn's group surged forward, as if wanting to get this done so they could return to the warmth inside the Coliseum. Flash bulbs popped as Jaclyn opened the door to the limousine. Once again, she popped her head inside.

"Good evening, Mr. Governor. Right this way, please."

Woodruff nodded and slid out of the limo, his white suit pristine and unwrinkled. He walked into the arena surrounded by Jaclyn and his security forces to a round of applause. They didn't say a word, and Jaclyn wondered if he knew he had to appoint several new judges. Once inside the arena proper a few minutes later, he waved and shook hands with people closer to the floor and the aisles that led toward the dais.

Jaclyn also wondered, as she walked back outside, what the response from the crowd will be when the candidates stepped out onto the dais a little less than thirty-five minutes from now. She put the dead judges out of her mind.

Several minutes later, the president arrived. Flash bulbs continued to go off as Jaclyn opened the door and slipped her entire self inside, closing the door behind her.

"Are you ready, Mr. President?"

"As ready as I'll ever be. This should be a snap," Forrister said. Jaclyn saw that he was dressed in a blue suit.

"Did the first lady and the vice president get back safely? I hadn't heard yet."

"They did. Veronica is at the White House now." Forrister took a deep breath. "I still don't know what I'd do if something had happened to her and you weren't there."

Jaclyn smiled.

"Just repaying the favor that you did for me in August, sir. And making up for what happened in Las Vegas."

Forrister smiled.

"Consider our debt to each other repaid, then. Let's go. I have a debate to win."

Jaclyn opened the door and found the president's Secret Service detail waiting for Forrister to emerge from the depths of Cadillac One. Forrister followed. Jaclyn took a step behind the president as they walked to the arena. Flash bulbs continued to go off.

"Sir, just walk into the building. Don't stop to shake hands," Jaclyn said as Forrister waved to the voters. Her HUD picked up nothing on its scan. "Bennett didn't, either. We just need to get you inside for security purposes."

"You got it, Jaclyn."

Forrister waved a few more times before ducking into the arena.

Jaclyn keyed her mike.

"The president is in the building. I repeat, the president is in the building. Secure the building. No one comes in or out without my say-so, and no one is allowed in the tunnels until after the president, the challenger and the governor are safely out of the building. Have I made myself clear?"

The president's Secret Service escort also checked their status into Washington while Jaclyn heard varying responses in the affirmative over her headset.

Despite the cold outside, Jaclyn felt herself grow warm as she led the president toward the Georgia Tech locker room. She could feel sweat—whether it be from nerves or from the heat inside the building, she couldn't tell—gliding down the crevasse of her spine. She didn't reach for it, choosing to ignore it as the president walked into the locker room.

It was time to pay close attention to the security around the arena. Jaclyn walked to her command center.

.

***

A few minutes after 8 p.m., the arena darkened to loud cheers before the spotlights danced and tumbled about. In the command center, Jaclyn snickered.

"I didn't know a basketball game was going to break out during this debate," she said into her headset. Several chuckled.

A voice boomed out over the public address system:

"Ladies and Gentlemen, on behalf of the entire Georgia Tech family, students and staff, welcome to the Hank McCamish Pavilion for this final presidential debate of the 2012 election season. Please welcome to the dais, the challenger, Dick Bennett, and the incumbent, Eric Forrister."

Polite applause rippled through the arena proper as the candidates finally took the stage. Jaclyn watched as the two men approached one another. They shook hands, she saw, and noticed they spoke to each other.

"I wonder what they're saying," she said.

***

The president took a deep breath and came out through the long black curtain in front of him, and immediately felt a spotlight come down on him. The lights were bright and he couldn't see the applauding audience. He remembered the instructions the stage manager gave him, and presumably gave to Bennett, as well: turn to the right and approach your opponent for a photo op and a handshake.

He saw Bennett. He tried to put on a smile—a fake smile, nonetheless—as he approached the Democrat-turned-Republican, his and Sarah Kendall's former White House Chief of Staff. He noticed that Bennett didn't smile as he approached.

He smirked, as if he knew deep secrets.

And then, as if time had accelerated, Forrister stood next to Bennett, looking each other eye to eye without the feeling that a boxing match was about to break out between the two political combatants.

"Good luck tonight, Dick," Forrister said.

Bennett's smirk didn't change one iota as he stared into his former boss's eyes.

"Fuck you, Eric. You and your pathetic administration are going down in flames tonight. Jeff will finally rest in peace after tonight."

Forrister grinned.

"We'll see who gets the last laugh, old friend," he replied, extending his hand.

Bennett took it and shook it twice before letting go, not responding to Forrister's barb. They stood together for a few minutes more as the photographers took their photos, then separated toward their respective podiums.

The candidates were about to have their final say before the voters went to the polls in four days' time.

Chapter 28
Georgia Tech's Hank McCamish Pavilion
Atlanta, Georgia
Thursday, November 1, 2012
10:10 p.m. ET

Jaclyn watched the debate and endured nearly two hours of political mudslinging. Bennett brought up her name on several occasions, namely for her work in Boston, London and Las Vegas. No one in the control room looked her way. She bit her tongue, even as the Republican challenger did his best to sully her reputation.

Yet she was proud of the way the president handled Bennett, using a nifty counter that gave Jaclyn goosebumps.

"Here's the funny thing about what Mr. Bennett is talking about, folks. At the time of Jaclyn Johnson's unmasking by this man," Forrister said, pointing an accusatory finger to the right, "he was a high ranking senior official in my interim administration with one of the highest security clearances in the world. His blatant disregard for security and, in the process, compromising the identity of one of our top agents, showed me and the rest of the country that he cannot be trusted with our nation's secrets."

"This is the same woman that, on your orders, Mr. President, assassinated a well-respected member of the Massachusetts state House of Representatives, Jeffrey Harper!" Bennett countered, slamming his hand on the podium.

"Which, of course, happened days after your friend Sarah Kendall died at the Quabbin Reservoir. Let me refresh everyone's memory to the facts, shall we? Harper leaked loads of information to the press in an attempt to win a Senate seat during this election. That information included a bailout of the Massachusetts Bay Transit

Authority and a secret arms deal that, if my memory is accurate, you instigated and negotiated on behalf of the late President Kendall. I don't deny that I ordered his assassination, Mr. Bennett. But I am curious as to why you haven't revealed your role in his death, or have worked to cover up your role in Sarah Kendall's administrative scandals?"

Jaclyn smiled as Bennett blanched on national television.

Forrister continued.

"Let me take you all back to that day. It was July 22, 2011. I was just informed of President Kendall's trip to Boston, and I was saddened by her death. In addition, by the power of the 25th Amendment and the line of succession, I was now the President of the United States—even though it was this man's suggestion, as I have since learned, who told President Kendall and the Attorney General not to inform me of her resignation that day. The next day, a Friday, the government had discovered that Jeff Harper had received financial contributions to his Senate campaign from several dummy corporations. It violated multiple campaign finance reform laws.

"But that wasn't why we had him assassinated.

"Over in the corner, it was Dick Bennett who had suggested killing him for what he had done minutes after the Chief Justice swore me into office. Mr. Bennett had more to gain with Harper's death than I did: Harper's revelations about his mother's scandals," he continued, and that revelation sent a series of gasps around the arena, "mysteriously disappeared after her actions made Sarah Kendall a national hero in the eyes of many. It also meant that Bennett was in the clear. Until now." Forrister smirked and looked right at Bennett. He didn't even put his hand over the microphone to stifle himself. "If I'm going down for murder, Dick, so are you."

The audience applauded.

Bennett's face had turned the color of raspberry ice cream.

"You are constantly protecting the CIA and their illegal—" he screeched, but Forrister interrupted him.

"The CIA is just as important as our military might," he said. "The CIA is the one that gathers intelligence for our military to execute. And I know where you're going with this, Dick, so let me stop you right now: If the CIA gathers intelligence for the military, then what use to this country is Jaclyn Johnson? Well I'll tell you: Jaclyn, and all of our covert agents, for that matter, is smaller than an attack cruiser and a tank. When we can't send a tank in to take care of a problem, we send Jaclyn instead. And from what I've seen, Jaclyn handles things with the efficiency of a tank."

"Yes, tell that to the British, who lost not only their national soccer stadium while on her watch, but an aquatics center, a destroyed limousine, but also unlawfully breaking into a building while there. And then when she turned her back on your order, she killed—"

"A couple of dangerous terrorists," Forrister finished. "She executed the mission and the criminals without prejudice. She would do so again, if her Commander in Chief asked her to do so."

"Which won't happen on my watch."

"You need to get the chance to have a watch before you're flaunting bills to weaken our country, Dick," Forrister said. The audience cheered. "It's slightly ironic that Republicans have historically wanted to bulk up our military and be aggressive when it comes to war, yet you have said, time and again, that the first thing you would do—after pardoning your running mate for crimes she committed in Las Vegas, of course, that has to come first—"

"There is no tangible proof that Jennifer Farrell did anything wrong in Las Vegas," Bennett shouted. "Jennifer

Farrell is a good, decent, hard-working public servant, who gave me the hidden information about the bill you signed."

Forrister, Jaclyn saw, froze as Bennett's words registered.

"Hidden information?" he said, recovering.

Bennett smirked. Even in the command center, Jaclyn knew he had just struck political gold.

"Yes, Mr. President. The hidden line items that Congress didn't question you on, such as the bailouts for the hotels and casinos along the Las Vegas Strip."

An audible gasp rippled through the arena.

Forrister recovered quickly, though.

"Oh, you mean the bailouts that Senator Farrell wanted in the bill before she even said she would support it, not to mention that she pushed it through without a reading." Forrister sighed. "I guess Republicans and Democrats are more alike than we give each other credit for: the Democrats force a health care bill through without anyone reading it, and Republicans do the same with a transportation infrastructure bill." Forrister brought his hands together in a mock applause. "Congrats to your side, Dick. Congrats."

Jaclyn smirked as the crowd applauded the president once again.

"He's going to win this debate so easily. I'm headed to the tunnels."

***

10:22 p.m. ET

Jaclyn figured Bennett would want to high-tail it out of there as quickly as possible, especially after the way Forrister had just thoroughly embarrassed him. However, she had everyone on a schedule, and she wanted to keep to that schedule: Bennett would leave second, after Governor

Woodruff and before the president. It was a somewhat convoluted schedule, she knew, especially with someone as important as the sitting president still in the building. But if it riled Bennett to keep him here just a few minutes longer—*He thinks so highly of himself,* she thought as she paced in the tunnels, waiting for the governor to emerge from the arena proper—than necessary, then she would do it just for the aggravation—and the entertainment—factor alone.

You can be such a devil sometimes, Jaclyn Ann, she thought, just as the crowd erupted in applause above.

Four minutes later, Governor Woodruff emerged through the curtain near the rear of the dais, clutching his stomach in the vicinity of his bowels. Bennett followed through the same curtain. Forrister emerged through a curtain further down the hall, and Jaclyn nodded to the man as his Secret Service detail swarmed him and led the president back to the Georgia Tech locker room. Peters also approached, his sport coat open. Jaclyn figured his sidearm was on his right hip.

"Agent Peters, please escort Mr. Bennett back to his locker room to wait while I escort the governor to his car," she said.

But Woodruff interrupted.

"I actually have to really use the rest room," Woodruff said.

It was then that Jaclyn noticed that the governor had his hands over his lower regions. A look of pain had washed across Woodruff's face, which accompanied a rather pale complexion.

"Eat something that didn't agree with you, Governor?"

Woodruff reluctantly nodded.

"Chili dog," he said. "Get Dick out first, I can wait."

"I don't think waiting is the issue, sir," Jaclyn replied. She jerked her head toward the bathroom. "Go on. Hit the head, we'll get Bennett out first."

"Thanks." Woodruff waddled away, ducking into the bathroom.

"Peters, change of plans. Get Senator Farrell ready to leave. She should be in Mr. Bennett's waiting area. Mr. Bennett can wait here. He'll be perfectly safe with me," Jaclyn said.

Bennett's spine went rigid.

Jaclyn smirked as she gauged his reaction.

"You got it," Peters said, smiling. He turned and walked away, the sound of his footsteps drowned out by the sounds of voices carrying down the hall. Above her, Jaclyn could hear the telltale sounds of people leaving the arena.

Bennett stared at Jaclyn, and she repaid the glance. Their gazes were locked. Jaclyn had to suppress the urge to pull her Foster Grants down to show the former White House Chief of Staff the whites of her eyes.

"Have fun tonight, Mr. Bennett?"

Bennett huffed.

"Like you care," he replied. "You're going to be out of a job come January."

"You still think you're going to win after what happened tonight?"

"Of course I'm going to win," Bennett said. "There's no way the American people elect someone who cheats the system like your boy Forrister did with the Las Vegas-Los Angeles bill."

"But they'll elect someone who lies and scares them into voting for them, right?"

Bennett grinned.

"It worked for Bush Junior, it'll work for me."

Jaclyn's expression mimicked his.

"I would think the American people are tired of that, to be honest Mr. Bennett. And they're tired of being scared by invisible enemies the Republicans conjure up."

Bennett's lip curled.

"Oh, shut up," he said. Then he pointed his right index finger in her face. "And don't for a minute think about collecting an unemployment check when I sign that bill that terminates your job in January."

Jaclyn rolled her eyes. She turned her head a fraction and noticed that Peters approached with Farrell and Daniel Ruebenstein in tow.

"Your girl is coming," Jaclyn said.

Bennett's mouth moved in anger, but no sound came out.

"Are you ready, Agent Johnson?" Peters asked.

"Only if Mr. Bennett and Senator Farrell are ready to leave."

"We are," the Republicans chorused.

Jaclyn nodded.

"Let's go then."

Bennett's phalanx of Secret Service agents were nowhere to be seen. This unnerved Jaclyn, and she paused the entourage and spun toward Peters.

"Where's his Secret Service protection?"

Peters seemed to stutter at the start, but the words soon rolled off his tongue.

"They went out ahead and readied his limousine."

Jaclyn shrugged. She turned and continued walking with Bennett and company right behind her. Her HUD scanned the area immediately in front of her, remembering her order from earlier that no one was allowed in the tunnels after the candidates and the governor were inside the arena.

As she approached the door, she detected an orange glow near the entryway. It didn't have the texture of a spotlight, nor was it small. Jaclyn felt her heart begin to thud in a more rapid fashion. Her forehead turned moist. She bit her lip a tad as her pace quickened, her footfalls matching her heart rate.

"Stay back," she said as she reached into her jacket to slap an area of her blouse just below her navel. She felt the Kevlar lining of her jumpsuit, which she had put on back at the hotel, form up. Then she unhitched the strap that secured her Walther P99. She never broke stride as she opened the door and stepped outside, her feet taking her several yards away onto Fowler.

Jaclyn felt the breath leave her as she surveyed the crowd, her HUD superimposing the images on the screen. Her blood had suddenly turned cold. Goose pimples prickled her flesh, even underneath the Lycra jumpsuit. The tiny hairs on the back of her neck came to attention.

She saw the Ku Klux Klan, each person in the group holding a torch while wearing full regalia, behind a cordon of Atlanta, Fulton County and Georgia State Police officers, all in riot gear, ready to withstand the KKK's numbers, which were great. She couldn't even begin counting the number of them as they stood several deep along the entryway to Fowler Street, cutting off access to 10th Street. They did not chant, choosing to remain silent. They stood statue-like, the front of their white hoods vacant of any expression, as if they were ghosts of a far-off time.

Jaclyn could only stare at them in return, as if mesmerized by their presence. All sound vanished into nothingness, so much so that she didn't hear Bennett yell for Farrell behind her. Her heart, though, thumped against her breastbone with a viciousness she never believed possible.

He has to be here, she thought, gritting her teeth. *Rayburn has to be among these sick, racist bastards.*

A body—a pair of bodies—collided with her right shoulder, knocking her aside and sending Jaclyn's focus away from the KKK and toward the pavement. Jaclyn groaned milliseconds after the impact. The duo continued moving toward the cordon at a rather rapid pace, the footsteps gaining speed.

Jaclyn recovered and looked at what had hit her from behind. Under her Foster Grants, her eyes narrowed, her eyebrows knitting together.

She recognized the man's back.

She recognized the woman's hair, too.

Somehow, Peters and Farrell had locked in a spoon-like embrace, with Peters right behind the senator as they walked.

"Peters? Peters! I told you to hang back inside!" Jaclyn yelled.

Peters turned, bringing Farrell around with him.

Her HUD immediately whined as he moved.

"Oh, shit," Jaclyn whispered. She reached for her unstrapped Walther.

Peters had his Sig Sauer P229 out and in his hand, but it wasn't pointed at the KKK. It was pointed right into Farrell's side instead.

Jaclyn whipped the Walther out and pointed it directly at Peters. She didn't have an open shot, as Farrell had screened the Secret Service agent perfectly.

"Stop where you are Peters and let Senator Farrell go," Jaclyn ordered. She lifted her foot to move forward.

"Don't move, Johnson," he countered. He edged toward the cordon, backing his feet inch by inch, step by step. "You can't save the damsel this time. Bobby Ray Rayburn's going to get Wally, and there's no way you can stop him. Now!"

Jaclyn couldn't answer. At that exclamation, the white-robed Kluckers grew enraged, their voices rising with their anger. So too did the torches. They pressed forward against the cordon, and the police did their best to contain the sudden burst of activity from the previously-comatose beings. She then watched, frozen in place, as Peters practically dragged Farrell toward the cordon, his elbow locked over her throat. Jaclyn noticed a look of panic had registered in the senator's eyes, pleading with her to save her. She saw that he now pointed the gun at her instead of the senator. He turned his head briefly and smashed through the riot police just as someone in the rear of the crowd fired off several rounds of ammunition into the air. A sea of white parted for a split second, then closed up again rather rapidly.

To Jaclyn's HUD, the way they had disappeared into the crowd made it appear as if Peters had taken Farrell into the gullet of Moby Dick, the KKK's white robes a humanized caricature of the great white whale itself.

She quickly found her breath returned. Her hearing had come back, too. She heard multiple voices over the headset, wondering just what the hell was going on outside, along with the voices of the Secret Service—a part of President Forrister's detail—noting they were headed for the entrance.

She couldn't answer as she turned her head to the sound of the door opening again. She whipped her head around.

"Alright Miss Johnson, I'm ready to go—oh, my goodness!" Woodruff said, walking upright until he, too, froze in place, his eyes widening by the heartbeat as he saw the KKK en masse, as if for the first time.

"Governor Woodruff, get back—"

Jaclyn's gasp came as she registered the danger in which the governor had placed himself. A red dot soon appeared on Woodruff's throat.

Under her HUD, Jaclyn's eyes widened.

"Get down, governor!" Jaclyn yelled, before she turned and launched herself toward him, her back still turned to the crowd.

A gunshot blistered the night. Jaclyn took the bullet in her Kevlar-covered abdomen, much in the same way she had protected the president upon her return from London. The force of the shot knocked her out of the air. Her shoulder collided with the governor's chest, knocking him to the asphalt.

Jaclyn landed right on his chest and bounced to the pavement, too, the impact knocking her HUD askew.

Just as the gunshot went off, the crowd screamed. Behind the cordon, the KKK began its mass retreat, causing chaos to tear the fabric of Georgia Tech's campus apart.

A booming voice, as if coming from a bull horn, then ruptured across the tar-filled chasm.

"Hey Wally, it's your good old buddy, Bobby Ray Rayburn! That's what we call paying the price for not issuing that pretty little stay of execution last weekend! Enjoy Hell, you fucking piece of slime!"

A laugh followed it before tires peeled away, headed toward the east.

Jaclyn finally caught her breath once the president's Secret Service agents busted their way through the door, their own Sig Sauer P229's out and at the ready. Except that all the fun had ended, the KKK leaving as fast as their feet could take them.

"What the hell?! The fucking Klan?" an agent said. "Agent Johnson, are you all right?"

Jaclyn didn't hear him. Her eyes, white and wide open, soon closed before she lowered her head to the black top. Her head pounded, the pain in her retinas slowly going away. She saw in her fuzzy vision the effigy in white hanging from a tree in front of the State Capitol Building.

She gasped as realization flooded her as she adjusted her HUD. The effigy came into focus. She took a deep breath and kicked herself up, then turned to the Secret Service agents standing next to her.

"Take Bennett and the governor to President Forrister's locker room immediately. Lock all three of them in if you have to, and that's an order! The shit just got real deep in Atlanta. We're up against a whole completely different ballgame now. Move, God damn you!"

The Secret Service didn't question her order. They helped Woodruff up before escorting him inside. Jaclyn didn't look to see Bennett staring at her, his face pale and ghost-like, and she figured that he would accuse her of letting the Klan kidnap Farrell in order to give Forrister a better chance to win the election; she knew Bennett and his antics all too well.

She power walked toward the police cordon and to the officers nearest where Peters had slipped through with his political prize, even though pain zipped through her rear end as she moved.

"What the hell happened?" she asked. "Did you see Senator Farrell get taken away by the Secret Service agent?"

The cop shook his head.

Jaclyn spat.

"Damn it," she said. "Fuck!" She paused before she continued: "Are you going to go after those fucking cowards in the white robes?"

"They'll all be rounded up by the patrols in the area, ma'am. Don't worry about that."

Jaclyn looked out and saw several white robes on the ground with police officers straddling their backs, placing steel bracelets on their reverse-turned wrists.

"Good. I want them locked up on federal hate crimes."

Jaclyn didn't say another word. She turned and walked back toward the arena doors, her steps hard and rapid. She punished the pavement for the knowledge she had obtained in the past two minutes, for she now knew everything about Rayburn's mind that Doctor Seminoff had spoken of the other day, and especially his motives.

She now knew who the escaped convict's target was after all.

Jaclyn pushed the doors to the arena open and powered her way down the hall, as if she had channeled Rayburn's mind and needed to stalk his target, too.

Wally, she thought. *That's who it is. That's why Rayburn screamed it. The attack on Air Force One was just a feint. God damn it!*

It was time for some answers from the one who could give them, because she realized that it wasn't really President Forrister who Rayburn had in his crosshairs.

Chapter 29
Georgia Tech's Hank McCamish Pavilion
Atlanta, Georgia
Thursday, November 1, 2012
10:31 p.m. ET

Jaclyn stormed into a room full of animosity and anger. The door to Georgia Tech's locker room banged off the wall, bringing the conversation to a halt.

Bennett seethed as soon as Jaclyn entered. She saw his eyes narrow, the eyebrows colliding with the other side.

"You!" he screamed before he launched himself at her with his hands up, aiming for her throat. Woodruff, too launched himself, but not at Jaclyn. His weight managed to keep the Republican nominee away from her. "You're going to pay for this, you liberal sheep! You've lost me my running mate!"

"She's only been kidnapped, Dick," Woodruff said. "We're going to get her back. Right, Mr. President?"

"Oh yeah, ask laughing boy," Bennett said. "Like he fucking cares that Jennifer has been taken by the Secret Service."

"Dick," Forrister replied calmly, "we're going to find her, won't we Jaclyn?"

Jaclyn nodded.

"Absolutely not," Bennett said before he turned back to shove a finger in Jaclyn's face from behind the governor. "It won't be that snot-nosed CIA punk who can't even keep her protectees safe. It'll be someone of my choosing, someone who'll—"

Jaclyn's fist came around the governor's right ear and drilled Bennett right in the nose. Cartilage snapped just before he staggered backward, the blow unforeseen. Blood soon flowed from his nostrils, coating the skin above his upper lip. He managed to maintain his balance and didn't fall to the floor.

She knew it wouldn't be long before he tasted copper.

"Bennett, I am through with taking your right wing bull shit. I will find Rayburn and the senator, regardless if it turns my stomach, and I will get her back into your boudoir by the end of the weekend. So sit the fuck down and pay close attention to what the facts are; we know how much you Republicans have a problem with doing that," Jaclyn said.

Bennett, still seething and breathing through his mouth, relaxed a bit. He pushed himself away from Woodruff, leaving a red smear on the governor's usually pristine white suit near the right bicep. He backed away from her, even though he never took his eyes off her.

Jaclyn let her gaze linger on Bennett for a few more seconds before she remembered what had happened outside. She reached around and, after feeling around the back of her blouse for a few seconds, picked something out of the Lycra.

She took a deep breath.

"Governor," she said, making the man in front of her turn abruptly. "Two things: First, Rayburn killed several of your judges earlier tonight. I didn't know if you knew or not. I'm sorry. Second, I have something for you." She held up what she had dug out. It was silver and gleamed in the artificial light. "I think this belongs to you."

Jaclyn grabbed his hand and held it open. She then dropped the bullet into his palm.

Woodruff blanched. Jaclyn noticed that his face muscles quivered slightly as he looked at what could have penetrated—violated—his body had it not been for her intervention.

She could see the wheels spinning in his mind, just from the way he looked at the bullet. She waited for him to recoil, to drop the bullet as if it had scalded his flesh, as if it had been freshly fired and ready to burrow its way through the palm. He had turned pliable, his jowl's quivering, and

Jaclyn knew that he would give her any information that she wished after what had happened. She tried to hide her smirk.

His eyes turned toward her.

"How are you still alive after that?" he breathed.

"It's completely classified, sir. I hope you understand that I can't answer that question. But I hope you can answer a few questions for me."

Woodruff blinked his confusion away.

"Of course, Miss Johnson. Anything," he replied.

Jaclyn crossed her arms underneath her breasts, her forearms coming to rest on the cool satin material of her blouse. She could still feel the Kevlar lining engaged.

"You're Wally," she said.

This time, Woodruff's face twisted into something unrecognizable.

"I detest that moniker," he said. "I am Wallace Wellington Woodruff the Fourth. I go by no other name."

Jaclyn mouthed the name.

"You know what I just realized? Your initials are the same as an Internet URL. That's totally cool, if you think about it."

Woodruff rolled his eyes.

"As if I hadn't heard that one twenty times already this week. Shall I plink another nickel into the jar?" He sighed. "What is your point, Miss Johnson?"

"You're Rayburn's target," she said.

Woodruff stared.

"I don't understand what you mean."

"Me either Jaclyn," Forrister said, quiet until that point.

"It's quite simple, sirs." She turned to Forrister. "Alex was wrong, Mr. President. You're not the target we were worried about. It was the governor all along."

Jaclyn felt the stunned silence reverberate throughout the room, radiating away from the governor and the president. Bennett, Jaclyn noticed, said nothing.

"Me?" Woodruff whispered. "Why?"

"You didn't issue the stay on Friday night," Jaclyn coolly replied. "The prison psychologist told my partner and I that in the days leading up to the execution, Rayburn had shouted the name Wally in his sleep. He also said that it all comes down to Wally, over and over and over again."

Jaclyn watched as Woodruff shuddered. Forrister stepped forward and consoled the governor.

"So I'm responsible for everything that's happened," Woodruff said. Jaclyn saw tears in his eyes.

"No sir, I don't believe so. If I had recognized the connection before this, I don't think it would have made one iota of difference. We would have probably put you under Secret Service protection, or protection of the federal marshals, but as we saw tonight, even with the Secret Service, things fall through." Jaclyn looked toward Bennett. "Mr. Bennett, I think we're going to need to give you a new Secret Service detail."

"Why?" Bennett said, his eyebrows lifting. "I happen to like my detail."

"More than likely, your detail is dead, or in some hidden room here in the Pavillion. Peters sold us all out. I don't know how the fuck he did it, but I have the feeling that he works for Rayburn. How he remained in contact with him—"

Jaclyn's eyes widened underneath her HUD, and her lips parted a centimeter. A gasp rattled her teeth. While her silence enveloped the room, Forrister turned to his detail and ordered them to fan out and search for Bennett's detail, and hopefully find them alive. Feet rushed for the door.

"That's it," she whispered before she brought her voice back to its normal timbre. "Rayburn used radio communication to inform the authorities about the kidnapping last night. I'm willing to bet that they used that to contact Peters and the other Klan members over the course of the past week."

"But can you prove all of that, Jaclyn?" Forrister asked. She sniffed.

"Not at all, but it's the best hypothesis we have."

The three men in the room looked as if Jaclyn's words had sobered them.

"Wallace, we'll give you any and all protection the government can spare, until this Rayburn bastard is brought down," Forrister said, bringing the attention back on Woodruff.

"But how is Johnson going to be able to protect Wallace when she's supposed to be looking for Jennifer?" Bennett said.

Jaclyn tried not to cough as she heard what Bennett had said, but the sharp intake of air went down the wrong pipe. She resisted sending her pinky finger on a spelunking spree inside her ear canal, too.

Apparently my decking him has knocked some sense into him after all, she thought.

"Why Dick," Forrister said, "I thought you were against the CIA and for all they're about. Is this a change of heart?"

This time, Jaclyn tried to suppress a grin. A tiny one showed as the president verbally bitch-slapped his opponent. Bennett tried his best to sneer, but that facial expression didn't emerge, and instead turned into a grimace.

"I was just thinking that you would order Johnson to find Farrell."

"I'm going to find the senator Mr. Bennett, like I already said. I don't need an order from the president for that," Jaclyn said. "We have to determine where she is. I'm ninety-nine percent certain that Peters worked for Rayburn, and that he's now holding her hostage. We need to draw him out somehow, with Farrell in tow."

"And how do we do that?" Woodruff asked.

"What's your plan, Jaclyn?" Forrister added.

Jaclyn tapped her fingertips against her lips as she began to pace slowly, her head bowed. The three men watched her intently as her clicks against the hardwood floor echoed.

She snapped her fingers as she brought her head up.

"Rayburn thinks that the governor is dead," she said. "He doesn't know that I took the bullet for him."

"For which I still don't completely understand why you're still alive after doing that, but I thank you for saving my life."

Jaclyn grinned.

"You're welcome. I want to burst Rayburn's bubble, Governor. And for that, I need you to do something for me."

She explained what she wanted.

The three men couldn't help but grin as she finished.

***

Hickory Flat, Georgia
Thursday, November 1, 2012
10:59 p.m. ET

The white van pulled into the driveway of Rayburn's dead parent's house just before 11 p.m. Rayburn leaped out of the side first, and ordered Peters and Carl to carry the senator inside. He watched as the bound and blindfolded woman struggled against Carl and Peters' meaty hands. They slipped into the house, and as Rayburn turned the television on, Carl and Peters tossed Farrell onto the couch, careful not to snap the valuable hostage's neck.

"Now, let's see just what leads the news: the debate, or what transpired afterward," Rayburn said as he sat down. He turned his head to Peters. "Take off the blindfold, but leave the gag on."

The corrupt Secret Service agent did as Rayburn ordered. He ripped it off. Farrell's hair tossed about.

Rayburn grinned as Farrell's eyes, cold and hard and full of fear—*yes*, he thought, *she fears me*—turned toward him.

"It's time for the news, senator." Rayburn grinned. He turned to the television.

The anchor began:

"Terror at the debate: The Ku Klux Klan causes chaos that led to the capture of the Republican vice presidential candidate, and the near shooting of Governor Wallace Woodruff. Now, on the WSB 11 o'clock news."

Rayburn's eyes widened as the words registered.

No, that can't be, he thought. *I killed him. I killed the bastard that nearly had me killed!*

He felt his eyes narrow as he returned his gaze toward the news.

"Breaking news to the WSB newsroom this evening: Georgia Governor Wallace Wellington Woodruff IV was nearly killed tonight just minutes after the final presidential election ended at Georgia Tech's McCamish Pavillion. Eyewitness reports indicate that not only that, but Republican vice presidential nominee Jennifer Farrell, a United States Senator from Nevada, was kidnapped by a corrupt Secret Service agent working for the Ku Klux Klan. We go live now to Georgia Tech, where Catherine Jackson is standing by with the latest. Catherine?"

"Trina, the activity began in a rush as the Secret Service and the CIA joined together to escort the players in tonight's debate, President Eric Forrister and Republican challenger Dick Bennett, as well as Senator Jennifer Farrell and Governor Woodruff, out of the arena to their cars after the event's conclusion. But with the Ku Klux Klan standing outside the arena entrance on Fowler Street, things heated up rather quickly."

Rayburn watched as the network switched to video, showing the viewers everything: of the woman's stand against Peters' passing with Farrell in tow, of Woodruff coming out to see the chaos caused by Rayburn's hooded cronies, to the woman leaping in front of Woodruff to take the bullet intended for him.

Then Rayburn heard his own voice. He sneered briefly, then brought his hands up to his chin as he leaned forward.

"This woman, who we understand to be Jaclyn Johnson of the CIA, the woman whose heroic acts have saved several cities in the past year and a half, leaped in front of the governor to take the bullet. But miraculously, she survived the attack and walked away. She—"

"Catherine," the anchor interrupted, "I see over your shoulder that President Forrister, Dick Bennett, Governor Woodruff and Jaclyn Johnson approaching a podium. Let's hear from them."

Rayburn's cheek twitched as his target came into view.

"Wally, you fat fuck," he said. "You're supposed to be dead."

The President of the United States stepped up to the podium first, Rayburn saw. He also noticed that both Bennett and Woodruff looked harried and frightened by what had happened. Forrister, though: Forrister looked cool, calm and collected, looking more and more like a Commander in Chief that had been in these situations before.

Rayburn couldn't recall when he had last seen a president like this: quite possibly it was Bush after 9-11.

Then, the president spoke to the cameras.

"My fellow Americans. Tonight, tragedy has struck Atlanta, and our great political system. As an agent of the federal government led out my former White House Chief of Staff Dick Bennett and his running mate, Senator Jennifer Farrell of the great state of Nevada, an agent of the Secret Service that had been an advance for the debate site, with the help of the Ku Klux Klan, created a diversion by kidnapping Senator Farrel, just before a gunman took aim and fired on the governor of the great state of Georgia, and my friend, Wallace Wellington Woodruff IV. If not for the courageous acts of a certain special agent of the CIA, Governor Woodruff would have died tonight.

"Our agent, Jaclyn Johnson, informed myself, Mr. Bennett, and Governor Woodruff what had occurred in the moments before and the moments after Senator Farrell was taken and before she took the bullet that could have ended the governor's life. She indicated to us that the man behind what occurred tonight is Bobby Ray Rayburn, a man who recently escaped from the Georgia State Prison system. He has been at large since the early hours of Saturday morning, and is considered to be armed and dangerous. We're asking the public to contact the Atlanta Police Department, the Fulton County Sheriff's Office, or the Georgia State Police, should you come in contact with Mr. Rayburn. In addition, I have ordered Agent Johnson to kill Bobby Ray Rayburn should she find him first, as well as find and rescue Senator Farrell."

Rayburn felt his heart skip a beat. He brought his body back into the chair before bringing his fingers together in the form of a steeple. His elbows rested on the armrests.

The president continued.

"Mr. Bennett and I stand together to condemn these attacks on an incredible public servant, and both of us promise to stand behind Governor Woodruff during this trying time. Dick."

The president stepped away from the podium, only to have Bennett take his place. The Republican put both hands on the sides of the podium as he looked out toward the glaring, bright lights.

"Thank you Mr. President for letting me stand beside you tonight. The acts of these people are deplorable and cannot be tolerated in a peaceful society. I stand in unison with the president because we both believe that acts of this nature are deplorable parts of our history. I stand behind the authorities here in the great state of Georgia to do whatever must be done to bring these cowards to justice. I also stand behind Jaclyn Johnson, a woman whose reputation that I have done my best to ruin. If she can take out Bobby Ray Rayburn and bring my running mate back to my campaign, I'll take back everything I've ever said about her. I've seen what she can do, and I know she is capable of doing this."

The camera panned to the left as Bennett turned his head and nodded to the blonde-haired woman wearing the dark sunglasses. Rayburn noted that she was the same woman in the photos his agent had taken a few days previous. He blew out a long breath as he watched Johnson stare at Bennett without a reaction.

Bennett stepped away. Governor Woodruff then took the podium. He, too, like Bennett, placed his hands on the sides and tried not to weep.

"I really have nothing to say tonight, only to publicly thank the president as well as Dick Bennett for putting aside their respective campaigns. I really appreciate both of their words, and I appreciate the work that Jaclyn did tonight." He turned and nodded to Jaclyn.

This time, Jaclyn nodded back. Woodruff stepped away, and Jaclyn stepped forward. She stared directly into the lens of the WSB camera.

Several miles away, Rayburn saw the stare Johnson gave and felt a chill squirrel its way up his spine. He felt like roots had grown out of his ass and had secured the lower half of his body to his dead father's old easy chair, as if the chair consisted of strong soil. He couldn't avert his eyes, no matter how much he willed his face to move.

Even though he couldn't see her eyes behind the dark sunglasses, he believed he saw his future in those lenses.

The only future he believed he saw was his death.

He blinked his fear away as she spoke.

"Rayburn, I'm putting you on alert right now: I will come for you. I will hunt you down. I will make you feel the pain that you have inflicted upon your victims, including the girl you kidnapped last night. I will make sure you feel the bite of my Walthers, and I will make sure you die a painful death."

Jaclyn reached up and pulled her sunglasses down, revealing what lay under them.

Rayburn felt himself shrink as he saw the whites of her eyes.

Peters and Carl muttered, "My God," when they saw her do this.

"You won't make it through the weekend, Bobby Ray. I'm going to treat you like I've treated all of my targets. I'm going to shoot off every finger and every toe. I'm going to make you cry for your momma, boy. And I'm going to make sure you suffer."

She slid the sunglasses up and stepped away. The president returned to the podium. He adjusted the microphone

"Rayburn, you have one day to give yourself up. Just one day. If you don't give yourself up, the manhunt begins. You have until midnight tomorrow—the time you were supposed to die last week—to turn yourself and your hostages over to authorities. You're going to die anyway, Rayburn. We're just giving you the opportunity to choose the manner of your own death: either by lethal injection, or by lead poisoning. It's your choice." He paused. "May God have mercy on you and your soul, and may God bless the United States of America."

Rayburn tuned the on-site reporter off as the president and the others turned and went back inside the arena. He stared at the television, the tips of his fingers now in his mouth and between his teeth. He gnawed at the skin the rested underneath his dirty fingernails. There was nothing on the news about the dead judges. He wondered when that would be brought up.

"Bobby Ray," Carl said. "What are we going to do?"

Rayburn snapped his head toward him.

"What do you mean we?"

"She's going to kill us, too."

Rayburn waved him off. He stared at the television again, his mind a tumult of thought, until he took a deep breath.

"Bring me the black bitch. Both of you."

They left the room, leaving him alone with Senator Farrell. He didn't speak at first, but instead glared at her.

Farrell, he saw, shuddered under his gaze.

"What do you think of that, Senator? Your friends are trying to secure your release." He got up and moved next to her. He sat down and loosened her gag. "Although I find it kind of funny: A Republican and a Democrat seeing eye to eye on something." He snickered. "I bet it took the president a lot of gumption to get him to agree to speak alongside of him, don't you think?"

Farrell worked her mouth to regain feeling.

"Dick Bennett is a visionary. I bet it was all his idea."

"But he said, and I quote, that he'd take everything he said about that Johnson babe back if he caught up with me and rescued you."

"Horse shit, you scum-sucking asshole. He's just playing for the cameras."

Rayburn grinned, a malicious gleam in his eye.

"Maybe you and I can play for a camera, too."

Farrell looked repulsed.

"I'm pretty good company," he said, reaching up and stroking her cheek. Farrell made a move to bite him.

Rayburn's lip curled. He reared back and backhanded her across the face, the crack echoing through the living room. Rayburn smiled as Farrell turned her face back toward him, tears forming in the depths of her eyes. The slap also drowned out the sounds of the young black woman struggling.

"Carl, let Nathan hold her while you keep the senator company," he ordered. Carl slid in where Rayburn had sat and wrapped an arm around Farrell. Farrell tried to push away, but the bald-headed ex-guard kept a firm grip on her shoulder. "You see, Senator Farrell, you're not the only woman who has enjoyed my Southern hospitality. This young woman is the one Miss Johnson spoke of a few minutes ago. Say hello to each other."

Roseann Teague tried to speak through her gag. Farrell said nothing.

"I know the nigger can talk," Rayburn said. "Now you say something, senator."

Farrell mumbled a hello before the tears rumbled down her cheeks.

Rayburn grinned.

"Good, now Senator Farrell, let me tell you something. I've had this bitch several times since early this morning, and she is the tightest bit of pussy I've ever had." He stroked her cheek just like he'd done to the senator. "I bet you your pussy's a little tighter."

Farrell bowed her head.

"Carl, keep her head up, I'm talking to her."

Carl grabbed her mop of hair and yanked it back. Farrell whimpered.

"Maybe y'all can have a little fun together, maybe a little show for me and my boys."

Farrell's tears came faster.

"I don't like other women," she whimpered.

Rayburn turned to Teague.

"How 'bout you?"

Teague shook her head, too.

Rayburn tsked several times.

"Shame. Such a shame. Beautiful woman like yourself, from Las Vegas, is that right?"

Farrell nodded through her tears.

"Beautiful woman, from Las Vegas, and you've never had another woman there in that big city of sin?"

Farrell shook her head.

"Shit, I tell you, I want to go to Vegas and get my dick wet with some lesbians. Wouldn't that be fun, boys?"

The two henchmen nodded and chuckled. Peters, Rayburn noted, took a step back and to the right of Teague, releasing her from his grasp. She stayed there, not moving a muscle.

Rayburn chuckled.

"Well, you know something? There's not enough room in my bed for two hostages who won't fuck each other, so I guess I should take care of one of y'all now and just relieve myself of this burden. Who to pick, who to pick." He tapped his chin, then reached into his coat. "Decision made."

He pulled out his suppressed gun and, after aiming it quickly, fired a shot that caught Roseann Teague between the eyes from several feet away. Farrell jumped in shock. She screamed. Teague fell backward, blood and brain matter erupting out of the mushroom cloud that poured from the back of her head. Her eyes, vacant several seconds later, stared at the ceiling without knowing Rayburn had shot her.

Rayburn tsked again.

"What a mess. You see what I did there, Senator Farrell? You're a little more valuable to me than she is. Besides, she was starting to stink a little, while you're as fresh as a daisy." He laughed. "No, I'm going to keep you alive, and maybe use you as bait for a little trap. I'm going to get Wally once and for all, and no little blind bitch is going to stop me from taking what is rightfully mine."

***

Hank McCamish Pavillion
Atlanta, Georgia
Thursday, November 1, 2012
11:14 p.m. ET

The quartet had returned to the Georgia Tech locker room after their impromptu news conference, a little more life in their faces than they had before they walked out to face the media. Woodruff was a little more chipper now that he had publicly thanked the three others in the room. But Bennett still looked a tad grim as he faced the president and Jaclyn. The report came in just as they returned: Forrister's Secret Service detail had found Bennett's detail.

Suffice it to say, Peters—or someone else close to Rayburn—had executed them with a bullet to the back of the heads. To Jaclyn's HUD, Bennett looked vulnerable.

"So the clock begins now," he said.

"He has twenty-five hours," Forrister replied.

"He won't turn himself in," Bennett said.

"I don't expect him to do that," Jaclyn said. "Rayburn is cunning and calculating. He's going to want to make his move at his time. We need to be ready for when he makes his move."

"And just what are we going to do then?" Woodruff asked.

"Just what we discussed before we went outside," Jaclyn said.

Woodruff closed his eyes, took a deep breath, and nodded.

Jaclyn walked up to him and grasped his upper arms.

"I may be considered a hero to some, but what you're going to do is pretty damn heroic, too."

Woodruff smiled weakly.

"It's alright to be nervous," she continued. "It's one thing to walk unknown into the path of a bullet. It's a completely different thing to do so willingly."

"It's been a while since I've seen live gunfire up close. I hope I remember how to act around it."

"You'll be safe, Wallace," Forrister said. "We'll make sure you're protected the entire time—if it comes down to that."

"I appreciate that, Mr. President."

"Jaclyn, you will make sure that the governor gets home safely, correct?"

Jaclyn nodded.

"Of course, sir. I'll keep my eyes on him and the house, so to speak."

Forrister smiled. He clapped Jaclyn on the shoulder before he bade both Bennett and Woodruff good night. He departed without another word.

Jaclyn turned and led Woodruff toward the door, too, but as she looked back into the Georgia Tech locker room, she saw that Bennett had sat down and was looking at his shoes.

She wondered exactly what the Republican presidential candidate had on his mind at that moment.

Chapter 30
Governor Woodruff's office, State Capitol Building
Atlanta, Georgia
Friday, November 2, 2012
11:59 p.m. ET

It had been the longest day of Jaclyn's life since September 11, 2001.

Her ability to thrive and be active without a great deal of sleep came in handy on Friday. With the exception of a small cat nap after escorting Woodruff to the State Capitol Building at 9 a.m., Jaclyn was awake and alert, ready for anything. Nothing came, though.

Jaclyn had escorted the governor back to the mansion, driving him to and from in her well-armored BMW. She checked the perimeter before checking the interior, her Walther P99 out, the safety off just in case one of Rayburn's cronies wanted to take a second chance at hitting Woodruff. Her HUD didn't whine or squeal, for which she was thankful.

In addition, she called Alex after she noted that the governor had turned out the lights to his bedroom.

"You've had quite the day, Snapshot," Alex said after answering on the second ring.

"You ain't just whistling Dixie, Chief. This has been the day from hell, and it won't end until Rayburn's in the crosshairs of my Walther." She told her that she was on protection duty.

"Got your coffee?"

Jaclyn fingered the plastic cover that held in the contents of her venti triple shot caramel latte. A bit of whipped cream had spilled through the tiny opening. She wiped it away with her fingertip and brought it to her mouth. She sucked it off.

"Yep. A little Starbucks should keep me awake, and I have a good book to read while the HUD is scanning away."

"What are you reading now?"

"Let me check. I haven't gone through my Kindle for iPad list in quite a while. I finished reading some Daniel Arenson, and I read some M.P. McDonald before Tom left for London. Did you know we're still waterboarding supposed terrorists? I've never done that."

"I did not know that, but I think you're reading fiction, correct?"

Jaclyn sat up a bit straighter.

"Yeah, and what's your point?"

"Never mind. Don't let the book distract you, Jaclyn. You know how much I like to live in reality."

"I doubt Rayburn's men will hit him tonight," Jaclyn countered, ignoring Alex's jab. "They're too amped up right now. Too many hits in a short amount of time would lead to mistakes. Rayburn doesn't make mistakes. He managed to hide away from the cops for three days during his original crime, and he's avoided detection for seven days since he broke out of prison. He won't make a mistake. Yet."

"I hope you're right, Snapshot."

"Me too," Jaclyn said after taking a quick breath. "Anything new with Tasha? She hasn't texted me in a couple of days."

"Nope, nothing to worry about. Just a lot of texting with boys and wearing a goofy smile. She has a date Friday night with one of them and then another with the other boy on Saturday night." Alex sighed. "I can assign an agent to keep watch over her if need be."

"No," Jaclyn replied. "Don't do that. She'll never trust you or me again."

"Maybe I'll send Tommy."

Jaclyn rolled her eyes.

"Secret Agent Tommy is worse than a regular agent. I really think he needs a girlfriend, and no, not Tasha. We don't need that kind of drama in our lives."

Alex chuckled.

"I concur. I'm going to bed. Check in tomorrow. Is the president on his way back?"

Jaclyn shrugged.

"To be honest, I don't know what he has planned. I think he's staying the night and flying back tomorrow morning. The backup Air Force One should be on its way by now, though."

"And Bennett was actually somewhat sincere in his remarks."

"Yeah, but give him five minutes and he may change his mind. Time to read, Chief. Good night."

Both hung up and Jaclyn delved into Misty Johnson, Supernatural Dick. She read for several hours, making several checks of the perimeter along with the governor's security forces. At 8:30 a.m., Jaclyn drove the governor to the State Capitol Building and escorted him inside before she returned to the Westin Peachtree for a shower, a change of clothes and a bit of sleep.

Later in the day, Jaclyn had received several reports: both Forrister and Bennett had departed Atlanta for Washington—on separate flights, Jaclyn saw, making her grin—and Rayburn had yet to give himself up. She didn't expect him to do so during the daylight hours. He would use every minute available to him.

Yet as the president's window rapidly came to a close on Friday night, Jaclyn had taken to pacing in front of Woodruff's desk. Her stride was slow and methodical, her hands resting at the small of her back, her blonde hair up in a ponytail. Jaclyn wore a blouse and long blue slacks. Her holstered Walther P99 was at the ready, but didn't expect—

Her HUD whined in warning.

"Get down!" she shouted, hitting the deck in front of the desk. The sounds of Woodruff banging his body against his desk clanged in the room.

So too did the sounds of breaking glass over to Jaclyn's right. The shattered glass tinkled off the hardwood floor like hailstones, and the brick that came through crumbled as soon as it collided with the floor, too.

Jaclyn forgot she had held her breath as she hit the floor. Nothing exploded, save the window imploding, but her HUD didn't sense a bomb, nor did she hear anything ticking. She got up and dusted herself off. She noticed the spiderweb etchings in the glass near the hole, which was only the size of a softball.

"Governor, are you alright?" she asked.

Woodruff gave a mumbled "Yes."

"Everything's okay, someone just sent a brick through your window."

"Is that all?" he said, poking his salt and pepper head up above the desktop. Jaclyn walked toward the brick. "I've faced worse stuff than that."

She turned to him.

"It has a note tied to it."

"They always do. Probably someone who wants a bill passed." Woodruff stepped around his desk.

"Or it could be from Rayburn and his henchmen."

Woodruff took a step back.

Jaclyn frowned at him.

"There's no bomb attached." Jaclyn picked up the note and pulled it open. The brick tumbled into pieces at Jaclyn's feet. "It's from Rayburn."

"What does he want?"

Jaclyn scanned the note.

"He wants you," she said, looking at him from the paper. She held his gaze long, even as she held Rayburn's words in her hands. "He wants you to meet him at the bridge in Piedmont Park at 6 o'clock in the morning, and he will leave Farrell there in exchange for you."

Woodruff's face spasmed as Jaclyn spoke. He tried moving his mouth to speak, but no words flowed.

"Relax, like I said yesterday. It's an honorable, heroic thing you're about to do. I'll be with you, though."

"He won't stay if you show up," Woodruff countered. "He'll bolt."

"Which is why," Jaclyn said calmly, "that I'll be there, but not in a place he expects. We'll get you ready before you go there. Just remember that I need a clean shot at him. I'll be in contact with you during the whole thing via a small earpiece. I'll tell you which way to move. You just make sure you get the fuck out of the way so I can take him out."

Woodruff gulped.

"Okay," he breathed.

Jaclyn smiled at him.

"You'll be fine. Trust me."

Woodruff nodded this time.

"Stay here. I'll send in your security. I'm going to scope out the park via computer." Jaclyn turned and left the room. She sent the security in.

I also need to get him that bullet-proof vest we talked about last night, she thought as she slid into the secretary's chair and booted up her computer. *And I need a nice little toy for myself. I'm going to keep him alive by any means possible.*

Chapter 31
Piedmont Park
Atlanta, Georgia
Saturday, November 3, 2012
6:01 a.m. ET

Jaclyn had arrived at 4 a.m., bundled in a warm black coat and armed with not only a Walther P99, but also a Barrett M107A1 sniper rifle that she had slung over her shoulder. She parked the BMW in the parking lot of the Henry W. Grady High School, confident that at this early hour on a Saturday it would be untouched by anyone.

She set the alarm and her personal entry code before she trotted across 10th Street Northeast and into the park. Jaclyn found it ironic that Rayburn had tried to kill the governor on 10th Street Northwest last night and would meet his own end, if she had anything to say about it, at its kitty corner on the compass rose.

The park was nothing like any other park Jaclyn had known. In D.C. and in her hometown of Seattle, the trees there were devoid of leaves by now, their skeletal forms rustling in the wind. Parks were no places at night or at 4 in the morning, especially if a pedestrian had a bit of a paranoid streak in them: the trees there looked ready to come to life and scoop up a potential victim, a Halloween nightmare come true. Piedmont's trees, on the other hand, still had plenty of leaves on their boughs, for the most part, and even in the darkness, Jaclyn looked for one with sturdy branches near Lake Clara Meer.

Lake Clara Meer was a small body of water in the middle of the park, shaped like a freshwater boomerang with its curve pointed to the southeast. Trees of all shapes and sizes lined its shore, and Jaclyn noticed there was plenty of cover in the branches for her to post herself. She slung the Barrett over her shoulder and climbed a tree near the bridge but close enough to get a good shot off, ready to begin her surveillance. She pulled out a black mask and covered her head with it.

Nearly two hours passed as Jaclyn readied herself mentally for this last gasp of the mission. She thought of every moment she could remember this past week. The cross burnings. The hanging effigy of the governor. Of kicking some Ku Klux Klan ass. And of punching Bennett in the face. She grinned as that memory stayed locked in her mind for a few minutes.

Jaclyn checked her chronometer. It read 5:50 a.m.

She keyed her microphone.

"Okay Governor, you should have that earpiece in and you can hear me. You can make your way into the park any time now."

A minute later, Jaclyn saw the governor's limousine pull up to the curb at 10th Street. She spotted the white suit in the distance and watched as he approached. He looked like he was nervous about what was going to go down.

And Jaclyn told him that.

"You need to calm down, Governor Woodruff. I'm right here, and nothing is going to happen to you."

She slipped a knob on her headset up.

"I'll try," she heard him say. She didn't reply.

Before she had left the State Capitol Building, she had helped the governor put on a bullet proof vest, akin to the one worn by police officers and almost like the kind she wore as part of her Lycra jumpsuit, with a blood vest on top of the Kevlar. It fit well, and from her perch in the tree, she could see that it didn't appear, from her vantage point at least, to add any bulk to Woodruff's form.

But what she didn't tell the governor was that she had a tiny omnidirectional microphone sewn into the Kevlar in order to pick up everything that he and Rayburn said to each other—if they talked.

I want to know exactly what Rayburn's last words are, she thought, *right before I kill him*.

Jaclyn couldn't help but smile as her cheek twitched.

She watched as the governor sat down at the bench on the right-hand side of the walkway. It curved toward the northeastern spur of the lake, allowing not only the governor to keep an eye on the area to the south, but it also gave Jaclyn a perfect view of the meeting spot.

She hefted the Bennett M107A1 and, after pointing it toward the bridge, looked through the scope.

The area looked accessible to her bullet.

The corner of her mouth twitched.

Jaclyn pulled out her iPhone and, with the gun resting in the crook of her arm, she texted Alex.

"Governor in place for the final move."

Veroop.

She then sent one message to Tom. She knew he would be awake as soon as she noticed that it would be just after 11 a.m. in London. Her fingers tapped out the message, which she hoped would not be the last one she ever sent to him.

"My darling, I'm hoping to take out a dangerous man this morning. He's evaded captured for a week. I don't know if I'll make it out, but I want to let you know I love you. Don't text back. I'll text you. JJ"

Jaclyn stashed her iPhone and readied herself for Rayburn's arrival. She checked the chronometer in her HUD. It read 6:05 a.m.

He's late, she thought, biting her lip. Her HUD scanned away, and nothing approached the bridge from any direction. She took a deep breath and let it out slowly.

She waited for 6:10, and then 6:15, and there was still no sign of Rayburn. She nearly reached up to key her microphone to speak to the governor, but then her HUD began to ping away warning tones. Then she saw the slim, bald-headed man as he drew his weapon, walking slowly across the bridge—with Nevada Senator Jennifer Farrell next to him, being dragged along by two men, her face scarred by running mascara. She knew one of them easily—Peters looked over his shoulder and all around, keeping an eye open for her, she figured—but the other one, also bald like Rayburn yet heavy set, must be the old guard that helped Rayburn escape his fate a week ago.

She pressed the button. "Governor, be calm. Rayburn is here. He's coming over the bridge with a gun out, as well as with the senator and two of his flunkies. They're about ten yards away from you."

The omnidirectional caught the sounds of footsteps as the escaped convict and his cronies walked to where the governor sat. She could also hear the governor's ragged breath, as if he were about to have a coronary. Then she heard Woodruff's breath come under control.

Jaclyn keyed the mike again.

"He's right there," she said before letting go of the button and hefting the rifle. She looked through the scope.

She watched as Woodruff turned and looked right at Rayburn.

"You're late, Bobby Ray," he said.

In the tree, Jaclyn blinked as the microphone picked up everything.

"I'm here, ain't I?" Rayburn said. "I got caught in traffic, Wally. You know how that happens here, right?"

Woodruff didn't laugh.

"Yeah, I guess you're right. But something puzzles me, Bobby Ray: Why did you take her? You do know that she's one of us, right?"

Through the scope, Jaclyn saw Rayburn blink.

"One of us?" He turned to Farrell. "Baby, you're Klan? Why the hell didn't you tell me that? I wouldn't have been so hard with you last night if you had told me that."

"That's not what I mean, damn it," Woodruff said. "She's not that kind of one of us, she's a Republican. Why did you kidnap a fellow Republican?"

Jaclyn's eyebrows knitted together under her HUD.

Just what the fuck am I listening to? she thought. *Is Woodruff on—no, I'm hearing this wrong.*

"I needed to create a diversion," Rayburn explained. "I had Peters slip you the note to make sure you knew to go to the bathroom. And with the DiVito broad out of state, we had to alter our plans and instead kidnapped her."

"And the diversion was to shoot me."

Rayburn snorted.

"You didn't exonerate me. You had to pay, Wally."

"If I've told you once, I've told you a thousand times, Bobby Ray: Don't call me Wally."

Jaclyn didn't reach for her microphone. She was too stunned to do that. She couldn't believe what she had heard so far, but she continued to look through the scope. She could have pulled the trigger at any time, but she wanted to see how far this would go.

How deep is this conspiracy? she wondered.

"I was actually surprised that you made it through," Rayburn continued. His tone changed. "I really wanted you dead, Wally. You could have saved us a whole lot of trouble if you had issued that stay."

"And then what, Bobby Ray? Burn crosses openly? Times have changed, damn it! We don't have to like it, but it's not right any more. We have to keep our feelings shut. The Godless liberals are too thirsty for Republican blood right now. We can't give them any useful ammunition. If you'd just listen to me like I've said before—"

Jaclyn's jaw fell open, but she maintained a grip on her rifle.

How in the hell—oh fuck, she thought.

"I don't give a damn about what you're saying any longer, Wally. I'm done with you, you see? I'm done with the lectures of the Grand Dragon. You don't have an effect on my young mind. Yeah, I listened to your speeches to the Klan a decade ago, but you've been warped too much."

"I am still your Grand Dragon, damn it."

"Fuck you, Grand Dragon Wally. It's time for a change. I'm going to re-invent the Klan in my image, and I'm going to turn it into a political party. The third real political party in the United States."

"You may have some stiff competition from the Libertarians," Woodruff said.

"I'm going to force our agenda on the American people. I'm going to insist that those black politicians and police officers all step down. I'm going to insist that the women go back to the kitchen where they belong. I'm going to lower costs on everything so the man can be the sole breadwinner in a family. I'm going to—"

"Shut the fuck up, I'm tired of this. You know the liberals won't stand for it. For any of it. They won't stand the return of the Klan."

Rayburn, Jaclyn saw, grinned.

"Oh but they will. They won't have a choice. We'll teach those stupid Yankee kids why we wanted to secede from the Union—the right reasons, not the trumped up reasons the Yankees say is why we wanted to secede. And then we'll teach them all to fear the niggers and all the people of color. Bring them up right. We'll develop a whole new generation of Klan, because you know as well as I do Wally that racism will never go away as long as someone is feeding the hate to the next generation."

Jaclyn saw Rayburn smile wide. She lifted the gun and fixed the crosshairs over his grin. She still didn't pull the trigger yet. He didn't have his gun up—yet she wasn't sure if she wanted to wait to kill him until after he killed Woodruff, or before.

Woodruff's a member of the Klan, she thought. *Holy shit. I should have recorded this.*

"End the hate, Bobby Ray. Turn yourself in and release the woman," the governor said. "There are government agents all over the park, ready to take you in. Listen to reason. Don't be fucking stupid."

"No, I won't listen. I'm done with you, Wally." Rayburn lifted the gun and pointed it at Woodruff's head. Jaclyn could now see he carried a Glock .22. "And if I'm so stupid, why do I know that you're wearing a bullet proof vest, you dumb fuck? Say hi to my ma and pa for me."

Jaclyn clicked in the laser target, just as Rayburn had done with the governor Thursday night. Through the scope, she saw that a red dot now appeared on the right-hand side of Rayburn's skull, near the temple.

She took a deep breath and held it as she pulled the trigger.

"Bobby Ray, get down!" Peters yelled. He let go of Farrell, rushed forward and dropped his left shoulder into Rayburn's right, the collision sending the ex-con off-kilter just as the initial gunshot registered throughout the park. Rayburn pulled the trigger as Peters whacked him, sending him to the gray paving stones they stood upon. He dropped the Glock, scraping his hand against the pavers.

Rayburn's gunshot met its target in the chest, and Wallace Wellington Woodruff IV fell backward, the bullet sending shrapnel and bullet particles throughout his torso. He bled freely, his eyes open. Soon, his gaze would be empty, his life concluded.

The shot Jaclyn fired, though, buried its way into Peters' brain. He slumped to the pavers and was motionless.

"Run Farrell, run!" Jaclyn yelled from the trees, noticing now that she was unguarded. "Run toward my voice!"

It took the senator a second to realize this, too. Jaclyn's call spurred her into action. She began to run toward 10th Street.

"Hey, come back here!" Carl yelled. He began to follow her, running as if he was a defensive end for the Falcons and Farrell was a quarterback for the Saints.

"Carl, stop!" Rayburn called.

Carl paid him no heed as his feet churned away.

Jaclyn followed the action from her branch and leveled the scope toward Carl. She drew a healthy bead on him, and as he drew closer to Farrell, Jaclyn held her breath once again.

She pulled the trigger. A thunderclap followed.

Half a second later, Carl Dane tumbled forward as the bullet hit him in the forehead.

Rayburn screamed and lifted his hands to his head.

Jaclyn dropped from the tree and raised the rifle. She immediately rushed toward Rayburn and stuck the barrel into his face. He didn't move. Jaclyn kicked his gun away several feet, out of his reach.

"I have an order to kill you, you know," she said. "Not only from Forrister—your parents want you dead, too."

Rayburn grinned.

"You have to do what you have to do," he said. "I'm going to die anyway."

"Yes, you are. Yes, you are. Where's Roseann Teague?"

Rayburn smirked.

"I think you know."

Jaclyn sneered. She keyed her headset. "Snapshot to Atlanta Police: Rayburn in custody at Piedmont Park. Repeat: Rayburn in custody. Come to the lake. I have him under guard. And call for three bodybags. The governor is dead."

Rayburn's sneer matched Jaclyn's, but he didn't say anything. To Jaclyn's limited sight, she saw that Rayburn knew the end had come. A needle awaited him.

Jaclyn's HUD also detected that Farrell came closer to the scene. Jaclyn breathed deep and let it out, all while keeping Rayburn under her rifle's barrel.

"Aren't you going to kill him, Agent Johnson?" Farrell said, her bravado returning to her now that she saw

Rayburn was under arrest. "You have a direct order from Forrister. Kill him."

"No, Senator," Jaclyn replied. She didn't turn toward her. "I'm going to let the state of Georgia take care of it."

Farrell snarled.

"You're insolent. I'm totally going to bring you up before my committee if you don't kill him this instant."

Jaclyn's HUD didn't move a millimeter.

"You mean if you don't get elected Vice President? I await the summons."

Farrell screamed and balled her fists as if throwing a childish temper tantrum, but that was as much as she could do. Cruisers converged on the scene, and Atlanta Police spilled out of the Ford Interceptors. They swarmed over Rayburn and cuffed him. While officers escorted the senator to an ambulance, Jaclyn watched as others led him to the cruiser. Within an hour, media helicopters would float overhead, looking for the best view of the scene below. She knew the media would want the scoop from her, but talking to the Fourth Estate wasn't in her job description.

She looked to the sky, took a deep breath, and smiled.

She got the bastard—again.

Chapter 32
Oval Office, The White House
Washington, D.C.
Sunday, November 4, 2012
10:00 a.m. ET

Jaclyn had found out all of the details that she needed to know before she returned to Washington later that day. Even without an attorney, Rayburn had spilled his guts; knowing that he would die soon, he waived due process and admitted everything, including how he contacted his followers, including Peters. He said the attack on Air Force One was a ruse to distract the feds. He told her about the plan to kill the judges that had sent him to prison, and did so with a smile. He told her where he had his followers stash the bodies—an Atlanta cop who was looking in was on the phone in moments, and Cobb County Sheriff's deputies had swarmed over Rayburn's parents' house minutes later. They found the bodies in the cellar, including the body of Roseann Teague.

And finally, Bobby Ray Rayburn was executed by firing squad—well, sort of. He had lunged and pulled out a cop's sidearm, inserting the barrel into his mouth, and didn't hesitate in pulling the trigger.

Jaclyn paid a visit to Jasmine Anderson's home, where she was able to gather her family together to hear the news. Anderson had told her that she wished she could have seen the bastard. She had also told Jaclyn that she was considering resigning, but Jaclyn had told her to give it some thought—and that she was sorry that she couldn't pull through on her promise.

Jaclyn hoped that if Anderson stayed in the service, this incident would help harden her heart against the criminals and the bystanders that crossed her path.

She had also paid a visit to the lieutenant governor of Georgia—now the Acting Governor—Tim Kappel-

Gauthier and explained everything to him. Then she flew home to Washington, landing at Reagan National at 8 p.m. Saturday night. Alex had promised her that she would keep Tasha over one more night to let Jaclyn sleep.

The next morning, Jaclyn's driver took her to The Cottage. Alex and Tasha met her there. Jaclyn spent a few minutes with Tasha before she and Alex ducked into the Oval Office to meet with Forrister and DiVito.

"So Wallace was a Klansman," Forrister had said when Jaclyn had relayed that to him. "I have to admit, I never saw that coming."

"He hid his past well, sir," Jaclyn replied. "His acting job was flawless. When I heard him and Rayburn speak of it, I have to admit, Wally played us all."

"Not only that, he played the voters," DiVito added.

"What do you think will happen next, Jaclyn?" Forrister said.

Jaclyn blinked under her HUD.

"I really don't know. The Klansmen they rounded up Thursday night, I understand, were given personal recognizance."

"Which means they'll disappear into the back woods of Georgia until everything blows over," Alex said. "Justice won't prevail."

"It will in one case, Chief," Jaclyn countered. "Rayburn is dead, ending a sad chapter in Georgia's history."

"Thanks to your efforts again, Agent Johnson," the vice president said. "You know, maybe you should think twice about that whole public thanks thing we talked about last Sunday at the airport. I saw you on television Thursday night. The camera really loves you."

Jaclyn and Alex shared a look. The director of the CIA simply grinned, lowering her chin a few millimeters.

"Yes, Madame Vice President," Jaclyn said with a smile. "I kind of knew that already."

***

Republican National Committee Headquarters
310 First Street SE, Washington, D.C.
Sunday, November 4, 2012
1:24 p.m. ET

Senator Jennifer Farrell had flown back to Washington before Jaclyn Johnson had departed Atlanta. Police had talked to her and even though she made no mention of her conversation with Johnson, she had told police everything that had happened between her and Rayburn after his henchmen had kidnapped her. She said it was a blur and that she had blocked out a great deal of what had happened, but she did tell the authorities that he did not rape her. A nice bruise had developed under her left eye though, and when police questioned her about that, she didn't reply. They let her go, a new Secret Service detail ready to escort her to Hartsfield-Jackson.

When she arrived at the GOP's campaign headquarters, she found Dick Bennett sitting in his office, deep in thought.

She walked in and slammed her hands down on the man's desk.

"What did you mean Thursday night when you said that you would take back everything you've said about Jaclyn Johnson? The woman is a conniving, back-stabbing, liberal CIA puppet! She refused to kill Rayburn when I ordered her to do so!"

"You don't have the power to order anyone's execution Jennifer and you know this," Bennett said.

"Are you developing a case of liberal goodie two-shoes-ness, Dick? You know I'll never sleep with you again if you are."

"You forget that I was once a liberal," Bennett said. "And you'll sleep with me, Jennifer. I have the goods on you, too."

Farrell crossed her arms underneath her breasts.

"The terrorism thing? Who cares, Dick? That'll be off the people's minds as soon as you sign the pardon. That was part of our agreement. I help get you elected, you sign the pardon on January 21st, you haul Forrister and Johnson before a committee and let our Republican brothers and sisters in Congress destroy them."

"I'm talking about the campaign finance and tax issues, Jennifer. The off-shore bank accounts to avoid taxes. The large endowments provided to your senate campaigns by several large Nevada corporations. I know all about them."

Farrell's face was passive, as if she played poker.

"You're bluffing," she said.

Bennett smirked.

"I might be, but then again, I may not."

"If you go to the press within the next forty-eight hours, our campaign would be fucked, Dick. Forrister and DiVito will win the election in a walk. Do you really want to do all that?"

Bennett smirked.

"No, I don't. Which is why you need to shut the fuck up and do as you're told. I can easily not sign the pardon and have you removed from office the next day, and then have you replaced with someone with a lot less to lose."

"In the Republican Party?" Farrell spat. She tossed her hair. "Good luck."

"Are you on my side or not, Jennifer?"

Farrell looked long and hard at Bennett, who had not stood up to defend his position at all. She nibbled at her lips. She knew that Bennett held all the trump cards. If they were elected and he didn't sign the pardon, she would have to face a judge. She knew she could be potentially found guilty for her part in Letts' schemes back in Las Vegas.

Johnson said she would testify for the prosecution. She had all the facts in line and would be hard to budge on a cross-examination. If she was found guilty, Farrell's political career would be over. Bennett would be able to replace her with someone else, just like Forrister had filled the vice presidential vacancy with Lucia DiVito.

In essence, Farrell was playing Russian Roulette, a political game of Chicken. She knew that Bennett held the smoking gun, and he would never blink before her. She was a pawn in this game she now realized, with men in positions of power destroying her, tearing her defenses down.

It's why she slept with Bennett to begin with. It's why she would lay motionless, soundless, the next time they had sex—now that she thought of it, it would be tonight, more than likely. They didn't risk a rendezvous in Atlanta.

It's why she made no noises and shed no tears when Rayburn and his henchmen took turns with her Thursday night into the early hours of Friday.

Farrell choked back tears. Her bravado was gone.

"I'm on your side, Dick. Yes, I am."

Bennett's smile was devilish.

"Good. Everything will be fine when we win on Tuesday."

Farrell nodded.

"When we win on Tuesday, yes."

Bennett smiled again. Farrell, instead of staying, turned and left the room. Her eyes, she noticed in a mirror, were red.

I need to get out of this arrangement as soon as I can, she thought, staring at her reflection. *I just don't know how to do it.*

She walked to the door, opening it and letting it slam shut in the cold November wind.

THE END

Like what you've read? Sean Sweeney has something for every member of the family: check out more books and stories!

For kids:

Furball And Feathers: The Cat Food Caper!
Furball And Feathers: The Birdseed Bugaboo!
Furball And Feathers: The Case of the High-Wire Horse!
My Sister Is An Alien…(I Think)

For young adults:

Zombie Showdown

For adults:

The Jaclyn Johnson, a.k.a. Snapshot series
Model Agent: A Thriller
Rogue Agent: A Thriller
Double Agent: A Thriller
Promises Given, Promises Kept: A Jaclyn Johnson novella
Federal Agent: A Thriller
Literary Agent: A Thriller

Redeemed
Royal Switch: A Major League Thriller

The Alex Bourque Small Town PI series
Cold Altar
Voir Dire (Coming soon)

The Obloeron fantasy Prequel Series

The Rise Of The Dark Falcon
The Shadow Looms (Coming soon)

Short stories
Belief Debt: Paid In Full (Part of Christopher Nadeau's Not in the Brochure anthology)
C is for Coulrophobia (Part of the Phobophobia anthology)
Red Christmas (Part of the Bump in the Night 2011 anthology)
Refugees: A short story of survival

Writing As John Fitch V

The Obloeron Trilogy
The Quest For The Chalice
The Return To Labergator
The Fall Of Myrindar

One Hero, A Savior
Turning Back The Clock
A Galaxy At War
The Mastermind: A novella

Short stories
Sidetracked
Amber Twilight
Vuvuzombie

About the Author

Sean Sweeney's love of reading began in 1988, when he was handed J.R.R. Tolkien's classic The Hobbit. His passion for writing began in 1993, as a sophomore in high school, when he began writing sports for his local newspaper. Born and raised in North Central Massachusetts, Sweeney has written for several newspapers. When he is not writing, he enjoys playing golf, reading, watching movies, enjoying the Boston Red Sox, the New England Revolution, Arsenal F.C., Gold Coast F.C. and playing with Caramel The Wonder Cat.

Visit Sean online:
www.seansweeneyauthor.com

Email Sean!
seansweeneyauthor@yahoo.com

Fan of Sean's work? Find him on Facebook
https://www.facebook.com/seansweeneyauthor

Made in the USA
Middletown, DE
03 June 2017